Being Bridie

The Diary of an

Aspiring Mother

Casey O'Connor

First published by Limelight Books, an imprint of
The Write Factor, January 2017
www.thewritefactor.co.uk

A CIP catalogue record for this book is available from
the British Library.

ACKNOWLEDGEMENTS

To my beautiful children and grandchildren,
J, A, I and W
Thank you for allowing me to be Mum.
I love you xxxx

My thanks to Lorna Howarth from
The Write Factor

'Our sorrows and wounds are healed only when we
touch them with compassion.'
– The Buddha

Contents

Chapter 1

Family Planning

1st November 1987

"Are you pregnant yet?" my mother asks me inquisitively.

"I'm afraid not, and we've tried just about everything,"
I reply. "You know, it's been three years now and you
name it, we've tried it: ovulation predictor tests, herbs,
aphrodisiacs, high-fat diets, low-fat diets, detox programmes,
hypnotherapy, abstinence..."

"We've even considered going into one of Aunty
Bernadette's retreats at the convent," chips-in Declan, my
long-suffering husband. I'm glad Declan changed the subject
here and didn't go into detail about the 'abstinence' issue as
it's been a bit of a bone of contention between us: I'd insisted
on keeping the window open as lower temperatures are better
for a good sperm-count, but Declan just moaned that he was
too cold for sex. Result? Abstinence – not exactly optimal
baby-making conditions.

My mother, as usual, is impatient. "Bridie – both of your
sisters had babies on the way at your age, and even Aunt
Susan, who was much older than you when she started her
family, had no trouble. You need to find out what the problem
is, straight away. Daddy and I will find the money to get you
the necessary treatment. You probably just need to stop trying
so hard or... maybe even, you know, lose a few pounds?"
ARGGHH! I want to scream. I've had enough advice to last me
a lifetime including:

1. Lose weight
2. Stop trying so hard
3. Acupuncture
4. Praying after sex (Aunty Bernadette in the convent is already doing the praying bit on our behalf)
5. Doing a handstand after sex (weird and rather messy)

Declan's getting annoyed with my mother. "Winifred! It's not like Bridie hasn't got any children – she's stepmother to little Bea after all and making a good job of it too."

I give Declan an appreciative smile, but deep down I know that being a stepmother isn't enough for me. I'm desperate – DESPERATE – to hold my own baby in my arms. This feeling is so strong it overwhelms everything else. I'm in maternal overdrive. The other thing that rattles me about being a stepmum to Declan's kids is that obviously, he isn't 'firing blanks' – and consequently, if there are fertility issues, and it's not all just bad luck or cold bedrooms, they're likely to be down to me.

As if she read my thoughts, my mother says, "I know, Declan, but Bridie needs her own child, her own baby – another grandchild for us. The twins and Mikey would love a new cousin and then me and Stanley could babysit for you just like we did for the other grandchildren..." My mother drifts into a reverie where she's surrounded by this imagined bevy of grandchildren, then just as quickly, she snaps out of it. "Come on Bridie! Hurry up and get pregnant. I'm sure you're not destined to be barren – you don't look the barren type to me, not like your Aunty Rene with her butch face and cold eyes." She never did have a good word to say about her sister Rene, who, with her preference for walking boots and workaday trousers (even when going out for a lunch date!), just wasn't feminine enough to have children, in my mother's humble opinion. Poor Rene – I always really liked her.

Everybody's talking over me as usual. It is true: I want a child so desperately it hurts. I feel inferior to other women for not having my own children; I feel lonely and angry every second of the day. Angry at God, angry at other pregnant women, especially those who have multiple children, angry at my body... What's wrong with my body? And that word 'barren' – it reverberates in my mind like an echo.

Gina, my best friend, had conceived her first baby at 34 years old, after only three months of trying. Three months! She'd said, "Oh, we didn't do anything special – I just came off the pill a month beforehand, stopped smoking, changed my diet around a bit and 'Bob's your uncle': a baby girl, nine months later." Christ on a bike.

Not only do I have to put up with Gina and her endless advice, but I'm starting to feel very awkward whilst in the company of mothers in general, like, for example, Declan's eldest daughter from his previous marriage, 21 year-old Flora. I mean, of course she could come and visit her Dad and little sister Bea when she was heavily pregnant. Of course she could – but how was I supposed to feel seeing her so... well, so happy and so bloody pregnant!

What I feel is guilty. Guilty that I hate her for being pregnant when I'm not. My feelings are so mixed up. I *am* happy for her, really I am, but I so want it to be me. Why can't it be me? I can hear that little whining voice in my head and I don't like it.

OUCH! Infertility hurts. It's making me bitter and resentful towards mothers. But, the thought of the fertility treatment my mother hinted at terrifies me. All those strange drugs and invasive examinations and injections in the bum... No thanks! I can't go through with that – can I? What a choice: remain barren or subject myself to the misery of fertility treatment?

Oh yes, I'd done my research and fertility treatment seems to me to be a trial of stressful, expensive and embarrassing medical procedures and often just failure at the end of it all.

Anyway, I never was one for taking drugs unnecessarily. I prefer the 'alternative' way of treating illness. My bathroom cabinet is stuffed full of homeopathic balms and salves and my favourite magazine is the obscure and fascinating *What Doctors Don't Tell You* (which turns out to be quite a lot actually). Needless to say, being a GP, Declan doesn't approve of this magazine at all, and we often have heated discussions about the feature articles it contains.

But say I was offered fertility drugs – could I cope with them? Could I do it, if it meant having a baby? My hair might fall out? Fine – it's quite short anyway, so it'd soon grow back. I could die from that condition where your ovaries are over-stimulated: hyper-ovulation or something ghastly like that. Sure, I could die from that, or I could die from heartbreak!

I can feel a little glint of light flickering in my closed mind about fertility treatment. Hmmmm. I don't know though, I'm not sure... It all seems so huge and scary and medicalised and not at all like the loving and romantic image I have of conception. But (isn't there always a but...?) I remember another side to the story, one that I'd stumble across from time to time in women's magazines: some rather more positive scenarios where women who'd endured fertility treatments had given birth to twins or triplets. Oh yes! Oh JOY. Maybe I could go through with it after all?

I find myself floating off on another reverie, imagining myself with twin girls. I'd call them Sienna and Maeve and I would dress them identically in flowery, blue dresses with delicate silver bracelets and their hair would be plaited with matching blue braids. As teenagers they would hang out with their cousins Saskia, Jaz and Mikey and their stepsister

Bea, and we'd all be one big happy family...

7th November 1987

My mother has arranged a thing called a 'Baby Shower' to celebrate the imminent birth of Flora's new baby. My father is not happy. He says it sounds too American. Anyway, we have arranged to meet at Dublin Bay Spa for a swim, a sauna and afterwards a cream tea. My sister Lee has suggested a bumblebee theme. "We need people to know how serious the threat is to our bees," she says. "All those sprays and all the land that's being destroyed... I want everybody to go away from the party with a packet of bee-friendly seeds that they can plant in their gardens."

My mother is not convinced. "Lee, darling is this not all a bit heavy? We're supposed to be relaxing and celebrating Flora's new baby."

Lee and mother are 'having words'.

That afternoon everyone is relaxing and chatting in the jacuzzi. Mum says loudly, "Oh, this is the life," but I'm not enjoying it one bit. I mean, just look at Flora – she's acting, appropriately enough, like a Queen Bee, and I have to admit to myself that I am jealous. Everybody is looking at her and asking questions like: "How are you sleeping?'" and "How much longer to go now?" and "Do you know the baby's sex?" Presents are given out, and Flora is delighted and moved to tears.

"This is lovely," she says. "It's so lonely with Brendan gone off to Afghanistan. This is really cheering me up."

I'm glad she's happy, I really am. I AM.

We all leave with seeds in hand. And bumblebee cake.

31st November 1987

It's after midnight and the phone is ringing. Declan answers it sleepily, but then his tone of voice suddenly changes. "You're what? In labour? Oh, Flora that's great!"

"Gone into labour," he whispers to me, as if I can't hear every word. Declan nudges me and says a little more loudly, "Wake up, Bridie – Flora's gone into labour."

I hide beneath the duvet for one final, warm second before I swing my legs out of bed and launch into action.

I'm Flora's birthing partner. Yes, she asked me once she knew Brendan would be in Afghanistan when the baby was due. *She needs me*, I told myself and it'll be good experience for WHEN I'M PREGNANT.

Fifteen minutes later, and I'm ready to go.

"Don't worry Bridie," Declan says from the warmth of our matrimonial bed, "this'll be good practice for you when it's your turn!" and with that he winks at me and snuggles back under the duvet. But his words do give me comfort, because he's thinking what I'm thinking isn't he? That my turn will come. He still has faith in me.

Dublin Maternity Hospital, 2am

URGGH! I'm tired and cold. Why do people always give birth in the middle of the night? It is so damn unsociable. I slurp down a cappuccino and flip through an old newspaper as I wait for Flora's labour to progress.

1 hour later

"Ohhhh... *owwww*... God that hurts! Brendan, you bastard, where are yoooouuu? I want Brendan!"

Flora is obviously in agony. Uncharitably, I think that if it was *me* giving birth, I wouldn't be making such a fuss. I'd be smiling, and feeling happy and calm. I wouldn't swear or scream, I'd just be glad to be giving birth – wouldn't I?

"Jesus, God argh, argh! Brendan where are you, you bastard? Brennnndaaan! Owwww, curse you!" Flora continued to moan and cry out.

"Are you assisting at this birth?" Iris the midwife asked me, rather too curtly for my liking.

"Er, yes – what can I do to help?" I ask, as I put down my coffee.

"Just try and make her as comfortable as you can. Hold her hand to reassure her; mop her brow with a damp cloth when she looks sweaty. Can you do that?" I nodded obediently as I put on a gown and reached for the blue paper towels.

Three hours later and Flora is exhausted.

"You're doing well! One last push – come on. Breathe... Brave girl, nearly there. Don't push until I tell you to..." Iris gave her clear instructions to a shattered Flora.

But then, "Ohha ahh..." Flora's voice is suddenly different, it is calmer, something's changed.

"I can see the head," beams Iris. "D'you want to see Bridie? Look..." All my resentment and self-pity evaporates as I watch the miracle of birth – the emergence of a tiny body streaked with blood and a kind of grey and white slime.

"Here she is! Well done Flora – you've a beautiful baby girl."

Iris does all the necessary checks on the baby and when she's happy that all is well, she says, "Right little one, go on to your mammy."

"Hello baby Mia, you are so perfect!" Flora says, holding her newborn closely and weeping as she offers her a pink nipple.

Later, back home, I gush enthusiastically to Declan about what a fantastic experience it was and how overcome with emotion I am. I don't mention my feelings of jealousy.

First week of December 1987

Flora and Mia come to stay with us whilst Brendan is away in Afghanistan. All of the family come and visit with flowers, cards and more presents. It's a lovely, precious time and the presence of Mia makes me even more determined to get pregnant.

MUMMY ENVY? Mummy envy.

8th January 1988

I'm still not pregnant but I'm exhausted from trying! I've even closed the bedroom window. God only knows how Declan's feeling. Personally, I feel like a complete failure, almost numb, with the 'b-word' ricocheting in my brain: barren, barren... Do I look barren? Do I look butch? Or do I look more like Fertile Flora? Barren Bridie and Fertile Flora.

It's no joke.

10th January 1988

My doctor has agreed to refer me to a gynaecologist.

I can't wait! Just maybe I will find out what is wrong with me and it can be dealt with without all this silly meditation and relaxation stuff. I ring Mum with the good news. She offers to buy me some baby clothes and another ovulation predictor test just in case. She will also visit Aunty Bernadette in the convent today and ask her to do some extra praying for a new baby.

21st January 1988

Today's the day of my gynaecologist appointment. My Happiness Factor (as Bridget Jones would say) is 9/10 because we may know the reason for our infertility soon – I may not be Barren Bridie for long. It's 7.30 and I'm up early, not being able to sleep what with the excitement of it all. Declan has to provide a sperm sample. I hear swearing and muttering in the bathroom then there is an eerie silence followed by a relieved call. "Bridie, I've done it. It's taken ages, so I hope all this is worth it! Yuk – ergh... what do you want me to do with it now?"

We both start giggling at the absurdity of the whole thing. "Just hide it somewhere out of sight and make sure neither Anna, Bea or the dog find it!" I warn, knowing that Anna, our Polish cleaner, has an uncanny knack of stumbling across things we'd rather she hadn't seen, like my ovulatory predictor kits.

To be honest, I was surprised that Declan even had to do a sperm sample, considering he's already fathered children, but apparently sperm count can decline with age. So it might not be all my fault after all – not that anyone's to blame in all this. We just need to find out what the hell's going on.

It's 2.15 pm and my journey begins in every sense of the word! I am full of HOPE. We're on our way to Dublin hospital, and I am all prepared: showered, clean underwear and armed with a flask of tea, a book and a newspaper (in case we have to wait ages) and a batch of sandwiches made with my very own homemade bread (in case we get peckish).

We are about half way there when suddenly Declan screeches to a halt at the traffic lights. "Shit!" he shouts, "I've forgotten my sample."

I become tense and cross. This is typical, and now we are going to be late. I shout at him, "Oh for God's sake Declan! Turn around and go and get it before somebody else finds it." I hope to God the dog hasn't found it. Fritz, our Jack Russell, has to date:

1. Taken a small bottle of Gaviscon out of my handbag
2. Found and shredded my secret packet of emergency cigarettes
3. Devoured a packet of chewing gum – seemed to have no ill effect
4. Nicked my mobile phone (an expensive luxury in 1988 I can tell you) and chewed it up.

It seems he is also into personal development, having stolen the Little Book of Confidence and also Buddha's Little Instruction Book from my rucksack. I found them in the garden along with other things that had mysteriously gone astray, such as a packet of jasmine joss sticks. I love him to bits, but he's a thief.

Suddenly I have visions of Bea or Anna or even my mother stumbling across Declan's sacred sample. How would we explain it to them? It would be Declan's worst nightmare for Bea to find something like that – he's such a loving, caring Dad and tries to protect her from everything since his split with her Mum. He doesn't want her to worry about having a brother or sister in the house just yet – we've agreed we will tell her we're trying for a baby, but not straight away.

We arrive back home. I nervously check the time. Oh, for

fuck's sake. Now we are going to be late. I panic when Declan says he can't remember where he put the sample and Anna is immediately very interested in the conversation. She pauses as she meticulously mops the kitchen floor. I see her crane her neck towards us.

"I can help you? Now what is it you looking for?" she says in her thick Polish accent.

"Nothing," snaps Declan. "I just wish people wouldn't move things..." He paces around the house impatiently, frantically searching everywhere, then – "Bingo!" he suddenly shouts. "Toothpaste. I had it when I was cleaning my teeth!" Hurray we've found our sample. I guard it carefully in my handbag.

Later at the hospital

We arrive stressed and 30 minutes late. I humbly apologise to the efficient receptionist who is amused by our story. I am here at Dublin Hospital to have a 'hysterosalpingogram'. The word is so difficult to pronounce I just call it a 'pingogram'. This is effectively an x-ray of my uterus. The young medic explained to me that a dye would be inserted via my vagina to check for polyps, adhesions and fibroids. He asks me if I had ever contracted any sexually transmitted diseases. I feel myself redden with embarrassment. "Certainly not," I reply indignantly. Declan nods his head approvingly.

The pingogram didn't hurt, but what with all the poking and prodding, it seemed my insides are no longer my private property. It's a bit like someone snooping around your house, not quite approving of your choice of curtains. This morning my HF was 9/10, but as I leave the hospital, I feel distinctly gloomy. What if they found something I'd rather not know about? My HF plummets to 3/10, and in my heart of hearts, I know this is just the start of things to come.

1st February 1988

Today I have another all-day hospital appointment for a laparoscopy, which is basically keyhole surgery consisting of a cut near my belly button so they can pump gas inside me to separate my organs allowing surgeons to have a good look around for any abnormalities. Help! It sounds too ghastly for words. I contemplate whether I could contend with being Barren Bridie forever, and just walk away from all this prodding. It's not an option, but the feeling that my body's not my own any more continues to weigh heavily on me. They never let on at school that conceiving could be this difficult: we were pretty much told that we'd only to look at a boy and we'd end up having twins.

1.30pm

Declan cuddles me, pecks me on the cheek and whispers, "Good luck Bride, it will all be worth it when you have that big bouncing baby boy in your arms!" and with that he folds up his Sporting Life magazine, looks at his watch and says, "I'm just heading off now for a decent cup of coffee," kisses me again, gives the thumbs-up sign and leaves. Declan's a great guy, he really is, but I have a feeling he's getting a bit bored of all these hospital visits. After all, being a GP, he already has his fair share of menopausal women and prostatic men to deal with. I can't blame him for taking his leave, but feel slightly resentful that it's me who has to go through all this palaver. HF 5/10: I'm glad we're getting to the bottom of our inability to conceive but scared stiff of what they might find.

By five o'clock, the laparoscopy is over and I am being allowed to go home but I feel dreadful. Somehow I've contracted a urine infection, I have a headache that's about to morph into a migraine and my stomach is so bloated I feel I could fart for Ireland. My mother, bless her, thinks that this is a sign of imminent pregnancy! I am certain that it is not.

3rd February 1988

Mum has been my constant companion since the laparoscopy. I've taken myself to bed as the procedure knocked me for six – much more so than I expected, but of course, it'll all be worth it in the end. That's what everyone keeps telling me: that's what I keep telling myself. Mum's brought me some zinc and ginseng capsules. She says she has read in *Good Housekeeping* that sometimes infertility is linked to a lack of zinc.

"It must be true if it's in *Good Housekeeping*,"

I say truculently.

Mother ignores me, but then she starts on about how I drink too much tea, and how that might be having an adverse effect on me. Whoever heard such rubbish!

Oww... I groan as I feel another twinge in my tummy. I feel a bit sorry for myself to tell the truth and feel a little sob develop in my throat. My mother looks at me sharply but stops short of repeating the old childhood mantra: "Remember, people called 'Collins' don't cry, my little Bridie Collins."

4th February 1988

Morning: still feel ill.
Afternoon: can't go on.

EURGHH! I contact a Chinese nutritionist, Dr Jian Li – recommended to me by my sister Denise – who fits me in straight away.

3.30pm

I am filling out a form and ticking boxes whilst Dr Li studies the spittle sample I'd provided her with a few minutes previously. Lovely.

The Questionnaire is easy-peasy:

1. *What foods do you eat on a daily basis?* Tea, coffee, bread, milk, cereals, eggs, cheese, cider (consider not putting that in but feel it's best to be honest), crackers, cake, chocolate.

2. *What health problems are you suffering from at the moment?* Reflux, ulcers on the tongue, indigestion, headaches, migraines, thrush, fertility problems...

3.45 pm

Dr Li has the results. "Right then, Mrs Kelly. Your blood tests show that you have candida, adrenal stress and low enzyme function. All of this contributes to your general health problems."

"But could this be why I can't get pregnant?"

I ask exasperatedly.

"I can't answer that question Mrs Kelly – I'm not a fertility specialist. But what I do know is that you have a very unhealthy diet indeed."

I feel a bit indignant on hearing this.

"Look at all the sugar you are consuming," Dr Li continued, "in cake, and chocolate and cereals, not to mention the yeasts in the bread and the saturated fats in the butter and milk. No wonder you have candida. You can either take medication from the doctor that will just cover up the problem and eventually make it worse, or you can do it the hard way – my way." She folds her arms and awaits my reply.

I don't like the sound of doing anything the hard way, but I don't like the thought of taking any prescribed drugs either – you never know what's in them. So I submit to her ultimatum and agree to stick to the following dietary regime:

Drinks: one cup of Redbush tea a day or two cups of green tea and one bottle of filtered water. Nothing else, no alcohol and no fruit juice as it's too sweet.
Food: no eggs, milk, cheese, bread or crackers for the first two months. Plenty of brown rice, pulses, lentils, beans, pumpkin seeds, nuts and green vegetables.

That's it.
Good God.

Dr Li hadn't finished there though. "Mrs Kelly, you are so stressed out with all this fertility treatment, you're spiritually exhausted. You need to meditate every day and take up yoga too. It'll really help to calm your nerves and give you a sense of general wellbeing. Have you thought about keeping a daily diary? It can be very cathartic you know."

"Yes," I tell her. "I do keep a diary. It's where I record all my thoughts and feelings about what I'm going through. I've been doing it for years." I am triumphant. At least I've got one thing right.

I still have my Holland & Barrett staff discount card from when I worked there before I got married, so I pay a visit to their huge store in the middle of Dublin and buy all the things

Dr Li suggested. My family seem impressed with my resolve, although I heard Mum on the phone to Lee a few days later saying, "Ah, but it's a passing fad. She'll be back on the fizzy drinks in no time."

Meanwhile, Declan and Bea keep complaining that the pantry is full of weird food and foul-smelling tea bags.

"Blimey Bridie, it's like a health food shop in here," said Declan as he studied the various coloured jars that had taken up residence on top of the microwave. "Could you not have just taken some antibiotics like normal people?" he smirks as he studies the list of ingredients in the supplements. I think to myself, *if you knew how much that lot cost, it'd soon wipe that smirk off your face, mister.*

I insist that it would be good for the whole family to eat healthily and shove bowlfuls of bean stew or miso soup under their noses. They visibly pale and reach for the takeaway menu.

Chapter 2

Fertility Treatment

7th February 1988

Hurray! I am back in control of my life. I don't have any health problems, the supplements and diet seem to have worked and I feel FINE – though I may just buy some chlorella for Mum and Dad. According to Dr Li, it's a Chinese herbal remedy that consists of about six green vegetables in one tablet, and it improves immunity. Can't be bad. At the last count I'm still taking five different supplements and one more can't hurt, so maybe I'll take the chlorella too. Just to be on the safe side.

28th February 1988

Hurray! We get the results of all the tests today and then it's full steam ahead for babies! HF 9.5/10. Mothercare here we come. Our appointment is at 1.30 pm with my gyneaecologist, Mr Willey. Yes, I know – it's an appropriate name. I find it hard not to giggle whenever it's mentioned.

1.45 pm

Mr Willey looks at us and refers to his notes and x-rays. "We've now completed all the tests and the good news is that there is nothing obviously wrong with you Mr Kelly, or you Mrs Kelly." He mumbles through results of hormone tests, sperm counts, and thyroid.

Declan nudges me. "Nothing's wrong! See, I told you – you just need to be patient and relax more and it will happen."

I glower at him.

Meanwhile the doctor closes his folder. "We don't know what the problem is – sometimes there's no reason for sub-fertility. But what we do know is that even for people with sub-fertility problems, pregnancy can surprise you when you're least expecting it. Why not go home and consider your options? Try to relax more or think about taking up yoga or meditation. Watch your diet, and be careful about too much stress or alcohol."

I want to scream. This isn't good news to me, it is totally disheartening news. The specialist can't find anything wrong with us... We have what is called 'Unexplained Infertility'. Oh my God. I am so disappointed. Why can't I have a diagnosis or something they can fix? I'm only 31 years old and I feel like a total failure – a freak, and a desperate freak at that. I am officially, technically, Barren Bridie. It's proven. I will never be a mum.

I sob into a tissue thinking of beautiful, cuddly, perfect baby Mia. HF 0.

Declan nudges me again with what I'm sure is a smirk and mutters something about my weird vegetarian diet. "I told you Bridie, that soya's lethal for fertility. You need red meat and lots of iron and protein."

"I'm a vegetarian, Declan!" I seethe.

Everybody is giving me advice again. Even Declan. Don't drink, don't smoke, don't eat anything even remotely tasty, don't bother having sex on non-ovulating days... My head is spinning with grief and devastation.

Mr Willey speaks again as he picks up on my desperation. "Don't be too disheartened Mrs Kelly. There are other ways into motherhood. Have you thought about adoption or fostering?"

Declan's face contorts and he sniggers, "I think my Bridie's too soft for fostering," and then (I could've slapped him), he pats my hand patronisingly.

"Do you want to consider fertility treatment? We could start you today on a small dose of Clomiphene, which is a fertility drug aimed at boosting egg production. Quite simply you just take one tablet daily and use a vaginal lubricant jelly each time you have intercourse."

We both feel slightly embarrassed as our sex life is discussed so clinically. Declan fiddles with his new mobile phone.

"Bridie, it may well be that you are not ovulating properly in which case Clomiphene would kick-start ovulation." Willey winks at me and continues, "There is a risk of multiple birth though. Other side effects include mood swings, and possibly mild ovarian enlargement. Nothing to worry about though. Success rate? Oooh let me see… at your age…. Well 60 to 70% of women will get pregnant, so your chances are pretty good, I'd say."

At that, Declan perks-up and squeezes my hand enthusiastically. He asks me what I think?

What do I think?

Well you can imagine after 36 months of roller-coaster emotions and failure, a fertility drug sounded like an exciting, positive option. All worries of hair falling out and damage to my body evaporate. Ha! Who cares? Feel the fear and bloody well do it anyway.

"I want to give it a try," I gush. "Motherhood is so important to me. I just, I just… want to be a MUM. I am going to be a mum. Whatever it takes, I'll do it."

I visualise Declan beside me as I struggle through labour.

He'd help cut the umbilical cords and hand me my newborn twin babies. We'd kiss and I'd cry with happiness. My family would visit with flowers, cuddly toys and cards. It would all be worth it, in the end. The prize of twin girls. Bridie would be complete and Barren Bridie would be extinct.

1st March 1988, 7.30 pm

I have now rung everybody and told them the news that Bridie Kelly is on fertility drugs and is going to be a mother one way or another. Reactions are varied: my sister Lee is cautiously optimistic but worried about multiple births having had twins herself. Mum and Dad are delighted – so much so that Mum declares she is going shopping to Mothercare, Toys R Us and Early Learning tomorrow, so she can be 'good and ready'. "Imagine, Bridie," she gasps, "there could be two sets of twins in the family. How fantastic!"

My best friend Gina is pleased for me but cautions me on how long the treatment might take to work. (That's right Gina – just rub-in the fact that you conceived straight away, why don't you?) Flora? Flora is delighted: "Come on Bridie, just get on with it then we can hang out together with the babies." My other sister Denise dampened my spirits a bit: "Er, Bridie – this motherhood lark is becoming a bit of an obsession with you, isn't it? Can't you just be happy with Bea and Sandy and Flora – and what about the twins and Mikey? They need you as well, you know. They love their Aunty Bridie. Heaven knows where this treatment is going to lead if you don't get pregnant... Your life just seems to be on hold all time until you get pregnant. You spend your time hoping and crying and being in despair. I am worried about you."

Denise had hit a very raw nerve. I snapped, "I think you're

just jealous, Denise. You can't stand that I'm getting a bit of attention."

Denise remained calm and replied, "Bridie, I'm just worried about you. It seems to me like you are on a huge emotional roller-coaster. You're up and down like a yo-yo. Just be careful, please. I mean, what next if the fertility drugs fail?"

I replied haughtily, "Well look, if I don't try, I might regret it forever. I know it's risky, but I say, 'feel the fear and do it anyway'. If the fertility drugs fail it's adopting for us."

I don't know where that all came from: neither the corny T-shirt 'feel the fear' slogan, nor the adopting bit... but I certainly remembered Declan's face in hospital when Mr Willey suggested fostering.

We'll cross that bridge if we come to it, I think.

7th March 1988

I start my fertility drugs today, and I am so excited. HF 10 out of bloody 10. Surely it will just be a matter of time before I am pregnant, now? I look at the magical little round tablets, kiss them, cross my fingers and pray they'll work. I place one in my mouth and swallow. Remembering discussions about fertility from Gina and Dr Li, oh, and Mum's advice from *Good Housekeeping*, I also popped a zinc capsule in my mouth along with fish oil and garlic. I then hopelessly try to meditate.

15 minutes later

Hey! This meditation thing's working: I didn't think of babies for three minutes but then Fritz started barking at the postman and the phone rang... Annoyingly it was a cold-caller.

Later

I'm reading a book on pregnancy and older mothers (40's not that old, is it – that's only nine years older than me?) and I play with the word 'preggers' – it sounded wonderful to me as it rolls off my tongue. "Preggers," I say. "Pregnant. I'm pregnant – oh, yes. You didn't know? Yes. Pregnant."

Even though I find meditation a trial, I can slip into a daydream no problem at all. This time, I imagine myself pregnant with quads. Everybody would be so happy for us. There would be presents and cards. Bea would have four more sisters to go with her other two, and it would help her to get over the feelings of her mum, Polly's, abandonment. Mia would have company. It can only be a good thing.

20th April 1988

Declan and I have to have a lot of sex over the first 12 weeks of taking the Clomiphene and we have to try different positions at least six times a week – something about 'optimising' our chances of conceiving. It's all quite tiring actually. Groan. On top of that, I am supposed to check my mucus levels regularly, use suppositories and calculate my body temperature before we even start! And yes, Declan thinks standing on my head after sex is a good idea because even if it doesn't work, he says it will be worth it for the laugh!

Despite his sense of humour, I notice that Declan is complaining that there's no romance left in our life; all this sex is so clinical and calculated. He says he feels like he has lost his sense of self and that he's just becoming a baby-making machine. I think he likes the one night a month when he's 'On Call' at the surgery and has to stay over to answer the phones and attend to emergencies – it gives him a legitimate night off from shagging! To be honest I am not surprised, because I feel a bit demeaned by it all too – but that old mantra slips out of my mouth to placate him: "It'll all be worth it in the end, Declan." I make a mental note to buy some extra zinc and ginseng – that'll perk the old boy up.

I'm on eight tubs of supplements now, plus a box of green tea. I'm dedicated to following-up every potential avenue to fertility, but my HF is about 4/10 because it's all such a bloody faff. And I keep mislaying my fertility tablets – I keep finding them in the most extraordinary places, like in the bread-bin yesterday. How on earth did they get there? Declan said, "BRIDIE – I know you've got a reputation for being disorganised, but this is ridiculous! Bea could've found them and then we'd have to tell her everything..." I can't blame the dog either, because even he couldn't open the bread-bin. Plus, I REALLY miss my daily mug of PG Tips.

15th May 1988

I'm not pregnant yet – just having a lot of dreadful hot flushes that leave me feeling not only barren but bloody menopausal as well. Bea, who now knows what's going on, says that I am a misery to live with and would it not be better to forget all about having a baby and just adopt a cute one from China? Wise words from a child of nine-and-a-half years.

31st May 1988

I'm feeling depressed because the doctor says that apparently, I'm not ovulating regularly, so I now have to progress to stronger drugs in the form of daily injections and horrible, horrible suppositories. I am not looking forward to having injections in my buttocks, that's for sure – and all my good intentions about never taking medication have just flown out the window. I've let my subscription to *What Doctors Don't Tell You* lapse. I can't face it any more.

The nurse advised Declan – who's going to be administering the injections – to practice injecting into an orange first. I frostily remind her that he is a GP, "for God's sake!" So it surprised me when Declan said that actually, he would have a practice first. Was he as nervous as me about all this? I then got a fit of giggles – God knows why – and Declan accused me of making fun of him saying, "Well anyway, I'm not likely to miss your big bum, am I?" The injection hurt and I wonder if Declan did it on purpose.

Another thing is the timing of all this fertility treatment – it is so, so inconvenient. The other day we were driving back from a lovely walk in sunny Bray Head with Bea and her friend Gilly when we suddenly realised that my mid-morning injection was due, right there and then. What were we supposed to do? Determined to pursue this treatment properly and keep to the timing, we searched for a nearby pub with a play area. I turned to the two girls and directed them into the ball pool.

"Now stay in the ball pool until I get back, girls," I told them. "No talking to any strangers whatsoever or going to the toilet on your own until I get back."

I returned to the car and retrieved my jabs. "Okay Declan – quick do it now," I ordered. I bent over the car seat, my head looking out of the back window, and braced myself for the sting of the huge needle.

As I did so I heard a knock on the car window. I looked up and saw two pairs of eyes peering at me inquisitively, and heard, "Bridie, Bridie, we're bored and Gilly wants a drink and the toilet... what are you two doing? Are you having sex?" They giggled and carried on staring at the red mark on my buttock, whilst I marvelled that they even knew what sex was at their age.

Embarrassed and irritated I explained the truth of the matter. "You know Mummy Bridie wants to have a baby don't you, and I need to have some injections to make it happen."

They listened intently and I watched as they skipped back to the ball pool, with Bea excitedly talking about a new baby sister or brother. If only I was able to deliver such a thing. I hoped I wouldn't disappoint her.

15th June 1988

I know it's not very cool or ladylike but I can't find my Prometrium suppositories anywhere. I expect Anna may have tidied them away after I asked her to do a deep clean of the bathroom. I can't really ask her where they are because I don't know Polish for suppository and I can't do a bloody charade as that would look rather uncouth! I decide I'll have to consult the dictionary for a Polish translation. It is czopek.

"Anna have you seen my czopeks? I need them you see – it's very important." I could have sworn I saw her smirk.

"No, I don't see it but I annoyed you dog, he shit everywhere." She angrily points to a pile of glistening dog mess in the sun lounge.

I explain to her that Fritz is a bit, shall we say, unruly. He came from a rescue centre, and we just don't know what kind of owners he had previously. He occasionally 'does his business' in the house for no apparent reason and we also have that problem with him stealing just about everything.

The vet said that it was probably due to the fact that Fritz came from a bad home and as a result steals things that smell of us.

Anna is unimpressed. "Not like bloody dog thing," I hear her say as she walks away.

3.30 pm

Still can't find my suppositories. It's so frustrating because everybody else thinks it's funny, but it's not. I need them!

Bea's curious: "What? You put them up your bottom?"

Later, Fritz is being really sick now. In fact, when I look closely, he is sicking-up my suppositories! Urgently, I ring the vet who laughs at the story and thinks Fritz will be okay. And certainly fertile, I think resignedly.

Off to the chemist I go for more suppositories. I could have sworn the pharmacist smiled, or am I getting paranoid now?

18th June 1988

Great excitement. We're going to the fertility clinic so that I can have a scan to check the presence of eggs in my ovaries. In my mind's eye, I keep thinking of the Easter Egg hunts we had when I was a child and I wonder how many they will find.

My ovaries are scanned but sadly there is not much sign of life and certainly no counting to be done.

"Mrs Kelly, your eggs are very immature and I can only find two," says a kindly, bosomy African nurse as she moves the scanner across my belly.

I am choked: all that effort and pain and inconvenience – for nothing. Everybody will be asking me how the fertility treatment is going and 'absolutely nowhere' is the answer.

I am annoyed, frustrated, stuck, and frankly, bored with the whole damn thing. Which way now to motherhood? Fostering? Adoption? Giving up altogether? Not likely! But why are my ovaries not co-operating? What am I doing wrong? Am I too stressed, too fat, too old...?

Whatever way I look at it, it feels like my body is letting me down again and a little sing-song voice inside my head starts humming, "Barren Bridie, Barren Bridie". I wish with all my heart that the scan had been to detect a tiny foetus, rather than a gruesome search for eggs.

All of July 1988

STILL no pregnancy but painful periods that last two weeks or more, mood swings, hot flushes and depression.

I am gloomy and ready to give up on fertility treatment. There must be another way? Surrogacy? Turkey baster? AID? IVF? Fostering? Adoption? Abduction? (Tempting...) HF 2/10.

On top of all that, I'm having problems with Anna. She has three different jobs and doesn't seem to be doing any of them very well. When I discuss this with her she exclaims, "But I come from Poland to make lots of money! You very lucky here. My family have no money."

Hmmm – I'm very lucky am I Anna? Then why don't I feel lucky? Why do I feel like there's a great big baby-shaped hole in my life?

1st August 1988

I spend a whole week in bed. My belly is bloated and I have agonising cramps all the time. I am utterly FED UP. I can only cheer myself up by imagining a surrogacy with Gina, or adopting a baby from China. I find myself more and more often fantasising about fostering or adopting, because at least it would release me from all this bodily pain and anguish.

7th August 1988

Mum and Dad have offered to pay for IVF! Surely that can't go wrong as well? You often hear of successful treatments, so perhaps we can be amongst them? I must admit that the glossy magazine that has arrived from the Lister Clinic in London looks very inviting. I can see bosomy, beautiful women nursing gorgeous, gurgling babies. Can I be one of them? Perhaps I'd have twins or triplets and never complain about being barren again? I can feel my gloomy state of mind begin to fade as I daydream of triplets and breast-pumps... I can almost smell that milky baby smell... I can almost feel my babies in my arms.

Chapter 3

IVF

7th September 1988

We have flown into Gatwick and now we are spending a celebratory night together in a posh hotel in London. Declan treated me to some special Body Shop bath milk and soap. I relax in my beautiful, soothing surroundings and dare to imagine that this is the start of a new life for us all. Declan joins me, perching on the edge of the bath with an opened bottle of champagne and proposes a toast that gives me the shivers: "Cheers! Here's to us and our new baby," he says optimistically.

It's like we've tacitly decided to ban any sceptical thoughts, and make the most of this romantic night in the 'city of dreams'. Seems quite appropriate really...

8th September 1988

We are at the Lister Clinic in London to see an IVF specialist, who much to my consternation performs a really embarrassing examination, and I've had some embarrassing examinations in my time. It is basically what amounts to a huge nozzle up my vagina and not all that discreetly either: "Mrs Kelly, is it okay if my students watch this procedure? They're young medics and could do with the experience."

I agree but secretly feel inadequate as a group of four

fascinated young medical students stare at my lazy ovaries and redundant uterus. I try to cheer myself up, thinking, *Hey, some of these young medics are rather fit!* Until I remember where they're actually looking...

5 minutes later...

So, the consultant has spotted a polyp on my womb. Could this be what's wrong with me, or is this, as I suspect, the result of many weeks of hormone drug treatment and three-week long heavy periods?

It seems the consultant can't be sure what consequences this little polyp has on my fertility, but wants to remove it to be on the safe side. He discusses how IVF treatment works and other options such as egg donation. We leave the clinic none the wiser really, but at least I'm booked-in to Dublin hospital to have the polyp removed and it feels one tiny step closer to conception.

21st September 1988

I have the polyp removed under general anaesthetic and wake up feeling queasy and disorientated.

"Be hopeful, Bridie," my mother says as she sits by my side in the recovery room." Just imagine your fallopian tubes all relaxed and ready for your IVF treatment. Shall I look for a hypnotherapist for you? It's all the rage now in fertility circles – something about tapping into the subconscious and relaxing the mind as well as the body."

"No thanks, Mum. I've had it with relaxation and hypnotherapy and all that malarkey. I just want the Full

Monty now. I want to get on with the IVF treatment as soon as possible."

12th October 1988

I have a consultation back at the hospital. The doctor is pleased with the results of the operation and my general health is good. He suggests to us that we can now start IVF and if that fails, egg donation, all at a cost of about £4000. (I silently bless my Mum and Dad for all their help and support.)

Declan is keen. "What do you think, darling?"

I agree half-heartedly because if the truth be told, I'm starting to dread the impact it will have on my body, but I don't see any other option. The consultant looks satisfied and Declan seems positive about the whole thing, and I'm so grateful to my parents and Declan and... I feel tears prick in my eyes. Denise was right. I am on a bloody emotional roller-coaster.

"Good, good," the doctor intercedes, keen to circumvent any hysterics. "We'll contact the Lister clinic to order the drugs which will arrive in Dublin next week, and then you can start immediately. Same routine as before; if you experience any severe side effects or upset tummies, ring me on my mobile." And with that he shakes our hands and wishes us luck. "I'll book you in at the Lister in a month for another scan and we can see what the state of play is then."

15th October 1988

Bea is 10 today. We celebrate with a horse-riding lesson and a sleep-over. Bea's mother Polly and her partner Pippa join us for tea and cake. Bea is embarrassed by the presence of her mother's partner. She doesn't quite understand bi-sexuality and her tenth birthday doesn't seem quite the right occasion to discuss the matter. I make a mental note to have a chat with Declan about this, but he is very evasive whenever the subject arises. It's like he's taken it as some kind of personal failure that his ex-wife and mother of his children is gay.

20th October 1988

Much against my better judgment and merely to subdue my mother's constant stream of advice, I start a yoga class this evening. Hmm... what to wear and when to eat? I've secretly always hated the thought of yoga. All that silence and stretching and stifling yawns... I traipse to Stillorgan village hall and roll-out my specially purchased yoga mat. Everybody looks very serious and the teacher is lovely. She reminds me of Joanna Lumley.

I listen to her words: "This is a time for you to let go any stresses and strains from today, and just relax..." Then there are lots of funny words like Nirvana, Asana, Upward Facing Dog, Downward Facing Dog, which Declan later thought hilarious. "Really? That's yoga? Sounds a bit, you know, saucy..." he sniggers.

I feel all the more determined to stick with the yoga, not to spite his sneers, but because, actually, I felt good afterwards.

1st November 1988

OUCH! I can hardly move today. All this yoga practice that I've been doing is certainly stretching me in places I didn't know needed stretching! I'm hobbling around like an old woman when I'm supposed to be lithe and graceful.

The tablets have arrived but I can't bring myself to take them. Once I'd read the leaflet about possible side effects like, for example, hair falling out, nausea, vomiting, ectopic pregnancy, multiple births (don't mind that one), I lost confidence. I've resorted to hiding them under the floorboards. I mean, I could even die from these drugs, and what about my hair? I take my hair very seriously. I colour it with a herbal dye and condition it every day. How could I risk taking a drug that might make my hair fall out? Then I would be Bald and Barren Bridie!! No, not happening.

Declan keeps badgering me, asking, "Have they arrived yet or has the dog got them?"

I lie and say that the post must have been delayed.

7th November 1988

I admit to Declan that the tablets have arrived but that I am not taking them. We argue intensely. He is cross with me for giving up, and confronts me: "I thought we were going to have a little sister or brother for Bea? What's going on Bridie? After everything we've been through? Don't go blaming me if you don't have a baby!"

"I'm SCARED Declan. I'm shit-scared!" I scream at him. There, it's out in the open. I'm shit-scared and I don't care who knows. I tell him about reading the leaflet that comes with the drugs, and all the side-effects. Declan kicks in to GP mode:

"Bridie, you won't necessarily get a single one of those side-effects. You could sail through the treatment and feel fine, it's just that the drug companies have to list any possible side-effects by law, but you won't necessarily have them."

I'm not convinced, and we're exhausted and emotional, so we drop the subject for now.

Later...

I suppose I'm a bit depressed really. I am so sad and tearful all the time. I keep wondering why this is happening to me. HF 0. After all the yoga talk, I wonder if it's 'bad karma' and if I don't actually deserve a baby. Maybe I did something terrible in a past life? My inability to conceive torments me day and night. I see young mothers smoking a cigarette whilst pushing their prams along, and it's all I can do not to go and slap their smug little faces and swipe the pram away. I mean, I don't smoke or drink any more, I practice yoga, get plenty of fresh air walking the dog, I support loads of charities, I have at least six tubs of supplements on the go all the time. I'm a good person. Admittedly I drink too much coffee but hell, you have to have some vices. Why, oh why can't Bridie Kelly get pregnant? Perhaps the whole thing is a judgment on me and I truly don't deserve it?

10th November 1988

I'm still not taking the IVF drugs. I feel that it's too risky for my health and I worry what effect all those drugs would have on the foetus. I can't seem to reconcile these worries. I just worry all the bloody time. Life is hell at the moment. I feel so isolated and alone. More and more of my friends are having instant families. Maudy, our neighbour who is 47 years old just got pregnant for God's sake. She already has four children and she is a grandma. To make things worse, she is calling this baby 'a mistake'. Well pass it on to me then, you stupid cow!

Then to cap it all, I watched a TV programme tonight called '10 Kids and Counting'. How? Please tell me how. Or, maybe, just give me one... You wouldn't miss the wee thing.

11th November 1988

We keep having conversations about whose fault it is that I am not pregnant. I'm not blaming Declan, but he's keen for me to accept that if I decide not to go ahead with the IVF treatment, then I can't bring up the subject of having babies again. Not that I would anyway because, it is all my fault, isn't it? I mean, I'm the one with no eggs; *I'm* the one who can't conceive; but I'm the one still having hot flushes, migraines and stomach upsets. If this is the result of the Clomiphene, which I stopped taking ages ago, then God only knows what the IVF drugs would do to me.

12th November 1988

On my mother's insistence, I start a course of acupuncture but I am not hopeful. It's not long before I am fed up of little pricks everywhere!

I ponder on what it is that makes some women fertile and why after years of trying, do some couples suddenly get pregnant? What's that all about then? Giving up? Is that what I need to do? Maybe I should just give up trying so hard, and just see what happens?

Suddenly, I realise that I have thought about every scenario and I have I experienced every emotion – except one. Acceptance.

Chapter 4

Acceptance

14th November 1988

Almost one year on from when all this fertility treatment started, and I have finally come to a decision. I am not going to have any more. I chastise myself for being a wimp, but I've found the whole thing pretty unbearable. I've felt like shit for a year, and I just want my body back, unadulterated. I joke with Declan: "I am taking my eggs and going home."

Declan is empathetic for once. "Oh, Bridie – I can see what all this has done to you. Maybe it's good to accept the inevitable? It looks like it's not going to happen for us, doesn't it?" He pauses dramatically and takes my hands in his. "Denise knows of somebody in the hospital – a Mrs O'Brien – she is a kind of a counsellor, and Denise thinks you should see her and discuss how all this infertility business has affected you." He squeezes my hands and then gives me a big bear hug.

Blimey, my husband sounds like a counsellor himself. I wonder when he has been discussing me with Denise – and do I detect a distinct note of relief in his voice? Note to self: make an appointment to see this Mrs O'Brien. You bet I need somebody to talk to.

15th November 1988

I'm at Grafton Street in Dublin as I have an appointment

today with Mrs O'Brien who is a bereavement counsellor, specialising in all sorts of loss. I feel half-angry that it has come to this, and half-devastated too – but there's a little chink of light in the gloom which is that maybe, just maybe, Mrs O'Brien can help sort out what has, to be honest, become a total obsession.

We talk about my infertility: the upsetting, invasive treatments, and the feelings of loss, anger, and shame. I explain how I love children and family life, but also how my life and thoughts have become overwhelmed by having children, like an obsession, an addiction. We drink tea together (PG Tips) and I fill out confidential forms.

During the session Mrs O'Brien encourages me to express and manage difficult emotions, and not bury them. "It's okay to feel sad Bridie. Feelings are like clouds – they come and go – so don't try to stop your feelings, but observe them. Greet them and accept that today, you're feeling overwhelmingly sad and that's okay." We do a 'spidergram' connecting feelings with thoughts.

Later we talk about Bea and her needs; her journey towards acceptance of her birthmother Polly and her new female partner. Mrs O'Brien asks whether Bea's presence could help with my feelings of loss and change? Could I, Bridie Kelly, actually be happy with a family of three: me, Declan and Bea? Does it matter that I've not actually given birth to her?

Mrs O'Brien talks about writing a letter to express my feelings. "Bridie, what would you say in a letter to your unborn child?"

I looked at her, astonished. How ridiculous. Or is it...? It sounds kind of weird writing to an unborn baby, but I'll give anything a try if it helps to get rid of this knot, this constant weight in my heart. I guess if Mrs O'Brien is recommending it, then it's the right thing to do.

The trouble is, this makes me feel like I am accepting infertility but I don't really want to! I can't yet imagine letting Barren Bridie win.

Later that evening

Homework: write a letter to my unborn child. Mrs O'Brien said that this will serve as a marker and help me to move away from the dream of being pregnant and having a baby. I find a quiet place in the house and laden with a box of tissues, chocolate digestives, a can of coke, crisps and a heavy heart, I settle down to the task in hand. Slowly, I write, redrafting the letter several times before I am satisfied. It feels very odd, but surprisingly cathartic.

Dear baby girl or baby boy,

I am sorry but I just was not able to find you. (I start sobbing at this point, munching hard on my digestives.) Who knows why it never happened? My health was good and your father to be, Declan, was already a Dad – but eager for some more children. We tried lots of treatments but they were very invasive and made me feel sick and gloomy. So, reluctantly, I have decided to say goodbye to you. **(I down the whole can of coke at this stage and start weeping hard.)**

I take a break and make a round of buttery toast.

20 minutes later

Back to the letter.

Bea, Declan and I are going to be happy as a family of three and I am going to enjoy being an Aunt to Mikey, Saskia, Jazzy and 'Grandma' to baby Mia. You will always be in my heart and it was not through lack of trying that we didn't meet.

I love you so much and I am sorry.

All my love – Mummy xx

I am wailing now.

10.45pm

Declan and I snuggle-up over mugs of hot chocolate and Pringles. I tearfully read out the letter. The word 'Mummy' sticks in my throat. It's so painful, but we both agree that it is time to move on and try and get our lives back to normal.

20th November 1988

I keep losing things and snapping at people. Declan complains that I am always starting a project and not finishing it. (I begin to take umbrage that he's referring to our fertility treatment, but let it go. I don't have the energy to argue.) He says that I am distracted all the time. Well, hello! Welcome to my world – and anyway, what the hell does he expect when I have given up my dream of being a mum? But I don't say anything because I am practicing just observing my emotions as if they're clouds, and letting them pass by. I am not at all sure I wouldn't rather shout and scream.

I'm still experiencing loads of hot flushes. Helpfully, (NOT) Denise says it's good practice for the menopause. Dr Li says I must take sage capsules three times a day and drink plenty of water. I go into the pantry and count the current number of supplements and tablets I am taking and can't quite believe that it amounts to 20. I hide some of the bottles from Declan.

Evening

I am also still full of 'mummy envy' which I was hoping by now would have dissipated a bit, especially since I wrote my letter. I am fed up. HF 0. I look at my body in the bedroom mirror; it's like my breasts and womb have betrayed me, and now they are redundant. I feel like I am not a complete woman and that I can't trust my body any more.

The phone rings, and it is Lee who has the reputation of being the 'strong one' in our family. "Oh, Bridie – yes, it's painful, but you have a beautiful step-daughter. She is such a gift, so cherish her: you're her step-mum, so put all your energy into that relationship. You need to take being Bea's stepmother more seriously. Just think how hard it was for Bea when Polly came out as gay and left Declan. She needs all your love and attention Bridie, so plough your energy into supporting Bea and it will distract you from your own worries."

I groan inside. I do love Bea – I love her to bits – but that doesn't for a minute reduce the desire to have my own baby. It's like the two things are totally unrelated. I don't think anyone who hasn't been through it can understand how I feel. My arms ache, they literally ache to hold my baby. So much for letting go...

Lee twitters on. "Do you remember that book you lent me ages ago? You know the one, *The Little Book of Confidence* by Susan Jeffers?"

"Yes."

"Well I'm going to pop it back round for you to read again."

"Actually, I didn't get round to reading it the first time – the dog's read it though," I say flippantly.

Lee ignores me. "It's all about your higher and lower voice. Your higher voice is about confidence and hope and your lower voice is negative and anxious and fearful. You need to recognise when your lower voice is speaking to you and tell it that you are not listening. You need to focus on your higher voice."

Sobbing and feeling very sorry for myself, I agreed to concentrate on Bea and read the book. "Oh, Lee," I say, "don't mention this to Mum and Dad yet. I haven't told them yet."

Later that day

I am taking Mrs O'Brien's and Lee's advice seriously and turn my attention to Bea. We decide to have a 'girly evening' and head for Dublin Country Club where we swim endless lengths in the sparkling and posh new pool. We then chill-out in the coffee bar above the pool and I make my opening gambit.

"How are thing's with your Mum these days, Bea?" I ask innocently.

Bea's cheeks flush and she looks down at her hot chocolate with marshmallow sprinkles. "Bridie, I am so embarrassed about Mum! Eurghh! LESBIAN! It's so uncool."

"But she can't help the way she feels Bea, darling. Lots of people have feelings for people of the same sex." I didn't think she'd understand the word 'gender', but her response surprised me.

"I do love her, and I don't really mind her being gay actually, I just wish she had told us instead of cheating on Dad, because now he resents Pippa and has a thing about lesbians. I suppose I haven't accepted it yet." She looks up and smiles at me.

Talk about 'out of the mouth of babes'... You could've knocked me down with a feather.

"Promise you won't tell anyone about mum being gay? Do you think I'll turn out gay?"

I laughed and reassured her that being gay is probably not genetic.

We talk about boys and hair and clothes – all the things ten year-olds are into – and I console myself that Bea and I are closer than ever today. I pretend that she is my real daughter and it kind of works. I'm proud of her and I think that nobody at the spa would ever know that we weren't mother and daughter.

Later, in bed, I read Susan Jeffers' *Little Book of Confidence*, which true to her word, Lee popped through the letterbox whilst we were in town. I diligently read and memorise the first quote. *'I open my eyes and heart and take in all the gifts that have been given me.'*

Do you know, that kind of makes sense. I have loving parents, a step-daughter (well, three if you count Flora and Sandy – but they're too old for me to mother now), beautiful nieces and nephews, a caring and patient husband, my beloved, thieving dog Fritz, and a beautiful home. I feel better already, even after reading one page.

28th November 1988, Mrs O'Brien – Visit 2

"Okay, Bridie – have you written your letter?"

I nod and meekly palm it across the desk to her.

"Can I read it?"

I nod again and she takes her time to read it through twice, but doesn't comment on it. Instead she rummages around in a capacious handbag, emerging with a pen and pad, and says, "So, let's create some options for you now, and then you can start to move forward."

Armed with her pen and paper Mrs O'Brien makes a list of possible options:

Option 1. Learn to be happy with what you've got
Option 2. Foster
Option 3. Adopt

I am dumbstruck as Mrs O'Brien writes these words, because after Mr Willey's mention of adoption and Declan's glowering response, all thoughts of such a course of action were banished from my mind. Now, whether she realises it or not, Mrs O'Brien has reignited the motherhood flame in me. I barely listen to her for the rest of the session as my mind races with possibilities. *Bridie Kelly is going to be a MUM, fertility drugs or not!*

Suddenly, I feel like me again.

20th December 1988

Mum and Dad have come over for supper. They don't know about the letter I have written, but they will soon, especially since Mum keeps going on and on about IVF. She's still excited about the treatment but what she doesn't know is that I never started it in the first place. She obviously doesn't understand how out of control and depressed I feel, otherwise she wouldn't still be talking about fertility treatment.

Over pudding, Bea innocently asks me, "Bride, are you still trying for a baby? It would be cool to have another baby in the family."

This is my moment and I grab it with both hands. "No, Bea, we're not still trying for a baby. Daddy and I have decided to accept that I can't have babies of my own. We've come to the end of that particular road." I am tearful but firm. What I don't mention is that I've got my eyes firmly set on another road altogether, but I haven't got the courage to face Mum, Dad and Declan with the A-word yet. Adoption.

My mother looks aghast. "BRIDIE! What do you mean? IVF can be really successful these days. Why don't you just give it one more try? Please, just for me?"

"I am telling you now Mum, I am not going through that drug treatment again. I'll probably end up with ovarian cancer at this rate. The fertility drugs were bad enough – they've given me hot flushes, migraine, irritability, depression... They're so horrible – you can't imagine. And anyway, I've been having a long think about everything... I have an announcement to make." Mum abruptly looked up from her coffee, her eyes narrowing. I went on. "After seeing a counsellor last week, I have decided to give up on the idea of fertility treatment forever."

Mother immediately became stiff and morose. Sniffing into her handkerchief she cried, "Bridie... it's no good just giving up!"

"I'm not just *giving up*, Mum. I really can't do it anymore. It's turning me into a nervous wreck. I'm sorry, but my mind is made up. I've written..." Tears spill over my cheeks, and I look at Declan for support. He nods at me and smiles. He knows what I'm going to say. "I've written a 'Goodbye Baby' letter, Mum... (sniff). I've written to my unborn babies, telling them that I love them, but that I just couldn't meet them. I'm sorry, Mum..."

With that, my mother left the house abruptly.

A little later my mother returns with Trixy her Jack Russell. She thrusts a small package in my hand.

"Bridie darling," she says tenderly, "you had better put

these with the Goodbye Baby letter. I bought them for you some time ago, just some little baby things, coats, booties and hats. I love this little teddy bear – I chose him myself..." My Mum stifles a sob.

"Mum, let's keep Roger Bear out as a symbol of hope. You never know what the future holds, eh?"

I place Roger Bear on his own on the sofa. "Perhaps Roger Bear will bring us luck?" I hug my determined mother.

22nd December 1988

I asked Mum if she and Dad would like to see the Goodbye Baby letter. I feel that I gave her a bit too much hope with the Roger Bear scenario earlier in the week. Dad says that it sounds a bit maudlin and that he'd rather not, but Mum said that perhaps we could quietly read the letter together and then move on. I am grateful to her for her understanding and I know that, in the end, she just wants what's best for me.

After lunch

I go over to Mum and Dad's house with the letter in my bag. Later that afternoon, on our own, Mum and I quietly prepare to read the Goodbye Baby letter. Mum makes a nice pot of Earl Grey tea and puts some homemade chocolate éclairs and scones on a plate. Dad has even given us his new batch of jam to try, but he then absents himself from the proceedings. The jam looks a bit runny and lumpy but it is a nice thought. Dad likes to keep himself busy with his jam- and cake-making, his regular letter-writing to the Guardian and his beloved fish pond.

After tea Mum reads the letter and sheds a few tears.

"Don't say 'never' Bridie," she admonishes. "It's never too late you know. You feel like this now, but if you change your mind tell me. Daddy and I will always help you, you know."

"Thanks, Mum," I say, admiring her indomitable spirit, and thinking that I'll have to get her on my side later, when I broach the A-subject.

Chapter 5

Moving On

Christmas Eve 1988

It feels good to have finally told everyone about my decision to stop all the fertility treatment. I swear my migraines stopped as soon as I did so. Declan seems to be in a much better mood too, and kissed me quite passionately under the mistletoe earlier today. It's as if we've suddenly remembered what it's like to be intimate with each other without a thermometer, injections and urgency.

Lee and Denise are very supportive, saying that we've made the right decision. Lee asks me if Saskia and Jazzy can come and stay for a couple of days after Christmas as she and Ned had been invited to a party in Cork. She says she didn't like to ask me before in case it upset me too much.

I was beginning to realise how much my fertility treatment has affected the rest of the family too – I just hadn't seen it before. "Of course, Lee – Bea would love it! We'd all love to have the twins to stay."

"They've missed you, Bride."

"What?"

"You've been... a bit distant with them."

I start to flare-up with an indignant response, but then realise she's right. "I know. I'm sorry, Lee. I've been so taken-up with all this fertility stuff, I've neglected the family I've got."

When the twins were born, Lee encouraged me to play a big role in their lives. We did so much together: going to the park, taking long walks with the double-buggy, just hanging-out together and sharing the love we felt having these two little lives in our midst. Where did that all go? It's like I'm seeing daylight for the first time in ages.

We're having such a lovely Christmas Eve. We went round to Mum and Dad's and everyone was there. Ned and Lee and the twins; Denise and Mikey, Flora and Mia who are expecting Brendan to return on leave before new year, and even Aunty Bernadette called in for a cup of tea. Only my brother Tim wasn't with us as he was away on a skiing holiday with his mates – such a perennial teenager, my brother, even in his forties!

There was no talk of babies, or treatment or hospitals. I had a large Baileys to celebrate Christmas, because I bloody well could now – I didn't have to deny myself anything just to keep in tip-top conceiving condition. That felt good. I had another.

We put on one of Dad's old Christmas records and sang carols together in the living room and the children were so excited they could hardly contain themselves. Bea, being the eldest, led Saskia, Jazzy and Mikey a merry dance as she proclaimed she could hear Santa's sleigh bells outside. We adults played along and all stood in the twinkling darkness, fairy lights in every direction, looking into the cold winter sky, to see if we could see Santa, his sleigh and reindeers. The only thing missing was snow – otherwise it would've been Christmas perfection.

Back home, after Bea has reluctantly gone to bed with threats of Santa not coming if she doesn't get some sleep, I have another large Baileys with ice, and pour Declan a glass of red wine, and then settle on the sofa. *This is nice*, I think.

"This is nice, darling," I say. "Wasn't Bea sweet tonight with the twins and Mikey?"

"She's a good girl really," her Dad says. "She doesn't seem to have suffered too much, what with all the fertility lark and everything you've been through, but I do feel we neglected her a bit."

"Do you?" I ask, genuinely surprised. "Ah, but she's a tough cookie really, Declan. She's had to be, since her Mum started 'batting for the other side'!" I laugh at my little joke, but Declan ignores me and stiffens visibly. "C'mon, D – I'm only joking," I say, and then out of nowhere, or perhaps out of my slightly alcoholic fug I put my foot right in it with, "she's going to need to be strong when we start adoption proceedings."

Declan's stiffness descends rapidly into something akin to rigor mortis. I see him sighing and shaking his head. "Bridie, we have had enough stress already, and Bea can be a handful – you know she can. She's getting to that age where her hormones will start racing around and she'll be endlessly nagging us to take her to parties and sleepovers, and she is going to need a helping hand to get her through school. Not to mention coming to terms with, you know, Polly's change of heart."

"Well, she's got the two of us to help her, Declan. It's not like you have to do it all on your own. We both love her and will help her."

"So, why isn't our little family good enough for you then? Why do you keep pushing, pushing – all the time...?"

"Because I... because I want a child of my own."

"But it won't bloody well be your own Bridie, if you're adopting or fostering or whatever it is you want to do now! It'll never be your own – it'll always be someone else's child. Always. And anyway, if you're adopting you need to be... well, organised and domesticated. They won't all be cute little vegetarians you know."

Something in me snapped. Call it the final straw of the

year from hell we'd just been through, but out it came. "It's adoption or divorce."

"Don't tempt me!" Declan replied icily and stalked off to bed, leaving me shocked and very much sobered-up on the sofa.

Where in God's name did all that come from? Has this adoption thing been so much in my consciousness since Mrs O'Brien first mentioned it that it just leaked out with the first alcoholic lubricant I've imbibed for months? I didn't intend to even raise the subject until the New Year.

I sigh and climb the stairs to bed. Declan has obviously decided to sleep in the guest room.

Christmas Morning, 1988

RESULT! I was awoken at 7.30am, not by Bea (who was miraculously still asleep) but by Declan, with a mug of PG and some buttered toast. He sat on the edge of the bed and it was obvious he'd been up for a while because he'd shaved and put on his Christmas jumper from last year.

"Look Bridie, I've been thinking… I know how hard it's been for you to accept that you can't have babies of your own. God knows, it's been hard, for both of us, and I don't want to take away your hope of ever being a Mum… But, I don't think now is the right time for any of us. What I'm suggesting is that we give ourselves a bit of time. We focus on Bea and being a little family, and we make the most of what we've got, and then in a couple of years or so, if you still feel the same… we can think again. How does that sound? Better than divorce?"

"Better than divorce," I say and crawl across the covers to give him a hug. "I love you. Thank you, Declan. You're a wonderful man. Let's take things one step at a time. You're right. I'll keep working on counting my blessings, and we'll see how we get on."

"I love you too," he says and hugs me warmly.

At that, Bea stumbles in rubbing her eyes, her hair a bird's nest on top of her head and asks, "Has he been? Has Santa been yet?"

31st January 1988

I think I have gone all Buddhist-y. I am trying to be happy with what I have got and, well, so far so good. My favourite quote of the moment from *Buddha's Little Instruction Book* is, 'When wishes are few, the heart is happy. When desire ends, there is peace.' This must be true because since I've started to accept that I can't have children and that as a family, we are not ready to foster or adopt yet, things do seem to have got much easier. Everything is falling into place and I'm feeling happier as a result. I know for sure that Declan is.

He was right: Bea is a huge consideration and we owe it to her to make sure she feels loved and secure, and not threatened by another child coming into the family. And besides, Declan is 49 years old with two other grown-up children and four small grandchildren. We already have a big family. As Lee has pointed out (many times, *ad nauseum*, frankly), family does not have to mean having a baby, and good old Susan Jeffers is right too: I must be thankful for all the gifts that I have been given.

The only cloud on the horizon is my mother who has not really accepted my intentions in the Goodbye Baby letter. She keeps saying, "I know you're still feeling maternal, Bridie, and that feeling won't go away." I think, no and neither will your meddling, Mother. She says that the personal development books are negatively influencing me and that Declan is a killjoy.

Time passes by, diaries are forgotten...

It's amazing how time flies once you make a decision and stick with it. Over the course of the next nine years, I learned to live with my childlessness and I reluctantly accepted my sub-fertility, although never a month went by that I didn't wish fervently that my period was late and that I was preggers. It never was late.

Sometimes I berated myself for being too cowardly to go through IVF, but just the thought of how terrible I felt when I was taking the fertility drugs reminded me that it just wasn't an option – my body couldn't have taken the battering. That, I am sure about. Do I wish I'd given it a go? Sometimes. Quite often in fact, but I think it would've killed me. And I stopped writing my diary too – it seemed I had nothing worth writing about, really – there was nothing I wanted to say.

Gradually, I accepted my fate and regularly re-read my Goodbye Baby letter, which was such a huge help in keeping me focused – and gradually my mother accepted it too. And it wasn't all bad, far from it, because we did thrive as a little family and I did enjoy being a supportive step-mother to Bea, whose teenage years were turbulent at times, but no more than any other girl finding her way in life and coming to terms with the changing relationship between her parents. She's become a keen horsewoman and a talented skier. I also had loads of fun being an Aunty to the lovely twins who are now 14 years old – I can hardly believe it. They've been a bit of a handful at times, what with Saskia's weed-smoking boyfriend and Jazzy's refusal to do anything except stay in her room and watch MTV. And, of course, baby Mia has been delightful too. She is eight and simply gorgeous.

But I yearned, oh, how I yearned. Never a day went by that I didn't have that feeling of emptiness inside – and no matter what I tried, it wouldn't go away. It felt like a void or a hole in my heart, but it was heavy too, a weight that was a burden I just had to bear. Nothing I could do made it go away.

Nine years passed, and I lived with that yearning for a baby, through every single moment.

Chapter 6

The Empty-Nest Syndrome

3rd January 1997

It must be all these personal development books I'm reading, but I'm feeling compelled to write my diary again. For years – eight years to be precise – it hasn't crossed my mind to do so, but of late, I find myself writing notes on any old bit of paper: on the back of shopping lists, on cinema tickets – just little thoughts and ideas, nothing massively significant, but I'm enjoying the process of writing. Last night, I dug out my old diary and read it from the beginning, reliving my agonies of childlessness, and it has to be said, rekindling some thoughts of adoption. I push them to the back of my mind – I've got very good at doing that – and instead, apply myself to restarting my diary. The housework goes unfinished as I become utterly absorbed with writing again. I've forgotten how much I enjoy this.

The quote of the day from the book I'm reading is: 'Failure is not about falling down, but making the conscious effort to get up again'. It's true in my case, because I fell good and proper down the hole of sub-fertility, but I did dig myself out of that hole and 'got up again'. But, I have also started reading another book called, *How To Coach Yourself* and I must admit, worryingly, that I am ticking quite a few boxes indicating negative behaviours. As a result I made a list of New Year Resolutions:

1. Talk less, listen more.

2. Turn negatives into positives, remembering that we are the sum total of our thoughts. (Apparently we have 90,000 thoughts a day and 60,000 are repetitive. In other words, we think the same thoughts over and over again. Erm, like, I can totally identify with that one!)

3. Try to see the funny side of life, and not hang on to criticism or negativity.

4. Don't burden people with my problems (this one worries me a bit as how would I be able to cope otherwise?). There's also a quotation that's stuck in my mind: 'Those who speak don't know; those who know don't speak'. Hmmm – I'm not sure about that one, but it keeps popping into my head when I'm rabbiting on to Lee or Gina about something insignificant, and it stops me in my tracks. Well, I'll *try* not to talk so much, but it won't be easy.

5. Exercise every day – that one's okay as I love taking the dogs on long walks. (My trawl through the diary brought back fond memories of Thieving Fritz, long departed. Now we have two bouncing golden Labradors – Hilda and Harry – who I adore equally and treat like my babies. They seem to have inherited Fritz's trait of stealing things too.)

6. See a glass half-full and turn lemons into lemonade. Love that one.

7. Work on my personal development every day. (I will try!)

8. Restart my diary.

I wonder how long I'll keep them up.

Later the same day

Reluctantly, as the evening wears on, I leave my desk and my diary to cook dinner for me and Declan. I'm still a vegetarian after all these years, switching my diet on the advice of Dr Li, and never looking back. I put a thawed-out vegetable lasagne for me, and a beef one for Declan in the oven, and pride myself that they are both homemade from the leftovers of the Christmas dinner, frozen into individual portions for easy use. I also open a bottle of wine, which has become a bit of a habit over the Christmas break, and still not something we're quite ready to give up just yet. Maybe for Lent?

Later we cuddle-up on the sofa. For once, the television is switched off and we're just gazing peacefully at the log fire.

"It's quiet without Bea isn't it?" Declan comments, echoing my own thoughts exactly. How intuitive couples get when they've lived together for years.

"It is! She's such a ball of energy, but at least she's happy at college. I was worried for a while that she'd get homesick and come back!"

"Me too, although I'm not sure whether my feelings are from worry or hope! But she really seems to have settled in Cork, doesn't she? She seems to like the city as much as the college. I expect we'll only see her now at Christmas and summer holidays."

"If we're lucky, Declan!"

The dogs snore at our feet and all seems well with the world.

19th January 1997

The house is so quiet today. Declan's gone to a GP's conference in Cork for a couple of days and is going to have dinner with Bea tonight, so it's just me, the dogs and my trusty laptop, on which I'm retyping my entire diary for safe-keeping. I've transferred all my entries into neat folders, filed per year, and I'm up to date. I can now just write to my heart's content.

As I type these words though, I can hear every noise in the house: the tap dripping in the bathroom (must go and turn it off properly); the dogs pushing their bowls around the kitchen floor (it's their signal to me that it's dinner time); even the feint roar of aircraft overhead – something I've never noticed before. It's so quiet...

28th January 1997

I picked up a leaflet in the doctor's surgery where I've been a regular visitor of late, seeing the chiropodist to get my verrucas treated. (I must admit to being a tiny bit disappointed to have picked up these contagious little warty things whilst at the posh environs of Dublin Bay Spa, which I thought would somehow be immune to such nasty diseases.) The leaflet is called 'Adoption and You' and its subtitle is: 'A journey to discover whether adoption is for you, and what kind of parent you might be'. I read it from cover to cover sitting in the car in the surgery car park, then stuff it in my handbag. I try to shove all thoughts of adoption to the back of my mind, but a flurry of words circle around like twittering sparrows in my brain: 'Adoption is a way of providing a new family for children who cannot be brought-up by their own parents.'

I get home to the smell of curry spices. Declan is in the kitchen with an apron on, whistling away tunelessly to himself. He is cooking dinner tonight and is experimenting with Indian cuisine, having just been on the cookery course I bought him for Christmas. I'm free until 6.30pm. Like an automaton, I head for the bathroom, lock the door and get the leaflet back out of my bag. I realise my heart is beating ten to the dozen.

At the end of the leaflet, there's a section on fostering. 'For those who are not quite ready to take on the life-long commitment and responsibilities of adoption, fostering may be a consideration. Foster parents look after children when their own parents aren't able to do so. Foster children usually return home once the circumstances that caused them to come into foster care have been resolved.'

Hmmm – even fostering appeals to me. I mean, it's usually short-term, so Declan can't get shirty about the 'forever-ness' of adoption, and I could be 'Mum' to dozens of kids. I envisage myself as an old woman, with an endless stream of my grown-up foster-children coming to visit me, their own children clinging to my legs as if I'm some kind of fairy godmother. I love the thought of it.

I run a bath and trickle in the expensive Tranquility Bubbles Declan bought me for Christmas. Too late, I realise that I have squeezed half the bottle into the foaming waters. I slip into the perfumed, steaming suds in a daze, my mind a tumult of thoughts and ideas.

I've rarely mentioned adoption to Declan since that row we had years ago when the 'D-word' – divorce – was mentioned. I recall the fear in his eyes and the tension in his whole body whenever I raised the subject – but fostering... now, we've never talked about that. Maybe we'd make great foster-parents and perhaps fostering would be a good compromise for us after all? Fostering is much more short-term. You just help people out for a while. Okay, you can get attached to the children, but we would be able to give them such a nice home; warm and loving. The children wouldn't go without a thing whilst they are with us, and Bea and the twins and Mikey and Mia would be great role models. I don't think D's ready for fostering yet, but I sure as hell am.

I languish in the bath in a reverie of children's laughter, autumnal walks and summer holidays, then realise the water is stone cold and Declan is shouting up the stairs that dinner is almost ready and will be served in ten minutes.

31st January 1997

We've walked for ages along the Howth coastal path, a favourite weekend walk of ours with the dogs. We found this beautiful area when we used to bring Bea here for riding lessons, and it's become a regular pilgrimage – something we both look forward to and really enjoy. We like to head north from the car park and after a couple of miles there's a little beach shack that does the most amazing coffee and cakes, then we turn around and head back, and finish off with a lunchtime drink or sometimes a bar snack in O'Connells. Today, we opt for lunch as we're both ravenous from the walk and the pub welcomes dogs. As we wait for our food, the conversation takes an unexpected twist.

"I saw that leaflet you threw in the bathroom bin."

I feel the colour drain from my face – I'm not ready for this: I haven't sorted my tactics out. Before I can reply, Declan continues, "I didn't realise you were back on the adoption trail again."

"I'm not," I say indignantly. "That's why I threw it away."

"Why did you pick it up in the first place though? That's what I'm interested to know."

"Oh, I don't know... I saw it in the surgery when I was having my feet done. Did you read it?"

"I did."

"And...? Are we ready to think about fostering, Declan?"

I think, *I'll throw him off the scent a bit and mention the F-word as it might be more acceptable than adoption.* Warming to the subject, I add, "I could ask Edna the social worker I contacted a few years ago to visit us?"

Declan looks at me and sighs. "You've obviously thought this all through then?"

"No, no, I haven't Declan. It's just that, I don't know... it's so quiet in the house with Bea gone, and I'm just kicking around now, writing my diary and doing the washing. I need something more in my life. You did say, years ago, that if I still felt the same about having children once Bea's grown up, then we'd think about it, didn't you?"

"Did I?" he says, looking puzzled.

"Don't you remember? After I'd written my Goodbye Baby letter?"

Declan's faced clouds over as he recalls that moment of deep sadness. "Look, I'm getting a bit old for all this malarkey, Bridie. I've had my family, my children – but you haven't. You've looked after my children, but you haven't had your own children. I know that's been hard for you. But if we do go down this route, then you've got to take the lion's share of the responsibility – my job's so demanding and I don't have the energy to deal with domestics at home on top of everything at work. And I think if we do this, we should start off with fostering first, just to see if we're cut out for it."

I beam at him – I can't believe what I'm hearing.

"Do you mean it, D? You'd be okay if I found out a bit more about fostering?"

He lets out a long sigh. "Bridie, if it's what you want to do, who am I to stop you? You deserve to be happy. You're a brilliant mum to Bea, so what's to stop you being a brilliant mum to other kids who need someone to love them? All I'd say is, make sure you know what you're letting us in for before there's any signing on the dotted line, okay?"

Two huge plates of food are plonked in front of us and conversation is cut off by talk of salt, pepper and an extra bowl of water for the dogs. But in my heart a great big ray of sunshine is pouring light into every cell in my body and I somehow feel more alive than I have done for years. I picture a small girl of six years old or so, arriving at our house with a suitcase and a teddy bear. I welcome her with open arms into the Kelly household and the whole family adores her.

An old name from the past – Barren Bridie – seems to shrivel and die under the burning glare of the sunlight in my soul.

Chapter 7

Deciding To Foster

13th February 1997

I think long and hard about what makes a good foster carer.
I always find it easier to think when I'm doing something, so I
decide to tidy the house and have a good spring clean, even if
it is a bit early.

Firstly, I consider where we might've done a bit better with
Bea, and I think being consistent with house rules would've
been a good starting point. Poor old Bea didn't know if
she was coming or going sometimes: I'd try being firm and
assertive about something like not wearing make-up to school
and Declan would undermine me with, "For God's sake, Bridie,
she's only expressing herself. She's had to witness a messy,
painful, divorce and she's acquired a step-sister courtesy of
her mother's new partner..." Declan never could accept that his
ex-wife Polly preferred the arms of another woman to his, and
I can understand that this could be a blow to his masculinity –
but what's it got to do with Bea wearing too much eyeliner?

Often, I would say one thing, and Declan would say
another: so I decide that with fostering, we've both got to
be 'singing from the same hymn sheet'. It's easy to be wise
in retrospect, but I do think we gave in to Bea too much,
to try and make up for all the chaos in her formative years.
For instance, I remember being exasperated that she never
emptied her waste paper bin in her bedroom (it always had
coke cans, chewing gum, Tampax packets and latterly, wine

bottles overflowing out of it) and she never changed her sheets unless I nagged her mercilessly. But if I mentioned it to her, she'd pit me and Declan against each other: "Daaaaaad, Bridie's having a go at me again," and D would say, "Oh, leave her be, Bridie." You know, now that I'm thinking about it, Bea would always call me Mum if she wanted something, and Bridie if she wanted to hurt me. It was her way of distancing herself from me to get what she wanted. Bloody hell – kids can be devious, and probably more so if they're coming from tricky family backgrounds.

I even contacted social services once, as I was so concerned about our parenting of Bea, but the advice we got from Edna Pritchard was that first, we should attend parenting classes to meet others in a similar situation, and if we were still worried, to come back to her. Needless to say, we never went and anyway, we just coped, as parents do.

As Bea got older, she was allowed to come home any time she liked, and on occasion she did so blind drunk. One particular night, I woke up to a kind of pitiful wailing coming from the bathroom and I found her practically unconscious beside the toilet with a half-eaten packet of crisps, a Chinese take-away and an empty wine bottle by her side. I wanted to have it out with her the next morning about how inappropriate it was to wake her parents, pissed out of her mind at three o'clock in the morning, but Declan's response was, "Leave it out, Bride – she's just trying to find her feet in the adult world." And to a degree, he was right because Bea has turned into a lovely young woman and her teenage wobbles were just that: wobbles. But, when we get our foster child, I want things to be different. There's going to be no good cop/bad cop this time because Declan won't have any hidden agendas and he's going to have to back me up 100%. In Declan's defence, he is a fantastic Dad to all his kids: warm, loving and good fun; he was just a bit inconsistent when it came to setting boundaries, and I do understand why.

I've made an appointment for Edna Pritchard to visit us in a week's time and between now and then I'm going to have a serious chat with Declan about house rules.

20th February 1997

Edna Pritchard, our link social worker, is coming to visit us today. I spend the whole day cleaning the house, walking the dogs and providing them with filled Kongs and smelly bones to keep them quiet whilst Edna is here. I am determined that we make a good impression.

After lunch, the phone rings. It's Mum, asking if she can come round to meet Edna. "I will be the grandma after all," she says in her confident 'let me sort everything out' voice.

"Okay, Mum," I say hesitantly, figuring that Edna may be impressed at my united, extended family, "but this is my big chance so don't go tormenting her or arguing with her before she's even started."

My mother feigns being hurt: "Bridie, that's not fair! I only have your best intentions at heart."

It's 2.30pm and Mum is knitting peacefully on the sofa, dressed in her best twin-set and pearls. She might look a bit conservative, but she certainly scrubs-up well and looks slim and rather glamorous, though I say it myself. Roger Bear, who is propped in the corner of the sofa, has survived many a tantrum and a cuddle intact, and has been machine-washed and dressed in new clothes – so keen am I to make a homely, child-friendly impression. My Dad, thankfully, has decided not to come. Mum said she left him painstakingly typing a vicious letter to the *Guardian*, because he is appalled at the divisions of wealth in his beloved England. "It makes a change from him writing about the CND," says my Mum disapprovingly. She's very catholic in her tastes and doesn't really believe in challenging authority. Declan is likely to be at work for the duration of Edna's visit, and I am glad about that, as I'm really nervous about this first meeting and I just want to see how we get on without making any decisions.

I continue to plump cushions nervously and adjust the display of child-rearing books on the bookshelf to best effect in the hopes that Edna will be impressed. The toilet is immaculate with Ecover sprayed around the edges, and I am leaving the *Guardian* newspaper, and a book on Personal Development on the coffee table beside where Edna will be sitting.

"Oh, do stop fussing," my mother tut-tuts.

The doorbell trills and the dogs bark nervously. I open the door to a plump middle-aged lady with blow-dried grey hair and black, horn-rimmed glasses. She smiles sweetly, her lips crimson.

I hold out my hand in formal greeting. "Edna" I say. "Pleased to meet you. Do come in."

She waves her identity badge in my face by way of reply and barges into the sitting room.

"Oh, very nice," she says approvingly, and I breathe an audible sigh of relief. She places her briefcase on the newly polished table beside Roger Bear and glances approvingly at the *Guardian*. (Well, I think it's an approving glance – for all I know she could read *Communism Today*.)

I dash out to put the kettle on and the dogs escape from the kitchen to see who the visitor is. They immediately disgrace themselves by jumping up all over Edna's black corduroy trousers leaving their fine white hairs everywhere.

"BRIDIE!" my mother shouts, "get those wretched dogs

back in the kitchen will you now, they're such a nuisance." And from behind her pink knitting my mother emerges and says, "Good afternoon, Mrs Pritchard, I'm Bridie's mother, Winifred."

Edna shakes my mother's hand and smiles. "Lovely to meet you, Winifred."

"I'm so sorry about Hilda and Harry," I say, grabbing both dogs by the collar and booting them gently back into the kitchen.

"Oh, but I love dogs," says Edna, and I wonder if she's this nice to everybody.

The rest of the afternoon was spent drinking tea, eating specially baked homemade scones topped with my Dad's runny jam, and discussing the idea of fostering or, hopefully, adoption.

Edna looked at me over the top of her glasses when I mentioned adoption. "Oh, so you're interested in adoption are you?" and my mother inches closer to ensure she doesn't miss this bit of the conversation.

"Well, we've talked about it," I reply, "but I think Declan, my husband – he's a GP, did I say? – I think Declan wants to take things one step at a time and start off with fostering."

"Well that's a sensible approach in my view," replies Edna, shuffling the vast pile of papers she's taken out of her briefcase. "You see, at your age you'd only be likely to be approved for fostering. However adoption could be a possibility depending on the kind of placements you get, and if they go well."

I try to take everything in, but there's so much to remember. I'm a little disconcerted at the mention of the 'age' thing. I know Declan's nearly 58, but he's young for his age and very fit and healthy, and I'm only 39... I'd assumed that we'd be a prime adoption family given our experience. I never imagined that we may be considered too old. This was a bit of a blow to be frank, but thinking about my positive New Year Resolutions, I resolve to cross that bridge if we come to it and not let age get in the way of my dream. I recall the furore our relationship caused when we first got together – anyone would think Declan was a paedophile, the way people looked at us when we were out together. Now, nobody takes a blind bit of notice at our age difference.

However, my mother was having no such truck with fostering first. "But, Mrs Pritchard…"

"Edna, please."

"Edna – could they not just get on with it and adopt, especially if age is an issue? They are wonderful parents – they've already proved that with Declan's children from his first marriage. What about from abroad – a nice little Chinese baby? A friend of mine adopted an 18-month old baby girl from Taiwan. Pretty little thing she was. She's brought them so much joy – she even went to university and now she has had her own children, making my friend a grandma at long last. Imagine that – me, Grandma to a little Oriental…"

I butt-in and stop my mother in her tracks before she says something really embarrassing. "MUM! This isn't all about you, in case you haven't noticed!"

Edna looks annoyed and disapproving but smiles a theatrical smile. "Winifred, adopting from abroad is expensive and difficult, and many of the babies are disabled in some way. There can also be a lot of future problems if the identity of the parents is unknown. But in answer to your first question, no, I don't think Bridie and Declan are ready to adopt yet. There are plenty of older children in Dublin that need short-term foster placements. Let's get Bridie and Declan on a 'Choosing to Foster' course first, and see where things go from there."

My mother mutters under her breath – something about

freedom of choice and not wanting to be saddled with an older grandchild. "I still think a little Chinese baby would be better than all this fostering lark. I mean, they are going to have to return home anyway, so what's the point if you don't get to keep the child?" With pursed lips, she attacked her fluffy knitting.

I felt a bit miffed to be honest. Miffed that I'd let my mother take over proceedings and miffed that Edna doesn't think we're up to adopting. How on earth did she think we managed all these years with Bea?

My mother had taken an instant dislike to Edna. She says that she is like a cross between a schoolmistress, Mrs Danvers from Daphne Du Maurier's *Rebecca* and Cruella de Vil! I suggest to my mother that it is probably better to co-operate with Edna than get on the wrong side of her, since she is our ticket to fostering and possible adoption, although to be quite honest, I didn't think she truly appreciated all the cleaning I'd done for her first visit. Nonetheless, credit where credit's due, she's booked us in to the 'Choosing to Foster' course, which is being held next week in Dublin.

27th February 1997

Declan and I are at the Fostering Course Introductory Evening, and we are on tenterhooks as we introduce ourselves to the three other couples who, like us, are considering the idea of fostering. We exchange stories about our lives and drink dreadful instant coffee. 20 minutes later we notice that somebody is trying to attract our attention. "Hello, hello!"

I turn to see Edna's face poking around the door.

"Excuse me everybody, but you're in the wrong room. The film 'Choosing to Foster' is starting now, so if you would like to be seated next door..." Edna ushers us into another big hall where several more couples were already sitting in a semi-circle in front of a projector screen.

Declan groans audibly and whispers to me, "Please tell me that is not our social worker?"

I nod that it is.

Declan says, "Winnie was right, she is Mrs Danvers. I'm going to have to call her Danny just like in the film!"

Unfortunately, as our film progresses Declan becomes more and more uncomfortable. Half way through he whispers in my ear, "Bridie, I am not at all sure I can do this!" whilst I am utterly sure I can.

1st April 1997

"Oh my God, Declan. You'll never guess what's happened? They've only gone and delivered two kids for us to have a practice fostering with."

There is stunned silence on the other end of the phone then a booming, "How dare they do that without giving us some notice first..."

"April Fool!" I interrupt.

He slams the phone down on me.

2nd April 1997

Tonight we have the first proper evening in the six-part fostering course. I am excited and restless: I can't wait. Declan, however, is less than enthusiastic, saying he is exhausted after a stream of patients with early onset dementia and that he is now feeling a bit demented himself. We are having a little tiff over what to wear. He is insisting on donning his oversize flat cap that makes him look like that old sixties singer – Donovan I think it was. I'm worried that may be a bit of a bad mark against us – I mean, we don't want to look like a couple of hippies, do we?

We compromise: he can take his hat but not wear it inside. We're friends again and set off for the meeting in reasonable spirits. We are put into three different groups and begin discussing various subjects with a facilitator such as: What sort of children usually need fostering; Getting started with fostering; Your first placement, etc. God, it's all so exciting! And to think, at the end of the training, if we are successful and approved, we will have a child placed with us. And if that goes well, we could look at adoption. Obviously, I'm keeping 'Mum' about the adoption bit, because Declan can't take it on board right now, but to me, only then will I become a mother. That is my ultimate aim.

9th April 1997

This week at our fostering course, we discuss parenting a difficult child. Again we assemble into groups and discuss different techniques. I am unfortunate enough to have Declan in my group and he is provocatively suggesting that kids don't need discipline and rules, they need to be free spirits. I can see that he's playing devil's advocate here, but it's really not the time or place. Why is he doing this?

"What about homework rules, Declan?" Edna asks. "Surely they're a good thing?"

Suddenly Declan gets all defensive. "Look, I'm a GP as well as a parent, and a granddad too. I do know a thing or two about children...

I am furious with Declan. What's he trying to do? Ruin our chances of fostering?

But Edna has not finished with him. She clears her throat. "So, Declan: difficult child, shouting, having a tantrum, what would you do?"

Most uncharacteristically, Declan is lost for words, and I wonder if he really was trying to tell me something about dementia last week.

"We would try to calm the child down and not respond to the tantrum. We would sanction them when they had calmed down and look at what had happened and how we can avoid it in the future," I intercede, reciting almost verbatim the techniques I had learned from one of the many parenting books I'd hoarded over the last few weeks.

Edna smiles her knowing smile and nods her head in approval. "Well done, Bridie. I can see you've been doing your homework." She gives Declan a warning glare.

As we drive home later, Declan says he's not going to any more fostering classes. "Bridie, I love you, but I am not being told what to do by Mrs bloody Danvers. Who the hell does she think she is? I'm a GP for God's sake – I know all there is to know about children."

"But why did you say all that tosh about children needing to be free spirits?"

"I don't think it is tosh, actually. What I do think is tosh are these god-awful classes about childcare led by a bloody spinster!"

"How do you know Edna's a spinster?"

"Well... who'd want to marry her?"

"Declan! Sometimes you're impossible!" I shout, and we drive home in silence.

16th April 1997

I am dreading tonight's meeting. Not only is Declan refusing to attend, but this evening, we will study the taboo subject of child abuse and I know I will find it distressing. Edna says that sometimes people leave the course after this week as it's all too much for them to take in. I am determined I will not be among them. Interestingly, I notice there are several other people besides Declan who are absent from the course and there seems to be a bit of a gloomy atmosphere amongst all of us. The tension is palpable. It occurs to me that Declan and I may not be the only ones who are finding this difficult.

A social worker from Child Protection is speaking. "As foster carers we must protect ourselves from allegations of abuse. Children in care may have memories of abuse that can be triggered by a new family. The following rules apply:

1. When having a bath, toddlers should be left on their own as much as possible with the carer looking on. We do not recommend playing games in the bath or telling stories in the bath. All bathroom doors should have a lock on them for the privacy and protection of older children.

2. At bedtime, read a story in the lounge, not in the bedroom.

3. Highly excitable, physical games are to be avoided between adult and child.

Christ. I didn't realise that we might be accused of abuse.

Later, a speaker from the NSPCC talks to us about the effects of child abuse on a young person. The man spoke for an hour and what he had to say was bewildering, depressing and incredibly sad. I resolve to fundraise for the NSPCC this year. I also promise never to raise my voice to a child ever again.

Later, at home

I return home to find Declan nervously hovering at the door.

"How did it go?" he asks, and I blurt it all out. We stay up late talking deeply about the desperate situation some poor kids find themselves in through no fault of their own, and I realise how much tonight's course affected me.

As Declan cleans his teeth in the bathroom, through the froth and whizz of his electric toothbrush he says, "Life is a challenge, Bridie, and we can't just fall at the first hurdle. I won't let you down with the fostering. These kids need us."

That little sentence is enough to lift my spirits, and as he climbs into bed, I thank him with all my heart for getting back on the fostering roller-coaster.

1st May 1997

My father is crying, literally crying with happiness as he watches the UK general election results on TV. "Bridie! Labour have won 418 seats! England has a Labour government. At last!" he stood up out of his chair and shook my hand. *My Dad shook my hand!* I giggled at the sheer incongruousness of his action, but Dad explained, "This means so much to me, Bridie. This is a momentous election. Look at Tony Blair walking the streets of London shaking people's hands. Now there's a true Socialist for you – you wouldn't catch a Tory doing that." He wiped his eyes, and continued, "I just *knew* I'd get to see a Labour government again before I died."

I was a bit shaken by this statement. Dad had never

mentioned his death before so I was a little taken aback.

"You're not ill are you Dad?" I ask nervously.

"No, but you never know when your time's up, do you?" He sat glued to the television with a huge mug of tea and a packet of Penguin biscuits. My mother, however, is disgusted. "Well, I prefer the Tories to the Labour lot. That Michael Heseltine's quite dishy."

"Mum, really!" I laugh. Then she and Dad begin a heated debate about the UK political system, which, to be honest, my mother knows very little about, apart from what she's gleaned from copies of the Guardian that Dad leaves lying around. In the end, my Dad loses his rag and says, "Winnie – I am not having this conversation with you, not today of all days. Today, it is a victory for Socialism – and that's something you know nothing about. Let's leave it at that."

My mother looks at me, raises her eyebrows, and then fishes in her handbag for her lipstick. It's an old trick of hers: if she needs to get the upper hand, on goes the lippy. It seems to give her some kind of inner confidence. I suppose there are bound to be differences of opinion in a mixed Anglo-Irish family. Dad's parents were originally from Norfolk but when Stanley was 14, they bought a run-down hotel in Dublin, and made a real success of it, despite some anti-English sentiment at that time. When they retired, my grandparents made a tidy sum of money, which eventually helped raise our family's standard of living considerably, but my Dad has always been a staunch socialist, despite this inherited wealth. I hastily say my goodbyes and make a quick exit. I had come to ask Mum a bit more about the Chinese baby her friend adopted, but I decide to leave it for another day.

12th June 1997

The remaining course sessions pass without incident. Declan was welcomed back into the fold with what seemed like genuine approval by Danny Danvers, and we didn't make any more *faux pas*. We had to write about why we want to be foster carers, and my new skills at the laptop came into their own.

The course has now ended and we are just waiting for references to come through. We also have to fill out lengthy forms about our own backgrounds, and write a Personal Statement about our intentions as foster parents.

29th August 1997

It's been a bit of a frustrating summer. The weather's been crap: rainy, windy and cool and it's dampened all our spirits a bit, and what with not hearing anything from social services about fostering, we've all been a bit snipey. Well, I have. I must admit that impatience has got the better of me on several occasions.

Like that time we went to the beach on the one sunny day of the whole bloody summer, and a family with about ten kids came and pitched-up right next to where me and Declan had staked-out our picnic blanket. I mean, they had the whole sodding beach and they plonked themselves two feet away from us. The whole afternoon, the mother just moaned and berated her kids for every little thing they did. One of them accidentally swept a bit of sand in the pizza and you'd think the kid had murdered someone the way that ungrateful mother of hers kicked-off. Bitch. I just couldn't help thinking, *if she's so stressed and unable to enjoy her children, why the hell did she have so many?* She set me in a bad mood for the rest of the day, and ruined our picnic with her endless grumbling.

My mother keeps making unhelpful comments too, like, "If you'd have taken my advice, you'd have a bouncing little Chinese baby by now."

I can see that Lee and Denise think I'm getting as obsessed about fostering as I did about my fertility treatment years ago, but I don't really care what they think. They lead their lives, and I lead mine. I love them, but we're very different people at heart.

But maybe I am a bit obsessed? I realised this as I leapt downstairs, two at a time, one morning to see if there was a letter from the Social Services (the SS as we call them) in the post. Nothing. Again.

The only light on our horizon this summer was a visit from Bea, back from college with her best friend Holly. They're doing the same course in Sports Science and Physical Education at the Cork College of Higher Education, and in Declan's words they are 'as thick as thieves'.

In bed one night, Declan turns to me and says, "Do you think Bea and Holly might be... lezzies?"

I chuckle at his old-fashioned terminology and his insecurities. "Declan, just because your daughter is best friends with another woman, it doesn't mean she's gay. They're not having an affair! A girlfriend is the best thing a young woman can have in her life, you know. I wish I'd got friends like that." The words came out of my mouth before I know it – but now I come to say it, I realise how having a friend to talk things over with might help with my own anxieties about fostering. I can't keep burdening Declan with them, and anyway, I get the feeling he's only half-listening most of the time. I make a mental note to call my old friend Gina tomorrow – it's been ages since we've had a chat.

31st October 1997

Today we have a 'Panel Meeting'. This involves us meeting members of a board of experts who ask us questions about our ability to look after children.

It's been so long since we heard anything from the SS that we get a bit over-excited as we get dressed.

There's an unexpected knock at the door, so I dash downstairs, still hopping into my trousers, to be greeted by my mother clutching two carnation buttonholes.

"I thought these might add a finishing touch to what you're wearing," she declares.

Declan, who by now is dressed and ready, roars with laughter as he plods downstairs. "Good heavens, Winifred! It's a fostering panel not the Queen's garden party!"

My mother is a little affronted. "Oh, well, if you don't want my help..."

"Come in, Mum, and have a cup of tea, I say," grinning at Declan who, I must admit, looks ten years younger than his age, and rather handsome to boot.

"Bridie, I don't think your husband is taking this seriously enough," Mum says but then her face softens, and she says to me, "Good luck, my darling. I know how much you want to be a mother, and we're all rooting for you."

Following an approved outfit inspection by mother, we walk nervously to the meeting and enter a large office where five people sit smiling around a huge oval table. We shake hands with each person and they do their best to make us feel relaxed and welcome. All seems rather hopeful. They read our notes and ask us lots of question about why we want to foster, and our various life experiences. We answer as honestly and naturally as we can, although occasionally, I find myself quoting from my personal development and parenting books.

There are smiles all round as they conclude the meeting and we are told that they will be in touch soon.

I can hardly bear the excitement. Will they approve us for fostering? Will we have a child with us soon? My Happiness Factor – that gauge of my personal wellbeing that I used to measure nearly every day when I was younger – is 9.9/10

Chapter 8

Here We Go!

1st November 1997, 8.45 am

"It's here!" I say to nobody in particular. "The letter's here. Oh my God, I daren't open it..."

"What letter?" asks Bea, who's home for a long weekend, and is putting on her eyeliner.

"The letter about fostering," I say tensely.

"Oh, that," says Bea, a little too disinterestedly for my liking. She's always been a bit lukewarm about our fostering plans. I can't believe it's jealousy at her age, but it might be?

"Declan!" I shout, "IT'S HERE!"

"Hang on," comes a muffled voice from the bathroom, and I hear the toilet flush.

I grab the formal-looking brown envelope and stare at it, kiss it and whisper to it, "Please be good news!" Then I put it down again and stare at it some more. I am so nervous: it's rather like waiting for the results of your O-Levels or a job application. After several more seconds of deliberation, touching wood and finger crossing, I decide on the 'rip it open and read it' approach. Without a minute to lose, I quickly tear open the formidable brown envelope and shake out the letter.

Declan gallops down the stairs, adjusting his tie, his hair still uncombed and a streak of toothpaste on his lip. "Go on then, what does it say?"

"Dublin Social Services, Foster Care Department, blah, blah, Notice of Approval..." I put down the letter and steady myself.

"NOTICE OF APPROVAL! Declan – we're approved!"

Declan grabs me around the waist and gives me a hug. I hear a grunt from Bea that I take to be congratulatory, and continue to read the letter aloud. "Mr & Mrs D Kelly, The Banks, Cothele Rd, blah, blah... The above-named are approved as foster carers for the following types of placements: Short term and long term; Fostering of 1 or 2 children; Age Range 0 -12 years; Either gender, but preferably female. Long-term placement with adoption to be considered after six months of short-term fostering... Ohhhhhhh! Oh. My. God!! We've done it. Declan, we've done it. I'm going to be a mum, I'm going to be a mum. It's like being PREGNANT!!!"

Bea stalks past, a haughty look on her face. "You are a mum already, in case you hadn't noticed!" She grabs her coat from the hall stand.

"I know I am, Bea, but you know how much we've wanted to foster – it's like a second chance at being a mum for me after all the IVF and fertility troubles we had."

"I know, I know... Congratulations MUM, congratulations Dad," she says pointedly. "I'm off into town. I'll see you later."

"Thank you, Bea! Thank you, God! Thank you, Baby Jesus and all his angels..." (I'm getting carried away) "I can't wait to tell the whole world."

I re-read the letter to make sure it's real and not a figment of my imagination. I then place it significantly on the mantelpiece. It feels like I have been awarded a degree or an OBE! I want everybody to see it and know that Bridie Kelly is going to be a real M.U.M.

I hug Declan again, who is still staring in disbelief at the letter. "So that's it then? We are through?" he says. "No more bloody courses... Now all we have to do is wait for a child to arrive. How long is that going to be?"

"Well, finding a good match for us is important so it could

take anything from one week to three months to find the right child for our family."

"That long? Ah, well – we've waited long enough. A few more weeks won't hurt, Bridie Kelly, mother and all round wonderful woman."

We hug again and I feel elated that this man by my side seems as happy as me about this life-changing bit of news.

"I'm off to work. Have a wonderful day – let's celebrate tonight."

And with that, I'm home alone with just Harry and Hilda for company. I promise to take them for a walk soon, but need to sit down and take it all in over a celebratory cappuccino.

By ten o'clock I've been on the phone for over an hour and have told every relation and friend I can think of the exciting news. Those that were not at home have a message awaiting them. I must admit the reactions have been a bit varied: Mum said she was thrilled but that said she had read something scary in the paper about fostering and did I not want to give IVF another go? (For God's sake mother – forget the IVF, please!) Dad said, "It's a lovely thing to do, Bridie, taking on a child who has had a bad start in life." Thank you, Daddy. Bless my father – he always has other people's best interests at heart.

My friend Gina – who is now a Christian counsellor — was pleased for me, I think. "Bridie, that is wonderful news. You are so patient with children; I know you will be fulfilled. It won't be easy though, Bridie – these kids haven't had the best start in life. You two are going to have to be extra-special parents to make them feel loved and wanted."

Gina continues in her new counsellor voice, which, to be frank, I find a bit condescending and annoying, "You know, Bridie, because of their chaotic first few years, foster-kids can sometimes be what's termed 'emotionally incontinent'.

They don't understand emotions like other children do. Also, because of their parents' backgrounds, sometimes there is drug addiction or even prison that they've had to contend with. Often the mothers smoke heavily or have addiction issues because they have ADHD themselves and then it's passed on, usually through the male line..." She was on a roll now and it was more than I could take in.

"Blimey. Thank you, Gina" I interrupt. "Emotional incontinence, drugs, ADHD and prison, all in one short phone call! Talk about bringing me down to earth!"

"Well, I'm sorry, Bridie, but you may as well face the truth. This is a roller-coaster you've embarked upon."

Hmmm – oh yes, I remember why I hadn't been in touch with Gina for such a long time. She's a know-it-all with a superiority complex. Note to self: find a new 'besty'.

My brother Tim was typically inept. "Wow, Bridie, how're you going to cope with little ones running around the house? I mean, you're so bloody disorganised, I can't imagine you being able to deal with foster kids too."

"Thanks for the vote of confidence, Tim!"

"Ah, only joking, Sis, it's just I know the little critters can be a handful..."

"Oh really? Do tell."

"It's just that... oh, forget it."

"No. What were you going to say?"

"Oh, it's just that a friend of mine tried fostering a few years ago and the kid they allocated to him was completely nuts. Poor kid had been in 12 placements before them and he was really unsettled and needy. In the end, they just couldn't cope with him..."

"Thanks, Bruv! That really is just what I need to hear."

"It's going to be tough, Sis, but if anyone can do it, you can."

Here We Go!

I love Tim, but he sure does put his foot in it sometimes.

Denise is pleased for me but remains cautious, telling me to try not to get too attached to them.

My other sister, Lee, really annoyed me. "Bridie," she said imperiously, "have you thought about how all this is going to affect Declan?"

"Errr – yeah! Of course we have, Lee. We've gone into this together, with open eyes."

"I don't know why you can't just be happy with Bea and possible grandchildren later on down the line. You don't have to do this to prove a point, you know. Remember in that letter you wrote when you said you were going to try and be happy just the three of you? Why isn't that enough for you? God, Bride, you eejit, you're a right glutton for punishment."

"Okay, Lee, you've had your say," I retort.
"'Congratulations' would've been nice." And I put the phone down on her, irritated as usual by my know-it-all older sister.

Finally, I ring Aunty Bernadette in the convent, who said, "Bless you, Bridie. I will pray for you every day."

Well, what did I expect? People have their own agendas, and not everyone is going to understand my motivations. Sometimes, I don't even think I do, really. I would have liked a bit more encouragement and enthusiasm from my siblings, though. Why are they all so heavy and negative? Do they know something I don't? I mean, I'm the expert here – I'm the one who's done all the courses.

It occurs to me that if I had been announcing my pregnancy there would have been flowers and cards, baby showers held at beautiful surroundings like Flora's in Dublin Bay Spa.

But do you know what? Nothing can dampen my spirits. It's like I've waited all my life for this day and nothing or nobody is going to take it away from me.

I pick up the dog leads and decide to take Hilda and Harry on an extra long walk in the woods to celebrate.

Chapter 9

The Foster-Shower

2nd November 1997

I wake up groggy, having hardly slept a wink. I am still as high as a kite. I now know what that old saying about being on 'cloud nine' means. I keep expecting the social services to ring us up and say that they have made a mistake with our approval. Periodically, I check the phone to see if there are any messages, again imagining that it's all some cosmic joke. Later, I read a book called *The Parents' Problem Solver* and wonder what problems we might face with our foster child: struggles with homework, bed times, food and then, if we get as far as adoption, in the good old teen years it'll be boyfriends, smoking, drinking, swearing... I've always known what a major responsibility it is to bring up a child, but that prospect now suddenly looms very large! But it's going to be worth it. I can't believe that after 10 years of trying for a baby, hideous fertility treatments, wholefood diets, fostering courses, arguments, tears and anxiety, a child is now in sight.

The phone rings and breaks my reverie. My body flushes with panic as I brace myself for the 'we've made a dreadful mistake' call, but it's Declan to say that as a special treat he has booked the whole family in for afternoon tea at The Beaches restaurant in Dublin in a couple of weeks' time, to be followed by a bracing seaside walk to Brey Head with the dogs. I'm too wrapped up in my thoughts to notice the date.

I run myself a hot bath, scented with lavender bubbles, and have a long and blissful soak, aware that this is one of the best days of my life. I resume my daydreaming and imagine the first day of being a foster mother – we're actually supposed to call ourselves 'foster carers' – with my new child. *My child.* Obviously there's bound to be settling-in problems but after that, I am certain that she will not look back and that she will flourish. (It never occurs to me that my child will be a boy.) My parents will want to babysit, of that I'm sure, and Bea and Mia can help her with reading, colouring, and schoolwork. Mia could even practice the violin with her. And then of course there will be holidays abroad to look forward to... Oh joy! I literally feel tingly with excitement – or is that just a sign to get out of the now cool and suddy bath? I am so full of hope and happiness. I LOVE LIFE.

Thank you, God. Thank you, Aunty Bernadette at Drumcondra Convent for praying for me. I kind of almost half believe in God now... I haul myself out of the bath, swathe myself in warm towels and wander down to the hall to check the phone again, because I may not have heard it ring when I ran the water. Come on! Please ring. Please ring! I wonder if I just stare at it and don't take my eyes off it, it might just tinkle? Please ring, pretty please... I can't wait!

I imagine myself further down the line as a mother, in the process of adopting. It's so exciting. We would have an adoption party of course with a juggler, live music and pink balloons and loads of delicious food – there would be no expense spared. As the good mother that I will undoubtedly be, I insist on plenty of chopped up salad and savoury food before the sweet stuff. The adoption would be permanent – obvs. I would be a Forever Mum to both Bea and my new adopted daughter. Hey, who knows I may even adopt another one.

This is such happy time for me. I hardly know what to do with myself – I have so much energy! I remember the old Happiness Factor thing I used to do in my diary. Well, today it's HF 10/10.

20th November 1997

I am dressed up in my best clothes for our afternoon tea in Dublin: my navy Laura Ashley skirt, my oh so comfy, oh so mumsy Echo shoes (which Tim calls 'Lesbian shoes' much to Declan's disgust), and my luxurious purple mohair jumper. I must look the part as I am going be a mum. Anyway, there is a double celebration this afternoon because it's my birthday and our fostering approval.

I am surrounded by my family, all smiles and sincerity, and we are discussing the incredible food on show: absolutely sumptuous sandwiches, fruit scones, lemon poppy seed cake, peach melba mousse and a glass of the best champagne to celebrate with. Saskia and Jasmine are here, so grown-up in their choice of clothes and a tiny bit of make-up, almost young women now. I stare at them in admiration, with their waist-length curly, red hair and their delightful personalities. How lucky Lee and Ned were to have such a straightforward family. I hope that my new family will be equally straightforward.

"We brought you these, Aunty Bridie," says Saskia opening up a large shiny bag with 'Birthday' written on it. Inside are two cards: one for my birthday and one with 'Congratulations' drawn on it. I kiss my nieces and thank them, feeling tearful with love that they're still not too old to draw me a card.

"So, you're going to have a new baby then?" asks Saskia curiously.

I explain that we were going to care for a child who doesn't have a family of their own to help them at the moment, and that it might only be for a few weeks or months at first, and also that it won't be a baby, but probably a bit younger than her. She seems quite satisfied with the answer.

I watch as the twins settle themselves and Mia in a corner of the room, the older girls with their teen magazines and Mia with her colouring books. They are such delightful children, so interested in everything and so gentle. I love all of them very much. Declan once said families were a 'genetic lottery', and that obviously the twins had inherited their parents' easy-going disposition. But, "If you look at Bea – now she is exactly the same as Polly: mad on the outdoor life and horses! You can't change it – it's just the way they are." This recollection sets me thinking: if kids are a genetic lottery and our foster-child is coming to us because their own parents are struggling for one reason or another – we were told at the course that it could be prison, or drugs or depression or illness – does that mean our child might express similar traits? Might our child be... a problem child? It's really the first time I've allowed myself to consider that all may not necessarily be rosy in the garden...

"Bridie, Bridie – look who it is," Declan nudges me out of my reverie and nods to the other side of the table, his face slightly puce from a little too much red wine.

"Bea! Oh Bea – you're here! I can't believe it." She's come home especially, just to celebrate my birthday and our good news, even though she was there when we got the letter.

"Hello, Bridie, hello, Dad!"

I'm made up! Our little Bea – not so little anymore – is here. The party is complete.

Mum waves heartily at Bea, who she loves like any other of her grandchildren although strictly speaking, she's not Bea's grandma. I notice Mum is wearing a matching grey fur hat and scarf and an expensive-looking outfit from East. She looks fantastic. After hugging Bea for all she's worth, Mum trots around the table to me.

"Happy Birthday, Bridie," she says and places a present on my lap. From the weight of it I can tell it is a book and I guess it may have something to do with motherhood. In fact it's four books! One on parenting, one called *Sibling Rivalry*, another titled, *Confident Children* and a brand spanking new day-to-day diary which is incredibly useful because actually, us foster carers have to complete a diary each day and I'd already decided to keep that one separate from the personal diary I've kept over the years.

We sit down together and browse through the books.

"Phew! It's a fair whack of reading," I joke.

Mum makes a face. "Umm... Your big sister Lee recommended these books. I personally think that they're a bit heavy going. I mean you're parenting, not giving them therapy, for God's sake!"

I laugh as she continues, "Bring back the old-fashioned days of childhood, with little girls in pink with lots of fluff and bows. That's what I say – just like when you were a little girl, Bridie. We had none of this introspective psychology stuff back then, and look at you – you've turned out alright!"

I hug my Mum. This is a rare compliment from her, and one that means a lot to me. I mean, I know she loves me, but she's not one for telling you that very often.

Declan stands up and tings the side of his champagne flute with a little cake fork, until he has everyone's attention. He then fiddles under the table and drags out an absolutely huge bouquet of white, pink and blue flowers with the word 'Congratulations' adorned in the middle in gold, plastic letters. He kisses me, turns to the gathered throng, raises his glass of Moët & Chandon and makes a toast: "Here's to my Bridie, and here's to our new family member, whoever they may be! Happy days!" and with that, we all take a gulp of the bubbles and chink glasses.

"It's just like Mia's Baby Shower, isn't it, Bridie!" Flora exclaims and hugs Mia to her. She's been such a precious gift to Flora since Brendan seems to be constantly posted in foreign climes. And I think that yes, it is. This is our foster-shower.

I don't think it is possible for me to be happier. No. It is not possible. The 'Congratulations' bouquet looks and smells heavenly as it rests on the white linen tablecloth. It is symbolic of HOPE, along with dear old patient Roger Bear waiting for us back home.

We take a family photo of this special day that I know will be cherished and displayed on my crowded mantelpiece along with all my other precious mementos.

A huge cake has arrived and somebody has dimmed the restaurant lights. I see Mia smiling and giggling. "It's coming!" she says, and suddenly everybody is singing 'Happy Birthday' and clapping, and there's a sea of happy, smiling faces in front of me. I feel on top of the world.

There are four candles on the cake and Mia watches animatedly as I blow them out. Weirdly, they stay alight, and try as I might, they won't go out. The twins explode with laughter and Mia explains that they're special candles that keep relighting themselves. They are all absolutely delighted with their trick.

"Speech!" says Tim, my brother, as he slurps down his champagne and bangs his hand loudly on the table.

I respond enthusiastically. "Okay, okay! Thanks everyone for helping us through the fostering process. As you all know we are now officially foster carers – and it's my 40th birthday, as well! Life begins at 40 as they say! But seriously, you all know what this means to me, to be able to care for children who aren't so lucky as our beautiful children here today..." I gaze benevolently at Saskia, Jazzy, Mia, Mikey and Bea, and am quite enjoying this speech-giving lark, when suddenly it's all over as there's loud and raucous cheering, Bea blows a tooter, Ned bangs on the table again and I hear someone muttering, "I hope she knows what she's letting herself in for."

There is just time for a brisk walk to Brey Head. The twins lead a dog each and ask if they can run on ahead to play with them in the sea.

"Woooowwww! Let's race – yay!" whoops Jazzy.

Lee congratulates me with a hug, "How's it feel to be starting this next phase of your life then, little Sis? Scary? Challenging? Amazing? Rather you than me, I must say, though I do admire you – it's a wonderful thing you're doing. What do you think it's going to be like, being a foster mum, Bridie? These two are enough for us," she said winking at me and looking at her two 14 year-old year old daughters as they throw a tennis ball into the sea for Hilda and Harry.

"Oh, I'm very happy – I've wanted this for a long time, but I'd be lying if I didn't say I was a bit nervous too. I really want to do this, but on the other hand I'm scared of measuring up as a, you know, parent *in lieu*. I know I can never take the place of my foster-kids' real parents, but I can give them lots of love. I think that's what most of them need really. Love, and security."

"But, Bridie, you do know that adoption's a whole different ball-game to fostering, don't you? Children who are adopted can be confused and hurt and quite possibly need sophisticated parenting. Are you up for that? I knew an adopted boy once who had something called Aspergers Syndrome and it complicated matters for his adoptive parents, even more than they already were."

"I know, Lee. It's a minefield," I said a little exasperatedly, "but we'll cross those bridges if and when we come to them. All I want to do is give a child a loving home, like you've done for your children. Everything else, we'll deal with together – me and Declan – just like we did for Bea. Things weren't exactly straightforward for us then, but we coped, didn't we?"

"You did a brilliant job, darling," Lee said affably.

We sit down together on a rock and share some chocolate. "They are lovely, Lee – your girls," I said indulgently. "They're so intelligent and kind. I always have such fun with them and they are never any trouble."

Lee smiles her big, wide smile and admits that she's been very lucky with her two daughters but that she had to be strict with them at times and consistent with rules. "Routine is the name of the game, Bridie. They hang their coats in the cupboard and put their shoes in the passage; they are not allowed sweets or fizzy drinks except for treats. I don't allow much TV at all."

Whilst the flippant side of me thinks *it doesn't sound like much fun in their house*, I admire Lee very much – in some ways she's always been a kind of role model for me. I want Bridie Kelly to be as consistent and assertive and damn well successful as her sister Lee. I do wonder though if I have it in me to be a strict foster-mother? Declan once said to me, "Bridie you don't much like conflict do you? You'll give-in just to make people happy." I've thought about this quite a lot over the years. I suppose I am a bit of a people-pleaser; I do back down and let others have their way, but when it comes to things that I think are really important – like the fertility treatment for example – I can be as determined, focused, assertive and consistent as anyone I know.

It's a beautiful walk with uninterrupted views of the sea,

and there's a kind of mist like a veil rising up in the distance. I can hear the dogs barking at seagulls and see the twins and Mia all holding hands racing up and down the sandy beach with Hilda and Harry in tow. Mikey is wading into the sea and skimming pebbles that get lost in the pounding surf. There is just time to build some sandcastles before dark. We manage ten little ones and they stand proudly in a circle each with a gull's feather planted in the middle. We draw circles in the sand and write "Good Luck! Love from Mikey, Mia, Saskia, Jazzy, Declan and Bridie". We write the significant date 20.11.97. The sea pounds in the distance, and far away there are fishermen attending to their boats in very rough and turbulent seas. My Happiness Factor is 11 out of 10! I love my family and it has been a perfect 40th birthday

Chapter 10

The Waiting Game

22nd November 1997

Mum has gone a little bit OTT over the fostering and she is on the phone now insisting that we take a trip into Dublin to drop into Mothercare and Toys R Us. "Just in case you do end up adopting and become a proper Mum – we need to have a little look at what's on offer. Not to buy anything you understand, just have a teensy-weensy look."

"But Mum, the child will probably be way older than Mothercare entry level," I say rather irritably. We still haven't heard anything from the Gestapo, I mean, the SS.

As usual, mother wins the day.

11.15 am

It's an unusually warm and sunny November day, more reminiscent of summer than autumn. Mum and I treat ourselves to a coffee and a forbidden cream cake in Bewleys, Ireland's leading coffee shop. The smell of the coffee beans is divine and for some reason it makes me feel happy, hopeful and nostalgic, all at the same time. I'm glad Mum insisted on this day out. We observe a young family seated beside us. "Oh, will you look at that one," whispers Mum pointing to a tiny little toddler with blonde hair and the bluest eyes you ever saw. The infant clutches a cuddly toy doggie. "Is she not a dote?" Mum smiles. "Hello, hello little one – aren't you lovely?"

The little girl smiles and then shyly hides behind her mother who acknowledges us with a knowing nod. We sit back in our chairs and chat about nothing in particular until Mum's passing shot: "So what sex do you want, Bridie?" My mother takes a bite out of a chocolate éclair and looks at me quizzically. I am momentarily taken aback until I realise she's not talking 'positions' but gender.

I sip my mocha latte, inhaling the cinnamon and chocolate sprinkles. "Well, I don't mind either way, as long as they're healthy," I say, congratulating myself on sounding just like a real mother, "but somehow, I've always seen my first child as a girl – I've never really even considered a boy. I don't know why. Do you know, I really don't care – I just want to get started with the fostering and then, if all goes well, maybe we can adopt at some point?" I smile and slip into a daydream: something I can do at any given moment these days. *Imogen Kelly, she'd be called, and I'd be just like all the other Mums, arranging birthdays, sleepovers, school uniforms...*

Mum squeezes my hand. "You'll be a good, loving mum, Bridie, but you wont know what's hit you once he or she arrives," she warns. "That's why I wanted to get you out of the house, so we could have a little chat."

"Mum! I'm the one who's done the fostering course," I say indignantly and put paid to her proposed purveying of wisdom. I don't want another lecture on rules and boundaries from anyone today.

12.30 pm

Despite my better judgment, I allow Mum to buy whatever she wants to buy for our forthcoming foster child, and arrive home, laden with bags full of toys and clothes, but Declan, who's popped home for a late lunch, instantly annoys me.

"Bridie – what were you thinking? We are only just approved – there may not be a suitable child for our family for ages. And, we might get a ten year-old boy – what good would this baby-grow be to him?"

I snap back. "Look, Declan, I have been waiting for more than ten years for this child, so waiting a bit longer is nothing to me! And anyway, these are Mum's presents to her new grandchild – I couldn't actually stop her!"

I turn tail and disappear back out of the door with my two surrogate children Hilda and Harry. We walk for an hour around Leopardstown racecourse and I regain my composure. If truth be told, I am absolutely desperately, overwhelmingly IMPATIENT.

I return home as the afternoon light is fading to darkness feeling sombre and thoughtful. I give the dogs their dinner and some water and then see in black felt tip pen some scrawly writing on a torn sheet of paper: Declan has written me a message. 'Edna Pritchard rang about fostering.'

Quick as a flash I bound down the hall to ring her office before it closes. Damn, the phone's engaged. It's 4.30 pm.

4.35pm. Now there's a bloody answering machine.
4.40pm. It's engaged again.
4.45pm. It's engaged! Oh, for God's sake. COME ON! JUST PLEASE, EDNA, *PRETTY PLEASE*, ANSWER THE BLOODY PHONE!

I feel my heart beating and a surge of adrenaline shoot through my body. I just know Edna will have gone home leaving me to wonder until tomorrow about a possible match. Why is everything so slow?

I ring again. Finally, I catch Edna just as she is about to leave the office. She sounds a bit miffed actually. "Oh, hello Mrs Kelly. Let me just switch off the answering machine... How are you? Well done with your fostering application, by the way. Can I visit you tomorrow to discuss one or two things?"

"Yes, of course, but can you tell me a little more now?" I ask eagerly.

"I think it's better to discuss it all tomorrow rather than going into things now, as it's quite late."

I agree straight away that tomorrow morning is fine, but inside I'm in agonies of suspense.

Later that evening

Declan and I snuggle up on the sofa with a glass of red wine and the promise of a good film on TV.

Declan sighs. "Of course, once we have a child there will be precious few evenings like this. There will be bath time, bedtime, story time, packed lunches to make, homework forms to be signed..." he was looking at me thoughtfully as if I'd neglected to think of this side of things.

"Yeah! I do know that, D! It'll be like it was when Bea was younger. Okay, there'll be the routine of housework, washing, tidying and all that, but once the child's in bed, there's no reason why we can't have nice, relaxing evenings like this." I give him a hug of reassurance.

23rd November 1997

I am up at 7.30 to make sure that the house is tidy for Danny Danver's visit, and recall the first time I met her when Harry and Hilda jumped up all over her black trousers. I find the dogs a roasted beef bone and and fill their Kongs up – with a bit of luck, this time that'll keep them quiet for the rest of the morning, at least until Edna has gone.

Being Bridie

By eight o'clock, I can feel a fierce migraine coming on – bad timing or what? I think it must have been that delicious cake I had in Bewleys yesterday or it may be the excitement and stress of the last few days. I make myself drink Barley Cup instead of my usual coffee, and take a couple of painkillers to get me through the meeting with Mrs Danvers – I mean, Mrs Pritchard.

At 9.30 on the dot, Edna arrives and I realise I still feel quite in awe of her. So much of my happiness suddenly depends on her.

"Is your husband here?" she asks without any introductory niceties.

"Er, no – he's at work." I reply feebly. "Come on in and have some coffee." Edna follows me into the sitting room and plonks herself down on our black leather sofa. Unfortunately, with it being a new leather sofa and Edna being rather a heavy lady, it emits a loud farting noise as she sits down. Edna doesn't turn a hair, but I find myself giggling nervously like a schoolgirl. I pinch myself hard and try to imagine something gloomy but it's not working.

"The coffee..." I manage to blurt out and dash into the kitchen to try and regain my composure.

"Mind if I eat my sandwiches?" Edna calls to me from the sitting room as I chuckle silently, rebuking myself that it is so childish to laugh at fart noises.

"Not at all," I shout back, thinking, *sandwiches, at 9.30 in the morning? No wonder she's a bit rotund and makes fart noises when she sits down!* And the hysteria bubbles in my throat all over again. I put it down to nerves.

Serenity regained, I troop back into the sitting room just as she reaches into her lunchbox and retrieves a huge baguette overflowing with cheese and pickle, and a flask. She takes an enormous bite of her baguette and puts it on the lid of her lunchbox. I sit down beside her and will myself not to laugh. Too late, I realise that I have left the kitchen door open and Hilda and Harry are loose and sniffing round the lounge.

Edna is impressed. "Oh yes!" she says though a mouthful of bread, "I remember your lovely dogs – very affectionate. I can see that they are well loved, Bridie."

Seconds later both dogs seem to be eating something: their tails are down and they are licking their lips and looking guilty. Harry has something white and creamy on his nose, which I think must be butter. There are lumps of pickle and crumbs on my freshly-hoovered carpet. Oh my Christ! They've eaten Edna's baguette, and what is it that's sticking out of Harry's mouth? I say nothing and usher the dogs back into the kitchen, hoping she doesn't notice – and pull the bit of string that's dangling from Harry's jaw. It's a tampon, still in its plastic wrapper – but whose? Edna's? Well... Edna doesn't look like she's that kind of lady. Harry must've been rootling in Bea's bedroom again. Christ Almighty.

I return to find Edna opening up a huge file of paperwork, that I realise is our 'case' and she explains to me that we will be contacted shortly by various social workers from different areas of Dublin, but that she, Edna, is our 'link worker' in charge of the fostering procedure. I feel a bit like a schoolgirl with my teacher standing over me telling me what I can and cannot do. Why can't they just bloody well get on with it and place a child with us? Still, my Happiness Factor is 9/10 as this is definitely one step forward and old Danny Danvers said 'we will be contacted shortly.'

As she packs up her things to leave, she looks around her for something – I presume it's the missing lunch, but says nothing – and she's off in a swirl of scarves and self-importance. I collapse on the offending sofa, momentarily overcome with fatigue from all the nervous tension.

Later, horror of horrors, I find a chewed-up tube of very expensive handcream hidden in the depths of Harry's dog-bed and realise that Harry must've nicked that from Edna's bag too – God only knows when he did that. So, it wasn't butter! Operation Fuck-Up or what? A handcream stealing, tampon-eating dog is not exactly the best advert for a stable home. Thank God Edna seemed oblivious to all this.

28th November 1997

I have still not heard anything from the SS. It's almost as bad as waiting for my period each month. Wait, wait, wait – that's all I ever do.

4th December 1997

It's less than a month until Christmas and we still haven't heard from the Gestapo. I go to the swimming pool to let off a bit of steam and manage 20 lengths. Not bad for a 40-year old.

I call in to see Sister Mary Anunciata AKA Aunty Bernadette on my way home. As I approach Poor Clare's Convent, Drumcondra, I can hear hymns playing and there's a really peaceful, spiritual air about the place, although it used to scare me to death coming here when I was a little girl.

Aunty Bernadette's chambers are austere. I sit down in silence and wait patiently to greet her. There are occasional whispers in the corridor, a grandfather clock ticking somewhere and the light patter of nuns' sandals on the wooden floors. The room is sparsely furnished but there's a strong smell of furniture polish everywhere.

Minutes later my beloved aunt appears from behind a thick black grille. Her face is round and shiny like an apple, her lips dry and colourless. She offers me her thin white bony hand, which I plump warmly, if only to try and get her circulation going.

"Welcome, my child," says Aunty Bernadette, "God bless you. I am praying for a child for you, Bridie." I look at her – one childless lady praying for another. The irony is not lost on me. We chat superficially for ten minutes or so. My aunt asks after everybody in the family. A little later, a bell rings which signifies the end of visiting hours.

As I turn to leave, Bernadette takes me to one side. "Next time you come, Bridie, you will have a little one by your side," and she gives me such a look of knowing that I think perhaps she does have a direct line to God, after all

Chapter 11
The Offer

5th December 1997

At 8.30 am I take an urgent phone call from Edna asking if she could come and see me today. OMG this could be it, and before Christmas as well! I picture a small blonde-haired girl with blue eyes. My mother was right to buy that present from Mothercare. Aunty Bernadette's prayers are working. Now then, I wonder how old she will be? 2 years? 5 years? 7 years at the most, but please, not a teenager – not for my first foster placement. *Just break me in gently,* I think. I am SO excited – I am high as a kite; my head's gone into overdrive and my mouth's dried-up completely.

9.30 am

Edna's here with her new mobile phone and she looks very flustered.

"Morning, Bridie," she says, delicately lowering herself onto the edge of the sofa. "I will come straight to the point. I have a 13 year-old teenage girl, whose mother's just been taken to hospital with an attempted suicide, and a father who is, you know," she mouthed 'inside' which took me a moment to realise meant prison. "Could you do me a favour and have her for a couple of days? It will be good practice," she added, as she furiously flicked through a huge big pile of notes and letters.

The Offer

I was dumbstruck. This wasn't at all what I had expected.

She peered at me from behind her glasses. My mouth went dry as I imagined Declan's face as he was told our first placement was a 13 year-old girl whose mother had attempted suicide and whose father was banged-up.

"Erm... well, I am not s-s-sure..." I stutter. "I had imagined us taking on a younger child as our first placement."

Edna looks very tense and she picks up on my nervousness. She sat upright and snapped her notes shut. "Bridie, you are foster carers – you don't get to choose what child you get – but let's look at the facts shall we? You've had experience of caring for your husband's teenage daughter, have you not? So you'll have plenty of skills and knowledge to draw on with this child." Her phone makes a buzzing noise. "I have to take this," she says, and marches outside and back into her car for privacy.

She returns ten minutes later looking more flustered if anything, but has obviously decided to go from bad cop to good cop. "Look, Bridie, cards on table here. You would be doing me an *enormous* favour if you could have her. This is an emergency situation, and it will look very good on your file," she gazes at me almost pleadingly, "especially if you want to adopt one day."

Suddenly there is an incentive I cannot refuse. And I've not come this far in my quest for a child to fall at the first hurdle.

"I'm sorry, Edna, but I really was expecting a younger chil..."

Edna sighs again and drums her fingers on the table. "Yes but that's not always possible," she interrupts. "You know, everybody wants a little one, but you have to ask yourself, what happens to the older children? They're still children, Bridie..."

"Yes, Edna, I know that, and I was going to say before you

interrupted me that I was really expecting a younger child, but that if this Kathleen – was that her name? – if this Kathleen is in desperate need then yes, we will take her." How's that for being assertive!

Edna breathes an audible sigh of relief. "Good. Good. Thank you, Bridie. Now then as I said, Kathleen is 13 and a bit of a wild child. You'll have to watch your purse as she is known to steal money and she smokes marijuana if she can get it. She can go to the local convent school whilst she's with you – that's the one Bea went to is it?"

"No, Bea went to Loretta convent... But Edna, if she's only going to be with us for a day or two, why are we worrying about school?"

"Ah, well, it's good for them to keep up the routine of school, even if it's a different one to where they live. It gives structure to their days. I'll be off now then, Bridie, I've a lot to organise. Someone will be in touch with you to sort out the placement and make sure you're happy with everything." And with that, Edna swept out of the house like a whirlwind, the only trace left of her being her expensive perfume.

10.30am

Thank God Edna has gone back to the family centre – I need time to think. I steady my nerves with a large, strong cappuccino and pet the dogs. I have a hideous vision of Declan walking out on me when he hears about Kathleen. But he'll support me in this, surely? Especially now I am so near to achieving my dream of being a mother. I'll just focus on the bit about her only being with us for a few days and this putting us in good stead for adoption: I won't mention the weed smoking or the stealing, or prison or suicide. Honestly! Talk about dropping us in at the deep end. I feel a bit sorry for myself to be honest, but the dogs comfort me with their unconditional love. I decide to go to the spa for a long swim (I actually did 50 lengths) and pray that Kathleen has a strong and dependable Aunt who steps forward to care for her.

1.00pm

I take a rather abrupt phone call from Edna to say that Kathleen will be here tomorrow to stay with us for four nights. Four nights! That's hardly a couple of days is it? God, this is all a bit scary – it's all happening too fast... Curse Aunty Bernadette for praying too much!

Okay, okay... how am I going to tell my family? I rehearse in my head what I'm going to say to Mum and Dad and to Lee and Denise, but Declan is my major worry: with the others, I'll just give them a brief resumé, after all, Kathleen will have been and gone in less than a week, so it's none of their business really. But Declan – Declan deserves and needs to know the truth. I feel like this is turning into one big nightmare. *After this placement I am giving up fostering*, I tell myself grumpily. *I will be happy with the family that I have.*

I prepare a special supper for me and Declan, to pave the way before I break the bad news.

"Ermm, I had a phone call from Mrs Danvers this morning," I begin.

"A child for Christmas?" he asks, his eyes twinkling at me.

"Yes, a child for Christmas – a thirteen year old girl."

"Oh."

"It's just for a few days, D. It's just an emergency placement."

"Bridie... what aren't you telling me? Why aren't you bouncing off the ceiling in excitement about all this?"

"I think you'd better take a look at the placement notes,"

I say, handing Declan the file that Edna's assistant had dropped round to me on her way home from work earlier this evening.

"Let me see then," he says, a resigned note in his voice. He retreats into the sitting room where I hear tuttings and 'oh my God's. Suddenly there is a loud noise as he slams the notes firmly on the table, and heads back into the kitchen.

"No. No that's not on. We're approved for younger children, not difficult teenagers," he said with a fixed expression on his face.

"It'll be okay, Declan. It's only for four days. I mean, what harm can she do in four days? She's in a desperate position, with both parents out of action. The poor thing needs a bit of security and we can give her that at least." I listen to myself, arguing for us to take on this girl who smokes weed and steals money out of purses. What's wrong with me? "I mean, that's what fostering is all about, isn't it? Reaching out to young people who are less fortunate than we are."

My husband is not convinced. "No, absolutely not, Bridie. We can't offer the support she needs, and you'll be too soft with her. You're a people-pleaser."

I bristle at that. "I've told them we'll take her, D."

"You what? Without discussing it with me first? Jesus Christ, Bridie – what next? A lad on heroin? *A junkie?* We're not equipped for this."

"Oh, don't be so melodramatic," I snap. "Of course it won't come to that."

"I'm going for a bath," Declan sighs. "I may be some time."

I spend the whole night in turmoil. Of course, it's up to us, in the end. We can say, "No, we're not ready for this," but that will be a black mark against my plans for adoption. Why, oh why can't things be straightforward for once? Why couldn't we have been matched with a little girl whose Mum and Dad had died in a plane crash or something? I blanche at that terrible thought. *God forgive me,* I think.

9.30pm

Declan still hasn't come downstairs. I think he must've gone straight to bed, and I don't blame him. What a bloody mess. I seriously think about giving up the idea of fostering and adopting altogether if this is the reality of it.

10.00pm

The phone rings. It's Edna.

"I'm sorry for ringing so late Bridie, but I thought you should know that Kathleen is going to an uncle's house instead. We do always like to place children within their own families if at all possible."

"Oh, thank God!" I hear myself say involuntarily, and then, "Thank you, Edna. I hope everything works out for her."

I breathe a sigh of relief and mount the stairs to tell Declan the news.

"Well, I can't say I'm not glad to hear that," he says, having taken to his bed. "But, Bridie, this is a shot across the bows for us. What if our next offer is much the same? Are we ready for this? I don't know about you, but I don't want a pot-smoking rebellious teenager in my house."

"I know, Declan. It's been a shock to me too. I've been fantasising about a cute little girl we can call our own, but to be honest, it doesn't look like cute little girls often come up for fostering..."

I get into bed, exhausted by the day's events, and sleep the sleep of the 'damned if you do and damned if you don't'.

6th December 1997

The SS haven't been back in touch with me since the 'Kathleen' incident. They'll probably never forgive me for being so ambivalent about my first foster-placement. I'm finding it impossible to relax because I feel such a failure, so I end up drinking more coffee to cheer myself up. I even sneak a crafty cigarette. I rarely smoke these days – probably less than 10 a year – but on occasions (like the sneaky one I forgot to mention after my 40th birthday party, or when I get hyper-stressed), I'll smoke a fag. Result: a big migraine. I ring Dr Li and order some liquorice supplements. I am under no illusions about my penchant for herbal remedies and supplements and my smoking habit – I know it's ridiculous. I currently have 23 bottles of supplements on the shelf above the microwave. I'm truthfully running out of space in the pantry. Declan and I often argue about it. "Bridie, for God's sake, can you move all these supplements, please – I can't swing a cat in here," and today, a rather terse, "Why can't you be like normal people and just get something from the chemist? Like Migraleve?" We are still not really talking to each other, but I won't threaten divorce again, in case he takes me up on it.

7th December 1997

The SS call, but this time it is a different social worker who has phoned me to talk about twin girls of seven years-old who needed long-term fostering and permanent adoption. I am suddenly back to my old, ecstatic self. This is more like it! Suzy and Daisy Smithson are identical twins currently living in a short-term foster placement in Listowel. Their birth parents are suffering from drug addiction and related problems (hmmmm). It is not likely that either parent will be able to care for the twins in the future. The twins are easy-going, lovely children with no learning difficulties; both read well and have won prizes at school. The birth grandma would like to have face-to-face contact once a year when the twins are adopted. (Adopted!)

They sound perfect, but (isn't there always a but), the poor little things have suffered physical abuse and as a result they often have scary nightmares and bed-wetting accidents. On the positive side, both children are doing well in their temporary family. Their health has improved and they are diligent students. Oh, my heart went out to them, it really did. Surely Declan will agree that they can come here and we can look after them? It's not like they're teenagers after all. Kieran, their link worker, has promised to send me their details in the post. I feel excited and high again, but I don't mention anything to Declan – I just can't risk him saying no.

8th December 1997

Further details of Daisy and Suzy have arrived in the post in an important-looking big brown envelope. I rip it open and feast my eyes on a sweet photo of the twins playing on swings. Do you know, they actually look like my twin nieces – how amazing is that?

I am suddenly aware that Declan is hovering over me pointing at the notes and saying in a threatening voice, "Who are those two then?" He swipes the details from me and starts reading them, shaking his head and tutting. I curse him silently, because I know he has rapidly gone off the idea of fostering – but its okay for him; he already has his own children. I don't.

"No, absolutely not. No, they're not suitable for us, Bridie. They're bound to have deep emotional problems after everything they've been through. It'll be a huge disruption for us. We can't take the risk Bridie. Please think hard on what I'm saying," he said before he rather abruptly threw the notes at me and slammed the lounge door. I then hear the sound of the car engine being revved up. Hilda eyes me wisely. "I want a divorce," I tell her. It seems so unfair that Declan is trying to stop me from helping these children.

As usual, I turn to my Mum and Dad for support in a time of crisis. Predictably, I am asked for chapter and verse on the recent turn of events with the SS.

"Oh, Bridie, no," said my mother. "You can't possibly take something like that on, especially if Declan is set against it. I mean, twins? It'll be double the work and double the trouble. That meddling Pritchard woman! I'll give her a ring if you like?"

"No!" I shout at Mum. "For God's sake, no – just butt-out, will you? I am stressed enough as it is." I burst into tears.

Dad knows what's good for the blues and drags me off to the pool for a swim. I energetically swim 30 lengths and feel much better for it especially when Dad buys me a mocha latte afterwards. Exercise always works to clear my head and settle me down. Dear old Dad – I love him so much. He's the perfect father. On the way home, he took my hand and looked at me straight in the eyes. "Bridie, my lovely, I hope you get a child soon, I really do, but don't take on too much too soon. Promise me? Look at the strain it's already putting on you. Two young, damaged children at once – Bridie, think about it, will you?"

"I think about nothing else, Dad," I say, feeling tearful again, "but I take on board what you're saying. I'll talk to Declan again."

The Offer

On my way home, I catch a glimpse of myself in a shop window. God, I'm looking old. Bea mentioned last time she came home that I'd got grey hairs showing. I'll cheer myself up, I think, and duck into LUSH and spend a fortune on hair products. Bea wanted me to have my hair professionally dyed, but I am not in favour of chemical dyes. So no, I will do things my way.

I get home and melt a brick-like slab of henna in hot water and plaster the hair dye all over my head and put a black swimming cap on for one hour whilst it does its thing.

Later, I come downstairs and do a twirl for Declan. "What do you think?" I ask.

"Well, I'd perhaps leave it on for half an hour less next time," is all he says, but he does give my hand a squeeze. What's this? A bit of a thaw in proceedings?

"Do you fancy going out for dinner to the curry house on Grafton Street?" he asks.

"Oh? Yes, that'd be lovely, especially now I've done my hair," I say, and dare to hope that we might try to get things back on an even keel.

Declan and I sit opposite each other with our drinks. Over poppadums dipped into delicious relishes with the soothing sound of Indian music I start to cry again. It's the fourth time today. "You want me to give up fostering a child, but I can't quit now, Declan."

Declan replies with his mouth stuffed full of poppadums, "I'm not asking you to quit, Bridie, just to think carefully about who we take on, and not just jump in feet first with the first offer we get. It's got to be right for both of us. I don't mind any child if it's the right match for us, but I am not having an older teenager coming in to disrupt our happy family and I think twins would be too much for us to cope with. Can't you see that?"

"But Edna says that there are very few younger children who come up for fostering," I whine.

Declan is adamant. "Well, we will just have to be patient then. I know patience doesn't come easily to you, Bridie Kelly, but in this case stand back from everything for a bit and take things a bit more slowly, will you? For me?"

"Okay, Declan." I agree, "I'll tell Edna that we can't take the Smithson twins, and I'll mention that we're looking for a child who's a bit less challenging for our first placement. But if you say no again, then I'm serious, I may just walk out that door and never come back again."

Declan looks at me, weighing up whether I'm actually serious or not.

I'm deadly serious.

Chapter 12

Desperate Measures

9th December 1997

I haven't heard anything from the Gestapo for a day or
two, but a really interesting magazine popped through the
letterbox this morning called *Children & Carers*, which I
remember seeing an advert for, on one of the foster evening
courses Declan and I went to ages ago. I'd forgotten all about
registering for it.

It's quite weird really though, because whilst it's meant
to place children with the best carers possible, it's designed
almost like a catalogue, so although in theory you can flick
through and pick out the children that are the best match
for you, what I actually find myself doing is focusing on the
prettiest of the girls, or the youngest of the children. I ring
my mother, slightly bemused. "Mum – can you come round? I
want to show you something."

"Show me what, Bridie? I can't just drop everything at a
moment's notice, you know."

"Well, I've got this magazine called *Children & Carers*,
where you can choose a child that needs fostering. There are
some really sweet children in it. They all look so appealing – I
can't decide..."

Mother cuts me off. "What? Children advertised in a
magazine? Good God, whatever next? I'll be right round."

Excitedly, I put the machine on to make us both a frothy
cappuccino with cinnamon on top (apparently cinnamon

lowers your blood sugar levels) and by eleven o'clock, Mum is at the back door, with two slices of chocolate cake and her reading spectacles. We spend the whole morning ploughing through the magazine.

"God, I can't believe how many children there are waiting to be adopted or fostered," I say to my Mum, "and they all look so special... Oh, bless their hearts. Look, there's even a picture of four brothers and sisters in a school photograph – look Mum..." My mother looks as me askance. "Oh! I'm not saying I want to foster all four of them! God forbid – Declan would definitely leave me – but what can have happened in their little lives that they have no mother or father or aunts and uncles to care for them...? It breaks my heart."

"Yes love, mine too," says my mother, with genuine compassion.

It's an odd feeling trawling through this magazine: something about it almost feels... wrong. It's like the ones who're a bit goofy, or fat or older – well, it's almost as if they know they haven't got a chance... they look somehow resigned to their fate. Oh, poor, poor little mites. I want to adopt them all.

Nonetheless, by 12.30 pm Mum and I have circled in red biro a little girl on page 14, aged four. I pour yet another cuppa and read out the details again. Mum sips her tea and smiles. "Dear little thing – she could be so happy here. All this fostering fuss isn't necessary, you know, Bridie. Stuff that Pritchard woman – just apply for this little girl! Be pushy. You should adopt this child – just think: another grandchild for us and a sister for Bea... She's described as cheerful, she likes dressing-up and there are no issues surrounding her health. She's PERFECT!" Buoyed-up by my mother's enthusiasm, I phone the number and ask to speak to the link social worker, Fiona Porter.

"Good afternoon," she says breezily. "I understand you want to know about Sara?"

"Yes please," I reply, smiling to myself and visualising Sara in the Kelly family.

"Firstly, can you tell me who your link worker is, and also, are you approved foster carers?"

I reply that yes we are newly-qualified foster carers and that Edna Pritchard is our link social worker, "but she doesn't know I've contacted you," I add hastily, and then feel guilty that I didn't discuss this with Edna first.

Fiona went on to describe Sara. "Well, she's a lovely wee thing – very gentle and likes to please. She eats well, loves bath time and her toys La La and Po, and, let me see now... No, no health problems, no learning difficulties so far but of course it's hard to say as she's only four years old. She had a normal birth, but has no contact with her birth family now. We are looking for a secure family that could give her a lot of one-to-one attention."

"I think she sounds like a perfect match for us," I say, specifically using the terminology I know social workers like to hear.

"Okay, Mrs Kelly, I'll speak with Edna Pritchard and we'll get the ball rolling. I'll be in touch soon."

I give the thumbs up to Mum and hug her. "We're getting there, Mum," I say tearfully. "God I am so excited – this seems like a much easier way to find a child doesn't it?" I say gleefully.

The phone rings and I answer it giddy with excitement.

"Mrs Kelly? It's Fiona Porter again. I'm sorry to tell you that I've found out Sara has been withdrawn, just this morning. Following a review, we are now looking at placing her back with a birth aunt."

I hide my disappointment and say, "No, no, that's fine – it's much better for her to stay with her birth family," but inside, my heart aches. Sara sounded just right for us.

My Mum is disappointed too. "Bridie, if you'd taken my advice and adopted a Chinese baby like my neighbour did, you'd be playing with it in the park today instead of these constant dead-end phone calls. I'm off for a round of golf with Stanley." And with that she stomps home. I think she's more upset than she lets on.

I'm determined not to fall at the first hurdle though. The next child I discuss with Fiona, Alexia aged nine, looks an absolute angel but when Fiona reads her 'Details Diary' to me, I nearly fall off my chair. I am so shocked and horrified. Alexia is only suitable for very experienced foster carers because – I can hardly write it down... She has experienced... No – it's no good. I can't commit those terrible words to paper. Suffice it to say that poor Alexia in her short lifetime has experienced more suffering than most people do in their entire lives. I can't stop thinking about her, but I know without a shadow of a doubt that we cannot give her the help she needs.

"Thank you, Fiona," I say as we agree that we are not the right placement for Alexia. "I'll have a think about things, and talk to my husband. I'll be in touch again soon."

But I have no intention of discussing *Children & Carers* with Declan just yet, as I have a feeling he won't approve, and in any case, if we can't find a suitable child, there's no point in discussing it at all, is there?

10th December 1997

The third child I fall in love with is Claire, an absolutely beautiful girl. Impulsively, once again I ring the link worker, this time a man called Adam Green.

"Hello, Adam, I am a newly approved foster carer in Dublin and I am ringing to speak to you about Claire, as a possible placement for her." I hear a distant phone ring and a ruffle of papers, and my heart is beating fast.

'Okay... Claire Connell – her name's been changed at this point to give her some anonymity. Now, let me see... Yes, she is a lovely girl, but I have to tell you that she was put into care after trying to strangle her sister with a tie." I heard him cough, but I couldn't manage to get any words out myself. "It is a lot to take in, and to be honest Mrs Kelly, we would not match you with Claire as a first time placement as we feel she would be too challenging for an inexperienced foster carer." (I bridle a little at the 'inexperienced' bit – but how is he to know about Bea and our family life without going back through my files, so I let it drop.) He continues, "A lot of these children have significant attachment disorders and Claire also has a syndrome called ADHD that can be very complex to deal with. The Reactive Attachment Disorder develops from a lack of nurture in the first few years, and the child may display such behaviour as lying, stealing and trust issues. As you can see Mrs Kelly, it's not as simple as just seeing a picture of a smiling child."

Could things get any more complicated and dark for these poor children? And what's ADHD anyway? I remember Gina mentioned it once... I made a mental note to look it up.

I agree with Adam that Claire is not a good first match for us and place the receiver down thoughtfully. This is all so emotionally exhausting, and I haven't even started fostering yet. I pick up the dog leads and call Harry and Hilda for a walk. I need to clear my mind.

On my return home, there is a prickly message from Edna.

"Bridie, I hear that you have been making enquiries about foster placements featured in *Children & Carers*? We need to talk about this. Why was I not informed? I'll call in for a chat on my way home from work tonight." No 'by your leave' or anything! Oh great – now I'm in trouble with Mrs Danvers.

And as good as her word, about 5.15 that evening, Edna rings my doorbell. I open the door to a very flustered-looking social worker, who marches in and plonks herself down on the dreaded black leather sofa to an accompanying soft trump. She takes out her notebook and studies me, looking at me over the top of her black horn-rimmed glasses to ensure ultimate intimidation.

"I'm sorry, Bridie, but it's really not on you ringing Children & Carers without consulting me, you know. They are in the magazine in the first place because they are usually older children, with complex backgrounds who are not at all suitable for newly approved foster carers like you. There are some terrible histories attached to these poor children and they need experienced foster carers who have undergone specialist training." Seeing my tearful eyes she reaches out and plumps my hand, smiling. "Dry your eyes, Bridie, nobody said fostering was going to be easy."

"So why was I given access to the magazine details at the fostering course then?" I ask petulantly.

"Oh? Well..."

I seem to have caught her off-guard, and feel a little redeemed.

"Well, that's inappropriate for an Introductory course," she said. "I'll see that it's removed. Now then..." she riffles through a pink file, nodding her head and muttering to herself,

"I do have someone in mind for you, but not until next year though... probably March time. She's a five year-old girl called Sinead who will need a three-month placement and possibly longer term fostering, even – ultimately – adoption, though it may be too risky to have her adopted locally..."

"I wouldn't mind," I blurt out.

Edna eyes me up and reads through the notes again. "Hmmm you and your husband may be suitable foster carers, but it is not going to be an easy first time placement, Bridie. She is an absolute sweetie but strong-minded."

I repeat the words in my head: *absolute sweetie but strong minded; absolute sweetie but strong minded...*

This time, I play it cool. "Any more details, Edna?" I ask.

Edna sips her tea and tells me a little more about Sinead. "Well, it's a very unusual situation... The thing is, her birth mother gave her away when she was two years old to a traveller friend called Margaret who already has seven other children. Sinead is very attached to the current family. In some ways Margaret's doing a great job, giving Sinead lots of love and attention and her other children adore Sinead. They spend a lot of time outside playing with the dogs near their mobile home," Edna stops to pat Hilda and Harry who escaped the kitchen and are now lying at her feet probably waiting for more baguette, "so she'll be fine with these two ruffians," she says looking lovingly at my prostrate dogs. "Sinead's not reading or talking that well at the moment except some basic words in Irish and her accent is so strong you can hardly understand a word that she is saying. She seems very alert and loves her little book – in fact it's the only thing she owns. She has had a deprived life up until now. I feel she needs lots of one-to-one attention and love, and help with reading and writing.

"Margaret is an experienced parent, and in many ways she's a 'good enough parent' but she has her own issues to deal with, which have changed again recently, and I feel that Sinead is somewhat neglected. That's why we feel she would be better placed in a quieter family." Edna peered at me. "She's not necessarily a good match for you or your family long-term, Bridie. It's best to be clear from the outset that if Sinead does come to you, it would probably only be short-term, so that you could give her the one-to-one support she needs at this tender age, but as she gets older, it may be that she needs to have a family with other children around, so that she has some sibling support. Just not seven of them."

Edna leaves, saying that she'll ask Barry Black, Sinead's social worker, to give me a ring.

I thank my lucky stars that I didn't mention any of the placements from *Children & Carers* to Declan, but make up my mind to tell him everything about Sinead when he returns from work.

When I hear his car pull up to the garage door, I pour two large glasses of red wine and wait with baited breath.

"What's this then?" he asks as he shucks-off his work jacket and flakes into a kitchen chair.

"It's to chill you out. I've got some news."

"A placement?"

"A possible placement, but not until next year," and I tell him the story of Sinead.

"Wow..." he takes a swig of the wine. "Gosh. Poor little thing. Why did her own mother abandon her?"

"I don't know... Mrs Danvers didn't say. What do you think, D?"

"I think... I think – well, it's only for three months isn't it, and she's only five, not like that weed-smoking teenager they wanted us to have! Poor little mite, in a caravan with seven other kids. It doesn't bear thinking about... Must be a hell of a squash. Sinead you say? That's a lovely name..."

I can't quite believe my ears. Perhaps he really took my threat seriously that I'd leave him if he put the mockers on another placement. But, I'm a fast learner, and I'm not going to jeopardise anything.

"Well, let's just leave it at that for now," I say, "and see what her social worker, Barry Black, has to say when he rings me."

"Barry Black!" Declan sniggers, spurting a bit of wine out between his teeth. "Barry bloody Black! That has to be a false name if ever I heard one! I wonder if he's really fat and sings Motown songs in his spare time!" Declan chuckles to himself and goes upstairs to get changed.

12th December 1997

Finally, Barry bloody Black rings me. Hurray! I don't think these social workers realise quite how horrendous it is to be constantly waiting for news all the time. OMG he is visiting us tomorrow.

I am so excited – it's all systems go for the obligatory house-clean and whilst I'm doing it, I realise I am constantly grinning like a Cheshire cat. OM effing G – this is the first step towards a placement. Roger Bear is ready and waiting in the lounge. I kiss him and plump him into his usual corner. Happiness Factor 9/10.

13th December 1997

It's 3 pm and Barry has just arrived. He is very plump and rather fresh-faced and, I guess, newly qualified. I am immediately impressed by his kind and measured manner. Declan (who has taken the afternoon off work to be here) and I sit down and wait to hear details about Sinead. We must make a good impression today, so I'm really glad D is showing willing.

Barry gets the interview going with, "So Mr Kelly, I know your wife is keen to take Sinead on, but how do you feel about having another child in the house again?"

"Well Mr Black..."

"Oh, let's dispense with the formalities shall we? Call me Barry."

"Barry – I know how much this means to my wife, and whilst I feel I've done my parenting, Bridie is desperate to have a child..."

"I'm asking how *you* feel Declan?"

I stare at Declan, willing him to say the right thing.

"Well, we didn't feel our first placement should be too challenging, to try and break us in gently, so to speak, but we realise that things aren't always straightforward with fostering and that you can't always get what you want, but then Sinead came along, and she's had such a tough life and she deserves some love and security. We can at least give her that, and a comfortable home for three months."

I let out an audible sigh of relief. Correct answer, Declan, if a bit long-winded!

Barry nods. "Yes, you're right – things rarely go exactly as we'd like with fostering, but Sinead is a sweet little thing and may actually turn out to be a good introduction to fostering. She is quite willful, but you've both had experience of young children, one way or another (he looks at some of our family photos on the bookshelf), so I shouldn't think Sinead will be overly difficult for you. You'll need to be firm with her though – you should see her boss everybody around in the Family Centre!" he laughs.

Declan frowns. "Oh dear, I don't like the sound of that."

"She's just a little girl, Declan – she just needs love and boundaries," I say and then, to change the subject I ask about her physical health.

"Okay.... Here are her Medical History notes," says Barry, shuffling through a raft of papers. "She's a little underweight, she's been prescribed glasses for her eyesight, but she hides them. She'll probably need some orthodontics work because she won't brush her teeth and was given honey in her dummy."

Declan winces at this catalogue of disaster.

"Her temperament is rather feisty. She can be a bit domineering if she doesn't get her own way and she's prone to tantrums and shouting at times." (My heart has steadily been sinking as Barry seems to just reel off one problem after another.) "She's not talking much yet, except some bits of Irish and some English words, but not sentences though."

Declan asked for more details. "Ermm – this naughtiness: is it normal?"

"It's quite normal given the circumstances of her upbringing so far, Declan, but it is one of the reasons why we want to remove her from the situation she's currently in. We want to give her the chance to learn about proper boundaries and behaviour and to be given coping mechanisms in a one-to-one, calm and loving environment – which is what we think you and your wife can give her."

That makes me feel a lot better.

Barry reads from a different file. "Now then, we'll be looking at a three-month short-term fostering placement, if and only if we get the Emergency Protection Order. That will go to court very soon. Murphy, her father, is a musician, but currently he's of no fixed abode so it is unlikely that they'll give him custody of Sinead, and Patsy, her birth mother, well... let's just say I am fairly sure she will not get custody, having given the child away in the first place. Then there's Margaret her current carer..." he made a nervous face and held his head in his hands momentarily. "Margaret is very keen to hang on to Sinead, but I will not be supporting her application, as I think she has enough on her plate with her own kids, all of whom have their own... challenges."

Declan interrupts. "What's the situation with Patsy, Sinead's birth mother?" he asks.

"I'm not really at liberty to disclose that situation," says Barry, but this doesn't assuage Declan's concerns.

"Look, Barry, I'm a GP and I know all about confidentiality clauses, but if there are mental health issues involved, for example, then we have a right to know, because this might affect our decision."

Barry sighs and looks Declan in the eye, and says, "Patsy has been in and out of care all her life, Declan. She was brought-up mainly by nuns in a convent near Galway, and she has made serious accusations against them, which I really can't go in to here. She is in with a bad crowd in Dublin – and I mean a really bad crowd – who take advantage of her because she has learning difficulties. Patsy gave Sinead away to a friend when she was only two – she just couldn't cope with the infant. These kinds of informal fostering arrangements are more common than you might think, you know. Patsy periodically makes noises about trying for custody, but to be honest, that's not going to happen. She's little more than a child herself in some ways."

Christ Almighty. My heart sinks again. This interview is a bloody roller-coaster.

Barry continues to read from his notes. "There are likely to be a lot of contacts with this fostering placement," he said. "Margaret is very likely to want to see Sinead, and we're also pretty sure both Patsy and Murphy will request to see her – and her relations do have a right to see Sinead whilst she's in foster care and for as many months as it takes to get her a permanent placement. Would that be a problem in your own house? I don't want you having to drive all over Dublin taking her to see different people every week."

"No, that won't be a problem," I say promptly, before Declan can intervene, without thinking of the consequences.

Declan says nothing.

"This seems a lot simpler than some of the cases I have read about," I lie, more than anything to try and put Declan's mind at rest. I went on to explain to Barry about having read about some of the children in *Children & Carers* whilst carefully editing out the phone calls and my run-in with Edna. Barry agrees that it is a difficult thing to find a suitable match and that *Children & Carers* placements are sadly the more challenging cases, but that often there are happy endings as long as the adoptive parents are consistent, flexible and prepared to attend further training courses.

"But, Bridie, Declan – Sinead's is not a straightforward case, and we have to be clear about that right from the start. It's only fair to you. In fact, Sinead's is one of the most complicated cases that I have ever had to deal with," he warns us. (*Bang goes my theory about him being newly qualified,* I think.) "There seem to be so many different relations suddenly coming forward and trying to claim Sinead." He lists them all: Murphy and his new girlfriend; Patsy her birth mother; Margaret; and Sinead's grandparents on Patsy's side. That's four sets of relatives that want Sinead, and then there's us, of course. Well, I want her.

Listening to all this, I hit rock bottom again, and my thoughts start spiraling: *This whole thing is ridiculous, like some mad competition! Obviously Sinead should come to us – isn't it obvious, Barry? Look, I have even bought educational toys and a daily planner to train her for routines at bedtime and in the morning. The bedroom has been newly decorated and carpeted. There's no competition. Sinead should come to us, she should come to the Kelly family.*

Declan puts down his cup of tea. He has a concerned expression on his face. "It sounds like a very challenging placement for us, Barry. What is the likelihood that the courts will find in our favour as foster carers?"

Our favour, I think. *That's a bit more promising...*

Barry replies, "Sinead has been assessed over many weeks at the Family Centre. At first, we were hoping that Murphy, her father, would manage to buck his ideas up and stop mixing with the 'wrong' sorts, but that is looking less and less likely. He's a musician and late nights playing in pubs and bars across the city isn't the kind of lifestyle that can accommodate looking after a young daughter. As for Patsy, she's very well meaning in her own way, but, well, she's had very little education and even less idea of how to parent. I think the courts will see that our case for foster care, and possible adoption in the longer-term, is in Sinead's interests."

A thought occurred to me, a recollection from *Children & Carers*. "Can I ask, was she ever, you know, ever hurt?"

Barry's face looks worn out as he reaches for another of the expensive Marks & Spencer's biscuits that I'd bought for the occasion. "Sinead has been passed from pillar to post in her short life, Bridie, and some of these people she's come into contact with are known drug users and addicts, some with mental health issues. They certainly present a high risk to Sinead, although we can't say categorically if she's ever suffered any physical abuse."

Declan sighs. "Poor little thing."

My mood lifts again: I'm so alert to Declan's responses and feelings. One foot out of place and the whole thing could go 'tits-up' as they say.

"Do you have a photo of Sinead?" I ask.

"Ummm... maybe I do somewhere," he mutters,

rummaging in his briefcase. He then pulls out a tattered black and white photo showing dozens of people all obviously saying 'Cheese'.

"Goodness, who are they all?"

"I'm not entirely sure," admits Barry. "That man there is Murphy," he points to a rangy man with a haggard face, who is covered in tattoos. "He has the dubious accolade of being the most tattooed man in Dublin!"

I laugh but inwardly groan at how my mother will take this news.

"And that lady there is Patsy, Sinead's mother. And those two girls are Peyton and Ginger, who are children from Murphy's first marriage, we believe."

"Yes, but which one's Sinead?" I ask eagerly.

"Oh, sorry!" Barry points to the only person not saying cheese – a little girl in ragged clothes who has her arms round a huge Irish wolfhound, her head buried in its neck so I cannot see her face. "That's Sinead," Barry says.

"Well, at least she'll get on with our dogs," I laugh, but inwardly the photo has been a shock to me. This is obviously a traveller family with a whole different way of life to ours. A little niggle starts to gnaw at me inside. Will she even like being with us?

Declan looks at the photo but says nothing.

"Can we keep the picture, Barry? When can we meet her?" I ask in a very determined fashion.

"Bridie! Can we talk about this first?" whispers Declan, but Barry doesn't seem to hear that.

"Next Monday any good to you?" he asks.

"Perfect. We'll be there."

Later that evening, I tentatively ask Declan how he feels about the whole thing.

"You're like a headstrong racehorse, Bridie. You won't be stopped until you get your own way," is all he says.

I can't argue with that.

14th December 1997

I am waiting on tenterhooks to meet Sinead next Monday. It's going to be the best Christmas present I've ever had. I know it is. Mum and Dad are cautiously excited for me although Mum says she thinks Sinead could turn out to be "tricky" and Dad warns me that if this offer is a non-starter then perhaps I should have a break from fostering for a while.

It's agony waiting. Everywhere I go, I am noticing five year-olds and their mothers. Just think, I might be part of that world sometime soon! I phone Denise.

"Hi, Denise! I am so excited to be meeting Sinead on Monday. Did I tell you she's five years old? I just keep looking at my watch and willing Monday to come sooner."

Denise is rather prickly. "Bridie, I have told you before – try not to get so obsessed about things. It might not work out – her Dad might get the court order. Have you thought about having some counselling? Just to help you deal with everything. You're so up and down... I mean, I know fostering and being a mother means the world to you, but it's not the be all and end all you know."

"It is to me, Denise," I say, hurt that my sister can't be happier for me. 'I've been thinking about a second name for Sinead – what do you think of Sophia, or Saffron, or Sacha."

"Too alliterative."

"What? Or Aoif?"

"Well, it's different, but could anybody actually spell it?"

I get the message, and tell Denise I have to go. She's not

able to share in my happiness, poor thing. Neither is Declan really. When I asked him if he's excited about meeting Sinead on Monday he says, "Excited's not really the word, Bridie. I'd say more, 'dreading' actually."

"But why, Declan? We could make all the difference to this girl. We can give her a good home, we can love her and cherish her."

"Bridie, love. You can do all those things. I will try. I honestly will. I love you and I will support you, but as I've always told you, if this is what you want, you have to take responsibility for the decisions you're about to make."

I resolve to wait out the weekend in dignified silence. I'll show them all.

Chapter 13

Meeting Sinead

15th December 1997

It's here! The day we meet Sinead. I know that this is one of the most important days of my life.

I'm trying to keep my anxiety, stress, panic and excitement levels at bay – I am not thinking ahead about family picnics and Christmases because this is all so uncertain with Sinead, but I can't help a little part of my brain obsessing about things: What if she doesn't like us? What if they give Murphy the residency order? *Shut up, brain!* It doesn't help that it is a very gloomy, cloudy mid-winter day. Even the Christmas lights don't lift the drear and Declan says that it matches his mood! Bad sign? H/F: I can't even tell.

We drive into Dublin, and find Ringsend Road where the Family Centre is based.

"There it is," says Declan pointing to a dark, depressing building rather like something you'd see in a horror film. "It's a bit grim around here isn't it," he mutters. "It's got one of the highest crime rates in the whole of Dublin."

"Oh, don't be daft, Declan! This is Dublin, not Beirut," I say checking my hair and lipstick in my pocket mirror. We park the car nearby and walk in silence to the imposing building, and I press the intercom button.

"Hello, Ringsend Family Centre. Who do you want to see?" The question takes me unawares and I freeze momentarily. "Erm... Er, we're here to see Sinead Riley," I say feeling sick to my boots with nerves.

"Who's the link worker please?"

"Oh, sorry! Barry Black."

"Thank you." There's a clunking noise and a bleep and the door opens. We make our way cautiously upstairs. The hall is grey and dark, the concrete steps chipped, and to add to that there is a faint smell of sick and lager. I'm completely out of my comfort zone. If we're allowed to adopt Sinead we'll take her away from all of this. She'd want for nothing: clothes, food, holidays, ponies, dogs and yes, if necessary, private school. Why not?

Edna and Barry are here to welcome us into Ringsend Family Centre and seeing familiar faces helps us to relax a little. We are given a remarkably decent cup of tea and some delicious, fruity barmbrack, before the obligatory guided tour of the Centre. I feel Declan's unease, but the staff are relaxed.

"See, it's not so bad here is it?" I hiss.

"'No, I'm *really* enjoying myself," he retorts acidly.

We both stop our sniping as we see a small, dark-haired toddler of about three years old, who is toying with a dolls tea-set. The little girl looks thin, scruffy, spaced out and somehow detached from her circumstances.

"Jesus, would you look at the marks on her arm," says Declan. "They are cigarette burns. Who could do that to a child?" he mutters.

It's devastating to see the evidence of somebody using a child as a punch bag. I want to take that little child home with us too and give her the life she deserves.

Barry is moving us next door to meet Sinead for the first time. My spirits lift as I recall the picture of her in my head: a small, vulnerable child with thick curly red hair. Where are you Sinead, my child? I know that we are destined to be together.

Suddenly there she is! Oh my... look at her... She is

smiling at us and waving. "Is mise Sinead, ello ello! Dia duit is mise Sinead."

Oh my God – she's speaking Irish. How amazing, except that I can hardly understand what she is saying, her accent is so strong. How unusual it is to hear a small child speaking Irish these days.

"D – look at her! Isn't she just adorable," I croon.

Declan nudges me with his elbow. "Slow down, Bridie!" he whispers, "let's just take it one step at a time."

I know he thinks I'm impulsive and emotional, but I do, I love her already. I want to pick her up in my arms and whisk her away. NOW.

My first impressions of Sinead are that she is quite tall and slender for her age, with shoulder-length, wavy red hair. Actually it strikes me that her hair is an amazing colour: it's not ginger-red, more a honeyed, maple syrup colour. Her eyes are almond shaped and green. I see determination and strength in them. She has big dimples in her cheeks and a bright smile. Her teeth don't look too bad: they're slightly yellowy, but hey, we could soon fix them with a good diet and regular trips to the hygienist. She is wearing old, boy's clothes and boy's black lace up shoes, poor little thing. God, I can't wait to buy her some new clothes from Next or Gap or Monsoon... I do, I love her.

I crouch down to meet her. "Hello, Sinead, I'm Bridie. I am very pleased to meet you," I say and reach out to hold her thin, bony hand. I smile at her and try to make eye contact.

She doesn't look me in the eye, in fact she seems very distracted, her eyes darting all over the place and I notice that one eye is bloodshot with a livid sty in the corner.

She breaks away from me and trots over to the other side of the play area, busying herself with a little toy iron and ironing board. Then she looks at me, and smiles! She smiles at me! Oh – hold on, it's more of a grimace... She's pointing to her wet pull-ups. "Toilet!" she says.

One of the female careworkers takes her off to the loo.

Declan whispers in my ear, "I like her, she's got character!"

"Really? You like her? Oh, D..." I hug him and feel a huge weight lift off my shoulders, but there's a commotion at the door and a big, burly man stumbles in.

"Ah, Mr Riley," says Barry. "We weren't expecting you until later."

"Well, I'm here now," says Murphy Riley, Sinead's birth father. "Here, child!" he demands of his daughter as she trots back into the room with the careworker.

Little Sinead stops in her tracks and looks at the careworker and then at Murphy. "Here!" he demands again as if he's talking to a dog, and I bristle with anger at this bully. Sinead starts to snivel.

"Stop that noise, girl," Murphy says. "Show 'em you're a Riley, not a mouse..."

Mercifully, Barry steps in. "Bridie, will you play with Sinead for a while whilst I take Mr Riley to the Waiting Room?" Barry nods to the play area and then very firmly leads Murphy back out of the door. I am impressed by his defusing of a potentially tricky situation.

Declan and I sit on the floor in the Wendy House. "Hey, Sinead, I have a little book for you to look at," I say, pointing at the pictures in her new book. "Do you want to come and look at them with me?" But all she seems to do is look around her distractedly and chat away incomprehensibly in her childish, disjointed Irish. Then she does a little burp and says, "Gabh mo leithscéal," which I gather means excuse me.

"Good girl" says Declan, and Sinead looks straight at him as if she's seen him for the first time. She is scratching her hair and making a face. I wonder if she is developmentally behind?

The twins were definitely talking in coherent sentences at this age and what with the Irish language barrier, I realise we will have to work hard with our communication.

"Sinead," I say, "shall we do some words?" I point at the dog in the picture. "Look, this is a dog," I say. "Can you say 'dog'?"

She inches towards us and looks at the book.

"Look, Sinead – here's an apple. Can you say 'apple'?" We carry on like this for a few minutes, but she doesn't actually say any of the words. Suddenly her happy mood changes and she marches off, frowning.

The door opens, and I am expecting Barry to return, but it is yet another suspicious-looking character.

"Nanna! Nanna! Love you!" Sinead shouts, as she runs towards the wizened-looking lady. *Ah, so she can speak a bit of English if she wants to.*

The woman responds by whisking Sinead into the air. "Phewee! You gotta shitty nappy," she laughs and pinches Sinead playfully on the nose.

Declan whispers to me, "She should be out of nappies by now, don't you think?"

Barry appears in the doorway and introduces us to the woman who is hugging and kissing Sinead. "Ah, I see you've met Mrs O'Driscoll, Sinead's grandma? She's Patsy's mother. I think it's best if we finish off with a debrief in the Visitors' Room," he says to me and Declan. "We'll leave Mrs O'Driscoll to have her time with Sinead now."

Barry whisks us off to another room. I turn and wave to Sinead and to my delight, she waves back.

"Well, all things considered, I think that was a successful first meeting," says Barry breezily. "I'm sorry about the interruptions from Sinead's relatives. They do love her in their own way. When Margaret brings her in to the Centre, we use it as an opportunity for Sinead to meet with other members of her family, but they never stick to the agreed meeting times! Oh, well. How do you feel, Bridie? Declan?"

"She's a sweet little thing," says Declan, "but shouldn't she be out of nappies by now?"

"She does have some developmental issues, yes," says Barry, "but we feel it's more a case of inconsistent supervision than anything underlying. Bridie?"

I am in a daze – there's so much to take in. "I love her," I say. It's all I can say.

On the way home, Declan and I are silent. It's been emotionally exhausting for both of us, but as we swing into our drive I say, "What are you thinking about, D?"

"I'm thinking I'd like to get Sinead away from those *shawlie* relatives of hers."

"Declan! You can't say things like that! But so would I."

19th December 1997

We have been invited to Sinead's birthday party today. I am so excited to see her again, but also churned-up with emotions and questions. Declan can't come this time because of work pressures so I invite Bea instead, who has just come home from college for her Christmas holidays.

"Okay, I'll come..." Bea says rather reluctantly.

"You are alright with us fostering, aren't you Bea?"

"Yes, of course Bridie, but Dad told me about your first meeting and it sounded a bit... mental. I mean, will her weird family be there?"

"I expect so – it is her birthday after all. She'll be six, I think.

At 3.30 pm prompt, we arrive at the party with a card and a small present of wax crayons and a colouring book. Sinead is playing with a huge red and white balloon – in fact, playing is a bit of an understatement as she's using the balloon to bat her careworker about the head.

"I get you little bugger," I hear her say. *Yup. She can definitely speak English if she wants to,* I think. She then pursues a small boy around the play area bashing his head several times with the balloon. To my horror, Murphy is joining in. "Ata girl, Sinead – get him." I want to reprimand Murphy for egging-on his daughter to be aggressive, but I feel it's not my place – yet. Bea looks bemused.

The other children are sitting obediently around the table, devouring white ham sandwiches, crisps and pink birthday cake. I can hear 'Happy Birthday' music playing in the background. Barry is sitting at the end of the table cutting the cake into small slices, and chatting amiably with the kids. He sees us at the door, smiles and beckons us in.

"Pleased to meet you, Bea," he says. "Let me introduce you to Sinead."

My lovely Bea kneels down to talk to Sinead who literally makes a bee-line for her, if you'll pardon the pun. It's quite amazing to see. How come Sinead will acknowledge Bea, but not me? I feel conflicting emotions: I'm so pleased that there seems to be an invisible bond between Sinead and Bea, but upset that Sinead has completely ignored me.

Barry picks up on my feelings. "Children seem to automatically know which adults are figures of authority and which are more like friends. I think Sinead has sussed you and Bea out already!"

"So, you mean, she knows we might foster her?"

"Not exactly, but I think she knows that you are part of the Family Centre system, and therefore, she's a little wary of you because the Family Centre represents change for her. It's all very subliminal, but you mustn't be downhearted. Most children seem to have this sixth sense."

Sinead is now opening our birthday present and speaking a mixture of Irish and English, "Tanks go raibh maith agat."

Bea is impressed. "Bridie, she's speaking Irish! That's amazing – I can't even remember French."

Nanna O'Driscoll is sitting in the corner wearing a thin blue polo neck jumper and tatty blue flared jeans. She has dyed her hair jet black, presumably to cover the grey, but it does nothing for her complexion.

"How are yuz, Bridie? This your step-dorter then?" she asks rather smugly.

"Yes, this is Bea," I say, introducing her to the throng. "She's home from college for Christmas," I add, just to wipe that self-righteous smile off her face. I don't expect she even knows what 'college' is.

Barry introduces me and Bea to Margaret, Sinead's surrogate mum, who nods back at us curtly. Margaret is a scrawny woman, with thin dyed blond hair, and sports an over-sized black leather biker-jacket which really does look a bit odd. "Sinead's my birthday girl," she says protectively. "Look at all the prezzies we got 'er. I bet she's sick as a pig tonight wit all that cake. 'Scuse me, I need a fag," and with that, she disappears out of the room. Bea turns to me, a slight look of alarm in her eyes. "Blimey... she's a bundle of laughs." And then, under her breath, "She stinks of weed."

"How do you know it's a weed smell?"

"Bride! I *am* at college!" she laughs as if that explains it. Ah well, I suppose she's experiencing all sorts in Cork.

The party progresses and we all manage to stay relatively friendly with each other. We sing 'Happy Birthday' to Sinead who is indeed six years old today. Sinead, with her mouth crammed full of birthday cake manages in one puff to blow out all the pretty pink candles.

On our way out, Barry thanks us for coming, saying, "I think you helped to diffuse a bit of tension between Nanny O'Driscoll and Margaret, you know. They don't usually see eye to eye."

As we get out of the door, Bea and I burst into hysterical laughter, partly from the relief of being out of that place, and partly the image of Margaret and Nanny O'D having a bun-fight. You couldn't put money on who'd win.

21st December 1997

Happiness Factor 100!!! Barry has phoned to say that the SS are in agreement that we would make ideal foster carers for Sinead, if we would like to take her on. Despite myself, I tell Barry that I will need to discuss it with Declan, but that I'll be in touch before they close for Christmas.

I ring Declan at work – something I rarely do because of his heavy workload and constant stream of patients.

"B?" he answers as the receptionist puts me through.

"We're approved to foster Sinead for three months in the new year, Declan! If you agree of course."

There's a long pause on the other end of the phone. I start to perspire.

"Declan? Do you agree?

"Of course I agree! Let's do it! Let's give Sinead the best three months she's ever had in her life."

"Oh my God! Oh Declan!" The tears are running down my face. "Thank you. Thank you!"

I phone Barry back straight away with the good news, then fling myself on the sofa and sob my heart out. I sob, and sob and sob. All the years of waiting, all the years of yearning, have brought me to this point. I am going to be a Mum to little Sinead. I AM GOING TO BE A MUM. I can't believe it. The Christmas lights on the tree are twinkling and sparkling through my tears. I hug Roger Bear, I hug the dogs who have picked up on all the excitement, and burst into tears all over again.

The front door slams and Bea trudges in. "Mum! What's the matter?" she asks, the concern in her voice amplified by her rare use of the word 'Mum', which is usually reserved for boyfriend heartbreak or visits to the dentist.

"Nothing, darling! We've just heard that they've approved us for fostering Sinead."

"Really?" she says, "Oh, that's amazing! She's a great kid. I'm really pleased for you, Bridie," and she gives me a big hug. "What's for tea?"

Chapter 14

A Bit Like Buses

6th January 1998

The unexpected has happened. Now, it seems they can't get enough of the Kellys: the SS have phoned to ask if we can take an urgent four-day placement of a young lad called Johnny – before Sinead comes. It seems his current carers need a break. A different social worker, Ellen O'Farrell has arrived to talk about Johnny. She seems very confident and well-organised and starts reading Johnny's notes to me and Declan. "He's small for his age and has Foetal Alcohol Syndrome. As a result of this, he is hyperactive and has difficulty concentrating. He is prone to huge temper tantrums. However he is a loving little boy who responds well to boundaries and consistency. He has just had his 11th birthday. He will need structure and lots to do. It is noted that Johnny can run off, so try to keep him in the house at all times. Also, Bridie, we do require you to keep a daily diary, because if we manage to find Johnny a permanent home, it will be useful to read these diaries to see how his placements went."

I nod obediently. I now have two diaries to keep!

She closes the file. "What do you think?" she asks, eyeing us both up cautiously. "It's only for four days, and as I understand it, Edna Pritchard wants you to have a bit of experience before going into the longer term fostering of Sinead Riley."

I turn to face Declan. "What do you think?" but Declan is

continuing to prove that he is Husband of the Year, as he says, "Of course we will have him. We can give the poor fellow a little holiday here."

Ellen shook our hands and told us that Johnny's carer would ring us next week and iron out the details so that he could be with us by 7th February. What a whirlwind! I can't believe it – my first placement, and it's happening much sooner than I anticipated.

"Are you really okay about this?" I ask Declan.

"Look, if it gets us in old Danny Danvers' good books, then I think it's a no-brainer! And in any case, it will give us a bit of practice for Sinead." And with that he buttons-up his jacket, and slips off to work.

Okay. So... where do I start? I am determined to make a success of fostering Johnny, even if it is just for a few days. I decide to find some suitable toys and games for a boy of his age from the charity shop and will see if I can arrange some swimming and a game of football with my brother Tim. I know Dad will bring his Lexicon round, or even Jack Straws. I must admit, I can't help feeling a bit proud of myself right now. Bridie Kelly – about to undertake her first foster placement. Who would've thought it, after all this time. MY FIRST CHILD.

I decide not to ring round all my family with the good news – once bitten, twice shy and all that. I do tell my parents though. Mum is confused. "Darling, isn't that Sinead one coming?"

I explained again that this is just a very temporary placement and make a mental note to speak to Dad about Mum's recent propensity to get the wrong end of the stick. I wonder if she's feeling alright...? She sounds disappointed. "But I thought it was just that dear little girl that was coming. I have knitted a beautiful pink scarf"

"That's okay Mum – it'll save till Sinead comes. It'll

probably be in March, so not that long now.

7th January 1998

Much sooner than expected, I get a phone call from Joyce, Johnny's current carer (the one who needs a break), who makes no bones about the fact that Johnny is going to be a challenging placement.

"He can be a sweet boy, but, well, let's put it like this: you'll need to be strict and have very firm boundaries with him. Watch everything he does and rein him in if he is cheeky. Keep a very strict routine throughout the day, because it's when he has nothing to do that he can go off the rails. Ask him to tidy his room, or clear the table and do a few chores round the house. He's a good boy and doesn't mind helping out. Any problems, give Ellen a ring. Okay?"

9th January 1998

It's eight o'clock and my Dad is on the phone. CRISIS. He's very upset; in fact he's in tears, which is unheard of. He thinks Mum is dying. Christ! I knew there was something wrong – I should pay attention to my intuition more. But my mother can't possibly be ill, can she? She's a tough old stick. I mean, I have seen her hands shake a bit, and I have noticed her forgetfulness, but she is only 70.

Close questioning of my Dad reveals that Mum has lost weight and developed a permanent shake of her hands; in fact it's so bad she dropped her cup of tea yesterday. He also thinks her personality is ever so slightly changing, as she is being more what Dad calls 'rude'."

"What? More so than usual, Dad?"

"Yes, love – more than usual!" We both chuckle, but it is without mirth.

Dad continues to tell me the full story. Apparently, her GP has referred her to a neurologist.

I try to reassure Dad that Mum is as fit as a fiddle and it is probably just an old-age tremor, but I feel secretly terrified. What if it's Motor Neurone Disease or Parkinson's? What if it's genetic?

I don't want to ring Declan at work, as I know what his response will be: probably not very reassuring, "Let's just wait until she's had the tests before we start speculating," so I ring Lee who always calms me down.

"Bridie, we have to face facts. They are not spring chickens any more. They're getting older – Mum's 70 and Dad's 80 – that's a good age you know. We've got to expect that things will start to wear out sooner rather than later. It's probably nothing serious and whatever it is, we'll deal with it as a family, like we always do." But this time, Lee has failed to reassure me.

I can't help it. I break our golden rule and ring Declan who also tells me to calm down because I am talking too fast, and that his father had Parkinson's for 11 years.

I blurt out, "So you are saying that she has Parkinson's then?"

"No! What I meant was that if it was anything serious, it doesn't mean that she's dying – she could live for years yet in reasonably good health. But it could be anything, Bridie – let's just wait and see what her doctor says, shall we?"

See.

I spend the rest of the day feeling very low. I am hijacked by the thought that my Mum is ill and will not live to make the most of Sinead and Johnny and all my other foster kids. We've been plotting and planning and waiting so long for this, and now it seems it's too late. How sad is that? Who will I ring with all my problems if Mum's not around any more? And what about Dad? How will he cope with her loss? HF: 0. I am petrified.

12th January 1998

Oh, for God's sake! A ridiculous situation has arisen: having signed myself up for Johnny, there is now strong possibility that Sinead could be with us at the same time. Declan is annoyed and weary. "Ach, Bridie – this is bad timing isn't it? As if we haven't got enough going on worrying about Winifred! I hope this isn't all going to be too much for you?"

"I know – it's bloody typical isn't it?" I say, feeling sorry for myself. "Everything comes at once, doesn't it? But I don't feel I can turn Johnny down, as his carer desperately needs a break and I have committed us to this placement." I munch on a family bag of crisps whilst downing yet another mug of strong filter coffee. The bottle of filtered water lies unopened in the fridge.

Later that morning, a ray of sunshine appears as I get a phone call from Mum to say that her shake has gone and that Dad was making a fuss. She then starts ranting on about Dad and his beloved Labour Party, and the ray of sunshine turns into a full-on sunny day. She must be okay if she's getting all political on me.

"Ah, Mum, it's lovely to hear you sound like your old self," I say, "but Barry Black is due to arrive any minute so I can't talk right now. But thanks for ringing – I'm so glad you're feeling better."

"There was nothing wrong with me in the first place!" she barks and puts the phone down.

I open the door to Barry Black feeling a whole lot more human. He looks exhausted.

"Come on in for a cup of tea," I say.

"Oh lovely. Thanks, Bridie," he says, pulling off his jacket and settling onto the sofa. I notice that interestingly, men don't seem to make the fart noise on that sofa. "Things are getting a bit difficult at the Family Centre," he says, raising his voice a little so that I can hear him from in the kitchen where I've found my special pack of M&S biscuits that I keep for his visits – I know he likes them.

"I am wondering if you could babysit Sinead once or twice before February 7th – that's before Johnny comes to stay with you? Would that be alright? Things are getting a bit sticky for Sinead at Margaret's – I can't really go into why – so we may have to bring her foster-placement with you forward. I would like her to get to know you a bit better before she comes for the placement. Otherwise, it will be a big shock to the system for her, and to be honest Bridie, I am a bit worried because she is not an easy child for a first-time foster carer." His eyes alight on the biscuits, and he takes two with his cup of tea.

Totally buoyed-up by my mother's phone call, I say blithely, "Oh, don't worry about me, Barry. I'm used to children, what with Bea and my nieces and nephew, and not to mention Declan's granddaughter, Mia... And in answer to your question, yes, we can have Sinead here any time. We're all ready for her – and there's plenty of room if it overlaps with Johnny's stay.

Barry nodded his head in approval. "Well, we'll try our best for that not to happen, as it may compromise the situation for both children. That will only happen as an absolute worst case scenario."

He didn't realise what music it was to my ears when he said the words 'foster placement'. I couldn't stop my big cheesy grin. Suddenly, everything was okay with the world. At that moment I loved Barry Black with his curly blonde hair and teenage complexion. He was making my dreams come true. I was going to be a mother of not just Sinead, but Johnny as well. How cool is that?

Later though, reality hits hard as I realise just what I'm taking on: two damaged children that I hardly know? I visualise the chaos and disorder that they might bring to the house, not to mention their propensity for tantrums and running away.

I ring Barry in a panic.

"Hi, Barry, er erm, it's Bridie Kelly. Ummm, I'm sorry about this, but I am a bit worried about coping with erm, well about Johnny coming as well as Sinead?"

Barry sighed and harrumphed. "That's understandable, Bridie, it's a big ask for you, but what we'll try and do is work it so that Sinead comes for her stays either before or after Johnny's been with you. How does that sound? So that you don't have them both at the same time."

"Okay thanks– I'd appreciate that," I say, feeling slightly relieved, but still apprehensive.

"It's normal you know. To feel nervous, I mean," says Barry reassuringly.

I think I might be a little bit in love with him.

I know it's unfair to trouble Mum with my worries, especially after her own little 'health scare' but I am so anxious about Johnny and Sinead coming together, that I give her a ring. But Mum is optimistic. "Bridie love – be positive! This is what you've always wanted – children in the house. Enjoy it. Rise to the challenge!" I heard her singing 'The hills are alive with the sound of music...' before she hung up.

She is right. I mean, how hard can it be looking after two young children for a week?

13th January 1998

Barry, bless him, has worked wonders. He must've understood the pressure I felt under with the whole scenario of the two children coming at once, so he has arranged for me to meet Sinead in town today – just me meeting Sinead (oh, and Barry will be there, of course). Barry says it will give me and Sinead an opportunity to bond. I can't wait. I dress in sensible blue corduroy trousers and my lesbian shoes.

I have arranged to meet Barry and Sinead outside Burger King at 2.30 pm (as long as he doesn't expect me to go inside the actual restaurant – I am veggie after all, and abhor those places). I am tense, and want a ciggie. In fact, if I had a packet on me I would be on my twentieth one by now.

They're late and I worry that Barry has changed his mind or that another, more experienced carer has been found?

It's 2.45 pm and there's still no sign of them. I am twitchy and nervous. Why does this feel like a blind date?

Christ... I recognise that woman... OMG it's Margaret, Sinead's surrogate mum. What the hell is she doing here? I do not like the look of her one bit and I turn away in the hope that she doesn't see me. I breathe a sigh of relief as she wanders past, and see that she doesn't have Sinead with her. She seems to know some people sitting on a bench who are drinking vodka. Shit. She's seen me. Now she's approaching me, smiling. I see her flick her rollie into the road.

"How are youz? You waiting to see our Sinead?" she asks with what I think is a slightly belligerent tone. I notice she's put on quite a bit of weight, but it doesn't make her look any more attractive.

"Yes I am actually – but they're late."

"Them's delayed. Should be here soon. Got trouble with Murphy," she says staring at me. She really is an odd-looking woman, with all that dyed blond, greasy hair, and a nose that has definitely been broken at some point. And, surprise, surprise, very few teeth. I'm certain she can't be much more than 40 but she looks 60. I mean really, who goes around with no teeth these days?

"I needs a fag. 'Scuse me," she says before deftly rolling and lighting up in front of me. It's all I can do to stop myself from blagging a rollie off her. She stinks of old fags and sour body odour. She then reaches into her leather jacket pocket and produces a round pink pair of children's glasses, a snow white doll and a dummy which seemed to have something sticky inside it. "These are my Sinead's, bless her," she says. "I always keep them on me. I loves her so much, I do."

To my surprise, I see genuine tears in her eyes, and feel a bit mean to have been so judgmental of her. What do I know of her life? Her past? What she's been through? Who am I to judge?

I was at a bit of a loss for what to say. Side with her? Ignore her? I opt for a change of subject and begin talking about Dublin, but it was her family she wanted to speak of.

"I have seven others you know – here's them," and she produces a crumpled up school photo with four children dressed in blue school uniforms, their arms around each other. Christ. It's the photo from *Children & Carers*.

"And these," she says and produces yet another tatty photo from her pocket, of three taller teenagers. One of them is poking a defiant middle finger at the camera. I half smile. Seeing me smile, she says, "Yeh, that one's Duane. He's at special school. Got the works, he has. ADHD, OCD and a bad, bad temper. Him and Sinead gets on a treat – luvs each other they do. Mind you, he's got a heart of gold. Kindest kid I got."

"They are lovely. You must be very proud," I say neutrally.

"You got none of yer own then?" she asks, eyeing me up

and down with a smirk on her face.

"Er, no. I have a step-daughter Bea – you met her at the party – but we want to foster to help other children."

"But none of your actual own then?" she repeats cockily.

"No. None of my actual own," I say, feeling inferior to this, this scrag of a woman.

"So Sinead'll be your first fer fosterin then?" she says, continuing her interrogation.

But at last, here they are, and Margaret backs off. Poor Barry looks exhausted, and he's literally dragging Sinead along behind him. I am so pleased to see them.

"Come on now, Sinead, chop chop! Let's go and have a drink." Sinead doesn't miss a trick however, and has seen that Margaret is here too.

Margaret elbows past me to get to Sinead first. How dare she! I stand feebly in the background and watch jealously as Sinead runs into Margaret's smoky embrace. I admit to myself that she obviously really loves this strange character.

"Margaret," says Barry rather tersely. "What are you doing here?"

"Seeing friends," Margaret replies, jerking her thumb back towards the reprobates on the bench.

"Shall we go in?" Barry asks pointing a finger towards Burger King. I do not want to say in front of Margaret that I am veggie – just imagine how she would sneer. I'll just have to put up with it.

"Erm, I have just eaten but you guys have something," I say. "I'll just have a green tea."

"What the fuck is green tea?" says Margaret defiantly, her lips curled in menace.

"Excuse me Margaret – no swearing in front of the child," Barry reprimands her.

She laughs in his face. "Can't wait to see what the *fooken* green tea is," she glares.

"Actually, Margaret, as you well know, this is a private meeting with Bridie and Sinead. So perhaps you'd like to go and see your friends now"

"Sure. See youz later Sinead," she says and slinks off to her vodka-lashed friends.

Barry and Sinead go to the counter to order something to eat, and return with a huge burger and fries for Sinead plus a large coke. Surely that's too much for a six year-old? Lee would have a fit! But Sinead begins to wolf down the burger, emitting a large throaty belch in the process.

Barry eyes me, but says nothing, and neither do I. Whilst Sinead is preoccupied, I ask Barry how come Margaret is here?

"I'm sorry, Bridie, it's my fault," Barry says, looking absolutely exhausted. "Margaret and Murphy have this one-upmanship about Sinead. If she's coming to the Centre, Margaret will boast about it to Murphy, then he'll turn up at the Centre and cause a scene. He's usually drunk. That's what happened today, only Margaret was still there, having dropped Sinead off. I just happened to mention that we were late and had to get to Burger King, and hey presto! Here she is. I expect Murphy will turn up any minute too."

I look around me nervously. That man gives me the creeps. "In her own way, Margaret is here to keep an eye on Sinead, you know," continues Barry. "She's finding it hard to let go of her, even though she can't really cope with her own kids. She has a strong sense of loyalty to Sinead." Just as he finished this sentence, we see Margaret at the counter queuing up, but obviously not for green tea. They don't sell it here.

And before we know it, Margaret has joined our table, and is taunting Sinead with what's left of her coke. She throws her head back laughing, revealing her scant number of teeth.

Sinead grabs the cup from her and gulps the remaining fizzy poison down and lets out another enormous belch. I can't believe that such a little girl can do such a loud burp.

"Thass my Sinead! Always belching and ferting! Keeps us amused anyways." Sinead does another burp and Margaret laughs, and I realise that this is some kind of ritual between them – probably the nearest emotion Sinead gets to love. I recoil a little, a bit disgusted to be honest, but Margaret's a canny one, and presses home her advantage.

"Always ferting this one. Always burpin'."

"Maybe she's got reflux problems or leaky gut syndrome?" I say, noticing that Barry has his head in his hands. "It's probably exacerbated by large amounts of fizzy drinks and fatty food."

Margaret stares at me and looked puzzled, and then shrieks with laughter, so that the whole restaurant goes quiet and looks towards our table. "What the fook is reflex? Youz and yer feckin' ekasserbated..."

Thankfully, Barry intervenes. "Bridie's right Margaret. Sinead shouldn't really have too many fizzy drinks or too much junk food."

Margaret tutted. "Never done her no harm. Youz bloody social workers no feckin' fun!" She laughs to herself and goes to light-up another fag, before realising that she can't smoke in here. But she's having too much fun to go outside right now.

"You can burp the bleedin' alphabet, can't you Shinny! Go on!" she eggs-on the little girl, cackling like a witch. I study Margaret's lined face – it has years of pain and hardship etched on it. Barry and I look at each other wearily, but Sinead is not playing ball. She's gone quiet and is perhaps picking-up that Margaret is using her as a pawn for her own petty vendetta against me.

"Hey, Sinead," I say, "shall we practice some other words for 'fert'? You can call it 'wind' or 'gas', or 'trump' or..."

"Trump!" Sinead says. "Trump."

Margaret looks at me like she could thrust a dagger in my heart, and stalks out for her fag.

"Would you like to take Sinead home for an hour or so, Bridie? If you can drop her back at the Centre by six o'clock, that would be grand. Margaret's due to collect her then, so it will at least give you two a bit of time to get to know each other.

We agree to meet back at the Family Centre, where I need to pick up a booster seat for my car, so that Sinead is safe for the drive home. When we arrive there and try to fit the seat, I cannot for the life of me get it to work. The seat belt is supposed to thread through the damn thing, but God knows how. Finally, I give up and ask Barry to show me. He is understanding.

"It's a bit old and rusty, Bridie. We all have a problem with it except Margaret. Enjoy the rest of the day." And with that, he leaves me and little Sinead to get on with things.

Every time I encourage her to get into the car seat she arches her back like a cat and shouts, "No! Off!" and shakes her head at me. On top of that, I am convinced that Margaret and Murphy are watching from one of the windows in that infernal building, laughing and judging me. I must look pathetic with my feeble attempts to befriend this six year-old girl. I feel near to tears.

"Sinead, please do as you are told. We are going to meet my mother for lovely afternoon tea," I say assertively, but this has no effect – in fact it makes everything worse as she lunges at me like a boxer and does that strange staring at things that aren't there.

"No! Want to stay with Magga!"

Then I have a lightbulb moment courtesy of my dear mother. I remember from childhood one of her distraction tricks was to change the subject. For instance when I used to cry as a small child my mother would say, "Bridie, look at that rabbit on top of the roof!" I would turn my head and search for the rabbit forgetting what I was crying about and, bingo! I was calm. Will this technique work with Sinead though? That's the million-dollar question.

"Hey, Sinead, there are some sweeties hidden in the car. Shall we see if we can find them?"

Hurray! I have succeeded in conning her. I am sure this is against every single one of the parenting rules in those bloody books my mother bought me, but I don't give a damn. It's works and she is in the car, and I know that I have some lemon-flavoured travel sweets in the glove compartment. Much as it is against my better judgment to bribe kids, I tell myself that this is the one and only time I'll do it.

Sinead is in her booster seat, sucking on a lemon travel sweet and all is well with the world. Right, let's go.

Exhausted and in a state of slight panic, I arrive at Mum and Dad's house. They're not expecting me, but they'll know what to do with Sinead, for sure. And I feel safe here.

"Hey, Mum, Dad? Where are you?" I shout as I let myself in. "Look who I have got with me."

"Well, look who we have here!" says my Mum as Sinead shyly stands beside me. Mum raises herself stiffly from the armchair and I notice that her thin little hands are shaking a bit. Mum bends down and gives Sinead a little stroke under the chin.

"Mum, Dad – this is Sinead," I say proudly. "She doesn't speak much English, mostly Irish."

"You'll be wanting a cup of hot chocolate I should think?" says my Mum. "Come with me – let's see what we can find." And just like that, Sinead holds her hand and they wander off into the kitchen. Amazed, and if truth be told, slightly irritated,

I watch them disappear into the next room, and hear my Mum jabbering to Sinead in the way that grandmas do – you know: the way that makes any kid feel safe, happy and loved. It seems to be a knack I haven't got – yet.

My father is fascinated and wants to know her background. I give him a potted history before Mum and Sinead come back in, Sinead carefully carrying a small plastic cup of hot chocolate.

Ten minutes later, Mum has persuaded Sinead out into the garden. It's getting dark, and it's cold, but it's something to do. However, the minute Sinead sees the dog she begins swearing at him.

"You fucker! Get lost."

Mum intervenes quickly. "Sinead, we don't speak like that in this house, darling." And to me, "Bridie, she knows more English than we've given her credit for!" But I see my Mum looking nervously around her and know that she is hoping to God the neighbours didn't hear the words of this little girl in her back garden!

Then I hear Dad's voice. "No, no – stop that now, Sinead. Be nice to the doggie. Leave the dog alone! Stroke her gently, like this... Shhh... be kind to the doggie, Sinead," and then the sound of a defiant Sinead roaring, "Mine! Off! Off!"

"Sinead, leave the dog alone," I say in my sternest voice as I attempt to dissuade Sinead from torturing poor Trixy. At first she ignores me but then we try the food approach, this time with chocolates, and it works. That's twice in one day that I've bribed her with sweets. Not good. And also, what's not so good is that I realise this little girl is too much for my elderly parents. She's too demanding for them – it's not going to be another Mikey-Jaz-Sassy-Mia scenario. Oh no – Sinead is in a class of her own, and that's not a place I can expect my parents to feel comfortable. Bang go my babysitters!

Boy, this first visit with Sinead is hard work. I am exhausted, but I can't relax yet – there's still over an hour to go. She just doesn't sit down and do things like the twins did; she is on the go the whole time like a Ferrari – I can't keep up with her. She's in the greenhouse now, kicking the watering can; now she's doing a kind of hopscotch on the garden path...

"Come on, Sinead, let's go back indoors," I say, but she ignores me. What shall I do with her? I try to remember bits from the fostering course. Bonding with your child; rapport; getting into her world...

"Ah, ah er me Sinead go home now see Magga."

Dad asks Sinead if she wants to play dominoes and to my surprise she agrees. She follows him back into the house and sits down on the rug by the fire as my father tries to teach her how to match the dots. But she is more interested in using the dominoes as building bricks, so they start to build a house. Every time if falls down, Sinead giggles and says, "Agen."

My father is a very patient man and plays this game with Sinead for twenty minutes or so, and she responds well to his one-to-one attention, until, for no reason that I can see, she is suddenly doing that odd stare at everything and nothing, and has lost all focus on the game.

"Come on then, Sinead," I say, "let's get you back to the Centre." I think that if I drive slowly, we'll only be ten minutes early and it won't look like utter failure.

As Dad helps to put Sinead's coat back on, Mum says, "Oh, Bridie, she's quite a handful for you isn't she?"

I am about to agree but once again Sinead has escaped and is ambushing poor Trixy, this time yanking her tail and leaving the poor dog howling with pain, her ears back and her tail submissively between her legs. Trixy has already had enough trauma in life, coming from a rescue home, and she doesn't take kindly to either children or rough handling.

"Sinead! No!" my Mum says, and Sinead stops long enough for Trixy to dash out into the garden, which by now is dark and offers a safe hiding place.

"Come on, Sinead, let's go," I say apologising to Mum and Dad. "I'll ring you," I say. "Don't worry."

Before Sinead can refuse to get in the car, I tell her she can look for a sweetie and she clambers in the booster seat, and to my utter amazement, she buckles-up the seatbelt. I smile to myself, thinking that this funny little girl just did something so easily that I struggled with myself.

I climb into my side and give Sinead her sweetie – the third bribe of the day – telling myself that next time, we will start over, no bribes, no swearing, no farting, no dog torturing... when my mobile phone rings in my handbag. It is Barry and I can hear the strain in his voice.

"Bridie, I am afraid things kicked-off rather badly after you left... " I was sure I could hear Margaret and Murphy screaming drunkenly in the background: "Feckin' social workers. I am getting meself a Barrister. Sinead's staying with me. She is not having our kid!"

"Can you keep her overnight Bridie, please? It's just temporary – we'll get an emergency protection order. She can't go back to Margaret's today..."

Christ. I was looking forward to a large glass of wine and a long soak in the bath tonight. But I am not falling at the first hurdle.

"Of course, Barry. She can stay with us for as long as necessary."

"Are you sure about this, Bridie? I'm asking for a court order of three months to give Margaret and Murphy time to cool down and get their lives in order, but from past experience, that's rather unlikely. I don't want to put pressure on you – only do this if you are absolutely sure about it."

I reassure Barry that Sinead will be in good hands. I don't mention that I am finding her hard work already.

Barry rings off, and I sit in the car, trying to take on the enormity of the situation, which has just accelerated beyond my wildest expectations. I have a child placed with me for three months. Oh. My. God. All the bravado has evaporated as I face reality: all the thoughts of toys and Mothercare and picnics and holidays seem like they're from another era. This is it. Me and Sinead. And Declan. Our new family.

Suddenly, another phone call comes in – my phone has never been so busy – and this time a different social worker tells me that we must return to the Family Centre immediately, where we are to be accompanied by a family support worker so that Murphy can say a proper 'Goodbye' to Sinead. God knows where Margaret is.

"Out!" demands Sinead.

"Okay, Sinead – we're going to the Family Centre," I say, and start the car. I am not looking forward to this bit at all.

In no time at all, we arrive back at the Family Centre – I have been rabbiting on to Sinead all the way back about all the people in her new family and what their names are, whilst she occasionally shouts, "Out!" or "No!" I feel so anxious, and my mouth's dry – this is all so unexpectedly dramatic.

The care worker meets us at the car park barrier and asks us to stay by her side because Murphy "may get violent". Shit.

She leads us towards the Family Centre, where I see a depressed-looking, tattoo-ridden, Murphy Riley standing outside smoking a rollie. He draws heavily on it and wipes tears from his eyes. A man standing nearby – one of his mates, I assume – hands him a can of Fosters which he gulps down furiously. As we get closer, I can smell the alcohol, cigarette smoke, and something sharp and pungent, which I assume must be weed or maybe even... shit. Despite his grimy appearance and obvious inebriation, I do empathise with him. He seems genuinely upset that Sinead is going into care, but I remind myself that the social workers have done everything they can to keep Sinead with her family, and that it is Murphy who has been unable to provide a place of safety for her. Poor Murphy, though – what a terrible thing to go through. On the one hand, I feel sorry for him but on the other hand, I am glad that we can give Sinead a new start. This is a major traumatic event for everyone.

He kneels to Sinead's level and wipes his nose with the back of his hand. "I am sorry I lets you down mo challín," the big man says, and dissolves into tears. He howls and shakes, as he grips Sinead tightly. "I don't wants to lose you."

Sinead cuddles him and stares at him curiously, dabbing his eyes. "Daddy you crying. Ahhhhh, i dont caoin."

"Come on Sinead, say bye bye to Daddy," says Barry firmly, who has just joined us. And with that, she lifts up her little hand and strokes Murphy's greasy hair. "Ahh," she says peering at him. "Why crying? Ahhhh, here kiss you."

It suddenly feels like Sinead is the parent. She carries on staring at him and stroking his hair. Finally she kisses him hard on the cheek and smiles at him in such a loving way it almost breaks my heart.

"Here, lady – these are yours," says Murphy to me, pointing to a crumpled-up black bin liner full of what I later discover to be rancid, filthy clothes, broken toys, half a packet of children's pull-up incontinence pants and right at the bottom, a moth-eared and obviously much-loved teddy called Snowy Bear.

By this time, Sinead is as absolutely weary as the rest of us, with all the emotional upheaval. I bundle her as quickly as I can back into the car, and this time need no bribes as mercifully, she is sleepy and exhausted. Before I leave, I ask if Barry can do me the huge favour of phoning Declan and explaining everything that's happened. At least that way, this won't be such a shock for him when we get home.

As I pull up to the garage, Declan is standing on the porch waiting for us, looking worried. He bounds up to the car, but I put my finger to my lips to signal that Sinead is asleep. He quietly opens the door and unbuckles her from the booster seat.

"She's a dead weight!" he whispers, carrying her up to bed.

"I'm not going to wake her for a bath or some food, D," I say, as we walk into Sinead's newly refurbished bedroom. "She ate a whopping great big burger this afternoon, and has had enough sweets to last a lifetime. Let's just get her into bed and we can work everything out tomorrow."

"She's got nits," says Declan.

"Thought so," I laugh, having already put two and two together with the head-scratching and occasional flares of bad temper. "We'll deal with them in the morning."

I collapse into an armchair, and gratefully accept a glass of wine from Declan. The irony of my having a drink and Murphy's drinking does not escape me, but this one's medicinal. I fill Declan in with the details of the day, when once again, my phone rings. It's Margaret asking to speak to her 'poor Sinead'.

"She's fast asleep in bed," I tell her smugly, "and anyway, how did you get this number?"

"The Social give it me," says Margaret. "I gots my rights, you know. I can talk to her when I gets a Barrister."

"That may be Margaret," I say, "but you can't talk to her now. She's asleep," I repeat in my best assertive voice.

"Well feckin' up yours!" she says, and the phone goes dead.

"Feckin' up yours too!" I say to the phone

Chapter 15

Waking Up To Reality

14th January 1998

Declan and I wake up early, although we're both exhausted from checking on Sinead every hour throughout the night, but at 8.30am she's still asleep, in fact she is snoring loudly. Declan leaves for work, and I am on my own, ready to face the day with my new charge. I wonder, should I wake her or just leave her to sleep for as long as she wants to?

But, there's no time to think about that as the phone rings. It's Edna asking how the dreaded first night went.

"You won't believe it, Edna, but she went out like a light. No problems there and she's still asleep now. She was so tired from everything that happened yesterday. But... can I mention something?"

"Go ahead, Bridie, that's what I'm here for."

"Well, I know things are very chaotic for her right now, but Sinead was very rough with me and my father yesterday, not to mention the dog! She also has nits really badly – am I allowed to nit comb her whilst she's in the bath?"

"Oh dear, that not a great sign – it means that she may have witnessed violence at some point.... Yes, it is okay to nit comb her whilst she's in the bath." I heard Edna sigh heavily, like a portent of gloom. "Right then, Bridie, I'll make a point to look in on you both tomorrow morning at about nine o'clock." Sinead comes stumbling down the stairs – perhaps the phone ringing has woken her? She looks around her, obviously trying to place where on earth she is.

"Come and sit at the table, sweetie," I say pointing at the chair, "and I'll make your breakfast." Without a sound, she does as she's told, her little head barely above the table. I busy myself making toast and boiled eggs, chatting inanely to Sinead. I then fetch a couple of cushions from the sitting-room to raise her up a bit, and am contemplating whether or not to let the dogs in and introduce her to them, when the phone rings again. This time it is Margaret.

"'Ello, Bridie, can I speak to my Sinead now?"

I reluctantly pass the phone to Sinead who is happily eating a boiled egg and soldiers. She grabs the phone with both hands and speaks into the wrong end.

"This way, sweetie," I say and redirect the phone to her mouth. Sinead smiles broadly on hearing the crackly voice at the other end. I put the phone on loudspeaker.

"Shinny, baby, it's Magga. I loves you. Do you loves me?"

"Ahh, er where you Magga?" Sinead's smile suddenly changes into a deep frown and she begins to cry and then screams loudly. I hear her say what sounds like an Irish swear word. "Cac damn nu air want Dada want Magga!"

Oh, for God's sake – now look what's happened. She was happily having her breakfast and now she's all upset. I prise the phone from her little hands as she continues to snivel.

"I'm sorry, Margaret," I say firmly, "but now is not a good time." I hang up and try to comfort Sinead, but she is having none of it, and just begins screaming even louder. I remember my diversion tactics from yesterday.

"Sinead, do you want to see the doggies?"

She stops crying immediately and gets down from the table and runs to the kitchen door. *She's a clever little thing*, I think. I open the door to the utility room and we walk through it and open the backdoor to the garden, where Harry and

Hilda are bouncing around at the thought of being able to come back in out of the cold. For some reason, maybe the size of the dogs, she's much more reserved with these two than she was with Trixy, even taking cover behind my legs and holding on to my jeans, which makes me almost melt with joy. *She's touched me, she sees me as a protector,* I think.

I introduce her to Harry and Hilda and tell her to be nice to the doggies and to play gently.

"Harry," she whispers. Harry gently comes up to Sinead, who equally gently pats him on the nose. Phew.

We are still having our calm session with the dogs when the doorbell rings and brings the moment to an end. It is Barry, and Sinead instantly recognises him, becoming loud and demanding again. "Ahhhhh hello hello Barry where Dada Maga Nana," and with that she rushes up to him and gives him an extended cuddle. I feel slightly deflated as she's never done that with me, but I tell myself that she hardly knows me compared with Barry. However, Barry's next comments do nothing to reassure me.

"Now, Sinead, just a quick cuddle and then off you go and play with..." he glances around the sitting room, "...the teddy bear over there," says Barry firmly, deftly turning Sinead around and propelling her towards beloved Roger Bear.

Barry explains, "She has no 'stranger danger' instinct, Bridie. She'll link hands and wander off with anyone – you'll have to keep an eye out for that. She has no real boundaries but also no real attachments either. She's bounced from pillar to post so much in her life that she sees almost any adult as family."

His words worry me, and I remember how readily she took to my parents. I would indeed have to keep an eagle eye on her.

Barry leaves us, and Sinead and I potter around for the

rest of the day in relative harmony, but mostly because I give her 100% attention. I say 'relative' because she does have a couple of minor tantrums: once because I asked her to wash her hands before we had a sandwich for lunch, and once because I said no sweeties today – but they were soon forgotten. Nothing else gets done – no washing or hoovering or shopping, and there's just time to get three 'ready-made by my own fair hand' lasagnes out of the freezer – it's just me and Sinead, looking at books together, or drawing pictures on the kitchen table, Sinead scribbling manically on every sheet of paper, as hard as she can, grasping the crayon in a most peculiar manner.

Declan comes home early, and for that I'm thankful as I haven't even taken the dogs for a walk yet and they are still sulking in the garden. I ask him to take them, even though it's almost dark. "You've had a busy day then?" he asks, nodding towards Sinead.

"Yes, but a good day," I say truthfully. It has been a good day. "I'm going to give her a bath now – Edna said I could stay in the bathroom to de-nit her hair, so I'll be a while. If we're not downstairs when you get back, can you check on the lasagnes in the oven and lay the table?" and with that, we go our separate ways. Not even time for a hug! It does remind me of how things were when Bea was little.

Armed with nit lotion and nit combs, I coax Sinead upstairs saying, "Shall we play with some bubbles in the bath?" She reluctantly leaves her spot on the sitting-room floor where she has been playing with some of the toys we've stashed away over the years that belong to the various children who've come to stay with us: Jazzy's old Tiny Tears doll, Mia's My Little Pony and of course, her beloved Snowy Bear. I even fetched down the lamb's wool comforter my mother bought on her mad shopping spree, which Sinead pounced on and cuddled mercilessly. I wonder whether nits can live on it?

I ask Sinead to get undressed in her room whilst I run a bath and read all the instructions about de-lousing. Sinead wanders back in to the bathroom naked except for her pull-up pants and a vest which looks grey and grubby. Note to self: we must embark on a shopping trip to Gap tomorrow to get her some new clothes. The bath is positively brimming over with bubbles, and Sinead is captivated by them, pushing her arm in and out of the iridescent clouds with little giggles of delight, and I realise she's probably never had a bubble bath. I help her get into the bath and leave her to play happily for a while. I am reminded of the innocent joy children take in the simplest of things.

"Sinead, I'm just going to spray some shampoo on your hair, okay?" I ask, advancing with the pungent nit lotion, but she's having none of it.

"No, no! Smells, get off, you cow!" she says defiantly.

"Sinead, that's not a nice thing to say to me. Let's just try and get your hair clean shall we?"

"NO!" she screams.

Oh, shit. Here we go... "Sinead, I'm going to put this shampoo on your hair, but then you can play with the bubbles for five minutes, okay?"

"NO! Fucker."

"Please don't use that word, Sinead – it's not a nice thing to say to me. I'm going to put the shampoo on now and if you can be still and count to ten, I'll put some more bubble bath in the water – how's that?"

She doesn't reply so I take that as an 'okay', and douse her hair with the foul-smelling liquid. "One, two, three... can you count with me Sinead?"

"Shit cow."

"Four, five, six..." I rub the lotion into her scalp and down the strands of her long hair. I notice that dirty-coloured drips stain the sparkling white bubbles and wonder when she last had her hair washed.

Sinead eventually acquiesces and lets me lather and rinse her hair, but I know the worst is to come. The dreaded nit comb. How am I going to get that through these long, thick locks? I know – conditioner.

I squirt the sweet-smelling gloup onto her hair and she visibly relaxes. Maybe Margaret has been through this rigmarole with her after all? I massage in the conditioner as I perch on the edge of the bath, and leave it on whilst I dash off to find clean towels, cursing the fact that I didn't have time to buy Sinead a dressing-gown or even a pair of pyjamas before she came to stay with us. She'll have to make do with one of my old T-shirts tonight.

I get back into the bathroom just in time to see Sinead crouch in the bath as if she's going to have a pee – or worse.

"Time to get out!" I say breezily and lift her onto the mat. "Do you want a pee?"

"Pee!" and she makes it to the loo just in time.

"We need to rinse your hair now," I say in a Maria Von Trapp way.

Sinead stiffens again. "No! Not now clean."

"Just lean over the bath Sinead, I won't be long."

"Nooooo! Nooooo! Ahhhhhhhhh cow!" she screams so loud I instinctively clasp my hands over my ears.

Sinead runs out of the bathroom and into her bedroom and slams the door behind her.

Shit, shit and double-shit. What do I do now?

I hear Declan coming up the stairs to find out what all the commotion is about.

"Okay, okay..." he says stroking his chin. "What would we have done with Bea?"

"Put the TV on, bribe her with treats, distract her whilst I comb her hair through and get as much of the conditioner and nits out as possible..." I suggest.

"That's what we'll do then," he says. Declan knocks on Sinead's door and speaks to her gently. "Sinead, Bridie's going down stairs to put the TV on and you can watch some cartoons if you want. And I brought some jelly babies home with me. You can have one after your dinner if you like..."

There is no reply from Sinead's room, but Declan makes a noisy exit downstairs saying, "I'll serve the dinner and you put the TV on."

I leave the T-shirt and a clean pair of pull-ups outside her door and also trot downstairs.

A few minutes later a little girl shuffles into the kitchen, her hair still dripping over the massive T-shirt that dangles well below her knees, Snowy Bear clutched in her hands. I pat the cushions on her chair and serve up the lasagne, which she literally makes a bee-line for. At least she's got a good appetite and she eats the whole lot in silence and with apparent relish.

"Cartoon!" she demands.

Declan has actually found an old Teletubbies video and puts it on in the sitting room. She sits on the mat – her favourite place, it seems – mesmerised by the colourful cartoons, whilst I rinse her hair into a bucket of warm water, spray on tea tree oil and start combing. Luckily, the conditioner has worked a treat and the comb goes through smoothly, but every pass through her hair reveals dozens of tiny black nits, some with their legs still wiggling. It's disgusting, and worse, to think how long she's had these things crawling through her hair and biting her scalp. For ten minutes or more, I comb, and she watches TV, until at last, the comb starts to run clean, and I think we can call it a day.

I leave her watching the Teletubbies as I go into the kitchen and chuck the nit-riddled water down the sink. "Yuck!"

"Bridie, should she still be using pull-ups?" asks Declan. "I saw the packet of them in the bathroom. I've noticed some of the kids that come into the surgery wearing them, but not at Sinead's age..."

"Everyone seems to use them these days," I reply. "Denise told me once that her neighbour's girl wore them right up until she was nearly nine years old – can you believe it? It's like some mothers have forgotten how to potty train their kids – or in Margaret's case, probably just can't be bothered." I regret saying that as soon as it comes out of my mouth. What do I know of how Magga brings up her kids? Who am I to judge? "Anyway, whilst Sinead's with us, we'll try and get her to use the toilet and get out of pull-ups," I say.

"Good," Declan says. "Wine?"

"Not right now, D – let's get her to bed first, eh? God knows I could do with one though!"

Declan and I wash up the dinner things together and feed the dogs who are definitely sulking with me because of the lack of attention. I've heard that dogs can get jealous if another family member comes into the house, and I wonder if this is the case with them. I give them both a big cuddle and a chewy treat each. The phone rings, and Declan wanders off to answer it.

I tip-toe back to the sitting-room, the silence being a clue that Sinead might have fallen asleep, and just as I thought, there she is, sprawled on the floor in my baggy old T-shirt, her hair still damp, clutching Roger Bear. Roger Bear my symbol of hope has waited eight years for a friend, and now he has Sinead.

Once again, Declan carries Sinead upstairs to bed, huffing and puffing under the dead weight of this strange little girl, who is already worming her way into our hearts, despite her tantrums and colourful language.

"Oh by the way, darling," Declan says, "that was Bea on the phone. She's coming home tomorrow – she's sprained her wrist playing squash and is taking a few days off."

"Poor thing! Well, it'll be good for her to get to know Sinead better, eh?"

We put the clean little girl in her bed with her dirty old Bear. She is already snoring gently. Exhausted, I decide to have an early night too.

15th January 1998

Sinead has slept right through the night, thank goodness, and again, is still fast asleep as we get up and go about our morning ablutions. It's nice that Declan and I have this quiet time together, but I wonder how normal this is? Most mothers complain about their children waking them up really early, but I'm not one of them. I rush around the house tidying-up before Edna comes. The hoover eventually wakes Sinead and I can hear bawling upstairs, "Nanna, Nanna, want Nanna!"

"It's okay, Sinead, I'm coming!" I call up the stairs, wondering why it is that this morning she wants Nanna and not Magga. Maybe it's an indication of how much she gets passed around from one to another?

"There's Mummy," she says pointing at me from her bed, as I walk through the bedroom door. Oh. My. God! Did she really say that? Or did I make it up from the sheer need to be loved by her? But no, I'm sure that's what she said! *Don't dwell on it*, Bridie, I think, *just act normally...*

Sinead jumps out of bed and grabs me around the legs for a second, then runs down the stairs shouting, "Dogs! Harry!"

"Gentle with the dogs, sweetie" I call after her. And so starts another day.

Edna arrives as Sinead is still eating her breakfast of porridge and yoghurt – I hope she approves of Sinead's diet. We then sit down in the lounge and observe Sinead for half an hour or so. It is not long before the dogs nose their way in through the door. Sinead shuffles towards Hilda and Harry saying under her breath, "Gently, feckin' dogs ciúin." It is all I can do not to laugh at her terrible language.

Edna is obviously concerned though – I can see it in her face – and there was I thinking we were doing such a great job.

"Hmmmmm, yes. I suspect she is going to be a handful, Bridie. I read the reports from the Family Centre this morning and they mention how strong-minded and angry she seems to be at the moment."

True to form and right on cue, Sinead suddenly demonstrates her volatility with Hilda, as she grabs the poor dog's ears and yanks them hard.

"No, Sinead. Stroke not pull, remember?" I remind her. "Look, like this," and I show her how to stroke the dogs gently.

"Off!" she shouts, glaring at me. "Get out you, want Nanna."

I decide to put the dogs in the kitchen so that she can't use them as collateral damage, but she chases after me pulling at the dogs' tails.

Nervous in front of Edna, I redirect her. "Where's Roger Bear, Sinead? Shall we show Edna?" I suggest, as I close the dogs in the kitchen, and wonder, not for the first time, how all this is affecting them.

"Roger Bear!" shouts Sinead and dives onto the cuddly toy that is perched in his usual place in the corner of the sofa.

Edna smiles an encouraging smile at me. "Well done,

Bridie," she says. "Although it's going to be a real challenge for you when Johnny arrives."

Christ! Johnny... I had forgotten all about him in the hullaballoo of Sinead's arrival.

"You must think about your boundaries, Bridie and not just about being kind to the children. With another child in the house, it will be really important for you to set absolute boundaries about the kind of behaviour you will accept."

Christ! Another child in the house... Forgive me for all my blaspheming Aunty Bernadette, but you can stop praying for me to have children now...?

"With Johnny, you will need to be very assertive and consistent."

"About Johnny, Edna... When... when will he be coming?"

"Oh, ummm – let me get back to you on that one. I think it's early February isn't it?"

Well, that gives me a few days at least to get used to Sinead, I think.

Edna leaves in a flourish of perfume and scarves, but the moment I close the door on her, Barry rings to tell me that Margaret and Murphy have both asked to visit separately tomorrow, each one for an hour and a half.

"Is that alright, Bridie?" I know it's short notice, but they are insistent that they want to see Sinead. What do you think?"

What I think is, *I might as well get it all over and done with in one day, because it's bound to be traumatic for both Sinead and me.*

"That's fine, Barry, but just make sure they don't both turn up here at the same time," I say.

Do you know, I'm exhausted already just at the sheer thought of those two reprobates in my house.

The phone rings once again. It is Pauline, yet another

bloody social worker.

"Hello, Mrs Kelly – I am Pauline Parsons, and I am Sinead's Guardian Ad Litem, which means I'm her legal representative in court. I wonder if it's possible for me to visit you today?"

I agree that today is as good a day as any, but bang go my plans to take Sinead into town to get her some new clothes. I know, I'll ring Mum and ask her if she can pop into Gap for me. But when I ring my parents' house, there's no reply, which is unusual.

I take Sinead and the dogs and my mobile phone into the garden to wait until Pauline gets here. It'll be good for Sinead to get some fresh air, and the dogs too, who once again are waiting for their walk. Thank God we've got this nice big garden for them.

"Here, Sinead, shall we throw a ball for the dogs?"

"Ball!"

I show Sinead how to throw the ball and she giggles in delight as Harry obligingly runs to pick it up and drops it back at her feet.

"Your turn," I say, and she lobs the ball a long way down the garden for such a little girl. She's got some strength in her. This time Hilda gets there first, and trots back and drops the ball at Sinead's feet. Sinead loves this game and runs round the garden throwing the ball which the dogs unfailingly deliver back to her.

I ring my Mum again.

"Hello, darling, how's it going with Saoirse?"

"Sinead, Mum. Quite well, I think, although she's an energetic little thing. Where were you earlier when I rang?"

"Oh... did you ring? I didn't hear the phone. I was having a snooze and Daddy's out playing golf."

Hmmmm snoozing at lunch time. It wasn't long ago that Mum would say only old people do that. "Mum, can you nip into town for me and get some clothes for Sinead? I haven't had time to. Six to seven years should be okay for her although she's quite tall for her age. She needs pyjamas, pants, socks..."

"Leave it with me, Bridie. I've got a discount card for M&S. I love a good shopping mission." And with that, Mother is off. It makes me smile to think how she'll enjoy her day.

Christ! Where's Sinead? I took my eye off her for a nanosecond and she's gone – but the dogs give me a clue. They are standing outside their kennel, wagging their tails. Sinead is inside, and she has done a poo in the dog kennel. She is smiling and pointing at it. "Ah h hah I dunna poo!"

I suppose it is good that she is aware of toileting but in the dog kennel? Is this normal at six years old? Probably not.

"Sinead, sweetie, if you want to go to the toilet, ask me and I'll take you to the bathroom, okay?"

I look around for a shovel and a poo-bag. What else can I do with it? As I lean into the kennel, I hear clonking noises overhead and guess that Sinead is trying to climb up onto the roof of the kennel. I bump my head as I reverse out of the kennel with a swinging poo-bag held at arm's length and attempt to coax her down, but it's not easy.

"Sinead, please get down. Shall we go and fetch Snowy Bear?"

She looks at me out of the corner of her eye. "Not off stay here!"

"Please do as you're told, Sinead. I think Teletubbbies are on and we can have a sandwich for lunch." I use positive language and encouragement as they taught us at the fostering course, but it doesn't work.

"No want dogs want Nanna stay here," she replies with a fierce expression on her face.

At that moment, the garden gate swings open and Bea

shouts across to us. "Hi, Bridie! Hi, Sinead! Do you remember me, Sinead? I came to your birthday party." Bea comes over to us at the most opportune moment, as Sinead slides off the roof and sidles over to me. She puts her little hand in mine, the finger of her right hand, up her nose, and looks up at Bea in awe.

"Hello, Bea!" I say, giving her a hug. "Shall we go and have a cuppa?"

Bingo! Sinead follows us into the house. She can't take her eyes off Bea.

It's lovely to catch up with Bea, and it seems her sprained wrist isn't too bad. "It was a bit of an excuse to come and see Sinead, to be honest," she says. "Dad told me all about what happened the other day when you had to give her an emergency placement – it all sounds very dramatic."

"It was a bit! Bea, could you just keep an eye on her a moment? There's another social worker coming round any minute, and I haven't even had time to brush my hair this morning."

"Sure, take your time. It'll give me and Sinead a chance to get to know each other, won't it little one?" she says.

"Not little one," Sinead says, "Roger Bear!" and off she trots into the sitting room, with Bea hard on her heels.

I go upstairs to make myself presentable. There is obviously so much work to do with Sinead. I don't know where to begin, so I try to remember some of the things I was taught on the fostering course. I consult my old folder and read some of the notes. *Reactive Attachment Disorder: develops from lack of nurture in the first few years. Indications are lying and stealing, and problems with emotional literacy.*

I wonder if Sinead has RAD? I continue reading my notes on the basic assumptions for parenting a traumatised attachment-resistant child. It says such children are likely to be controlling and have a younger developmental age than other children. I promise myself to read more on this later and do some research. I want to help this little girl the best way I can.

Pauline has arrived; a young, blond-haired lady with a fresh face, and disarming smile.

"Pauline Parsons," she says, waving her identity badge in front of me, which makes me smile in turn, as this seems to be the Social Services equivalent of a handshake.

I lead Pauline into the sitting-room, where Sinead and Bea are playing with the scant few toys we have in the house. Pauline gasps when she sees Sinead.

"Hello, Sinead!" Pauline says and Sinead promptly runs across to her and sits on her lap, saying something unintelligible in Irish.

Pauline and I exchange glances. It is not long before Sinead wanders back to Bea and her toys. I ask Bea if she's okay to stay with Sinead whilst Pauline and I go into the kitchen to talk, and Bea readily agrees. What a godsend she is today.

"Bridie, she looks really well already," says Pauline, which makes me swell with pride. "What are you doing with her? She can be a little madam in the Family Centre you know. I've seen her swearing, and hitting people and she makes that terrible 'ah ah' noise all the time which can be very wearing... Whatever it is you're doing, you're doing something right. You must be so patient! And she's only been with you two nights."

Part of me wonders if Pauline is 'buttering me up' because, let's be honest, Sinead has nowhere else to go, but I say, "It's been a 100% one-to-one process so far, Pauline. I've done absolutely nothing else except be there for Sinead. Actually, I am a bit nervous about the whole parenting thing though, especially as Sinead is... she has some... strange ways."

"Bridie, look, I've known Sinead for three years, I can tell you everything you need to know." Pauline opens the notes she has brought with her and begins to tell me more about Sinead's life. "She has been neglected all her life, although to be fair, I don't think it's intentional on her parents' part. I mean, they themselves had poor parenting, so they had no positive role models to draw on. They just knew nothing about childrearing. For example, Sinead was given sugary tea and coffee as an infant. She was often left on her own for hours on end. When she was older and lived on and off with Murphy, a relation heard him threaten regularly to lock her in a cupboard. There were also marks on her arms suggesting force was used on her. Before she was first taken into care, the police were often called to Patsy and Murphy's caravan, for all sorts of reasons, but most often domestic affray. On one occasion when Sinead was about a year old, the police found out that Murphy had been on a drinking binge and just left the baby with a mate who is a registered drug addict. The poor child did not know whether she was coming or going most of the time. The whole situation was very unstable and the attachment that Sinead should have had with her parents was insecure. That's why we must be very careful where she is placed." Pauline paused and looked at me.

"Bridie, this is a hard one, but I would advise you not to think about anything long-term with Sinead just yet, because her family situation is always so complicated. Let's just take it one day at a time for now. I am very happy to see Sinead so settled though."

"But, might adoption be a consideration in the future?" I ask.

Pauline studies my face carefully. "Bridie, you have to ask yourself, do you want to adopt a child, or do you want to adopt this child in particular?"

I feel like this is a warning from Pauline, and alarm bells

are ringing in my head. I wave Pauline off with mixed feelings: she's very pleased with progress so far, but she's keen to impress upon me that this is early days, and things may get worse. But I can't bear the thought of Sinead being taken away from me. I love her so much already.

Later, after we've had dinner and Sinead is in bed, Declan picks up on my distractedness, so I tell him of Pauline's warning.

"Well, I must say, I am very worried about all these local relations that are threatening to descend on us, Bridie," he says. "They'll probably run off with the family silver!"

I burst into tears, because the truth of the matter is that the bloody relatives worry me more than Sinead does.

16th January 1998

It's the dreaded day of visiting. Margaret is coming at 11 o'clock and Murphy is coming at two in the afternoon. I don't know which one I'm dreading most. Sinead and I walk to the local shops to buy chocolate biscuits and teabags, and I brace myself for the onslaught. I have Sinead on a wrist strap, which she does not seem to mind but it's rather like managing a Rottweiler on a lead. She is so strong and energetic all the time. We chug along the Leopardstown Road and I try to name things to extend Sinead's vocabulary. This distracts Sinead from being 'difficult'.

"Bus– can you say 'bus', Sinead?"

"Dog," says Sinead.

"Yes! Good girl! There's a dog. And there's a lady. Can you say 'lady', Sinead?" I ask.

"Dog."

I sing 10 Green Bottles and Sinead hums along to it. Then,

Sinead says, "Me sing Nanna nice song 123 mother caught
a flee put it in her tea." As she sings, I notice her face come
alive as she remembers Nanna. I have to remind myself that
she loves Nanna O'Driscoll and that this is natural and good.
People look at us rather strangely as we sing these silly songs.

At the grocery shop, Mrs Castle talks to Sinead. "Are you
not a little dote," and to me, "Does she really need those wrist
straps, Bridie? I would have thought they were a little old
fashioned these days? Especially at what, six years old?"

I explain to Mrs Castle that Sinead is very headstrong and
could run off at any time. Mrs Castle looks bemused and not
at all convinced.

As we walk along the narrow isles of the little shop, Sinead
keeps putting sweets, crisps and coke in the shopping basket.
In fact, she is opening up and eating a bar of chocolate.

"Sinead, no, you are not having too much sugar today.
It's bad for your teeth. Put it in the basket and you can have
some more tomorrow. Let's put these thing back," I say to her
gently, replacing the coke and crisps on the shelves.

"No! Sweeties are mine," and with that she snatches the
bar of chocolate back and stuffs it in her pocket, looking at
me defiantly.

"Sinead, I have to pay for the chocolate. If you put it in
the basket, you can have some more when we get home." (I
don't say when and I certainly don't intend for her to have any
more today.)

"No! Mine."

"Sinead. Please put the chocolate back in the basket so I
can pay for it. We can't go home until we've paid Mrs Castle."

I point to Mrs Castle who is watching this little
fiasco unfold.

"No. No. No. No. Bugger."

Mrs Castle visibly blanches.

"Sinead!" It's the first time since she's been with us that I have raised my voice. Sinead instantly puts the chocolate in the basket, and starts quietly sniveling.

"Thank you. Good girl," I say.

We trudge home in silence. No singing on the way back.

When we get home, I persuade Sinead to go and have a little sleep in her bedroom. She doesn't want to, but I tell her that she can take Snowy Bear with her and she can have a hot milk drink when she comes back down. That does the trick. I peep my head around her bedroom door after she's been up there for ten minutes, and she has got herself into bed and is fast asleep. I want to do the same, but I need to have a quick tidy up before Margaret comes.

Ten minutes before Margaret is due, I wake Sinead and explain that Magga is coming to our house to visit. Predictably, Sinead comes alive at the mention of Magga's name. She abandons Snowy and rushes to look out of the window, singing, "123 Nanna caught a flea." Oh, bless her cotton socks.

She is suddenly very animated and happy. She is chatting away as if she's having a conversation with someone, in her half-English, half-Irish childish language.

"Who are you talking to, Sinead?" I ask curiously.

"Bobby," she replies. "He's my friend. Bye Bobby Magga here now."

And she is right. Margaret waddles towards our front door, with Lesley her eldest daughter and Jade, a family support worker. Margaret is laden with presents I don't approve of: Wotsits, bars of chocolate, and a bracelet of nasty coloured sweets on an elastic band.

"Look what I gots for you, Shinny!" she says thrusting the presents at the little girl and giving her a big hug, whirling her around and around. It's not for my benefit. She obviously really loves Sinead, like one of her own..

Despite my wariness of Margaret, I can see that she has had a very hard life and that in her heart of hearts she wants to be a good parent. Sinead certainly worships the ground that she walks on.

"Come on, Lesley, let's get 'er out of 'ere an goes a walk, have one of me fags," Margaret says.

Lesley searches in her bag for a lighter and belches loudly.

"'Scuse me," she says and Sinead giggles delightedly.

To my horror, Margaret is allowed to take Sinead out on her own. I enquire why this is, and Jade reminds me that Margaret is seeking a full residential order and that she is allowed open and unsupervised contact with Sinead, whilst Sinead's birth parents must be supervised. I feel tearful and resentful as Margaret waltzes off with Sinead who does not even look back at me. The three walk away together arms linked, singing some silly song. I see Sinead patting Margaret's belly, which I think is a bit inappropriate.

At one o'clock on the dot, Margaret, Lesley and Sinead return, but Sinead has had a fall and cut her knee and is hysterical. I dress the graze with a plaster, making a big fuss of Sinead while Margaret and Lesley glare at me and swear under their breath. Jade writes up her report and I hope she mentions their lack of supervision in letting Sinead fall. (Later that evening I write up my own diary, complaining that Sinead obviously loves Margaret, and how can I compete with that?)

"You got her pull-ups on wrong way round," Margaret reprimands me.

"Well, she shouldn't really be wearing them at her age," I snap. "We're toilet-training whilst she's here, and she's doing very well without her pull-ups." I don't mention the poo in the dog kennel.

"Oooe, toilet training is it? Fancy that!" Margaret mocks.

Don't rise to the bait, Bridie, ignore her – I tell myself.

Sinead is having what can only be described as a volcanic tantrum. She screams and cries, throwing anything she can lay her hands on across the room: her toys, her books, Roger Bear... Suddenly it's like a war zone in here and the tension in the air is unbearable. Only Margaret can calm her. I discreetly study her parenting style. She crouches down to Sinead's level and tells her a little story about a girl and her mummy. Sinead responds well to Margaret's hypnotic, smoky voice. I see them clap hands together and eventually, Sinead calms down and begins to laugh. How I wish I had that bond with Sinead.

Sinead starts up the Flea Song again, ending it with a big throaty belch that Magga heartily applauds.

"See, her loves her family, don't ya, chicken?" she says ruffling Sinead's hair.

"Love Snowy Bear!" says Sinead.

For a fleeting moment, I am in awe of Margaret: she has seven children, no washing machine, is stuck on state benefits and one child is at special school, and yet she has enough love for this little girl who is not even her own.

I watch as Margaret and Sinead play with little bricks and finger puppets that Jade has brought with her.

"Oh, by the way, Sinead has a friend," Margaret winks at me. "He's invisible is he not, chicken?"

"Yes, Bobby," I say. "We've been introduced."

Margaret looks a bit crestfallen, but I take no pleasure in such one-upmanship. It's pointless because Sinead loves Margaret like a mother, and probably always will, and I have to admit that Margaret loves Sinead too. Is that not what every child wants and needs? Okay, she lives in a filthy caravan with seven other children, but doesn't love conquer all? Isn't love all you need? I wonder if it's not best if Margaret gets custody of Sinead after all and I call a halt to this fostering lark and we all go back to normal.

Margaret and Lesley are just about to leave, when suddenly Lesley slaps Sinead across the back of her legs.

"Little bitch pinched me fags!" she screams. "Give 'em 'ere."

"No, I gots 'em," says Margaret chuckling. "Silly cow."

Jade doesn't notice as she's already getting into the car. But I do. No, that isn't right – they might love her in their own way, but they've no right to hit her. Lesley and Margaret leave, chuckling to themselves about the fags but Sinead is confused, being left with the sting of Lesley's slap and the name-calling. As the car pulls out of the drive, Sinead has her second meltdown of the day and I am the target. She is hysterical, crying and trying to hit me. She is overwhelmed with emotion. Nothing I do or say works. Think... Distraction, rapport, emotion...

I crouch down and reflect what Sinead might be feeling. "Sinead, you sound so sad and upset about Margaret leaving. Do you want to talk to me about it?"

I see Sinead take in my words, and a calmness comes over her. Eventually she says, "Miss Magga an Nanna an D-d Dada an Pey, Cissy..."

I feel annoyed that she misses Magga, but I hide my feelings. And who the hell is Cissy? "It's okay to miss them, Sinead. It means you love them. Let's draw a picture for them, shall we?" We draw a beautiful picture for Nanna – fair enough, it looks like an exploding dustbin, but it's the thought that counts.

Murphy and Edna will be here soon, and I want them to come into a house that is calm and creative.

The doorbell trills and the dogs rush to greet Murphy and Edna. However, Hilda immediately starts growling at Murphy who is obviously in a glum, low mood. ("Well," as Declan rather loftily says later when Bea is out of the room, "she can probably sniff the drugs on him.")

Sinead hears Murphy's voice, and comes running towards him, her arms outstretched. "Err oh ahhhhhhh see my Daddy Dad," she cries. "Love you love you." She trips over the washing basket and emits a loud, pitiful wail.

Here we go again, I think. *Welcome to the rollercoaster.* But Murphy chucks his cigarette out onto the drive, smiles at his daughter and throws her onto his shoulders, and twirls her around in a big circle, most affectionately. For a minute, Murphy has energy and life about him.

"Sure has anyone seen Sinead Riley?" he asks in his strong Irish accent. I watch Sinead's expression – she is suddenly in heaven; the happiest I have ever seen her. Margaret and Murphy mean the world to her. That much is obvious.

"Got her these," he says humbly, placing a packet of fruit gums on the table. It looks like he's already eaten a couple of them! But barely ten minutes into the contact, Murphy has lost interest in Sinead, his new-found energy gone. Sinead persists in prodding him with her books.

"Read this one Dad like this one," she persists.

"Oh, I don't like reading, girl. Fág mé alon."

The carer later tells me that Murphy is illiterate.

Murphy catches my eye. "Bridie, any chance of a cuppa tea and a biccy? Had a skinful last night – playing the fiddle all night I was – I'm knackered," and with that he too lets out a long, throaty and very smelly alcohol belch.

"Owerr, that's better," he says, patting his chest and then, for God's sake, he lifts his leg and does an equally long and tortuous fart.

"'Scuse, sorry, sorry!"

Sinead cackles with glee. "Daddy trump!" she says, and I feel proud of her choice of words.

Edna however purses her bright red lips and glares at him like a wise old owl. "Then perhaps you should cut down your drinking, Murphy. We don't expect you to attend a contact under the influence of alcohol."

Murphy makes a face. "Yeah, yeah, yeah," he says, obviously having no intention whatsoever to cut down his drinking.

I make the tea whilst Edna supervises the father and daughter session. When I get back in, Murphy is slumped on the infamous leather sofa and is fast asleep, while Edna is playing 'dolls' with Sinead. We quietly drink our tea and watch Sinead as she chats away to herself (or to Bobby) and her father snores blissfully on the sofa.

Eventually, he wakes himself up with a loud snore. "'Cor, best bit o' kip I had all week – been sofa surfing, homeless see." He shifts his weight and I realise I was wrong about men not making the sofa fart noise, as Murphy coaxes out a lengthy squeal from the leather.

Edna looks away again in disgust but Sinead cheers and screeches, "Pohee yaayyy Daddy farted! Phoeeww Daddy is a stinker stinker yeh yeh!" She runs around holding her nose and fanning the air.

"I didn't – honest!" Murphy looks at me askance. I can't be bothered to explain about the sofa, and I'm a bit disappointed that Sinead has reverted to the 'F' word. What do they say about pride coming before a fall? My mother would be shocked at this show of rather uncouth behaviour from Sinead and her father, that's for sure.

Murphy reaches for his cold cup of tea. "Ahh, this is the life," he says washing down a handful of biscuits with the tepid drink.

He looks at me perversely. "Course, I got a record as long as me arm. Nothing I don't know about prison," he says grinning like a Cheshire cat.

I don't really know how to answer this one, so I just don't reply and concentrate on Sinead. I am interested in her even if Murphy is not. The contact session drags on relentlessly, but 50 minutes later Murphy and Edna have gone.

Thank God, I think, *I am going mad – I feel like a cross between a probation officer and a cafe owner.*

Chapter 16

One Direction

20th January 1998

"Oh, Bridie – for God's sake, I think I've got nits!" Bea examines strands of her long, dark hair in disgust. "I have – I've caught bloody nits from Sinead."

"But I de-nitted her only a few days ago," I say defensively.

"Well where else would they come from?" she demands, and stomps off to continue her packing. She's off back to college today. I must say, I'll be very sorry to see her go – she's been so helpful with Sinead: a really lovely big sister and Sinead has got quite attached to her already. Not only that, but now I've got another nit session to look forward to with Sinead.

Declan is insisting that I cancel Johnny's placement, and I must admit I am not looking forward to having two demanding children at the same time, so I agree to ring 'Mrs Danvers' as D still calls her, to discuss the situation.

I pluck up courage and finally manage to get through to Edna on the phone and ask her rather falteringly if I can cancel Johnny's stay, especially since Sinead is already here. "I don't think I'll be able to cope with both of them, Edna," I plead.

Edna takes her time before replying. She lets out a long breath and says, "No, I don't think so do you, Bridie? His carers have their holiday booked and by God they deserve it. We can't let them down Bridie, not at this late stage."

For a moment I wish it was us going on holiday and Sinead

and Johnny were staying with them, but I give in as I usually do. Anything for a quiet life.

"Okay," I whisper resentfully. It will be a journey into the unknown when Johnny comes.

Later that evening

Declan comes home from work early so that he can take Bea to the airport. "What did Danny Danvers say?" he asks.

"She said we'd be letting the carers down and that they really need this break."

"Jesus. What about our needs?"

"Well, I think we'll cope, D – it's not like it's forever, it's just a few days. We can do it."

"If you say so, Bridie, but it's you who's at the coal-face here. You look knackered enough already," he says, running his fingers through his thinning hair and rubbing his scalp.

"Thanks. Love you too."

I give Bea a tearful hug goodbye. I am sad to see her go.

I think Declan's got nits.

25th January 1998

Two nice things are happening today: I am allowed to take Sinead to a Mothers and Children group in Dublin, and Lee and the twins are coming around tonight to meet her for the first time. As a treat I am baking my special coffee cake, fruit scones and vegetable samosas. Sinead is helping me too – she is getting ingredients out of the cupboard, and mixing the cake batter. She makes loads of mess but I don't mind because she is chatting away quite happily to me and we sing along to some of the songs we know on the radio – well, I do.

Sinead just kind of warbles in her endearing way.

Just after lunch, as Sinead takes her regular nap – at least that's one good habit I'm getting her into – there is a call from Pauline Parsons asking if Declan and I can attend an important 'Directions' meeting next week. Sinead is not allowed to come but they will arrange for another carer to look after her whilst we're at the meeting. I don't really know what a Directions meeting is, but I'm told there will be barristers and solicitors there as well as Murphy, Patsy and Margaret. Oh great. That's a pretty daunting prospect. I leave a phone message for Declan saying that he has to get the day off next week for this meeting then dash off with Sinead to the Mothers and Children group.

Sinead is excited to see other children. She points to herself and says, "I go now." I register Sinead with the play leader and I feel and act like a real MUM. I fill in a form about Sinead, her link workers, doctor, health visitor and her disposition as a child. It's lovely to see Sinead running around with other kids. I see her smile and link up with all the boys with whom she seems very much at home – I suppose because she's used to her foster-brothers at Margaret's. Half and hour later and it looks like Sinead is well and truly in charge, in fact all the other children look rather intimidated by her. She has her scary face on and she is running at all the other children and herding them away from the sand pit saying, "Off mine go away."

Now she has found herself a playmate; she looks like she wants to own him. Aww! They're holding hands – hang on, now she's dragging him along like a reluctant puppy. I must say he does not look very happy. I must speak to her about being gentle with other children like she's gentle with the dogs.

It's time for a tea break. Sinead looks excited and bangs

her cup loudly on the formica table. "Mine, mine, me hungry thirsty me first!" I watch her and intervene just before she snatches a drink from Milly, a little girl sitting beside her. Minutes later all the children are singing 'The Wheels on the Bus' very loudly, in fact Sinead has the loudest voice of all!

Suddenly, there is a vile, rotten smell and several of the parents are tittering and whispering. I find myself going red – I know that it is Sinead who is responsible. Sinead's done a poo in her pull-ups. I blame myself; I should've checked if she needed to go to the toilet, but what with all the hullabaloo, I forgot. I discreetly whisk her off to the loos, change her pants and tell her to have a pee. We go back into the playroom and I find myself hoping and praying she doesn't start singing that rhyme about the mother and the flea.

Now she's playing in the sand pit with a lovely little girl called Annie who is four years old. Well that's progress in itself: friends who are girls. Before we know it, it's time to say goodbye, but Sinead doesn't want to go home. I stand around looking silly as I try to coax her out of the playroom. She folds her arms and stamps her feet. "No not off get off shit staying here with Bobby." Oh great. My six year-old is swearing and talking to her invisible friend. Other mothers politely look away, but some of them are smiling smugly and whispering to each other. "Apparently she's a new foster carer," I hear one woman whisper to another.

Embarrassed, I try the food distraction trick but this time with ice cream and Teletubbies when we get home. It works. Phew! However, I find myself dry-mouthed and panicky, and cross that I've resorted to yet another bribe. Everything seems to be such a trial.

We go home and I give Sinead a small scoop of the ice-cream bribe and plonk her in front of Teletubbies – recalling that I once swore I'd never use the TV as a convenient babysitter. I laugh bitterly at my naivety.

The twins and their Mum arrive and are eager to meet Sinead.

"Girls, this is Sinead," I say, pointing them in the direction of the sitting-room where Sinead is scrawling a colourful picture. She runs into their arms as if she's known them all her life, and cuddles them. "Love you argh argh," she says, stroking their hair and cackling in her strange Anglo-Irish language.

"Oh, Aunty Bridie – she's so sweet. You have lovely hair haven't you, Sinead," says Saskia.

"Cac, shit 123 mother caught a flea," she sings to the twins.

"No naughty words, Sinead, please." I reprimand her but it is a big mistake.

"Shit shit silly little fucker," she says smiling wickedly and defiantly at me.

The twins look shocked and are trying not to giggle in front of Lee. Lee intervenes sharply, whispering in their ears, "Don't respond when she does that swearing. Look the other way, or walk away and do something else. Then she will soon get tired of it if she doesn't get a reaction." The girls nod obediently.

A bit later on, the twins sit down quietly and read John Burningham's book *Would You Rather* to Sinead. It is a miracle – 20 minutes of peace, leaving me and Lee to relax and watch the endearing scene. Sinead is engrossed in the book.

"Would you rather eat slug dumplings, snail squash or mashed up spiders?" Sinead is fascinated and makes huge "errgghhhh yeuch" noises and everyone laughs.

Then my worst nightmare happens as Sinead does an enormous fart and says, "Err err done a fert I can burp the alphabet look," and God forbid, she starts to burp the bloody alphabet. The twins are hysterical with laughter – they just can't help themselves. Lee is very shocked, but says nothing.

"Sinead, please don't use that word. It's rude. Just say 'Excuse me' that's all. And please stop doing the burp alphabet. It's not nice."

Sinead says, "Shut up cow," and the twins blanche. To my surprise, Jazzy says, "Sinead, please be nice to Aunty Bridie." At that, Sinead starts to snivel and grizzle. Time for bed, I think.

I thank Lee and the girls for coming round, and apologise for Sinead's behaviour.

"Oh, don't worry, Bridie," Lee says, "we've heard worse. (Although I doubt they have.) She's a lovely wee girl and she's only been with you a couple of weeks. I'm sure you'll soon stop all the burping and trumping!" and at that, all three chuckle their way down the drive, leaving me feeling like an utter failure. I resolve that I will help Sinead to put this uncouth behaviour in the past.

As Sinead is having her bath and happily playing with the bubbles, I read my *Parents' Problem Solver* book, and to my surprise, it has a section on 'socializing your child' and in particular on the problem of breaking wind (or belching) in public. God, it must be a more common problem than I thought. "*In private family situations, breaking wind or belching is often found amusing and will make parents or siblings laugh. Laughter can break the tension or atmosphere and a child can perceive laughter as approval or love. If excessive, you can speak to your foster-child in a non-confrontational way by saying, 'You seem to be belching a lot today. Why do you think this might be?'*"

Later when we are both quiet and relaxed, and Sinead is tucked-up in bed, I tackle the belching issue. "Sinead, do you remember when the twins visited us today and you made some rude noises? Why do you think this might be happening?" I know she doesn't speak that well but she sure as hell understands most things.

She looks at me, shrugs her shoulders and says, "Dunno. Ask Bobby." And with that she fell fast asleep with Snowy Bear and invisible Bobby, presumably.

6th February 1998

Dr Li is sending yet more supplements, this time not for me but Sinead – to try and tackle her belching and flatulence.

Sinead is going to Mrs Doyle's today and no, she is not a character from Father Ted but an experienced foster carer who will take care of Sinead whilst we are at the dreaded Directions meeting.

"I have looked after over 40 children of all ages and sizes and none of them have been much trouble," she says proudly on the phone. *Good luck with Sinead then*, Mrs Doyle, I think.

We duly arrive in Leopardstown Drive to deliver Sinead to Mrs Doyle's house, complete with Roger Bear, Snowy Bear and some books. Sinead is wary and I wonder if she thinks she will be abandoned again. I see her expression change from happiness to anxiety.

"Don't worry, sweetie," I say. "We love you, and we'll be back in a little while." I reassure her with an extra big cuddle.

"No! Stay with you," she says squeezing my arm. "I be good."

I am absolutely bowled over that she's asking to stay with me, but of course, I have to go. I am firm but warm. "We'll be back soon, Sinead. Have a nice time with Mrs Doyle."

But it is no good. She throws herself to the floor and refuses to move, clinging to me and arching her back like a cat. Mrs Doyle comes up to us and bends over Sinead and says, "I've got a big fluffy donkey in the house, Sinead. Do you want to see it?"

To my great relief, Sinead lets go of me, puts her hand in Mrs Doyle's and says. "See donkey. House brostaigh."

As we drive to Ringsend Family Centre, Declan says, "What's a Directions meeting anyway, Bridie?"

"I'm not really sure, but it's to do with Sinead's future."

Declan looks thoughtful. "They may not allow her to stay with us you know. We may be too old, or just not have enough experience."

"You're arguing for our limitations," I say. "Anyone would think you don't want her to stay."

Declan says nothing.

At the Directions Meeting we are all assembled around a huge round table. I see Patsy for the first time, accompanied by her solicitor. I can see Sinead in her looks, but she is a haggard waif of a woman; she looks confused and distracted and painfully, painfully thin. Margaret and her barrister are here too, as is Murphy and his solicitor, a Social Services barrister and also Nanna O'Driscol.

It takes me a while to realise that Margaret has a baby in her arms and I find myself staring at the bundle.

"A'right Broidy?" Margaret asks. "This 'ere's my little Branna. Only two weeks old, she is." Margaret hoists the bundle towards my face, in what can only be described as a triumphant manner, and of course, Branna is a beauty, as all babies are. But I'm the one who's looking confused now. I didn't even know Margaret was pregnant – how can she have been pregnant? I mean, she'd put on a bit of weight, but she was still scrawny. I suppose after – how many kids has she had? – she just pops them out now... Maybe this was what Barry couldn't tell us, and the reason why Sinead was put up for fostering? I have to admit, I am bitter and jealous of this fecund woman and her bundle of joy.

Pauline the Guardian Ad Litem, Edna, Barry and Jed Walsh, Margaret's social worker, are also present. And us, of course. It's like being in court and I suddenly get very nervous and reach for Declan's hand. He squeezes mine reassuringly, but there's a very formal, edgy atmosphere.

Declan and I do not know what to do or say – this is all so new to us. We awkwardly find the seats with our names written down on little cards on the table in front, and then forms are passed around which we are asked to sign.

"Erhhem," Edna is clearing her voice, "if we could all sit down please. Welcome everybody and thank you for coming today. Could we start off with introductions please." She points at me and catches me totally unawares.

"Erm, I'm Bridie Kelly and this is my husband Declan. We're foster carers for Sinead."

We move on to Margaret who says rather curtly, "Margaret, current carer for Sinead Riley," but Barry interrupts her: "Excuse me Margaret, but you're not actually the current carer are you? Mr and Mrs Kelly are."

Margaret stares at him and swears audibly, "Bastard," under her breath. Patsy stands up and dreamily announces that she is Sinead's real mum as she is her birth mum. Murphy drags himself up from his slumped position in his chair, coughs, snorts, but mercifully, doesn't fart, and lethargically describes himself as a musician and then, as if he's just remembered what he's here for, says he's also Sinead's Dad. Edna tells us that she is Sinead's link social worker. Pauline brightly declares herself the social worker representing Sinead in court. Then follows Barry Black and Jed Walsh who are working on Sinead's case.

Edna starts the meeting. "We are here to discuss the

future of Sinead Riley who is currently in temporary foster care with Mr and Mrs Kelly. Can I ask Bridie to report on the situation with Sinead at the moment, please?"

Declan nudges me.

"Ermm, hi! Yes, well..." I am at a loss. Nothing comes to mind at all so I start jabbering. "Sinead eats huge amounts of food, concentrates quite well for a short while, but then loses her focus, she reads a few words with me in her children's books, she sleeps really well and she is starting to talk more in English as well as Irish. She has been to a Mothers and Children group with me, in fact I couldn't get her to come home..." At this point everybody titters, and I relax a little and get into my stride. "Erm... she has met all my family and behaved very well, although she was a bit rough with the dogs at first. She seems to like to play with other children, although she always takes charge and is a bit bossy. I'm giving her some supplements to help with her digestive problems..." All the social workers are furiously scribbling down notes whilst Sinead's family members look utterly bored. Murphy is even picking his nose.

I am quite enjoying myself now, and about to continue, but Margaret has stood up and is saying, "I would like to inform you that I intend to seek a residential order for Sinead. I loves her like she's me own family."

Patsy takes her cue from Margaret and also stands up to say her piece. "As Sinead's real mother, I would like Sinead to stay within my own family so as I can see 'er. If you won't let 'er stay wiv myself, then my mother, Mrs O'Driscoll over there," Patsy nods at her mother, and we all suddenly realise that she has been totally overlooked and not introduced, "my Ma will 'ave her for me." Mrs O'Driscoll nods, but says nothing, and Patsy, clearly anxious, sits down abruptly, biting her nails.

Murphy who seems to be asleep is given a nudge by his

solicitor. "I just wants Sinead to have a good 'ome," he said with dead eyes. True to form, Murphy sways and belches, his rancid alcoholic breath enveloping all present. I see his solicitor prod him again and hiss, "You are not exactly giving a good impression here, Murphy."

Edna takes the floor. "I think we all need to be thinking what is best for Sinead at this moment in time, and given the, um, the difficulties that the plaintiffs are currently presenting, I move that the current short-term fostering placement with Mr and Mrs Kelly is the best option."

However, Margaret has also taken the floor. "Shinny should be 'ome with my family an' able to see Patsy and Murphy every day she wants. Bridie's got no children – Sinead will be bored sick wiv 'er."

I felt acute pain at that jibe. She had hit a raw nerve and she knew it.

"But, Margaret, you've just had a baby yourself – which you failed to mention to us until six weeks ago. Don't you think that this will impede your ability to look after Sinead?" Barry Black asks.

"Baby's no bother," Margaret replies, and it has to be said that the little mite hasn't uttered a sound during the whole meeting.

"The fact remains," Barry continues, "that you now have eight children, one of whom is a newborn. We need to assess whether you can give Sinead the attention she needs, given your new circumstances."

The room remains silent for a while, as people busy themselves with their laptops and box files.

Then, to my delight, Edna announces that the short-term foster placement with us will stand and that the meeting would reconvene next month to review the situation.

Bloody hell – they're leaving Sinead with us! Declan was

wrong – we are good enough. She's staying with us!

The kettle has boiled and strong tea or bad coffee is being served although Murphy, Patsy, Margaret and her newborn, and Nanna have gone outside for a fag. We hear a car horn beep and a bit of commotion in the car park and, just to make small-talk really, Declan says, "I bet that's Sinead coming to cause trouble." I kick him in the shin, thinking it's an inappropriate comment but sure enough, moments later, an exhausted and flustered Mrs Doyle barges in with Sinead and her whole family in tow.

"Goodness me, what a handful this one is – she's very bright, but she's into everything!" she says to me. "I've fostered over 40 kids," she mopped her sweating brow, "and none of them have been as naughty as this one."

"Sinead, what have you been up to?" I ask.

"You don't want to know, but I'll tell you anyway. She put my shoes in the washing machine – lucky she couldn't work out how to turn it on! And I think she's broken the TV.... You're going to have your work cut out with this one," she says ruffling Sinead's hair. "Here, have her back," and she pushes Sinead in my direction. Sinead leans against my leg, hands on her hip in a defiant battle of wills against Mrs Doyle, and to my utter joy (and Edna's I assume), she says, "Wanna go home now, Bridie."

Margaret throws me a look that could kill, but Patsy and Murphy are having a row that is getting more heated by the second. Barry ushers them out and the meeting's over.

I am triumphant. Bloody well TRIUMPHANT.

Chapter 17

Johnny, Be Good

7th February 1988

Unlike Sinead, I have not slept a wink – in fact last night I had nightmares about Johnny coming to stay with us. I know I wanted to be a mum but two foster-children, at once, when I'm only just accredited? I am trying to visualise a happy four days ahead, with Sinead and Johnny bonding like brother and sister but I can't convince myself. You see, the problem is that not only is Sinead hyperactive, but Johnny is as well. I can't imagine how I am going to cope? As the old saying goes, I'll need eyes in the back of my head.

I ring Denise for a bit of moral support – I've not been doing that so much lately, I realise.

"Oh well, just focus on the positive, Bridie – you did want a child and now you're getting two, and a chance to prove yourself. If you do well with Johnny, then there might just be a chance that they will let you adopt Sinead."

Ah, that's a nice thing to say, Denise, I think.

"And Brides," she continues, "you are going to have to stop being so needy now you're their foster Mum. They are the needy ones, not you."

Talk about a slap in the face! Before I could respond, she makes her excuses and rings off.

Oh my God. Am I needy? I didn't think I was, but maybe I am? Maybe this whole thing is about me trying to fulfill my own need to be loved, and not about wanting to help children after all? How do I stop being needy? Is being needy the opposite of being confident?

Denise's comment niggles me, but somewhere deep down, I know she's got a point. This whole thing really has been about my needs and my wants. I've pushed for it even though I know that Declan would prefer a quiet life. He's been amazing really, standing by me as I pursue my needs: my need not to be Barren Bridie anymore, when it boils down to it. (Note to self: remember to thank D and buy him a nice present.) But, I think I'm changing... I really do. I want to help these kids, out of a genuine sense of love and concern for them. It's starting to be less about me, and more about them – I think.

I set about tidying up the house for the imminent arrival of Johnny and his social worker, Ellen – and I warn the dogs that there are going to be lots of distractions today. I plan on taking Sinead and Johnny to the beach once all the introductions and formalities are over, because I figure, that's a fairly safe place for them to let off a bit of steam, run around and get to know each other. It's even quite a warm, spring-like day today, so it should be fun.

In fact, I've actually planned out the whole four days right down to the minutest detail, like a *proper pedigree parent*.

Day 1: Introductions – Johnny to Sinead – followed by the rest of the day on the beach. Memo: make healthy picnic, e.g. salad Niçoise (don't forget tongs), fresh tuna, a savoury tart with anchovies (good for hyperactivity), and a huge selection of fresh fruit like papaya, mango, kiwi (papaya good for enzymes and digestion). Bath/shower. Evening story: talking book CD Part 1, something like Swallows and Amazons (check what's on Bea's old bookshelf).

Day 2: Swimming in the morning (NB: Johnny – trunks?) Healthy lunch at pool or maybe chips as treat? Followed by 101 Dalmations plus light snacks (apple/celery/carrots if they had chips). Bath/shower. Early night. CD Part 2 story again. Practice some English vocabulary with Sinead particularly. Maybe make a classical CD to go to sleep with (supposed to stimulate intellect).

Day 3: Long walk along coast path and picnic. (Make cheese/onion pasties?) Check if they have wellies. NB: ask Declan to get picnic basket out of loft. If bad weather, consider skating rink – ask Declan to accompany? Bath/shower. Early night and CD Part 3.

Day 4: Pack-up Johnny's things (hurray!) Lexicon or jigsaw games, drawing, Play-Doh, etc. Long dog walk. Late lunch: special treat, homemade pizza? Ellen collecting Johnny at 3pm.

I re-read my itinerary. We'll be fine.

It's 11am already and Johnny and Ellen are due any minute. I find myself pacing up and down the room nervously peeping around the curtain every few minutes. Sinead is happy and full of expectation.

"Here now?" she asks every five minutes. "Daddy coming too?"

Sinead has made up a funny little song, which is actually quite catchy and we sing it together as she dances around the room very eccentrically, swinging Snowy Bear to and fro.

Little Johnny coming to stay
Going to have a friend to play

Sinead's getting rather hysterical with excitement and suddenly, out of nowhere, she punches Snowy Bear in the mouth. As she does so, her whole face changes from a cheerful little girl to a sullen and angry one. I wonder where this aggression is coming from and whether Snowy Bear is reminding her of anything from her life at Margaret's. (After all, he does stink of smoke and chip fat). Memo: sneak Snowy Bear out of her bed tonight and put him in the washing machine.

Her little tantrum is soon over though, and hey ho, here they come. There are footsteps approaching the door and the sound of a high-pitched chattering voice. I brace myself as the doorbells rings, which makes the dogs bark madly. Sinead is now utterly high and I am tense. I wonder if we could pretend we are not in? For a moment I am tempted to do this!

I open the door to a small boy who actually looks like a minute black-haired leprechaun. He has a long pointed chin a high forehead and huge brown eyes.

"Hello, you must be Johnny! Welcome." His eyes dart nervously around the room as he does a most peculiar thing: he shakes my hand vigorously.

"Where are the dogs and who's that girl over there?" he demands in a loud, shouty voice. I'm quite taken aback that he can string a sentence together.

Ellen reins him in a little. "Johnny, Johnny! Look at me – what do you do when you meet new people? You say hello and tell them your name." She mutters under her breath that it may take him a couple of hours to calm down as he is very excitable today.

"Say hello to Bridie and Sinead, Johnny. Then we can show you your room and you can put your pyjamas under your pillow and your toothbrush in the bathroom. Do you need the toilet?"

I study Ellen's manner – she is very firm and concise. Could I ever be this kind of Mum: no nonsense; no doing things just to be popular with the children?

"Hello, Bridie. Hello, Sinead," he says. "No, don't need the toilet."

As the children size each other up, Ellen quickly gives me some tips and advice. "Don't let him go outside just yet as he needs to settle-in first. Talk with him and try to bond a little bit. Take an interest in his belongings especially Rupert Bear his 'cuddly'. Perhaps make Sinead and him a drink so you can all do something together. He likes tea and cake would you believe! Positive language only – that's what works with Johnny."

We take Johnny up to his bedroom which has bunk beds in it left over from the days when the twins used to visit more regularly. Johnny loves his bunk and immediately starts jumping up and down on the mattress.

"Johnny, please remember that your bed is not a trampoline," says Ellen with a firm, authoritative tone. I notice her positively re-directing him. "Show Bridie and Sinead your new suitcase," she says smiling, "and you can get Rupert Bear out. Your Aunty Mary gave you that, didn't she?" I notice Johnny's face light up at the mention of his Aunty Mary and make a mental note to mention her name if he gets upset or homesick. Ellen is a supreme example of 'cool, calm and collected' and I find the way she works with the children very inspiring. I want to emulate her and make another note to re-read some of my Personal Development books tonight.

Just as we are starting to settle-in, Ellen gets an emergency phone call and has to dash off and I am left home alone with Johnny and Sinead.

Impulsively I plan an immediate getaway to the beach with my high-class picnic, forgetting entirely Ellen's advice to keep Johnny inside for a bit – which I now recall thinking was a bit too much like getting a new kitten. Fortunately, Sinead is mesmerised by the new visitor, which gives me some time to finish packing the picnic bits and bobs.

"Wos' your name then?"

"Johnny..."

"Gunna play with me?"

"Okay..."

She clings on to the new visitor like a limpet. "Johnny, do you live here?"

"Don't know..."

Sinead is speaking brilliantly and I congratulate myself on her progress so far.

"Children," I say feeling a little bit like Mary Poppins, "shall we go to the beach and have a picnic?"

Sinead starts jumping up and down and clapping her hands, and then Johnny joins her.

"The sea! The sea! Get dogs! Let's go!" Sinead gleefully demands. To my utter surprise, Johnny starts singing, 'We Are Sailing' with a big smile on his face.

It's not too long before we are all settled in the car and the two dogs are cuddled up in their cage in the back. Johnny and Sinead are chattering away to each other and seem to be getting on like a house on fire. Now they are singing 'One Man Went To Mow' very loudly and getting the words all wrong! Still it's good to hear children enjoying themselves. Let's face it, kids just need boundaries and fun, don't they? Maybe I was making a fuss about nothing with Johnny coming? Lee always says that I exaggerate about everything! Who knows, perhaps she is right – how hard can it be to foster two children?

Now Sinead is singing that song about a mother that caught a flea – oh, that reminds me, I must do a nit check on Sinead tonight. I certainly don't want Johnny getting nits before he leaves us! That would not do at all! I allow myself to be a bit confident, because so far, so good. Johnny and Sinead seem quite happy together and even the dogs are excited at this unexpected excursion.

We pull into the car park by the beach and get out of the car. Granted it's a bit chilly but we can find a sheltered spot and sit down together for the picnic.

"Bridie, I'm hungry," says Johnny.

"Bridie, *I'm* hungry," says Sinead immediately, mimicking Johnny and she barges in front of him to try and look in the picnic box.

"Shall we find a nice spot to eat?" I suggest using diversionary tactics. "Let's get onto the beach and then we can find somewhere out of the wind to eat."

"I get wind," says Sinead, which makes me laugh out loud.

"Good girl, Sinead," I say. "That's right, sometimes we all get wind."

Johnny looks on a bit bemused. We walk towards the beach, the kids hand in hand, and me holding the two dogs on their leads in one hand, and the picnic basket in the other.

"I have to eat all the time, with my metabolism," says Johnny suddenly.

"Do you? I must remember that." I am genuinely surprised that he knows such a word but I guess he's heard it from one of his social workers. I make a mental note to relay this little anecdote to Declan and my fostering diary, as it may be important.

"This is a nice spot isn't it?" I say to the children. We've walked up to a lovely little family area where we've picnicked before. It has half a dozen picnic tables and is in the lee of one of the low cliffs, so it gives us a bit of seclusion from the wind, and we can see the vast beach and the sea in the distance.

"Okay, let's eat. I have made some nice tuna salad and we have a lovely quiche too..."

Sinead looks greedily at the food and then spontaneously hugs me.

"Thank you, Mummy Bridie," she says and I nearly melt with joy. I kiss her and cuddle her back, then whisper foolishly in her ear that we will stay together come what may. Immediately, I could kick myself. One of the cardinal rules with foster-children is that you never promise them anything that you might not be able to deliver. Oh, Bridie, what if you can't keep Sinead? I'll be just another adult that lets her down. Damn.

At this point however, Johnny distracts my reverie. I think he may be a little jealous of Sinead's show of affection and to be honest, I think she's doing it to provoke his jealousy. I'll have to keep my wits about me.

"I only like Wotsits and jammy dodgers," he says moodily. "I hate salad."

"Well Johnny, I think with your metabolism, salad might be better for you," I say assertively, hoping that reflecting the word 'metabolism' back at him might be reassuring. "Would you like to try some? It's very yummy,"

"Ummmm," says Sinead provocatively, "yummy, ummmm." She's munching on a slice of quiche and is waiting for me to dish out the salad. I'm grateful that she will eat pretty much anything that I put in front of her.

I offer Johnny some fresh tuna salad and homemade coleslaw. "Yuk! Not eating it – I'm allergic to it. It stinks!"

"Do you think so, Johnny? I think it smells lovely. What about a bit of fruit then?" (*Positive language; recognition of their personal likes and dislikes...*)

Johnny is refusing to touch any food, but Sinead seems to have devoured everything in sight, even the radishes!"

Okay, so the picnic seems to be only a partial success, but Johnny's bound to feel unsettled, poor little thing. Perhaps if they're good, I'll buy them both a small ice cream each – surely that won't hurt? I feel a little worried about Johnny's metabolism, especially if he has to eat regularly.

As I pack-up the picnic, both the children run down towards the sea together, with their buckets and spades in hand.

"Not too far please!" I shout after them. It's a lovely sight – my first two foster children enjoying themselves on the beach. I feel genuinely happy – I do, I feel fulfilled. I catch up with them and take lots of photographs so that I can remember this special day, and show Declan and my parents and sisters: I'm so proud.

"Smile, Sinead! Smile, Johnny!" Both of them smile, then make faces and jut their chins out, making each other laugh. Bless them! Oh!

"I'm going to sit here and read my magazine whilst you two make some sandcastles," I say, spreading a rubber-backed rug out on the sand. It's blustery but the sun is shining and it's not too cold. "Don't go too far please."

"Can we take the dogs?" asks Johnny. Hilda and Harry have already curled up on the rug. They don't look like they want to go anywhere.

"If you throw the tennis ball for them, they might come with you," I say to Johnny, "but don't throw it in the sea – it's too cold for them."

"Okay, Bridie."

Awww! Sweet! I'll remember this day forever, I know it. Look at them with their little wellie-boots and woollen hats! "Try not to get wet and look after the dogs," I shout.

I watch as they gallop around the beach, throwing the ball for the dogs, who are playful but gentle with the children.

It is a lovely sight. I try to relax and read my *Marie Claire* magazine, but I don't really want to take my eyes off the children. I have to be vigilant at all times, but I do feel proud to have achieved even this much.

I notice that another family is walking towards Sinead and Johnny – they must be saying hello. But then, Sinead follows them as they walk away. Hmmm – Barry's words filter into my brain: 'she has no awareness of stranger danger'...

"Sinead, darling! Can you come back now please? Mummy wants to talk to you." (Is it alright to call myself Mummy so soon? I must ask one of the SS.) I abandon *Marie Claire* and the picnic and tear after the unsuspecting family. Why is she not responding to me?

"Sinead!" I run after her and grab hold of her hand, but she yanks it away.

"Get off want Nanna Dadda gread leat."

The family looks at me suspiciously as if I am a child abductor rather than a foster carer.

"Come with me please, Sinead," I say in my newly-practiced authoritative tone. "Stay with me." And to the bemused family, "She's my new foster-daughter," as if that explains everything.

"Why's she speaking like that?" asks Johnny. "Is she still a baby?"

"No, Johnny, Sinead just speaks in Irish sometimes. Can you go and get the dogs please and put them on their leads, and bring them back? There's a good boy. Thank you."

Johnny takes the leads out of my hands and wanders off towards where the dogs are sniffing something on the beach. I turn back to Sinead.

"Shall we go and join Johnny and the dogs, Sinead?" I ask in my best conciliatory voice, hoping that she will be compliant and won't make a scene.

"No! Get off bugger! Not going with you."

Oh God! I thought she was bonding with me earlier – why is she suddenly treating me like a stranger?

"Sinead. Please don't use that language. Come with me now."

"NO! No, no. Ag fuck ar!"

"That's enough Sinead!" I say and grab her hand. "Sorry," I hiss to the family who are rapidly backing away from us, their own children looking absolutely horrified.

I march her back towards where our belongings are but Sinead is having none of it. OMG! Now she is screaming "Shit! Cac!" at the top of her voice – thank God the beach is nearly deserted – and she's kicking me hard.

"Ouch, Sinead – that's not nice." I am being assaulted by a six year-old. So much for bonding and staying together forever! Let's just say this picnic is not quite going to plan.

I hate myself for it, but I say to her, "If you calm down, Sinead, we can go and get an ice cream. Would you like that?" Finally, she starts to come to her senses. It's like she's possessed by some chaotic spirit when she has these tantrums. Then, as if a switch is flicked (usually by a bribe of sweets or food) she is fine again, but it's very traumatic for me when she's having an episode.

"CHRIST! Where's Johnny? Oh God, oh God..." The dogs are still there sniffing whatever the hell it is they're sniffing, but where's Johnny?

"Johnny!" I shout. "Johnny! Where are you? Time to go home now?"

"Johnny! Johnny!" Sinead shouts at the top of her voice. By God that child's got a pair of bellows for lungs.

Panic flashes through me, my legs are wobbly and my mouth is bone dry; my body is awash with adrenaline. A terrible scenario of police sirens, ambulances and Edna looking aghast and disappointed, flashes through my mind. Oh no, no.

"Johnny! Johnny! Bridie wants you to come back please." I am running distractedly down the beach, then turn around immediately. I can't leave Sinead.

"Sinead, darling can you come and help me find Johnny?" Amazingly, this little girl seems to know when the shit has seriously hit the fan. She instinctively links hands with me and Team Hilda, Harry, Sinead and Bridie start running back towards the picnic area, leaving a trail of magazines, napkins and the dogs' ball in our wake. We search and search for Johnny. He is not in the picnic area, he is not in the car park, he is not in the toilet block which is locked anyway. (*What if Sinead needs a pee?* I think.)

"Sinead? Do you need a pee?" I ask her.

"Dun a pee," she says sweetly. Christ. So much for the toilet training. Good job I've got some more pull-ups in the car. I imagine myself in trouble with the police and social services. I would bring disgrace on my family. Declan would divorce me. Bea would disown me. Oh God.

The dogs know something is up. I let them off their leads. "Find him, Hilda! Find him, Harry!" I say and somehow, my lovely dogs seem to know what to do. They bound back up the beach sniffing at everything but it's just the tennis ball they return with minutes later.

I am at a loss. I don't know what to do. A tear runs down my cheek and I sniff and wipe it away.

"Don't cry, Mummy Bridie," Sinead says.

Oh, you're suddenly all sweetness and light now, I think. *If you hadn't caused a scene in the first place, none of this would've happened.*

"I'm not crying, darling," I say. "I've just got a runny nose." My heart is pounding, and I feel scared. I am still clutching

Sinead's hand. "Where is he?" I ask aloud. I am responsible for him. Oh God, what was I thinking of, bringing him to the bloody beach when I hardly know him – especially as Ellen told me to keep him indoors. I was too hooked-up on some romantic notion of being a mother... I'm totally useless... I silently chastise myself. I hope to God he hasn't run into the road or even worse, been abducted by a paedophile. Or one of Murphy's bloody mates! I am mad with worry. I imagine the headlines in the *Irish Times*: 'Young Lad in Care Drowns on Brey Beach. Foster Mother Guilty'.

"Johnny there Bridie," Sinead is saying, tugging at my hand. "Johnny in the sea amaideach..."

"What? Where?" Oh, thank God – I can just see him, miles down the beach, paddling quite far out in the sea. Thank God. *Thank God*.

"Can you run Sinead?"

"Run down the beach!"

We set off at a fair pace, but he's a long way away. The dogs think this is a great game. Sinead and I both get puffed-out quite quickly, and slow down to a jog.

As soon as we are within earshot, I shout angrily, (thinking *foster carers should use a firm, non-aggressive tone*) "Johnny! Come here THIS INSTANT!"

Johnny looks at me blankly and so do the dogs. I don't think they've ever heard me so cross.

"This instink!" echoes Sinead.

"Johnny, come on! We're getting cold. Let's go," I plead. I'm going to give up this bloody fostering lark, I really am. This is too much... "Johnny, I asked you not to go too far away. The sea is very dangerous you know," I say, catching my breath. I instinctively reach out to give him a hug, but he backs away from me. "I was worried about you, Johnny.

The dogs and Sinead are now bouncing about in the

waves, having fun. She is splashing water at them and they are biting the droplets as they cascade down. She thinks it's hilarious.

"I wanted to play in the sea," Johnny looks very worried. "I forgot to get the dogs."

"That's okay, Johnny, but next time, please stay with us. Don't go wandering away, okay? We couldn't find you. We thought you might have got hurt."

"I'm okay."

Relieved and grateful that he's not dead, I say, "Shall we go and get some ice cream?"

"Yeah! Ice cream! Yeah!" shouts Sinead, whose ears always prick up at any mention of food.

"I love ice cream," says Johnny.

"Come on then!" We walk back up the beach and Johnny falls into step beside me.

"It's nice here. Can I stay forever?"

"On the beach? You'd get a bit cold, Johnny."

"No, I mean with you. Nobody else wants me," he says, patting Hilda's head.

My emotions take over and I bend down and put my arms around him. This time he doesn't wince. "Oh, Johnny, it's really lovely to have you here with us, but you know that it's only for a few days, don't you?"

We get our ice creams from the stall in the car park that is painted with big blue and white stripes. Sinead wolfs hers down and then starts playing with the dogs again, thrashing the sand with a long stick and teasing them with it.

"Tell me a little bit about yourself, Johnny," I say.

He is silent for a long time and I think he's not going to talk to me, but then he says, "I live with Joyce but she is old and boring and makes me tidy my room and clean my teeth for three minutes. We never go out like this. Its fun here.

Where is your husband? Can I call you Mum and Dad while I'm here?" he speaks so fast and asks so many questions I can hardly keep up with him.

"I think you should call us Bridie and Declan whilst you're here with us, Johnny, because we're not really your Mum and Dad are we? We're your foster-carers."

Johnny shrugs his shoulders and looks at the ground. "'Spose so," he replies.

I have an idea that might just set us all back on the right track, even though it wasn't on the Itinerary.

"Shall we go and see my Mum and Dad?" I ask him. "Would you like that?"

"Yeah!" says Johnny with such enthusiasm, I just have to hug him again.

"Come on then! Come on, Sinead!" I shout.

We bundle back into the car, and I start to breathe a little more normally again. I feel traumatised by this afternoon's events, but nothing terrible actually happened, and me and Johnny have at least talked a little. On the way there in the car we practiced Knock Knock jokes. Johnny is good at them, but Sinead doesn't quite get them.

"Knock, Knock," she says.

"Who's there?" we say.

"Me!!!!" she screams.

I laughed all the way home just like the little piggy who went to market. As we wait at a red traffic light, I notice Johnny staring jealously at Sinead who is now snoozing in her car seat.

"Is she staying with you forever?" he asks.

"She is staying for three months," I say breezily.

"Why can't I stay for three months?" Johnny asks.

I'm a bit lost for words. "I think it's very complicated, Johnny," is the best I can come up with.

We arrive at Mum's house and I am mentally exhausted but feeling positive. Today has been good with some terrifying bits. I decide not to say anything about Johnny getting lost on the beach.

"Cooee! Dad? Mum?" We are here – all three of us," I say, giving them just a bit of warning. They'd obviously been fast asleep on the sofa and were surprised to see us.

"Stanley, put the kettle on would you, and get out that special chocolate cake. Now then, who are you?" says Mum, studying Johnny.

"I am Johnny," he says and pats Trixy affectionately.

"Hello, Johnny," says my Dad on his way to the kitchen.

"Hello," says Johnny and extends his hand for my Dad to shake. My lovely Dad shakes his hand. "Pleased to meet you. And where's Sinead"

Sinead comes over and leans against my leg saying hello to my parents very politely. I feel so proud of her. I'm sure she's improving even in the short time she's been with us. A surge of love for her overwhelms me.

Johnny and Mum are having a little tête-à-tête.

"Where are you from?" she asks kindly.

"Gunduggan Estate," he replies. I notice my mother's expression change from optimism to pessimism.

"Oh, I see," she says, sniffing and looking at her watch.

"You're very wrinkly, like an elephant."

Mum stiffens up and checks herself in the mirror. Then she wanders over to me. "Did you hear what he said, Bridie? He thinks I'm wrinkly. I'm not so bad am I?"

"No, Mum! He's just a kid. Anyway, they're too truthful for their own good half the time. Watch this," and I turn to Johnny and say, "How old do you think I am then Johnny?"

"About 200?"

We all laugh, Johnny and Sinead just a bit too boisterously

and I wonder if they're getting tired.

Dad wanders in with the chocolate cake and a pot of tea on an enormous tray and plonks it down on the table. My Mum then begins to slice and pass the cake around.

"What's wrong with her hand? Why is she shaking so much?" Johnny asks me. "Is she going to die?"

"Johnny!" I can't help but reprimand him. I whisk him aside and tell him that it's a bit rude to suggest an old person is wrinkly, or that they're shaky, and it's not nice to ask if they're dying either.

"But I really like her. She is a nice Mum. What's wrong with her? She shakes like a jelly." Johnny then starts wobbling his head and shaking his body and Sinead, who has cottoned on that something is happening starts mimicking him.

"Stop it you two, and eat your cake please," I say. I am shattered.

Luckily, Mum and Dad don't seem to hear this conversation, or at least, they've decided to ignore us, and I'm glad because although he didn't mean to hurt her feelings, he certainly picked up on something that I'd been trying not to notice. Mum's shaking is getting much worse.

I figure it is time to go, but then Sinead says her first coherent sentence since she's been with us. "We went to the beach today and Bobby came. Hilda and Harry did a poo, poo, poo!"

No. Please don't mention the crisis...

"123 mother caught a flea..." and Sinead is now singing her little song.

"Bridie, you are a natural," says my Dad. "Look at her – she's talking so much better than when she first came here."

"Thanks, Dad!" I say, but I see that Mum has snuck off to the kitchen. I think this little visit has upset her more than she's letting on. She's a very proud lady.

We finally get home, and Declan is waiting for us.

"Hello, young man!" he says to Johnny who, true to form, extends his handshake. Declan is charmed.

"How was your day?" he asks.

"Great!" the children chorus.

"We went to the beach and had ice cream and I lost the dogs," says Johnny.

"Then we lost 'im," says Sinead, prodding Johnny quite viciously.

Declan raises his eyebrows at me.

"Tell you later," I whisper, but it's too late.

Sinead lets out a loud and lingering belch and says, "Pardon. Hilda and Harry did a poo poo ooh and I love Mummy Dadda Nanna Murphy. Went to beach and ran away."

Declan and I just burst out laughing. "I will tell you later," I say.

After dinner, Sinead asks if she can watch Teletubbies so I pack her off into the sitting-room with Roger Bear, Snowy B and a glass of hot milk. By the time I have cleared the dishes whilst Declan runs a bath for Johnny, she is fast asleep, snoring gently. I love her for that: important things like eating and sleeping are easy with Sinead. I prise Snowy B from her arms and throw him in the washing machine along with the kids' sodden socks, trousers and towels.

Whilst Johnny is in the bath, I recount the day to Declan.

"Honestly, D, I know nothing terrible actually happened, but the thought of it, and the thought of being responsible for it filled me with terror. I bloody well hope that tomorrow isn't going to be so traumatic."

"It happens to us all, Bridie – don't be so hard on yourself. Do you remember that time I lost Bea in Woolworths? We'd drummed into her that if ever she got lost in a shop she should go and stand by the front doors, and I scoured the whole shop high and low and didn't even think about looking there? And when I eventually found her she was as cool as a cucumber and I was about to call the Garda! You're doing brilliantly. Give yourself a pat on the back."

I burst into tears. "Thanks, Declan. You're always so supportive. Thank you for believing in me." I hug him tightly. He is my rock.

"Johnny's a nice enough boy, isn't he?" Declan says. "Is he still in the bath, by the way?"

"Oops!" I run upstairs. "You alright Johnny?" I can hear a lot of splashing noises and he's singing 'I am sailing, I am sailing, home again, across the sea...'

"Hurry up now, Johnny, come on, it's eight o'clock. Bed time." No reply. I try again "Johnny – bed time now!" The problem is, he has locked the bathroom door, which you are encouraged to allow your older foster-children to do.

Declan runs up the stairs. "There's water dripping from the kitchen ceiling Bridie! What the hell is he doing in there?"

Declan tries his loud, scary voice "What on earth's going on in there, Johnny? Open the door young man, now! There's water dripping down from the ceiling. Come out immediately."

There's no reply for a few seconds, then we hear the toilet flush and the door opens gingerly. Johnny is standing there smiling, with bright red shiny cheeks and wet hair.

"Whoa! I love that bath – it's like a swimming pool. I've been practicing!"

Oh dear. Johnny has flooded the bathroom. It turns out that he put more water in after Declan left him and then switched on the spa whirlpools. It seems he's had a great time. Declan, with a face like thunder begins to mop-up. I wonder if he thinks I'm doing so well now.

Jesus, Lord, Aunty Bernadette – please can tomorrow be a bit easier than today?

Chapter 18

Two's Company

8th February 1998

I wake up still immersed in dreams – well, nightmares really – about flooding, drowning and child abduction. But a brisk shower wakes me up, and the positive thought that we are already a quarter of the way through Johnny's stay cheers me up. It's not that I'm not fond of the little chap, but two foster children at once, for a novice like me, is a real challenge. I resolve to keep Johnny out of Declan's way as much as possible, until the flooding incident is history. I think Declan's 'scary voice' upset Johnny a bit and they are giving each other a wide berth at the moment. Later today we will go to the pool for a swim, but first I have to sort out swimming nappies and water wings. It occurs to me that I may not be able to get a big enough size for Sinead, who at six years old should really be out of swimming nappies by now.

At breakfast, Johnny and Sinead sit happily around our kitchen table, and what with the radio in the background and Declan humming to himself as he stirs the porridge, I have a moment of serenity. I gaze at this family of four – well, six if you count the dogs – and have a wonderful feeling of accomplishment, but still, there's a low-level anxiety that something could go wrong at any minute. Declan dishes out freshly made porridge, boiled eggs, and toast and I watch the children eat in silence, momentarily. Then, Sinead claps her hands and starts singing her new doggie song.

Johnny seems a bit agitated. "Can I have those Coco Pops? I don't like this porridge."

Declan looks at me with raised eyebrows, but to head off the scary voice, I reply, "Coco Pops have a lot of sugar in them, Johnny. If you can eat a bit more porridge, you can have a small bowl of Coco Pops."

"I'm allowed them at Joyce's," he says defiantly. I give in and dish him out a small bowl.

"I want some too, please, Mummy Bridie," Sinead pipes up.

The word Mummy totally seduces me and I dish out a small bowl for her too. Declan shakes his head wearily and I feel as if I'm just pandering to them. Would I do anything for a quiet life?

It's not long before Declan sets off to work and I am alone with Johnny and Sinead, but they seem to be playing happily for the moment, so I take the opportunity to sort out the swimming costumes – I'll just have to buy the expensive swimming nappies at the pool shop. Moments later, Johnny is desperate to get out of the house.

"Wanna go out – 's boring here. Why's the door locked? Where's the keys?"

I take a deep breath and think of a distraction quickly. "Johnny, please can you go and find some towels – and did you bring any water wings with you?"

"Okay, but I don't need no waterings."

I smile, finish getting the swimming gear together, put the dogs in their kennel and find my keys.

I have the usual trouble getting Sinead in her car seat. "Sinead – look at me. We are going swimming and we need to get there in the car. Shall we sing that funny song whilst you get in?"

She just looks at me blankly and replies, "Nope," and shakes her head. Her defiance at getting in cars does make me wonder if anything traumatic had happened to her in a car at some point in the past.

Tactic 2: I ask her if she wants Bobby to join us. Bingo! Her little face lights up and she jumps in and buckles up her seat. Brilliant. They are both in the car and singing the 'Flea' song too. Phew! As I shut the door, I notice Sinead scratching her head vigorously. Note to self: do a nit check soon and probably on both of them.

Yes! We have arrived at the pool — I feel utterly triumphant at this small achievement. Both children are thrashing around joyfully in the shallow end, though Johnny can actually swim pretty well without armbands. I join the children and we play in the water together. They each hold on to one of my arms and I swing them round in circles, which makes them scream with excitement. Wow. I, Bridie Kelly, have done it. I am fostering two challenging children and have taken them swimming. I breathe a sigh of relief and smile smugly.

Now then, the itinerary allows for 60 minutes of swimming before lunch and my plan is to use food as a bribe to get them out. Before I know it, it's midday and I am starting to get hungry, so I implement my exit strategy.

"Johnny, Sinead – its time to get out of the pool now. Let's go and have some chips, shall we?" I say, clapping my hands loudly. No response from either of them. I repeat myself in a school teachery, no nonsense tone. "Come on. Out now! It's lunchtime. Quickly – get on with it or I'll start counting...1... 2... don't let me get to 3..." I wait again, but both children seem deaf to my request.

Tactic 2: I get out and ask the lifeguard to pretend that the pool is closing. The nice young lad winks at me and nods, saying he is happy to help me. I have rather pathetically explained that I am a foster carer and that my children are a bit of a handful. I am reassured to have somebody – anybody – on my side.

I try, "The pool's closing now!"

Nothing.

I try again. "Johnny, Sinead – come on now, the lifeguard needs to close the pool," and the lifeguard gives two short blasts on his whistle and comes over to stand by me. It's enough for Sinead to haul herself out of the pool and sit on the edge trickling little puddles of water all around her. I pray there are no nits in those rivulets. But Johnny has now decided to swim underwater for the whole length of the pool. I can't even see him now let alone talk to him. Panic hits me like a train. OMG – I hate my life.

Shit. He is now on the second level of the diving board.

"Get down now please, young man," says the lifeguard, "children under 12 are not allowed on the diving boards."

"But it's fun – can I dive?"

"No! Get down now Johnny," I shout, but he is oblivious to my warning.

"Want to stay here. It's fun. Not hungry yet," and with that he jumps into the water and swims furiously to the opposite end of the pool, then he sticks two fingers up at me and laughs loudly.

"Stay here please, Sinead," I say, and leave her on the side of the pool. With the help of the lifeguard we pursue Johnny, at last cornering him in the shallow end of the learner pool. The lifeguard wades in. "Come on young man – out now!" he says severely.

Suddenly I hear a crack and a deafening scream. I look around to see Sinead flat on the floor rubbing her head vigorously. My first thought is that she's found some nits, but then I realise that she's slipped over and bumped her head. My heart is in my mouth as I run over to her (knowing that running is not allowed in the swimming pool area). *I can't do it, I can't manage two kids! I curse. I knew that two children was too much for me – what the hell was Social Services thinking? Two kids – two hyperactive kids – and one novice carer. It's too much!*

I scream at Johnny. "GET HERE NOW! Look what's happened!" A different lifeguard helps me to comfort Sinead and check that she is okay, and her wailing subsides. She seems to perk up immediately with all the attention and I briefly wonder if her fall was to distract our own attention from Johnny. Meanwhile a kindly lady swimmer is trying to assist the lifeguard with Johnny. He points Johnny in my direction. "Your little sister has fallen over," says the lifeguard. "Go and help your Mummy will you?"

"Errr, she ain't my sister – I hate her – and that ain't my Mum and you touched me! Stranger danger!" he yells. "Paedo stranger danger! I'm ringing Ellen!" he shouts in a highly excited voice.

The lifeguard backs away immediately, and the woman pales and looks at me aghast.

"Paedo stranger danger!" Johnny repeats in his sing-song voice, but he doesn't seem quite so sure of himself now that everyone's watching him. I feel my face redden and my body freeze. I don't know what to do. I just don't. I am torn between Sinead and Johnny. I can't bloody well be in two places at once. But in the end, the lifeguard prevails.

"Listen to me, Johnny," he says in a quiet, but firm voice, "my job is to keep you safe. That's what I'm trained for. There's no stranger danger here – I'm a lifeguard and I look after hundreds of children every day. Let's get you out of the pool – look you're cold and shivering. Didn't somebody mention chips?"

Reluctantly, Johnny hops out of the pool and dashes into the

changing rooms before I can chastise him further.
Somehow we manage to get through lunch without any
further shenanigans. When I ask Johnny why he accused the
lifeguard of stranger danger, he said, "Joyce told me not to
talk to strangers."

"But there are certain people who are here to help you
Johnny," I say, "like policemen and teachers and lifeguards.
You may not know them, but they won't hurt you. Try not to
shout at people and call them bad names, okay?"

He shrugs his shoulders and stuffs his chips down like
there's no tomorrow. Sinead, luckily, has been sidetracked by
the chips too, and has forgotten about the rather livid bruise
that has appeared on her forehead. Bloody hell, what if a
social worker sees that?

We get home and I am exhausted, both mentally and
physically. I'm too old for this. I can't do it. I'll have to ring
Ellen and tell her to find some emergency care for Johnny
for the final two days. Sinead on her own, I can just about
manage, but Sinead and Johnny? No. I am a nervous wreck.

I can feel a migraine coming on, and need a bit of time
to just relax and recover, so I ask if Johnny and Sinead would
like to watch a video. They jump at the chance and squabble
about what to watch. Johnny wants Batman and Sinead wants
Teletubbies, but in the end, thank God, they agree to sit and
watch Babe: A Pig in the City, and as I put the kettle on in the
kitchen, I hear Sinead laughing heartily.

My head throbs and tears spill down my cheeks. I didn't
know it was going to be this hard. Denise was right. Lee was
right. Declan was right. Why couldn't I just be satisfied with
my little family of Declan and Bea, and the twins and Mikey...?
Why did I have to push us all down the fostering road, and
end up with two kids from hell? Oh, that's not fair – I actually
feel great love for them both, poor things. God knows what

they've been through in their own lives, it's just... it's just that I feel so ill-equipped for this. I should've gone on more parenting courses first, but I thought, after Bea, you know, I thought I was quite experienced as a step-mother... But it's different with foster children because you have no idea of what makes them tick. I mean, NO IDEA...

All of a sudden I realise it's gone quiet in the living room, and my 'crisis radar' goes into overdrive. Shit! I dash in to find Sinead glued to the film, but no sign of Johnny. Double-shit.

"Sinead sweetie, where's Johnny?"

"Dunno. Outside."

"Wha..."

"Key was on the table."

Oh, Jesus, Mary and Joseph! I'd put the car keys on the hall table, and the front-door key was on the fob too. He's only gone and let himself out. The search is on for Johnny again. I drag Sinead along with me and we run towards the park which I remembered Johnny had pointed out when we drove past this morning, pathetically asking people if they've seen a dark-haired little boy of about 11 years of age. Nobody's seen him.

"Mummy Bridie, can we sing songs?" Sinead asks as she trots along beside me.

I love it when she calls me Mummy Bridie. "You sing me the Flea song sweetie, and I'll keep looking for Johnny," I say – and she does, and somehow, it comforts me. Hand in hand, we make our way towards the play area at the end of the park.

"Excuse me," I say to a mother who is obviously local, "have you seen a little boy with black hair – small for his age, about 11 years old?"

"Yes, he's with the big lads over there. He's been shouting and swearing at the little ones – is he your boy? You should really talk to him about his language. Quite shocking... look he's over there by the youth club sign."

"Thank you. I'm sorry, he's not my... sorry. I'll speak to him about his behaviour."

Sinead calls out to him, mimicking me: "Johnny! Come 'ere, get 'ere now! Naughty boy!" Even in the heat of the moment, I'm impressed that she's not using Irish words so much now, and she's stringing more sentences together.

I can see a gang of lads smoking and jeering. Surely Johnny's not smoking? Oh God, he is.

I use a stern, no-nonsense voice. "Johnny, come here right now, please. Running off like that makes me very worried. COME. HERE. NOW!"

He stares at me and shouts, "No. You prefer Sinead – you don't want me. Declan hates me!" And with that, this time he gives me the middle finger. His newfound friends look suitably impressed, and to add insult to injury I hear them egg him on and call me Grandma, for God's sake.

"Up yours, Grandma!" they laugh as they swig back their cans of Coke emitting loud, forced belches as they do so.

"Burp, crush, throw!" says one of them as he lobs an empty can into the flowerbed.

But I respond to Johnny's pain, remembering a book that Lee had given me. In it I had read about deep listening and empathising with the emotion being expressed, not denying the feeling or accusing the child. "Come on, let's go home and talk about everything shall we, Johnny? You sound hurt and rejected. Do you want to do some dog-training in the garden with Hilda?"

His eyes light up and he hurls his fag into a puddle (which I notice he hasn't taken a drag of and hope is just a status symbol amongst the big boys). He suddenly becomes confident and introduces me to his new mates."

This is Bridie, my foster carer, and this is my pretend little sis, Sinead," he says to his friends. They shuffle about, seeming a little bit embarrassed.

"Hi, everyone," I say.

"Hi!" says Sinead, and she inches towards the smoking teenagers who grunt, "Alright?" at her and scuff their shoes along the ground.

"Come on then, Johnny," I say brightly. "Let's go and sort those dogs out. They'll be missing us."

"Okay then," Johnny responds positively and I breathe a prayer of thanks. "See you later," he shouts to the lads, who have by this time totally lost interest in the whole thing and are climbing the swings and hanging upside-down like a pack of monkeys. I realise Johnny is just a curiosity to them and will be soon forgotten.

Back home at last, I feel I have to tackle Johnny's propensity to run away and his rudeness too. "Johnny, before you go and play with the dogs, I'd like to have a little chat with you." He makes a grumbling noise, but I continue. "It's very worrying for me when you leave the house without asking me first, or when you don't do as I ask, like when we were in the pool. I'm responsible for your safety Johnny, and I need to know where you are, and that you're okay. Do you understand?"

"'Spose... but I was just playing."

"I'm glad you like playing Johnny, but if you want to do anything in future, please ask me first."

"Okay. Can I go and play with the dogs now?"

"In a minute. I also want to talk to you about being rude to people. It's really not nice to call someone a 'paedo' you know. And it's not nice to stick your fingers up to me. I'd like you to think about how this can hurt people's feelings. You wouldn't like it if people did that to you, would you?"

"Declan was rude to me yesterday."

"He wasn't rude, he was cross. There's a difference. He was cross because you'd overflowed the bath and flooded the kitchen, and when we asked you to come out, you ignored us. He doesn't hate you, okay?"

"Okay. Can I go now? Just me, without her," he points to Sinead, his brotherly love of earlier seemingly evaporated.

I watch out of the kitchen window as he plays with Hilda and Harry in the garden. He chases them round and round and they love it and prance around him. He can't quite catch them. I creep out of the back door to enjoy the charmingly normal scene, and hear him say, "Sure I am gunna train ya, ya little eejits!" Suddenly Johnny's softer side comes out as he strokes each dog and talks to them. He has more empathy with the animals than Sinead does, that's for sure. He looks up and sees me watching him. I smile but he says defensively, "I'm not going nowhere!"

"I know – I was just watching you playing with the dogs. You have a lovely way with them."

I feel like I've got a serious migraine coming on, I can hardly stand, but I've got to keep going, at least until Declan comes home. I break the habit of a lifetime and take two Migraleve.

It's funny, but despite the ups and downs, I am actually getting to like this little fella. I know his mother was a heroin addict who drank heavily and I know he also fell – or was pushed – out of a bedroom window and was in hospital for weeks, poor little mite. Perhaps he's never experienced love before? For a brief moment I imagine that Johnny is mine. I would teach him relaxation exercises and get him a little pet of his own that he could love – a rabbit or a tortoise perhaps. He would have chores to do around the house, and we would work on his low self-esteem and hey, maybe I could teach him to read and write. Maybe even him and Sinead would start to bond like brother and sister? In the garden, Johnny and the dogs are pretending to be at Crufts. I haven't seen him so animated before.

"Bridie," he shouts, "she likes me! Look, and she can jump – watch!"

I watch as Johnny manoeuvers Hilda in and out of some bamboo poles he's poked into the lawn, and over small jumps made out of his scrunched up jumper and a sack of compost.

"Now hide the rubber ring and let her sniff it out," I suggest. Sometimes I amaze myself with my brilliant ideas. Johnny spends the rest of the afternoon hiding Hilda's yellow hoop and Harry's tennis ball in different places. The dogs absolutely love the game. Wow – there seems to be a really positive bond between Hilda and Johnny. That's something we can build on. I realise my Happiness Factor has crept up a bit. Say, 5/10.

In the evening, after his bath – with Sinead once again crashed-out in front of Teletubbies – I gently approach Johnny about his life.

"Joyce makes me do everything. She is really strict, not like here. She never goes out and is always tidying-up. She makes me tidy-up all the time. It's really boring there. They are looking for a forever family for me and I have had a few weekends away but nobody wants me yet."

"Be positive Johnny," I say, trying to cheer him up, "there are lots of experienced foster carers out there looking for a little chap like you. It would be nice if you stayed on a farm maybe? You could play with lots of animals then. Don't give up hope."

"Can I stay here, Bridie? Can you be my forever family?" he asks, looking at me so hopefully. My heart goes out to him, it really does, but I know that I can't cope with the two of them, and I have already committed to Sinead.

"I'm sorry, Johnny, but we already have Sinead staying with us and we don't have enough experience to look after two children at the moment." I look at his distraught face and wait for the rage, which comes in the form of a hard door slam.

"Hate it here anyway! I want to go back to Joyce now."

I feel nervous and anxious. Please don't run off again... But Johnny is roaming the house saying that he is hungry and that Joyce lets him have snacks whenever he wants them. I make him a small healthy snack of apple, cheese and crackers, and as a special treat, let him eat it in his room before bed.

At about nine o'clock, with both children in bed, I collapse on the sofa and discuss the day with Declan, who is equally exhausted by his own long and arduous day in the surgery.

"Bridie!" I hear Johnny shout down the stairs.

"What now Johnny? Go to sleep – it's bed time."

"I feel sick – can I come downstairs?"

"He's pushing his luck," says Declan. "Shall I use the scary voice?"

9th February 1998

3.30am

I am awoken by Johnny knocking boldly on our bedroom door, which he then flings open, and comes bouncing into our room.

"Time to get up. Wanna do dog shows again."
Declan stirs and groans. "What the Dickens? It's 3.30 in the morning. Go back to sleep, Johnny."

"No it's not – my alarm clock has gone off!" Johnny trills. "I'm gunna train the dogs – Hilda! Hilda! You can watch again. Bridie. You said I could..."

Angrily, Declan studies the alarm clock Johnny is holding. "You've altered the time haven't you?"

"Have not! Bridie told me to set it early," he says, smiling with his arms folded.

God, this kid is wide awake at 3.30 a.m.

I see Declan's body tense up and his lips purse. He kneels down to the lad's level and says in an utterly scary voice, "Go back to your room now, Johnny. If you can't get back to sleep, then read a book, and keep the noise down."

Sulkily, Johnny walks back to his room dragging his slippers on the floor. He plays noisily with his toys and talks to himself until 6.30 am. It is only later as I get up myself, that I remember that Johnny can't read. What are you supposed to do with a hyperactive 11-year-old who can't read or write? Everything I suggest lasts for about five minutes, then boredom sets in – he has no concentration or focus. After a rather testing breakfast where bad tempers seem to be the order of the day, I resort to dog training: Part 2.

"Go and hide Hilda's bone and ask her to find it," I suggest. But by 8.30 am, dog training is over, and he is bored again.

"What we doing now?" he asks. "Where are we going? I'm bored."

"I'm bored as well," says Sinead who is playing with Roger Bear and Snowy B and doesn't look bored at all.

I start to dread the long day ahead of me. I can't go to Mum's as I know the kids are too much for her. It makes me sad that after all the years she's encouraged me in my dream to be a Mum, when I eventually get there, she can't share the highs and lows with me. She's just not up to it.

Seeing the strain on my face, Declan comes to the rescue. Thankfully, as it's Saturday, he hasn't got to go to work. "How about you and me take the dogs and go for a nice long walk up to Howth?" he says to Johnny.

"Are you sure?" I whisper.

"Yes – he can muck about with the dogs; it'll tire him out."

Oh joy! No Johnny for a whole day. Just me and Sinead, and she seems like the easiest child in the world in comparison. I instantly relax and switch on the kettle for tea, and rewind Babe for Sinead to watch again. I check on her regularly during the course of the morning and after the movie, she is engrossed in playing Babe with all the toys and dolls she can find. She comes in for lunch, sleeps for an hour afterwards and insists that I put Babe on again when she wakes up, and she resumes her games. I feel slightly guilty that I'm using the TV as a babysitter, but mostly I don't care, because I have just had the best day for weeks. I've done absolutely nothing.

Johnny and Declan are back after a successful trip (or so they tell me).

"Declan gave me sweeties, and we got some stickers, and we walked all the way to that castle thing and the dogs love me!" he blurts out before he's even got his coat off.

"How was it?" I ask Declan in a quiet moment.

"Okay – we just walked and walked, and he played with the dogs. We stopped for lunch and ice cream, and just kept going. I'm knackered though, and so are the dogs," – we admire them as they lie crashed out by the fire – "so Johnny must be too. Oh, by the way Bridie, Bea phoned. She's calling in for an hour tonight. She's going to Isla's engagement party – do you remember her? The best friend from primary school?"

"Oh yeah... she's getting engaged? Bit young isn't it?"

"That's what I thought. Anyway, Bea's going to pop in and say hello, but she can't stay long. Okay with you?"

"Of course it's okay," I say, thinking, *My God, all three of them together in one room. There could be fireworks!*

Later that evening I help Johnny to re-pack his suitcase ready for when Ellen picks him up to go home tomorrow. On the one hand, I'm relieved that we'll get back to normal with Sinead who, to her credit, has taken Johnny's visit in her stride – who has in fact been a paragon of virtue – but on the other hand, I feel so sad for the little chap who has no family. Will he ever find his Forever Family?

Would you believe it, just when its time for him to go home, Bea and Johnny are bonding over music.

"Can I borrow your Walkman?" he asks Bea. "Can I listen to your music?"

"It's Prince – you won't like it."

"I do! I do like Prince."

"Whoa! You like Prince? You little freak! Can I call you Freak?" Bea asks jokingly. I'm not sure I approve at all of the way this conversation's going, but I like the way the children have become animated, now Bea's here.

"Yes, if you'll go out with me!" he says, smiling and blushing at the same time.

"Course, Freak," she says ruffling his hair.

"Cool! My first girlfriend."

"Go out with me too!" howls Sinead.

"Yeah, yeah – we'll go out too," says Bea to the little girl who has crawled onto her lap and who is pinging Bea's earrings in awe of their sparkliness.

"So why are you here, Freak?" Bea asks inquisitively. It's all I can do to stop myself from asking Bea not to call him that name, but somehow, he likes it. It's like a badge of honour for him.

"'Cos nobody wants me and I have foetal alcohol syndrome, and can't read or write. Nobody wants me." He spouts that line like it's a mantra he's learned by heart.

Bea responds as I expect. "That's so wrong! You should stay here with Mum and Dad."

"Nah, can't. Got to get back to Joyce's. She'll be wondering where I am," he says, suddenly remembering his stable current placement. "Joyce is nice, she's okay really, but it's no fun – not like here. She ain't got no pets an' we never go walking like with Declan..." his eyes look sadly towards Hilda and he goes over and strokes her gently.

Sinead, indignant that Johnny's getting all the attention again, jumps off Bea's lap and barges in front of Johnny, and roughly pats Hilda on the head, so that the dog winces and retreats under the table.

Johnny follows her and gets under the table with the dogs. "I love Hilda. She is so sweet and she's got soft ears, haven't you girl?" Hilda leans her head on his knee and he continues stroking her soft, velvety ears, wiping the tears from his eyes with the back of his hand. "I wish I had a dog – I wish you were mine..."

Bea and I exchange glances. It is the saddest thing we've ever seen. It is all I can do not to promise him the world; to say we'll be his Forever Family and Bea can be his older sister. But I know in my heart that this fragile little boy would test me to my limits and beyond. I can't give him what he needs. It breaks my heart.

10th February 1998

6.30am

Johnny is awake early again because he knows he is going home today. But, I'm awake early too. What the hell is wrong with me? Now I'm crying because Johnny is going home.

I can't bear to think of the little chap not having a proper, caring family. I want him to stay here, and suddenly feel all broody.

I don't say anything to Declan, but one look at my puffy eyes and runny nose and D says, "No Bridie, he can't stay. Let's just focus on Sinead for now. Let's give Sinead 100% eh?"

I nod and sniff.

At breakfast, we give Johnny a card that we've all signed – well, Sinead did a sticky paint hand-print – and we watch as he unwraps a black and white spaniel cuddly dog toy, the nearest thing we could get to Hilda's likeness. Johnny doesn't seem quite sure what to do with it. Bless them, Mum and Dad pop around and sweetly say, "It's been lovely to meet you, young man. Good luck." Secretly, my parents are glad he has only hours left at our house.

By midday, Ellen is here and wants chapter and verse about the placement, including a look at my diary. I focus on the good bits, and brush the bad bits under the carpet, but I do stress that Johnny has said that he would like a pet in his new forever family. Ellen assures me that they are looking for a new placement for him as soon as possible.

The time has come to say goodbye to Johnny. I'm glad that even in her obviously hung-over state, Bea has called in on her way back to college to see him off. We all wave goodbye to Johnny who looks away to hide the big salty tears that are ambushing him.

"Bye bye, Hilda, bye bye, Harry. Bye, Bea, bye, Declan, bye, Bridie. See you again," he says, like butter wouldn't melt in his mouth.

I note that he did not say goodbye to Sinead.

Chapter 19

A Bevy Of Mothers

1st March 1998

I can't say that Johnny's placement with us was a total success, but it did cement something between Sinead, Declan and me. It made us realise that even during the short time that she's been with us, we have become parental figures to her, and she has begun to open up to us. The sibling rivalry that arose when Johnny was here propelled her into our arms for comfort or reassurance, and that changed something, inexorably, for the better.

I'm not saying that everything in the garden is rosy – far from it, because the flip side of Sinead's jostle for ascendancy and associated language and emotional improvements has been a slump back into a more childlike and non-verbal state now Johnny has gone. It has made me wonder if Sinead needs brothers and sisters around her to help her development, and if that may be more successful than the one-to-one attention I can give her.

There's never a dull moment here, and today's no exception as a psychologist is visiting with Patsy, Sinead's birth mother. I know that this is going to be very disturbing for Sinead, who hasn't seen any of her extended family since before Johnny came to stay. The idea is that Patsy's mothering skills will be assessed objectively, in a stable and safe environment – our house. I feel rather disgruntled about this, because it's us who have given Sinead a semblance of normality, and Patsy who's getting the benefit from it. Ho hum. As I normally do, I fill up the kettle and make up a tea tray with a plate of biscuits. Whilst we wait for the impending visit, Sinead and I work hard on her reading. I haven't told the little girl that Patsy is coming, because I know she would go into overdrive and be totally over-excited.

Is it my imagination or is this child learning to read, like, literally overnight? Is she a genius? When she first came to us, she only had a few words in her vocabulary, like shit, fuck, dog, poo, cake, love, and later, "where's Johnny," and also, a lot of Irish words. But her use of words has improved dramatically. Yesterday, Sinead said to me, "Bridie Mummy, can I have a skipping rope?" I really hope the psychologist notices.

Dr Janet Forsyth has arrived. I did wonder what a psychologist looks like, and now I know. She's about my height with reddish auburn hair and glasses. She wears sensible shoes and a matching handbag. Her face is freckly and she wears no make up. She's not in the least bit intimidating. We sit down to discuss Sinead and Patsy's relationship.

"Do you see much of a bond between mother and daughter?" Janet asks me.

I reply that Sinead barely knows her mother, and when I have seen them together, Patsy tends to torment Sinead with negative 'No' language.

Janet nodded. "Patsy has already been assessed in my clinic and it's clear she struggles with parenting. But it's my job to watch and report back on what contact Patsy should receive after adoption."

I reel at the 'A' word. Is the SS thinking in terms of adoption? I haven't dared to think that far ahead... But before I have time to ask, Patsy arrives with her social worker. She looks much smarter than last time I saw her, and her teeth, I notice, are no longer yellow. She looks brighter – she looks like she's clean. I am vaguely alarmed by this transformation in case Patsy redeems herself as a mother too. She has brought some wax crayons but also lots of inappropriate toys for older boys, and cheap sweets aplenty. I groan, as these treats make Sinead very gassy and hyper. I just hope we don't have any more burping and farting displays – I was hoping they may be a thing of the past! Note to self: check probiotics supplement stock and order some more.

After coffee, Patsy is invited to play with Sinead as if in a normal contact situation. We withdraw enough to allow mother and child to feel relaxed, and observe their behaviour and language.

"Come here, Sinead. Hello, girl. How are you?"

Sinead seems almost shy, and remains coy and silent. Patsy attempts to hug her daughter but Sinead kicks-off and looks distressed. She elbows past Patsy and pinches her hard on the arm.

Patsy responds, "No, no, no, you little bugger!" and rubs her reddened arm. "That's not nice, Shinny – be nice to yer old Mum." Patsy tries to further impress her daughter with Haribo sweets and finger puppets. Sinead is suitably bribed – but who am I to judge? I've done much the same myself to gain the girl's affection.

I'm in the kitchen making more coffee. As I set up the tea tray I play over and over again in my head, the words, "after the adoption, after the adoption..." It becomes a chorus in my head. Would Sinead be mine or would they move her on? I panic – I still don't have confidence in myself as a mother, but I cannot lose her now.

The psychologist, Patsy and her social worker leave at last after what I consider to have been a fairly successful contact for Patsy. Sinead eventually warmed to her mother and they played quite happily for an hour or so without any dramas. I feel a little deflated, and even more so on Janet's parting shot, "It'll be nice for Sinead to see her grandmother too."

"Excuse me?" I say. "What about her Nanna?"

"Well, she's arriving any minute, isn't she? For her own contact?"

"That's the first I've heard of it," I sigh. Surely this has got to be too much for a six year-old child? Two intense contacts in one day, for goodness sake. Nanna O'Driscoll arrives with her son David and they are allowed to take Sinead to town. I feel so frustrated and jealous. However, my HF is 6/10 because the word 'adoption' has been mentioned. Whilst I await their return, I amuse myself by planning the adoption party – and then realise some time later that these flights of fancy that I'm prone to are becoming fewer and farther between.

An hour later, the wanderers return and Sinead's old defiance with it. She throws a huge tantrum when Nanna O'D and Uncle David leave, and refuses to speak to me or eat her dinner. The up-side is that she's so exhausted by the day's events that she falls asleep at the dinner table, her macaroni cheese untouched, and Declan carries her up to bed.

2nd March 1998

It's my mother's birthday. We celebrate at her home with presents, cards, flowers homemade chocolate fudge cake that Sinead and I cooked, and all the family gathered. Sinead is delighted to see the twins again, although I can't say that feeling is mutual. Mikey joins them at the kitchen table where they play 'Cheat' – a card game that takes Sinead a nanosecond to get the hang of and at which she's really good.

I wonder again if this girl is highly intelligent underneath all the emotional scars. There are gales of laughter as the game progresses and it keeps the kids occupied all afternoon.

Me, Lee and Denise sit on the sofa and chat about daft things like Lee's latest haircut – very chic – and Denise's new job at the Council. We don't mention children, childcare, or adoption at all. It seems so... normal. I feel like I've joined their 'Mum's Gang' somehow. OMG: the kids are playing, and we're drinking a glass of bubbly to celebrate Mum's birthday. How good is that?

We give Mum her birthday present which we've all chipped in for.

"Oh no, you shouldn't have," says Winifred as she opens the large shiny blue envelope. "A Pamper Session at the Spa! Next week – oh, how lovely," she says in her poshest voice. "Thank you all so much, it's just what I need."

Mum's deliriously happy with her present, and Dad repeats his oft-quoted joke that he cannot compete with Winifred's wealthy children in the presents department, as if this somehow lets him off the hook with his own rather eccentric present of a new fork and trowel for the garden.

I decide to bite the bullet and get out into the open, something that's been troubling me for a while. "So, how's the shaking Mum?" I ask.

Silence falls over the room and the tension heightens as everyone looks towards Winifred. She's either going to hit the roof and tell us to mind our own business, like she has done in the past when we enquire about her health, deny anything's wrong, or come clean. I'm glad when it turns out to be the latter.

"Well love, it's my wrists... they don't seem to work anymore and my arms are like a pair of knitting needles, they just won't bend... I don't really like to talk about it though, as your father gets upset. He keeps saying, 'Winifred if anything happened to you, I just don't know how I would cope.'"

"Well, I don't..." says Dad despondently.

"But Dad, we'll all support each other, just like we've always done," says Lee. "You're not on your own. We have to try to get to the bottom of what the problem is with Mammy – don't you agree?"

"Yes, I do. I've been worried sick, if truth be told," Dad admits. "I'm going out to feed the fish and let the dogs have a roam in the garden," he says, and slopes off, leaving the rest of us to discuss what's best for Mum.

Sinead has sidled into the room. She has an uncanny knack of knowing when people are upset, and just like she did with Murphy that first day she came to us, she tries to help. As she watches me dab my eyes with a Kleenex, she says, "Why crying Mummy Bridie?" She climbs onto my lap and we hug – and I see Lee and Denise smile at each other, as if they've longed for this scene too.

"I'm okay, sweetie. We need to get you a slide for your hair, don't we?" I say stroking her auburn locks away from her eyes, pleased that they are now nit-free and shiny. "Why don't you go and find Stanley – he's in the garden feeding the goldfish."

She laughs and goes off to find Dad. She mimics me and I think I hear some more new words. "Find Stanley feed the goldfish."

"Sinead's very bright, isn't she?" says Lee, once she's gone out of the door.

"She picks things up in a flash," I say, "she's almost too quick – sometimes her brain is like a Ferrari! In fact, she speaks so quickly I can hardly understand a word she is saying, but at least it's mostly in English now, and not Irish."

We talk to Mum about her health and she agrees that

she'll make another appointment at the GP surgery and that Lee will go with her, but not until after her Spa day. We all understand intuitively that she's saying if there's any bad news, she doesn't want to know until she's had her special day.

We leave Mum and Dad's house, and I feel a strange mixture of happiness at the whole family having been together yet tinged with sadness that Mum's facing health uncertainties. And if I'm totally honest, I'm missing that little lad Johnny. He was hard work, but his vulnerability made me love him deeply.

5th March 1998

Murphy was supposed to be coming today but he has cancelled with a bad back. Great – as usual, I didn't tell Sinead, and it leaves us free to go to pre-school, which is something I consider to be very important as, whether she's with us or not, Sinead will be going to primary school in September, and she needs all the socialising she can get.

Before we go, I put up Sinead's lovely hair into bunches tied with sparkly bands. "What a pretty girl you are," I say to her. "Perhaps you will make some new friends today?" I sincerely hope so as it would be nice to have someone to come round and play with her, or even have a sleepover.

As luck would have it, later that morning Sinead gets her first party invite. It's not until 29th April, for little Iris who will be four years old – but Sinead is invited! It worries me a bit that Sinead is so much older than her little friends at pre-school, and she can be a bit... let us say, robust – but as long as I keep a careful eye on her, all should be well.

Whilst I'm busy doing a bit of housework, the phone rings.

"Hello," I say cheerily, "Battersea dogs' home."

Edna answers but she is in a serious mood. "Bridie, there's a problem. Can I come to visit you, today?"

She takes me by surprise. "Oh? Okay... Sinead's asleep. Can you come now?"

I tidy up the house and leave Sinead's achievements dotted around the place: potato print pictures, the party invite, her reading books, the hand prints from Johnny. Shortly after, Edna arrives looking flustered and... what? Upset?

"Tea?" I say.

"No, not today." She swallows and clears her throat, and I feel a flutter of anxiety in my guts. "It's about Sinead. I'm sorry, Bridie, but I think we are going to have to review the case and possibly move her on. She is getting too attached to you, and we are worried that we may not be able to get you an adoption order. We can't have her getting close to you if she's eventually got to leave."

I freeze and then the shock registers.

"Oh, no, no!" I sob. I knew it was all too good to be true. My life is shattered, and I feel drained and distraught. "But Edna, she's doing so well here. She's happy. Her speech is so much better, and she's stopped having so many tantrums. She's safe here – she's okay here. She can read a few words now, and she is nearly out of nappies you know. Did you know that?"

"I know how sad this is for you, Bridie, but it may be for the best in the end. It may not be such a good idea after all to place her with a local family, as there will always be the birth family connections to deal with..."

"But I don't mind that, Edna..."

Edna excuses herself and pops to the toilet.

Calm, breathe, focus. I say these words to myself, but already I can feel myself losing control. Sinead is slipping away from me. Why is life so painful? How on earth can I say goodbye to that vulnerable little girl? I could hardly manage to say goodbye to Johnny and that was only after a few days of caring for him. How could they move Sinead on after we had bonded so well? How could they do that to her? But then, I knew this would happen, didn't I? This is what fostering is all about – as usual, I've been jumping the gun and thinking of adoption, but this is just my first fostering placement and Sinead, is just my first foster child.

At this point Sinead calls out from her bedroom upstairs, "Mummy Bridie, can I have Teletubbies on now?"

As Edna comes back into the room, she looks annoyed. "You are not letting her call you Mummy are you? Oh, Bridie, that's the first rule of fostering – that they don't call you Mummy..." she shook her head and stared at me.

"I know, but she just started calling me Mummy Bridie and, and... it just felt so nice..."

"Look, I know what a fantastic job you have done with Sinead, but this is a very difficult case and we are concerned that you two are getting too close. We have to make decisions in the best longer-term interests for Sinead, and if we can't get an adoption order, and she goes back to Margaret or Patsy, what then? The separation from you further down the line will be painful for you both."

"But it will be painful now," I wail. I pathetically start to weep again.

Sinead who has trotted downstairs looking sleepy and cute is worried. "Why cry again? Don't cry Mummy Bridie."

Edna leaves, telling me that nothing has been decided definitely about Sinead's future, and that I will be informed of their decision in three weeks or so. In the meantime Sinead must not call me Mummy.

6th March 1998

I am devastated and shell-shocked, and you know what, so is
Declan. We discussed Edna's visit and in the cold light of day,
we can see that the SS are only trying to do the right thing
for Sinead as they see it. But as we see it, she should stay
with us, where we can give her love and a safe, stable home.
I cry every time I look at Sinead, and she has picked up on
my emotional state because she is now starting to have her
old meltdowns again. I feel I can't cope with the horrendous
countdown to D-Day. I question why I ever started this
fostering lark. I should've known it would be painful. Didn't
they say in the training that we shouldn't get too attached
to our foster-children...? I suppose my overwhelming desire
to have children of my own just trumps everything. One shot
at motherhood – even as a foster-mother – and I'm already
putting her through university and planning what to get her
for her 21st birthday. It's all my fault... I'm too needy...

Happiness factor 0 /10. Meltdowns 7: Sinead 3, Bridie 4.
I wish I was dead. I hate those bloody social workers. I resort
to the old, needy Bridie, and ring around everybody and
behave like a victim. Only Lee puts me straight: "Bridie, this is
what fostering is all about. You knew all along you were only
fostering her, not adopting her. Channel your energy into
an adoption course, then maybe you will be able to adopt
properly at a later date. Use your brain for God's sake – you
are too emotional right now. You need to be in control. Bridie,
remember the phoenix and rise up again."

Declan, bless him, is as upset as I am (and there's me
thinking he wasn't 100% with the fostering idea). "I don't
know what the hell they are playing at, Bridie. The child is
happy with you."

I mention what Edna said about us living too close to

Sinead's real family – her birth family.

""Hmm…" he says stroking his chin, "that is a fair point though, don't you think? I mean, they're a colourful family to say the least, aren't they? But you know what Bridie? For every problem there's a solution. We could always move house. I could relocate to a rural surgery in Wicklow or bloody Dingle for that matter."

I love him.

14th March 1998

We have taken Lee's advice and Declan and I have been accepted on an adoption course in Dublin. It seems like a step in the right direction, but I am filled with despair that it may not be Sinead who we're adopting. It was so, so hard to correct her this morning when she called me 'Mummy Bridie'.

"Just call me Bridie, sweetie," I say.

"Why?"

"Ummm… because it's my name. It's a nice name, don't you think?"

"Is Sinead a nice name, Mu… Bridie?"

"I think Sinead is the best name ever."

I am going mad. Margaret is now asking for a report on her parenting skills; she's probably had a set-to with Patsy and found out Patsy's been here with Dr Forsyth. Oh, for God's sake, I really don't need this. Like Patsy, she is allowed her own social worker and a psychiatrist to report on her attachment to Sinead.

I get a phone call from Margaret.

"Ello Broidie, alroight? Did ya know tha my barrister is

gunna 'elp me get my Sinead back? I get assessed in your 'ouse."

"We'll see about that Margaret. I'm not giving her up without a fight," I say and gobsmack myself. I've been feeling like a doormat in all of this, but when push comes to shove, I can fight like a bloody lioness. If the Social Services think that woman is a better mother than me, then I will prove them wrong.

Later, over a cup of tea at my parents' house, Dad says from behind one of his newspapers, "Bridie love, don't you think Sinead's acting a bit differently? I notice that she doesn't look me in the eye very often any more and sometimes when she talks, it's like half the time its almost robotic..."

I am defensive. "No, she's alight. It's just all this fostering business Dad. She knows something's going on – God knows all her relatives descending constantly isn't helping – and she's just withdrawing, bless her. Actually, she has a fantastic vocabulary compared to what she was like when she first came here – don't you remember? I know the tantrums are bad at the moment, but that's just because she is confused."

"Hmm... – I'm just saying, that's all."

Sirens ring in my head but I silence them quickly.

18th March 1998

I prepare the house for the psychiatrist and Margaret's visit. I am in a daze, my life is in turmoil but I will cope, I have to. Eventually, the psychiatrist arrives – a different one this time – and I observe her perhaps like she observes other people. She is very overweight with a severe blond perm. She wears expensive chunky jewellery and she is Scottish and incredibly loud.

"Pleased to meet you. I am Heather Innis," she holds out her hand and smiles at us.

I offer the customary tea and biscuits, and she asks for Earl Grey with a slice of lemon. Pish posh as Bea would say. Declan who has insisted on taking the afternoon off work to support me, takes an immediate liking to her and the two of them sit with their tea and biscuits gabbling on about the state of farming in Scotland, for some obscure reason. It turns out her father is an organic farmer.

Shortly after, Margaret arrives, minus baby, with her social worker, and Sinead goes into overdrive.

"Magga, Magga! Magga here!" and Sinead runs into her arms. I get an overwhelming urge to prise them apart, but recognise too that Sinead is not this loving to anyone else, even me.

"Oh goodness me yes, I must focus..." says Heather, scrabbling around for her notebook and clipboard. She sprang into action. "If I could see you, Bridie, with Sinead," she said starting up a fresh page of writing.

"Wha...?" says Margaret, "'s my time with Shinny."

"Just for a moment, Margaret," says Heather. "Please join me on the sofa."

Margaret reluctantly does as she's told, but Sinead does not respond much to me, although she does keep eye contact with Declan and a big bouncy ball he has suddenly acquired.

"Okay. Thank you, Bridie. Now, Margaret let me see you and Sinead for half an hour please."

Margaret plays up to Sinead with cuddles and sweets and she responds, "Love you, Magga. Where Bobby? Can I see him at your house?"

"Erm... who is Bobby?" asks Heather.

"Sinead's imaginary friend," I say.

The psychiatrist scribbles down notes furiously and nods

her head approvingly. Then it is my turn again. I am asked to play a game with Sinead. God, it feels like I am acting in some ghastly competition.

"Hmm... Bridie why don't you try to bond with her a bit more? Develop some rapport... Allow her to sit on your knee for example – give her a cuddle. She has missed out on physical contact in many ways."

"But we were told by the social workers not to show too much affection or physical contact."

"Oh, what tosh. I suppose it explains why she has not bonded with you that much..."

To be honest, I don't know whether to be mortified or relieved. If she hasn't bonded with me that much, then perhaps they won't revoke the foster placement, but on the other hand, does that make me a bad foster mother?

The afternoon drags on interminably, and to me, it's obvious that Margaret is the one who has all the rapport with Sinead. But just as it's time for them to leave, something happens that gives me a shred of hope. As Margaret puts her coat on, Sinead comes over to me, holds my hand and says, "Bye bye Magga, see you next time." No tantrums, no shrieking, just a calm acceptance that Margaret is leaving. Surely Heather can see that the child is settled here, at the very least.

At last they've gone and Declan rushes off to walk the dogs before it gets dark. Sinead is on the sofa with Roger Bear and Snowy B watching her beloved Teletubbies, which, to be honest I'm trying to wean her off. I'd rather she watched Babe, because at least they talk properly in that film, but she just loves the Tubbies and after such a traumatic day, I think she deserves it.

After I've settled Sinead, cleared up the tea things and washed the dishes, I notice that Heather has left her notebook on the hall table. She must've left it there when she was putting her coat on. I seize it and read it, knowing that what I'm reading is confidential, and tears of anger and sadness spring to my eyes. I hate her, the stupid bitch. 'Sinead has bonded well with Margaret, and there is great attachment. I feel that Margaret could be a 'good enough' parent. Mr Kelly has an easy way with Sinead; the two of them seem quite close. Bridie is rather stiff and formal with Sinead, almost as if she is afraid of getting too close.' Aghh, the traitor, the turncoat, the hypocrite! Wasn't it the bloody specialists who told us not to get too close in the first place? Not to go in the bathroom with them, not to get too attached. I do as I'm told and they throw it back in my face. I sling the notebook across the kitchen in a fit of temper, just as D returns with the dogs.

He picks up the pad and reads Heather's notes. "Silly cow," he says and comes over and gives me a hug. "If all else fails, Bridie, we still have each other," he says.

Out of nowhere, I remember something I read in one of my many self-help books. 'I will rejoice and meet all challenges with open arms.' That and a cup of tea help me to regain my composure somewhat.

At seven o'clock, Heather returns rather shame-facedly, for her notebook. "Silly me," she says," I hope you haven't read it!"

"What do you think?" I reply, hand her the book and shut the door in her face.

Chapter 20

Gobsmacked

23rd March 1998

The adoption course starts this evening, and whilst I am not exactly full of hope, it does give me something else to focus on apart from the situation with Sinead. I know Sinead has noticed that I am not so close anymore. I think she feels abandoned yet again. Yesterday she had a major meltdown during which she jumped on me from behind and yanked my hair. The pain was excruciating and sadly, I actually felt quite scared of her. It made me think of the Bertha Mason character in Jane Eyre! I try to explain to Sinead as best I can what is happening, but I don't think she understands. She's just getting more and more confused. Her latest little ramble to herself is, "Stay here go Magga's". It breaks my heart. I feel like my journey with Sinead is nearly complete and that soon, she will be gone. This is how foster carers the world over must feel. I am most worried about where Sinead will end up and what horrors she might witness.

I think about Dad's observations. Is there something wrong with Sinead? Are her development problems more than merely circumstantial? I am still pondering these unknowables when the phone rings.

It is Sinead's Guardian Ad Litem, Pauline. "Hello, Bridie, I have some news for you."

"Right..." I say, bracing myself.

"At the team meeting yesterday it was decided that it is in Sinead's best interests to remain with you and Mr Kelly as her foster carers for the foreseeable future."

My mind is reeling... but what about Heather's mean report? What about Sinead's family being local and all the safety issues that ensue? What about her not bonding with me...? But all I can squeeze out is, "Do you mean it? That she can stay?"

"Yes, Bridie."

I was on cloud nine, I was floating on air, I was high as a helium balloon. Sinead can stay! Sinead can stay...

Pauline went on, "It might be a good idea to change your phone number, just so that Sinead's family can't keep constantly ringing, and I'd advise you to get an email account if you can..."

"Pauline, I, I can't take all this in right now," I stammer. "Can we talk again tomorrow and do all the finer details then?"

"Of course, Bridie – enjoy your day!" says Pauline, and rings off.

Right on cue, Sinead wanders out of her bedroom where she's been playing 'Caravans' with her toys, and stumbles downstairs saying, "I'm hungry, want food now."

"Okay sweetie," I say, "Mummy Bridie will get you some pizza as a special treat. How about that!"

"Don't say Mummy Bridie!" says Sinead sullenly.

"I think it's okay to say Mummy Bridie now, Sinead," I say and give her a hug, desperate as I am to improve my bonding with her.

"No! Off Bridie. Pasta."

"Okay, you can have pasta," I say, shaken by the way she vehemently pushes me away. "What's the magic word, Sinead?"

"Shit."

Suddenly anxiety takes over. Now that I get what I want,

I'm full of concerns. Sinead will be okay won't she? I won't be scared of her as a teenager, will I? No, no NO!! Christ, maybe – she scares the hell out of me sometimes even now, and she's not even six...It'll be okay, it'll be okay. She just needs watertight boundaries.

I pull myself together, make lunch, and ring Declan.

"Well, let's hope they don't change their minds, Bridie," he says in a non-committal whisper.

"Why would they do that? And why are you whispering? She's obviously better off with us than Mad Margaret. And once we've done the adoption course, we can set the ball in motion to adopt her."

"One step at a time, darling," he says, which really bloody annoys me. What does he think I've been doing all my life? I ring off and instead, do a mini-ring round just to close family, to tell them our news. To be honest, they all seem to be a bit bored with the whole thing.

Rather than celebrate the good news that Sinead's foster placement is secure with us for the time being, that night we attend our first adoption course. There are seven couples aged between about 25 and 50 years of age, making Declan feel a little more comfortable about his age. He immediately latches onto a couple beside him who are farmers and adopting for the first time.

Edna is running the show tonight and she's asking everybody to stand up and introduce themselves. Ughh... Don't you just hate these courses?

It was my turn. "Hello, I'm Bridie Kelly and this is my husband Declan. We have a grown-up daughter Bea who's at college in Cork, and two dogs. I was worried about going through IVF, so we decided to foster or adopt."

Edna beamed at me and said, "Thank you, Bridie."

Another lady stands up. "Hi, I am Carol and I would like to foster now my own children have left home." A single man stands up and shocks Declan by saying, "Hi, I'm Paul and I'm a Youth Worker. As a single parent, I am looking to foster a toddler to keep my 13 year old company." Another couple aged about 30 who have had seven rounds of IVF have now run out of money. They tell us their story. "We just so much wanted a family of our own, but it's not going to happen. We are spiritually and financially broke." I added a silent, "hear hear" to their story. Then there is a lesbian couple who want to adopt a group of three children to try and give them a better life. Declan whispers something about not being sure if lesbians adopting is a good idea. I kick him hard under the table and accuse him of being a bigot. "What about Polly and Pippa? They have a child together and that was not exactly conventional was it?" I hiss. Declan nods his head submissively. "Yes, but they had to go to England to do it – they couldn't do it here in Ireland."

Declan is looking at his watch and visibly wondering how much longer before this is over.

24th March 1998

It's another of Mad Margaret's contact days – but at least this morning, it's just her and the social worker, and there are no charades in front of psychiatrists about who loves whom most.

"That psychiatrist lady says I am doing okay, y'know," she says. "There's a good bond between me and Shinny she sez. Shins should be back home with her family in Dublin not here, in this posh 'ouse," she said pointing angrily around my sitting room.

I gaze at her haggard face and see again the hardship and

pain she has endured. I don't know if she's breast-feeding Branna, but she sure as hell looks drained of all energy. She must really love Sinead to be putting herself to all this extra hassle. The thought unsettles me somewhat, despite our recent good news.

She goes on, "My barrister sez that I can go to the High Court to get Sinead back – I can get 'elp from the Legal Aid Board, see."

As gently as I can, I say, "Margaret, the Social Services want Sinead to stay with us, for the foreseeable future. This is her home now."

"Not feckin' likely! She belongs with us. She's not from your sort of posh family – she won't fit in," she roars as she squares up to me.

I look at her wearily – it's all too much. I blink back the tears. Why oh why is everything such a fight? Getting rid of Barren Bridie has been such an uphill battle.

But perhaps Margaret in turn has seen my pain because she says, "Any rate, no use fightin' you. T'int you I need to fight."

Over a cup of coffee and a cigarette, Margaret starts to describe her home life. "Sure, I don't even have a washing machine. I've eight kids of me own plus Sinead if she comes back, and no partner – it is hard," she said thoughtfully, "but as long as I get my little Sinead back, I don't care. They all miss her – she's special to us." With that she took out Sinead's soft zebra toy that she's bought with her and stares at it as tears form in her eyes.

Sinead has wandered into the kitchen from the sitting room where she's been playing with the social worker. It does occur to me that Margaret's not doing much bonding today.

"Sinead, pass a biscuit to Magga, would you," I say, suddenly witnessing Sinead's concern at Margaret's sombre mood. Margaret takes a bite out of the biscuit but not before dunking it for several seconds into her strong tea.

"Magga's got no teeth Sinead, look," and she shows Sinead a worn set of dentures. I feel instantly repulsed but it lightens the moment.

"Erugh, wat's that?" says Sinead, pointing at the dentures. We all laugh and then I withdraw so that Margaret and Sinead can spend some quiet time together. I vow to make sure Sinead uses dental floss, interdental brushes and an electric toothbrush. Furthermore I will insist on a savoury diet, with fizzy drinks only on special occasions. I've got a thing about good teeth.

"Roight then me darlin', Magga's gotta go. See youz layter!"

Once again, to my relief, Sinead stands by my side and waves goodbye to Magga without making a song and dance about it.

Sinead also has a visit with the paediatrician today. They will assess her physical and cognitive abilities over two gruelling hours. The paediatrician is pleased with Sinead's physical development but a little worried about her unusual behaviour, and also, Bobby.

"So, Bridie, what do you notice most about Sinead?"

I breathe and then let out a long sigh. "Well, I love her to bits, but she can be such a handful. She is defiant and often angry, but I am imagining that the fostering is taking its toll on her. She talks really fast and sometimes repeats herself a lot, and when she gets stressed, she reverts to the use of Irish words. She talks to her imaginary friend Bobby everywhere, even on the toilet. If I ask her to brush her hair or get dressed – well, it's a minefield and I never really know how she's going to react. She does eat and sleep really well though."

The paediatrician let's out a "Hmmm..." and studies his notes. "Of course, you know that both birth parents have learning difficulties? We do not know how that will manifest itself in the future for Sinead, but she seems very bright and alert. Are you aware that invisible friends may be associated with Asperger's Syndrome? And from what you have told me about her moods, aggression and difficulty socialising, we may be looking at a child very high on the spectrum. Her hearing test is fine though. A report will be sent to Barry and the Guardian Ad Litem, and I'm sure they'll share it with you in due course.

So, Sinead could have Asperger's Syndrome. What the hell does that mean? I must ask Declan about it; see if he's heard of it.

The phone rings, and it's Margaret. My heart sinks, but totally out of the blue, Margaret tells me that she is not now going to fight me in court for Sinead. To use a phrase my mother hates, I am gobsmacked.

"I see Shinny's 'appy with you, sure I do. God love her. I miss her but she should stay with you. An' I got my Branna to look after now – I got me own troubles..."

Quite what caused this change of heart I don't know.

"Thank you, Margaret," is all I can say.

"See youz around Broidy."

29th April 1998

Declan's knowledge of Asperger's Syndrome is fairly rudimentary. He is of the opinion that it is just another label that psychiatrists like to give to people who don't behave according to social norms. He doesn't believe children should be labeled with syndromes, because he thinks it makes it harder for them in later life. He has a point. Nonetheless, I have ordered a book from the library about the subject.

Edna has called and given me a rather stern talking to. "You do realise that if you do succeed in adopting Sinead – and that's by no means a foregone conclusion even though the fostering placement is secure – it will be in yours and her best interests not to go into Dublin; evidence is emerging that Sinead may have been in the company of various drug dealers there in the past. Therefore, it is crucial that you keep her away from Dublin until she is 18 at least."

Bloody hell.

"Well, Declan did talk about the possibility of us moving to the country, so if things get difficult in that respect, it's something we're prepared to do for Sinead's sake." I refuse to be daunted by Edna.

As I show Edna to the door, she turns and says, "By the way, Bridie, I thought you'd like to know that we have found a forever family for Johnny. Apparently, although it's very early days, it's all going very well so far. I just want to personally say thanks for what you did for him – he mentions you a lot and he raves over the photos you sent him. He asked me to say hello to you all."

OMG! I feel so happy for Johnny! That's such great news. And I also feel a fleeting moment of pride that between us – me, Declan and Sinead – we succeeded with a difficult foster placement. My Happiness Factor is momentarily 10/10.

Later in the afternoon I drop Sinead off at Iris' house to celebrate her 4th birthday party. I am anxious about leaving Sinead on her own for the fist time, but Edna has reassured me that it is fine, that it's just for an hour or so and that Sinead needs to be able to find her feet in these kinds of situations, especially as she'll be going to school soon. I am a bag of nerves and so is Sinead. She clings to me as I turn to leave, and I fear a tantrum is about to erupt, but a little boy called Declan, funnily enough, tugs her sleeve and says, "Come and play on the trampoline," and that's it. She's gone.

I resolve to drive home, have a cup of tea and a hoover around the house, and come straight back. 45 minutes max.

As I get home, Lee's car is in the driveway – it's very unusual for Lee to visit during the day as she's usually at work. I see her sitting in the spring sunshine on the garden bench, and go and join her.

"Hey, Lee..." I say, but then notice she's crying. "Oh my God... what's wrong?" Lee never cries.

"It's Mum, Bridie. She's got Parkinson's Disease..."

"Oh God, oh no..." We hug each other and sob noisily.

"How did she take it? How's Dad?"

"I think they both knew, to be honest. They seemed to take it in their stride. The doctor said it's very early stages and that with the right medication, they might be able to keep it under control for a few years before it really takes hold. But there's no cure, Bridie. She's not going to get better..."

"You know, Declan tried to talk to me about Parkinson's Disease only a week or two ago. I think he'd realised too. I told him not to be so negative and that just because he was a GP there was no need to see the worst in every situation."

"Ah well, he's a good man your Declan..."

"What do we do now, Lee?"

"We just keep everything as normal as possible. We make sure she takes her medication and we keep an eye on her, but for now, we act as if nothing's changed. We'll take one day at a time, and we'll face whatever happens in the future, as a family."

I hug my big sister, and we talk about our love of our parents, and reminisce about our childhoods.

"Oh shit! I have to go and pick up Sinead. I'll call round to Mum's on the way home. Thanks for coming, Lee," I say, and jump in the car to get back to the party.

I needn't have worried about Sinead. She was definitely King of the Castle in every respect, and was lording-it over the bouncy castle as I entered Iris' garden. She'd got all the children to queue up in a line, and then one by one, to jump onto the castle and bounce over her; they all seemed to find it hilarious. Despite the bad news about Mum, this scene raised my spirits, and I joined the other Mums in the kitchen, where we kept one eye on the children and the other on our waistlines, as we gorged on left-over birthday cake, jam sandwiches and fizzy drinks.

Chapter 21

An Unfortunate Encounter

1st July 1998

I am allowed to enroll Sinead in the local school and playgroup. I feel giddy with excitement and am determined that Sinead will grow up with a good education and a social conscience – it's not going to be all private schools and ponies. Far from it. In fact, I think when me and Sinead go into Dublin today to pick up Mum's dry-cleaning, we'll go and donate some food items and a few coins to some of the homeless people on O'Connell Bridge – I want Sinead to understand that we can always try to help those worse off than ourselves.

I know we've been advised only to go to Dublin if absolutely necessary to avoid any unforeseen encounters with those who have known Sinead in the past – but my Mum is ill and I consider helping her out to be a priority right now.

When we get into town, I pretend that Sinead is my daughter – well she nearly is – and I practice some of the assertive stuff I've read in the parenting books.

"Sinead, I need you to stop pulling on the wrist strap now," I say. I point to various things that we can see: the big bridge, the buses, the River Liffey, boats, families, birds... I'm doing my best to improve Sinead's vocabulary and I'm enjoying myself.

Sinead is suddenly fascinated by somebody curled-up fast asleep on the pavement. In fact she is staring at him.

Oh... now he is standing up and swaying.

"Got any spare change, Mrs?" he says with tired, sunken eyes. Sinead dutifully puts a few coins into the navy woollen beret at his feet. She claps and smiles as she stares at the gentleman.

Suddenly I freeze, and my mouth goes dry. Christ, it's Murphy, Sinead's father. No wonder Sinead is staring at him – she has half-recognised her birth father, filthy and fast asleep on O'Connell Bridge.

Panic sets in – what to do? Too late... the damage is done. Murphy has suddenly come alive; he is standing up straight and trying not to sway.

"That's my... my... is it? Yes, it's SINEAD! Sinead innit! Jesus, on me fuckin' life!" he says triumphantly, looking at his daughter.

I have to respect Sinead's feelings and I have no problem with Murphy really – he is Sinead's birth father after all – but I had no idea he was so down-and-out. I knew he was a musician and that he'd recently become homeless, but the truth is harder to bear. The man is destitute.

"It's Murphy isn't it?" I say calmly, though I would recognise those tattoos anywhere.

"Tha's right, tha's right, Mrs," he says, and with that he smiles a rather crooked smile, more of a grimace really, and beckons a bunch of his mates over from the other side of the bridge, to come and meet his 'dorrta'.

"Tha's my kid, my dorrta Sinead," he says as they totter over. "I love yas, Shinny."

"Get on..." says one of the men with thick blonde dreadlocks and a kind, ruddy face. "How are youz, Sinead?" he says. "It's me, Raz – do you remember me? I remember you as a little kiddy in the Family Centre. You was there with my Jimmy but they fuckin' took him an' all..." Sinead stares at all these familiar faces, but she does catch hold of my hand, which touches my heart. Meanwhile, I'm desperately trying to think of an exit strategy.

A scary-looking red-haired female with masses of piercings and tattoos eyes me up and down sharply. It looks like she is Murphy's girlfriend. She pauses to swig from her can of cheap lager and takes a puff from her rollie. There follows a loud, phlegmy sniff.

"Murphy, if that's your dorrta, sure, why's she not with us now? Feckin' social workers, I hate 'em. They bloody took her away did they not? For no reason. No, she's ours, right?" I could tell she was out of her head drunk, as she drew on her rollie again and violently spat at us.

Sinead started crying. "Scared Mummy Bridie. Don't like it. Want to go home, see the dogs. See Hilda, see Harry."

"Get away from us, please," I say to the scary woman as she inches towards Sinead and me.

"Feck you, and your entire family!" the woman spits at me, as she turns back to rejoin her friends on the other side of the bridge. I expect she's a friend of Margaret's, and she'll report back that Sinead was in town. This is exactly why the social services told me not to take her into Dublin – but did I listen? I chastise myself silently.

"Take care, Murphy," I say, feeling stunned by the pierced woman's vitriol.

"Look after 'er Mrs," he says, stumbling towards Sinead as if he's going to give her a hug. She instinctively clasps my leg, and I wonder if she knows that he's had a bit to drink. "She's my dorrta she is..." he says, and with that he smiles his feeble, crooked smile and waves his hand childishly and then he looks me in the eye and says, "Thank you, Bridie. Thank you."

He obviously knows who I am and that Sinead is safe with us. My heart goes out to the poor man.

Suddenly, Sinead changes her tune. "Want to stay here with Dad," she says.

"No we can't do that today, sweetie," I say. "Are you hungry?"

My distraction tactics, so hard-learned, are successful. Thank God for Sinead's wonderful appetite.

"M'ungry," she says and I usher her into Bewleys, just down the street, for a milk shake and a piece of chocolate cake – food that I hope will distract her from the tragic memory of meeting her down-and-out father on the bridge.

"But where's my Da? Want him to come here. Get him a drink, Mummy Bridie," she whines.

I know exactly the sort of drink Murphy would like and it's not going to be a milkshake.

"Maybe we'll see your Dad another day, Sinead," I say, thinking to myself how love is blind. Not for a minute does it occur to me that I am also suffering from the delusion.

7th September 1998

Somehow, and I can't work out how, both Murphy and Patsy have got hold of our new telephone number. Now Patsy keeps phoning me and hanging up – I know it's her because our phone has one of the new caller display functions. Yup, this is beginning to feel like stalker territory.

After the fourth call, Patsy plucks up the courage to say what it is she's been trying to say. "Bridie, I's pregnant again."

Oh for fuck's sake – they're all at it. I don't know how to help her, or even why she's telling me this. I ask if she's okay and if she's been to see a doctor. She answers yes to both questions then rings off abruptly. I decide to ring Edna because, well, what else can I do? Edna sighs, as if this is just going to add a whole new dimension to her workload, and says she's not surprised.

10th September 1998

We are still going through the interminable bureaucracy of fostering Sinead. It is a never-ending series of meetings, phone calls, form-filling and box-ticking. Today we are due at a meeting to discuss Sinead's safety now she has a permanent foster placement with us. Declan and I arrive at the Family Centre, to find the Guardian Ad Litem, Pauline, and Edna already in the meeting room, sitting there stony-faced.

"We are here to discuss the implications of Sinead being fostered locally and we need you to sign a form and agree not to allow Sinead to go into Dublin city centre unaccompanied."

"Of course not – she'd always be with us. We wouldn't let her go anywhere on her own, not at her age," I say, confused.

"Sorry Bridie – when we say 'unaccompanied' we mean unaccompanied by anyone who is not registered as her legal carer. So for example, she must not go into the city centre with Declan's daughter Bea, or with your parents."

"I see... But, what if there's a school trip to the theatre?" asks Declan.

"Well, if she is supervised, then that may be acceptable, but you will need to register her visit with us in advance."

"So, we can go to the out of town shopping centres and the spa and coast?" I ask.

"Yes Bridie – just not the city centre unaccompanied. Will this be a problem for you?"

"No, no," I say quickly. "Where's the form?"

Edna goes on, "Your phone number needs to be changed – ideally your address too, but we can't do much about that now can we?" she jokes.

"We've already changed the numbers once," moans Declan.

"You did it too soon, Mr Kelly. You should've waited for us to give you the go-ahead. Our administration staff didn't realise your change of number was for the purposes of anonymity."

"Well that explains the ongoing calls from the Rileys then," I comment exasperatedly.

"Do you feel you can keep her safe? If not, now is the time to say," Edna asks, looking at us earnestly.

"We love Sinead," I say. "We can keep her safe. If push came to shove, we would move house to keep her safe." I dab my eyes with a tissue. How much more can we take of this endless questioning and soul-searching?

The Guardian ad Litem is stoical. "It's just that it's much better to be honest and say it now, rather than that the placement breaks down in say a years' time. This child is going to be a challenge to you both. Please take some time to think about it, discuss it together and give me a call in two days time to confirm your willingness to go ahead. Here is my mobile number. And please get those phone numbers changed again," she jokes "or you will have Patsy, Murphy and the new baby moving in."

Chapter 22

Saying Goodbye

1st October 1998

We are now into the routine of school, which Sinead loves one day, and refuses to go to the next. Her teacher, Mrs Allerton tells me she is fitting in very well, but that she needs to work hard on her reading and writing to catch up with the others, and that she sometimes gets a bit boisterous with the other children. I read that as a euphemism for aggressive, but Mrs Allerton's too kind to say so.

I'm planning a special party for her on 19th December, which is her seventh birthday. It seems like a long way away, but time flies, and I want it to be special. Note to self: Ask Mrs Allerton who her best friends are and invite them to the party. I'd like to give her a middle name on her birthday too. A name we've chosen for her: something that's hers, from us.

Also, I must make damn sure she doesn't give everybody nits because my mother's insisting that she caught them from Sinead now. I was sure she was nit-free, but the buggers keep coming back. Mum says she's not coming around our house any more!

3rd October 1998

We have a nice quiet day playing with Sinead and walking the dogs, visiting Mum and Dad on the way home. Sinead is now devoted to my father who insists that she is, "coming on," but to be honest, she's still a real handful. I watch them hug each other lovingly and then they proceed to feed Granddad's fish in the pond at the top of the garden. It's frowned upon by the SS to call foster-relatives 'Auntie' and 'Granddad' but I have encouraged it with Sinead. I think it's partly my need to have a normal family, and partly because I'm sure in my bones that Sinead will be with us forever – so what's the problem?

"Yes, you sprinkle the pellets and then they come up to feed. Watch... here they are!"

Sinead screams with delight. "Granddad! Do it again, more feed. Granddad look at this one – argh that's Creamy! He's happy arrgh!"

"Now then, Sinead, come along – let's do some growing," says my lovely Dad. "Put these little cress seeds in the greenhouse and then you can eat them for your tea in a few days time."

Sinead clumsily spreads the seeds into the compost making "ahh oooee" noises. "Yummy! Eat them!"

I relax with Mum on the patio and watch the two of them: Sinead, my foster-daughter and her Granddad. Bless them. They actually get on well for a short space of time. Sometimes Dad will get a little annoyed: "No, please don't throw stones in pond Sinead, there's a good girl."

Sinead always responds badly to negative statements such as this. In my experience it's better to turn it around to a positive statement, which is certainly not always easy.

"How's the old Parkinson's Mum?" I ask.

"Oh, it's gone! Those doctors are all wrong –I think its getting better unlike the nits!" she says scowling as she scratches her fine grey newly set hair. "I mean it, Bridie, I will charge you if this hairstyle is ruined by all this wretched nit combing!"

Poor Mum. She's in denial about her diagnosis, which is understandable, but as for the nits – Jesus, Mary and Joseph – when am I ever going to get the better of them?

4th October 1998

Sinead's drawn a picture for Granddad. It looks like a big orange fish but Sinead insists that it is a picture of "Mummy Bridie".

A letter came in the post today informing us of the court hearing to rubber-stamp our foster placement. I recall the adoption course we did, and wonder whether it was just a waste of time. After all my fuss over these official-looking letters when we first started fostering, this one barely passes muster. It's a formality. Nothing more.

That evening, my lovely Dad brings round a surprise for Sinead. He has brought her a rabbit. It's a huge great thing with long floppy ears.

"My rabbit, mine!" Sinead says, immediately clasping the poor thing to her chest.

"Be gentle with him, Sinead," says my Dad. "What do you want to call him?"

"Bobby!" says Sinead.

I am about to say that might get confusing, but then think better of it. If she calls her rabbit Bobby, maybe the other invisible Bobby will begin to disappear and she can talk to this real Bobby instead.

7th October 1998

We have a bit of a worrying day because my Dad's been

feeling ill with indigestion and pain. Sinead's upset as we can't call round there after school and feed the fish, and Declan seems rather concerned when he speaks to Dad later on the phone. "Stanley, go and see your doctor – you can't take any chances at your age."

"It's nothing," my Dad says, "just a touch of heartburn." We try in vain to persuade my father to visit the doctor but he refuses saying his new doctor doesn't listen, but merely produces a prescription pad and tries to put him on drugs which he knows will have even worse side effects.

8th October 1998

I am trying to arrange for Sinead to make some friends. The twins get on well with her now, but there's such an age gap that they don't really want to come round much, and the children at the school seem reluctant to visit, even though we ask often enough. Sometimes in the playground, parents will turn away from me and make subtle remarks about spoiled children and too much money. This upsets me a bit because, whilst we're not short of a bob or two, we're not exactly rich. Declan's worked so hard – he has a strong work ethic, that's all.

The other day Sinead asked me rather sadly, "Mummy Bridie, why don't people like me? Mia don't come round to play."

I replied jokingly, "Don't worry, Sinead – I love you, and Declan loves you, and all the family loves you and Bobby the rabbit luuuurves you!" (To be honest that is a lie. Bobby hates her and lopes back into his hutch whenever she approaches – I think it was that day she tried to teach him to sit and lie down!)

But her question does worry me. Why can't she make friends? She's a tomboy and can get overly bossy, but she's not a bully, I'm sure of it. Perhaps her birthday party will encourage a few friends and maybe once she has the security of knowing that she is a 'forever child' her aggression and moods will start to dissipate?

I ring Edna who pops round for tea and cake.

"You look a bit stressed, Bridie – what's the matter? I thought you would be settling down to fostering by now?"

"Oh I am! I'm really happy. It's just that nobody wants to play with Sinead, and it's upsetting her. They all find her too quirky and bossy. Actually, Edna, I want to tell you about something she did the other day... She went to the toilet in the downstairs loo, and she smeared poo on the walls... That's not good, is it? And she quite often goes outside to do a wee in the dog kennel. Then yesterday, I caught her stuffing herself with raw sausage and when I tried to take it away from her, she actually snarled at me..."

Edna looks thoughtful and nods her head making "hmmm oh dear" noises.

Before I know what's happening, I dissolve into tears and reach for the box of Kleenex. I hadn't realised how worried I've been about all this – I've just buried it in my subconscious because God knows, I can't start moaning about the situation now I've finally got what I asked for. I blub on, "And she's full of nits – her hair is so thick and curly, I can't get rid of them. I've tried everything..."

Edna speaks clearly and slowly so that I take in every word. "Bridie, what I am hearing is that this child is controlling you. Many foster-children express themselves through controlling and dominant behaviour, and everything you've told me relates to that. I think we had better look at referring you to a Child Psychologist. I think that will really help."

I'm so glad I had the courage to speak with Edna about my worries. I've got to get a grip of her behaviour, before it starts to become ingrained and she gets the better of me. Edna leaves me with some reading matter: Basic Assumptions for Parenting and Treating Traumatized Attachment Resistant Children. That's my bedtime reading sorted then.

10th October 1998

The child psychologist has slotted us in at 5pm for a 'quick chat', after being briefed by Edna. Sinead is being particularly difficult at the moment – I don't know why – but I suppose it's good that he sees her at her worst. It's never a good time for her at the end of the day. I try to distract her with games and cuddles but she wants to be outside all the time.

"Don't wanna be here – let's go home! Not waiting, out now!" I feel the Riley anger rising.

The CP directs Sinead to the Wendy house and momentarily she is content. We begin our discussions, but suddenly there is a noise like an orgasm emanating from the Wendy house: "Argh oooow argh argh!"

Sinead shouts out, "Mum – I've had a baby, look! " She points to a baby doll in her arms.

That's the first time she's ever called me Mum. I look over my shoulder to see if the CP had heard, as I'm sure it would be frowned on, but he seems distracted with his paperwork.

Five minutes later the tantrums and torments return. "Want to go now!" she says pedantically, as she pokes me. The tantrums erupt and become volcanic. She attempts to bite me. "Go home! Don't like it here!" she screams in anger.

"Okay, Mrs Kelly, I can see why you are finding the tantrums hard to handle," said Dr Morgan, looking at me.

"Yes... they... they really scare me," I reply.

The doctor talks to Sinead for quite a while in a different room. Then he comes back to me with his notes.

"Mrs Kelly, as you've probably realised, Sinead is very bright (hooray) but she is also hyperactive (boo). She's obviously very fond of you (thank God) and her friend Bobby (ahh, so much for my theory about the rabbit). She is lively and charming but she may be high on the Autistic Spectrum and possibly ADHD. It's hard to say at this stage but we will have to see you regularly and do further tests and try and support you and Sinead.

"Unfortunately the first four years of Sinead's life were difficult for her, and this is when attachments form. In Sinead's case the attachments she made are not part of her life anymore, so she will be grieving for a while and that's expressed in some of her unpredictable behaviour like smearing faeces on the toilet wall. It's understandable really, Mrs Kelly. She has lost her whole family. Try to recognise her pain. Try to extend her emotional vocabulary. For example, when she is expressing anger, frustration or hurt say to her, 'Sinead you sound really hurt, do you want to talk about it?' This will help her understand the different ranges of her emotions. Build on her self-esteem: catch her doing something right and praise her. Reward rather than punish. Stay positive, Mrs Kelly."

I am overwhelmed and relieved. Poor, poor Sinead. She is grieving. Why didn't I think of that? I cry and cry myself, for the pain she must be going through and doesn't know how to express. That little girl has probably experienced more pain and grief in her few short years, than I have in my entire life.

31st October 1998

We are having a Halloween party and are also (belatedly) celebrating Bea's birthday all in one go – it's exhausting but fun getting everything ready. Bea's come home for the weekend from college and she's dressed up to the nines with an alarmingly low cut dress that Declan disapproves of. She has a 'Birthday Girl' badge pinned dangerously near her cleavage.

"Your dress is a bit low-cut," says Declan.

"Dad! Chill out – it's called fashion," she laughs and blows her Dad a kiss.

The twins arrive and they are dressed up in scary Halloween costumes like Sinead, who is on a screaming great high, bordering on a full-scale tantrum.

I try to remember what the consultant said. Oh yes, reflect the feeling.

"Sinead, is this exciting for you?" I ask.

With that she calms down and agrees, "Yeyeeee! I am so excited I can't sit down!"

Well done, Bridie, I commend myself. Moments later, Sinead relapses and I become an incompetent mother who is scared of my bullying daughter, who is now standing on the sofa and lobbing things at me. She is just so impulsive and can't seem to control any of her emotions.

The twins rescue me. "Don't worry, Aunty Bridie," says Saskia. "Come and dance with us."

"Sinead, don't throw things at Bridie," says Jazzy. "It's not nice," and with that, both twins drag me away from her. But, rejecting Sinead is unwise: she runs up to me and before I know it, she has punched me in the stomach. I double-up in pain and the twins are horrified.

Sinead howls and screams. "Nobody likes me. Not fair!"

"Well people will like you even less if you hit them, Sinead," says Saskia. "It's really not nice."

"Cow bitch. Go home!" Sinead howls and the party silences around us.

I want to go to her and comfort her, but Declan intervenes.

"Upstairs to bed, young lady!" he demands, "right now."
It's too late. I know he's lit the touch-paper.

"No no no no no. Fucker!' she screams, and twists on her heels, picks up the first thing that comes to hand – which happens to be a plate of sandwiches, and lobs it at Declan.

He ducks and the plate shatters on the floor, salmon and cucumber sandwiches strewn across the polished oak boards.

Everyone present seems frozen in time, eyes wide, and drinks held in mid air. It's like a scene from a dreadful film. Then the tension breaks and attention resumes on the previous topics of conversation, but Declan and I are mortified. Sinead has shown her true colours tonight.

We try to redeem the party, but Bea and her friends make excuses to leave and leg-it down to the nearest pub – who can blame them – and my family soldier on for a bit, but eventually take their leave too, bidding us goodbye with pitying, *'We told you so'* looks.

1st November 1998

The party has cast a shadow on us all. We are morose and distant with each other. Bea has decided to go back to college; Declan mutters constantly under his breath about "appalling behavior," and something about leopards and spots; Sinead is grizzly and uncommunicative and spends most of her time taunting and prodding the poor rabbit mercilessly.

I am riven with self-doubt. Am I just a really bad mother, or is Sinead beyond help? The CP told me that she could be autistic, but I have no idea how to handle that, or how to help her.

We are a bit gloomy and I can't even turn to my family for support because let's face it, they did all warn me against this course of action. I suddenly understand why the fostering process is so long and bureaucratic, because maybe everybody goes through the kind of doubts I'm currently experiencing. I don't know if I can cope with this in the long term. I don't know if we can be her forever family. I don't know if I even want to adopt her...

10th November 1998

Bobby the rabbit is urgently rehomed in the middle of the night. I just had to do it. Sinead has been bullying him and giving him 1-2-3 time outs! I tried to explain to Sinead that rabbits can't count or understand the concept of time, nor indeed can they 'sit' like a dog. But she can't seem to comprehend this.

"Bobby been naughty!" she says defiantly.

I worry about how she torments him when I'm not there to watch her every move, so reluctantly, we have given him to the animal rescue centre. Bye bye, Bobby.

19th December 1998

Sinead is seven years old today. After the debacle of the Halloween party, I decide not to throw her a birthday party. I think it would be overwhelming for her, and anyway, she hasn't got many friends to ask, except little Wayne, who is like her shadow these days. Instead, I take Sinead for a swim and a special lunch at the Spa – which is far enough away from Dublin city centre to be a safe day out – and then we drop in to see Aunty Bernadette at the convent for blessings.

My beloved aunt is patiently waiting for us with a calm smile on her face. "Welcome, Sinead. Happy birthday to you and I hope you'll have a very happy Christmas. Be good for your mother and father."

Initially Sinead is bewildered and in awe of Aunty Bernadette but she soon becomes confident. Too confident.

"Why you got that on?" she says pulling hard at Bernadette's wimple.

"Sinead, please leave it alone. Tell Aunty Bernadette all about the dogs."

"Hilda and Harry – I love them. And Bobby but he has been murdered by Mum."

"Ah Sinead, that's not true, now is it?"

"It is! I saw you killed my rabbit," she says with mischief in her eyes.

I apologise to Aunty Bernadette who is not in the least bit fazed by my apparent act of murder.

"I had to rehome him," I whisper.

"God bless you both," says Bernadette, and I take my cue to head on home.

7th January 1999

Somehow we managed to get through the festive season without too many minefields and tantrums. We purposefully kept it quite low-key so Sinead wouldn't get over-wrought. We spent lazy mornings watching films on TV and long afternoon walks with the dogs. I think we literally tired

Sinead out and she was in bed by 7pm most nights, leaving Declan and I some quality time to recover our energy for the following day. Thankfully, we've regained some of our former equilibrium before the Halloween meltdown, and I'm cautiously beginning to feel that perhaps we could adopt her after all.

Today Sinead goes back to school and I'm sure things will continue to improve once she is focused and structured and back in her routine. I have her Stillorgan Primary School uniform all ready for her to put on: a blue jumper, matching skirt, white shirt, tie – hmmm, one of us is bound to be strangled by this wretched tie – black shoes and tights.

I tell Sinead to get dressed, and then we can read a Topsy & Tim story about going to school after breakfast.

"No! Miss Bobby and Magga."

I recognise that this is her anxiety about going to school that is surfacing, so I give her something to look forward to.

"Sinead, after school, we'll call round and see Grandma and Granddad, okay?"

The phone rings and I leave Sinead to get dressed as I scoot downstairs to answer it.

"Is that Mrs Bridie Kelly?" says a strange, serious voice.

"Yes. Who is this please?" I say with new-found assertiveness.

"Its the Garda here... Erm, could you come now to your mother's house please?"

"No, I can't right now – it's a bit difficult actually as it's the first day back at school for my daughter..." I gabble.

"Mrs Kelly, if you could just come right now – its very important"

I'm suddenly filled with dread. "Why? What's happened? Has there been an accident? Has Mum wandered off?" My mouth is dry and my heart's beating fast.

"Just come over as soon as you can please," he repeats for the third time.

"Declan!" I scream up the stairs, "something's happened to Mum. Can you give Sinead her breakfast and take her to school?"

Declan opens the bathroom door in an instant, his dressing gown hanging loosely around him. "What is it now?" he asks.

"I think something's happened to Mum. I've been told by the police to go round immediately... What do you think's happened? Oh My God – why can't things go smoothly just for once...?"

I dress quickly, grab my handbag and keys and dash out the door. I even forget to say goodbye to Sinead. I am filled with panic. What's happened to my Mum? Oh God... Something's wrong – she's going to die I know it. It's that shake, it's worse than we thought... she's obviously had some sort of heart attack or died from the Parkinson's – but Declan said that people die with it not of it... My mind is racing as I drive like a lunatic round to their house.

I arrive at my parents' house where two police cars are stationed. Christ! As I rush in the back door, I hear the stairs creaking and see my mother walking downstairs ever-so slowly, her eyes red and puffy.

"Bridie, Bridie... Daddy's dead... He died in his sleep – we don't know why..."

I am stunned. It's not Mum – it's my Dad. Noooooooo, please, no. God, no – not Dad...

"I just went to bed as usual, and then the alarm clock went off at 6am like it always does and it just went on ringing. I got cross and said to Stanley, 'Turn the bloody thing off,' but he was..." Her voice broke. "He was cold. Gone – just like that. He seemed well enough – only last night we went dancing! He looked well; he seemed fit as a fiddle... Only the other day he said he thought that he would live to 100..."

"It's okay Mum, ssshhhh," I say, my voice returning. I hug her to me as she makes it down the last step.

Shock and confusion set in. We head for the sitting room, but are met with the spectacle of yesterday's crumpled *Guardian,* with his glasses placed on top. It's too much and the tears begin to flow. Even Trixy looks upset.

"He can't be dead Mum – are you sure?" I ask stupidly.

"I'm afraid the paramedics pronounced him dead about half an hour ago. Do you want to see him, darling? He's going to be at the Dublin mortuary for a while. For the post mortem?"

"Post mortem? Why?"

"Because he died unexpectedly love, for no good reason..."

I collapse onto the sofa and wail, distraught at the thought of my poor dear father's body being opened up. His organs would be examined and removed... Oh my God – oh no...

"Sure now, I'll get the kettle on," says my Mum. "Lee and Denise will be here in a bit."

She pats my hand and tries to comfort me. "It's the shock of sudden death that is so distressing, love. Sit down now and just relax a little."

"Unexplained death," says the policeman. "It's just procedure. Give it a couple of days then they will sign the release papers and then the funeral company can collect the body."

Collect the body, collect the body...

The phone rings – it's Declan. I tell him the news and I hear him gasp and then moments later sniff.

"He's gone, D. Please come as soon as you can."

The phone rings again – it's Lee. She too is in shock. "I can't believe it, Bridie, I just can't believe he's gone. I'm waiting for Ned to come home – he's got the car. Then we'll be round..." There was a pause and a sigh, and nose blowing. I hear the twins crying in the background.

As we wait for the rest of the family to get here, I experience huge swings of emotion. I feel grief-stricken and then angry. I am so angry with my Dad. How could he just pop off like that? It feels like he's walked out on Mum, on us all... Why, Dad?

God knows how I'm going to break this to Sinead. She loved her Granddad and their time feeding the fish and gardening together. This will be a hard loss for her; another betrayal by an adult is how she'll see it.

12th January 1999

Okay, so we know now that dear old Dad died of a heart attack. It came out of the blue – just like that: totally unexpected, and really there was nothing anybody could've done about it. Even if he hadn't argued with all his doctors, and even if he hadn't taken all those aspirin – it would probably still have happened.

Lee, Tim, Denise, Mum, Bea (who returned home the moment she heard the news), Declan and I decide that we want to visit the mortuary and see Dad's body to say goodbye. Sinead will stay with the twins, who we agree are old enough now to look after her for an hour. I try to calmly visualise the body but I am distraught and in overdrive.

It's a terrifying experience. I try to control myself by breathing, but it's too much. I feel dizzy and I am overwhelmed with heart-wrenching sorrow. "I can't see my father dead, I can't!" Mum picks up on my emotion.

"Bridie," she says sharply, "it's not what Dad would have

wanted – he hated people making a fuss. Now come on –
'Onward Christian soldiers'..."

It makes no difference. I am not stoical like Mum. I am still
a blubbering wreck. Lee, Tim and Denise are a different kettle
of fish altogether. They remain calm and composed as they
make polite conversation about funeral arrangements.

In the mortuary, we gather around the trolley bearing
his body.

"Oh, he does look fine does he not?" says my Mum.
"I thought he... I thought he would be..." she sobs as she
kisses his shiny, forehead. The rest of the family and I survey
the body.

Sniffs and sobs echo in the clinical room. Then Bea
breaks down.

"Why does it have to happen, Dad? Why do we have to
lose what we love? It's not fair..." and with that she flees the
mortuary weeping.

The mortician, a bald, bespectacled, tired-looking man
knocks on the door politely and coughs. "Ahermm. Please take
as long as you like with Mandy. Just take your time and give a
knock when you are ready."

Suddenly, everybody is beside themselves with laughter.

Tim calls out, "Who the heck is Mandy? This is supposed to
be my father!"

It breaks the tension and allows us all a moment to
breathe and recoup. Immediately there are lots of jokes
about sex changes and cross-dressing. Here I am, seeing my
father's dead body – my first dead body – and I am hysterical
with laughter. It's strange how death brings every emotion
to the surface. Bea, who has composed herself and returned,
moans about what all this crying's doing to her mascara.
Declan and I decide not to tell Sinead until we've got over the
shock ourselves.

Chapter 23

Life Goes On

17th January 1999

It's a seriously gloomy day. None of us has any energy and Sinead is a nightmare. Mum's not feeling well either; she is staying in bed to listen to a radio play – which is most unlike her. Her shaking hands are more prominent now and I see she is not eating well since Dad died. I am worried for her health. Please God, don't let her die too. Later, the whole family – minus Mum – assembles to discuss the dreaded funeral.
I feel so upset and overwhelmed that I can't think straight anymore. Lee says that I must not give in to grief; that things need to be organised after a death, like: death certificate and funeral arrangements (Lee's job); solicitor (Denise's job); newspaper announcements (my job); friends and relatives to be informed (Tim's job).

"See, Bridie, there's so much to do and Mum needs us to be strong and organised. We are going to have to think about who looks after Mum now as well – she can't live on her own."

Jeez. I hadn't thought of that. My mind wanders and I become emotional again. I imagine Dad returning home with a packet of chocolate digestives, and a Guardian newspaper. Oh why did he have to leave us, why? I'd give anything to see him one more time; to play one more game of Scrabble with him. I start weeping again. My world is shattered but I must stay strong for Sinead. I am a parent now.

We decide to have a wake for my father before the funeral.

One of Tim's friends is going to arrange some Irish folk music. Declan is going to play his tin whistle (he's very good) and the twins are going to have a go at joining in with their violins. But first I have to explain to Sinead that Granddad's dead and she'll never see him again. I'm not looking forward to that.

Armed with Roger Bear, paper, photographs and crayons, Sinead and I talk about death. It's not easy. I am crying inside and this just makes everything harder to bear, because I can see Sinead struggling to come to terms with what I'm saying. I feel so sorry for this little girl who has already had to say goodbye so many times: Patsy, Murphy, Margaret, Bobby and now to Granddad as well.

We talk together about flowers dying and fish dying and Sinead perks up. "One of Granddad's fishes dieded!"

"Yes that's right. Well, that's what's happened to Granddad. He was very old and he died – but he is in our hearts forever."

Sinead remains serious and looks around. "Where dieded?" We are both crying now. I wipe my eyes and try to calm myself down.

"Well, Sinead, tomorrow we are going to have a big party with Irish music and dancing, and you will have a chance to see Granddad if you want to. I will hold your hand and we will see him together, but only if you want to." The word party fills me with dread. Will this one be even more traumatic than Halloween?

"But he's dieded...?"

Christ, how do you explain a wake to a child?

Note to self: arrange immediate appointment with Edna. It's clearly too much for her to take in.

When I get a quiet moment, I sneak outside for a quick cigarette. I've been hitting the old nicotine a bit too often since Dad died. I promise myself that after the funeral, I will quit again, and this time for good. I phone Edna who offers the following advice:

1. Get plenty of sleep: both of you.
2. Keep a strict routine going.
3. Do whatever comforts or sustains you both.
4. Let her talk to Bobby – don't discourage or encourage it.
(She never stopped talking to imaginary Bobby as I'd hoped,
and had no problem distinguishing him from the rabbit!)
5. Ask her if she wants to see the body and explain what it will
be like. Tell her he is asleep and will never wake up.

18th January 1999

It's the day of the dreaded wake. I don't know how I keep
going – I just want to run away, but Lee and Denise are being
very stoical and brave about it all, so I suppose I've got to be.
Declan keeps saying things like, "He had a good life," and "He
lived to a ripe old age," which doesn't make any difference.
He's DEAD.

There are lots of sandwiches, sausage rolls and cakes to
make. My mother has said acidly that the whole Irish folk
music thing sounds ghastly.

My dead Dad is in our lounge. It's a bit of an eerie feeling
having him so close – yet never has he been further away from
us. My heart breaks all over again.

Bit by bit, I warm to the lively music once the wake starts.

Tim – who seems to have taken Dad's death the best of all
of us, perhaps because he's lived all over the world in his time
and hasn't stayed so close-knit as us girls – is jigging along
to Finnegan's Wake with his pint of lager. He beckons to me.
"Come on, Bridie – go and get Sinead and Mum and lets have
some fun."

Sinead throws herself somewhat alarmingly into the dancing. "Come ON Grandma," I hear her say as she attempts to drag my mother's thin, withered little body onto the makeshift dance floor. I am on tenterhooks that Sinead is going to fly off the handle and cause a scene. Somebody has started up Galway Boy, and triangle ham sandwiches, fresh scones, and cups of tea are passed around.

Later, we all gather beside the body and talk about Dad. I see his hands clasped across his chest – it's such an unnatural pose... and words of comfort are spoken: "Ah sure, he had a good innings and went very quickly," and "God bless him."

I ask Sinead if she wants to see Granddad and she nods her head slowly.

"I am gunna read him a poem."

Tim thinks this is a bad idea (the memory might haunt her), but Aunty Bernadette and the other nun Marie encourage it. "Let her have a while with him. She loved him; he was a special friend to her."

Sinead stands timidly beside my father's coffin and allows herself a quick peak at him. I see her gasp and mechanically read out her 'poem'.

"Granddad I miss you; look after Bobby if you see him." And with that she flees, to find some food and a dancing partner.

Some more visitors have arrived. They shake our hands and say, "Sorry for your loss." There are flowers and cards everywhere.

I feel like I'm in a dream and not really participating in any of it. My emotions are drained and I'm like an automaton. I smile and make small talk, but nothing's sinking in – it's like I'm floating under the ice of a lake, watching everything as it happens from a distance, but underlying everything is this pain; this ache of loss that's taken hold of my body. It's so utterly sad, almost unbearable.

Dad's coffin is staying with us overnight until the funeral tomorrow and his sister, my beloved Aunty Olive wants to keep a vigil. She promises to watch over him and I can't think of anyone else I'd want to do it.

19th January 1999

How am I going to get through this day – the day of my Dad's funeral? My limbs feel like lead. I'm finding it hard to be present, but I notice Sinead doing little things like putting Roger Bear in my lap, or stroking my hair. It's her way of comforting me, and it does. It really does.

Sinead doesn't come to the funeral. She's had enough to cope with already, without the harrowing rigmarole of it all. She's gone to Wayne's house for the afternoon. Thank goodness for her one and only friend, Wayne.

The funeral is actually quite comforting. We sing familiar hymns and say prayers together and then lay my father to rest in Stillorgan churchyard. We will visit him as often as we can.

We are all feeling depressed and we can't stop talking about Dad. Later that evening, Sinead has several meltdowns, but amazingly, we talk about how she's feeling and she snaps out of them quite quickly. It's obvious they're to do with loss and the grief she's feeling. She keeps saying, "Mummy Bridie, feel funny. Don't like it." I know exactly what she means.

Me and Denise keep saying, "If only..." If only he had gone to the doctors, or hadn't taken so many aspirin, or not quarreled with two of the doctors... would he still be alive today?

At night, after Sinead's gone to bed, I take Edna's advice to heart. I've found a way to sleep: 2-3 glasses of wine and a comedy video. It works a treat. Laughter therapy. So far, me and Declan have watched all of the Father Ted series, Dave Allen (very appropriate, Dad loved his 'lefty' humour), The Good Life, Butterflies and Absolutely Fabulous.

14th February 1999

As if one death in the family is not enough, we had to have Hilda put down today. Both Declan and I had noticed that since Dad died, she'd slowly gone off her food, refused to go with Harry on their daily walks and was just sleeping all the time. We took her to the vet last week and he took blood samples and x-rays, and today he confirmed our worst fears. Late-stage cancer. As we didn't want her to suffer any more, we asked him to put her out of her misery there and then. It was so peaceful...

When we got in the car, we both cried and cried. I can't bear to see Declan cry and that just set me off even more. When we got home, we had to break the news to Sinead – something we were both dreading – and she went into complete meltdown. I tried to see her ranting and swearing as just an expression of her grief, but when she kicked-out at me and caught me square on the shin, I wanted to hit the girl. I literally saw red, something that's never happened to me before.

"Sinead! You little bitch!" I say, before I can stop the words coming out of my mouth.

She turns towards me slowly and deliberately.

"You killed Hildy like Bobby rabbit. Hate you!"

Oh, for fuck's sake.

Chapter 24

The Change

14th March 1999

Happiness Factor: 5/10. This might sound as if things are not too good, which is not true. We have all slowly got back to some semblance of normality now – even Harry seems to be getting used to life without Hilda – but oh, how I wish I could get Sinead to do as she is told. She seems to take a great delight these days in doing the exact opposite of what I ask her to do. Okay, she's not taking a poo in the garden shed any more, and she's not constantly swearing at me in Irish and both of those things are a huge bonus, but if I ask her to turn the television down, she will turn it up, and look me in the eye, just challenging me for a fight. I won't rise to the bait, but sometimes it's hard.

Take this morning for example. I ask Sinead if she can clear the breakfast things off the table and put them in the dishwasher. So what does she do? She gets more plates and cups out of the cupboard and puts them on the kitchen table. At first, I think she just misheard me.

"No, Sinead," I grumble. "I said, 'Clear the plates and put them in the dishwasher'."

"Yeah. I know," she says petulantly.

"So why didn't you do that?"

"Don't wanna."

Declan intervenes and as usual, things escalate. "Sinead! If Mummy Bridie asks you to do something, please will you do as you're told." I know he's only trying to help, but it doesn't.

"NO! DON'T WANNA!" she repeats and runs out of the room slamming the door.

"That girl is a law unto herself," Declan hisses. "She's so unruly, Bridie."

"I know, D. I don't know what to do. She seems to take a great delight in being naughty and provoking us. I could've done with her help this morning after being sick like that. Jeez, that's not like me. I think it was that prawn curry last night."

"Or the couple of glasses of wine you washed it down with."

"Declan! That's the first drink I have had for days, and you were the one who opened the bottle. I was quite happy with sparkling water."

"I know, darling. I just wanted to celebrate my little promotion."

Oh, I forgot to mention – Declan has been asked to become one of the senior partners at the surgery. Doctor O'Connor, who founded the surgery over 30 years ago is retiring, and they've asked Declan to take his place. We are utterly delighted, needless to say, and it's no more than Declan deserves. He works so hard.

Later, I rather nervously ring Edna – she always makes me feel like a child at school for some reason – and discuss Sinead's recent behaviour.

"She's just pushing the boundaries," Edna says, sounding wearisome. "That's what kids do. She wants to know how far she can push you before you snap. But my advice is not to retaliate and make a big deal out of it, because if you can do that, sooner or later, she's just going to get bored of the whole thing. All I can say is just keep things on an even keel for now Bridie. Just be grounded with her. Routine is important."

16th March 1999

Even though I feel like I'm doing well and getting over Dad's death, Declan's insisting I have a couple of bereavement counselling sessions with Mrs O'Brien at the hospital. I am grateful that he has pushed me to go on the one hand, because she really helped me come to terms with things last time, but on the other hand I'm curious as to why it's only me, out of the whole family, who needs help?

Session 1 – Mrs O'Brien shakes my hand and says, "Sorry for your loss". It's enough to cause an out-pouring of grief in me that I wasn't expecting. To be honest, I thought I was getting over it and didn't really need these sessions, but it seems D was right all along. She asks me to describe what has happened and what my feelings are. I explain how the shock of his sudden death has thrown me out of kilter and that I can't stop thinking the same thoughts over and over again: that it's my fault somehow. I also tell her how I can't cope with visiting poor old Mum because everything in the house reminds me of him. Again, I hadn't even realised I felt that way. God, these sessions are good.

"Anything else you'd like to discuss Mrs Kelly?"

"Well..." I hesitate, "I don't think it's really your department, but I think I'm menopausal. My periods have stopped and I'm putting on weight, and I feel nauseous all the time."

"How old was your mother when she started the menopause?" Mrs O'Brien asks.

"She was about 52, I think... A lot older than I am now."

"Thought so. You seem rather too young to be menopausal, I'd say, but it could be peri-menopausal symptoms or even some kind of post-traumatic stress disorder. I really wouldn't worry too much, Bridie. Your periods have stopped because of the shock, and the excessive drinking you mentioned just after your father died will mean you have put on a bit of weight. PTSD is easy enough to treat providing you are committed to attending the appointments and practice the exercises I give you. And I would advise that you restart your meditation practice. I have it here in my notes that it's something you've found helpful in the past. Things won't improve overnight, but they will improve. How's young Sinead coping, by the way?" she looks concerned.

I reply that her behaviour is the same as it's always been – very, very difficult but with little bouts where she's totally angelic so that I forgive her everything. If truth be told I haven't a clue how to parent her and don't know if I'm actually doing anything right at all.

20th March 1999

I have started a 'Thought Dairy' where I just write down my thoughts when I get the hamster-wheel brain, and it's really helped me to realise that it's just futile to keep going over old ground like this. I even found myself getting bored of my own thoughts the other day, and found myself thinking, *God, not that old chestnut again!* So maybe that's a good sign?
I also read a book on sudden death and it's brilliant. I now understand the grieving process I'm going through and think I've been through denial and anger and am maybe getting somewhere near acceptance now.

3rd April 1999

I've just had my third session with Mrs O'Brien and the

bereavement counselling has come to an end now. I feel much more confident at being able to control my overwhelming feelings of grief, and also accept them for what they are. I can also accept that everybody deals with grief differently, and even though Lee and Denise, and Mum to some extent, seem to have breezed through it, they may still have their own version of this process to go through. It's amazing how just 'unpacking' things can be such a relief. Mrs O'Brien says that I must keep busy but find time to acknowledge and honour the loss of Dad and Hilda. She even suggested that we busy ourselves with a new puppy. "You wont have any time to be maudlin when you have a labrador pup to train," she laughed and I can't help but agree.

Since Dad died, there's been talk of Mum moving in with us, although she seems very hesitant about doing so, understandably I suppose – after all, she lived her whole married life in that house. Declan helped to get her house on the market just to see if there was any interest in it, and already there is a couple who want to come and see it. When it sells, we've offered her our little annexe so that she can have her own space here with us, but still have her independence. She hasn't formally agreed (or thanked us), but she has got the keys for the annexe now, and when she comes to see us, she goes in there and sits in a chair by the window for hours at a time. I think she's trying to envisage how her life might be if she lives there. She came back from one of these vigils yesterday and said, "I don't know what your cleaner gets paid for Bridie. I could write my name in the dust in there." Note to self: get Anna to spring-clean the place and open all the windows and give it a good airing.

I'm thinking: *Mum and Sinead. Really? Is this a good idea?* Declan thinks it will be easier for me in the long-run if she lives with us, as I won't have to keep going round to her house to try and cheer her up (not possible) and be confronted with all the memories of Dad. He could have a point.

7th April 1999

The new puppy is arriving tomorrow. I can't wait and Sinead is absolutely beside herself and can talk of nothing else. She is a beautiful extra-small labrador bitch from a breeder in Dublin. We have chosen the name 'Carly' because Sinead's alternatives were just a bit too, well...dull. Bea was hysterical with laughter on the phone when I told her about the names Sinead had chosen: Susan or Derek.

"You are joking, Bridie? You can't possibly call a dog Derek! Imagine calling him in the park: Derek! Derek! Everyone would think you'd lost your husband, for God's sake!"

I have made a list of things we need for the new puppy: a crate, soft toys, puppy food, a tiny, teensy collar and a lead, training pads, rubber bones, chews, a brush.... Note to dairy: this is really therapeutic – keeping busy works.

Later I practice my relaxation exercises. I must admit I am feeling a lot more chilled and at peace with everything. HF 7/10 – why not? Life is short, so it's best to fill it with mindfulness, positive thoughts and relaxation. Declan and I enjoy a romantic early night. Say no more!

8th April 1999

Let the mayhem begin! We are besotted with Carly and I am training Sinead to treat her gently and kindly. Sinead thinks she's like a living Roger Bear or Snowy B, but I'm determined that she will understand that this is a creature with feelings and needs. To give Sinead her dues though – she's learning really fast, and notices if the water bowl is empty or if she's done a little pee somewhere. Harry is resolutely not amused by this bundle of fluff that tries to clamber all over him, but he is good-tempered and tolerant of her. Like all puppies, Carly has needle-sharp teeth!

I'm back on the supplements big time, to see if they'll help me with this nausea I keep feeling: multi vits, fish oils, spirulina, glutamine... I can't say as I'm feeling any different, but it makes me feel better mentally for looking after myself and taking them. Mind you, I've had about 10 crafty ciggies since Carly got here. Declan knows what I'm doing, but just raises an eyebrow. I'll get there in the end. I'm reducing my intake gradually.

12th April 1999

Whilst I am coping with the bereavement I feel like I am failing abjectly with Sinead. Fight, fight, fight – that's all we do. She is very physically strong and it worries me sometimes, because there have been occasions when she's gone to hit or kick me. I'm still big enough that I can stop her and keep her at arm's length, but for how long? Her temper seems to erupt from nowhere. We can be having a lovely time walking Carly and Harry or doing some cooking together, and suddenly over the tiniest thing – usually involving me misunderstanding something she's said – she's volcanic with rage. At these times she starts ranting on about Peyton, Cissy and Ginger, her half-sisters who seem to have been occupying her mind so much of late. When she starts these rants, she also lapses back into Irish. Apparently, the trick is for me to transfer the attachments from them to us, but it's like on one level she knows what I'm doing and refuses to play ball.

The other day she was in one of these rages and she said, "Wanna go back an live with Peyton. NOW!"

"Sinead, you live with us now. This is your home."

"Not my home. Home is Peyton an Ginger an Murphy. And Magga," she adds, though quite how Magga can be part of that equation, I don't know.

"Shall we have a look at some of the photos of us we took on the beach?" I ask, hoping this will calm her a little.

"No! Stupid photos of stupid Bridie and stupid Declan!"

"Sinead, please don't be rude," I ask her.

"Gabh suas ort fein!" she says, which I think means 'piss off' in Irish.

Once she is calm, I ring Edna to speak with her about these worrying turn of events.

"Why has she suddenly dredged up all these names from the past, Edna?" I ask.

Edna sighs (something she seems to be doing a lot of lately, when I talk with her about Sinead.) "The thing is, Bridie, we felt that this attachment to her half-sisters was something that was better not to be encouraged. Before Sinead was born, before Murphy and Patsy got together, Murphy was on the road with his own extended family for many years, and he had a relationship – we don't know if they were married – to a woman called Mary. They had three children together as far as we can ascertain – Peyton, Cissy and Ginger – all much older than Sinead. But then a terrible accident happened and Mary was knocked down and killed by one of the vehicles in the convoy they were travelling in and it sent Murphy over the edge. He couldn't stand to be near the children, because they reminded him so much of Mary. He started drinking and causing havoc in the community and, eventually, they kicked him out. He was kind of ex-communicated. The children live with their maternal grandmother, although they are in their mid- to late teens now, I would think. Once or twice, Murphy has gone back to try and make amends, taking Sinead with him – usually when he and Patsy had had a row – but each time it ended in tears, usually because he was drunk. Murphy seems unable or unwilling to fit back in with his old traveller community and so we are not encouraging Sinead to keep that bond going, for obvious reasons. Murphy's child from another, non-traveller, relationship would not be so welcome. But Sinead has an amazing memory. She seems to remember these two or three visits really vividly, and she's embroidered them in her dreams to become something far more exciting and loving than they really were. From what we can tell, Sinead was not really welcomed with open arms."

Edna's revelations leave me reeling somewhat. I really feel for Sinead. They didn't want her... Well, I do. I want her and I love her. But my God, she tests me to my limit.

3.00 pm

Carly the puppy serves as a distraction but even that is complicated. Sinead snatches Carly from me and calls Carly 'my mine puppy'. The poor little thing shakes with terror and does not know whether she's coming or going.

In desperation I phone Wayne's mother and ask if Wayne can come over for a few hours to play.

"Well... it's a bit difficult," she replies. "I'm just about to go out so his older brother Rory is looking after him. But yes, Wayne can come round to yours if you don't mind Rory coming too."

"Sure, that'll be fine," I say, somewhat relieved that Sinead will have two friends to keep her occupied.

When I tell Sinead that she'll be having visitors soon, she is suddenly high as a kite. "Wayne's coming! And Rory! I love Rory – he's a big boy. He's better than Wayne. We can get my mine puppy and play with her."

"Sinead, she is not your puppy, and she is a baby," I quietly explain. "Carly needs peace and quiet so that she can sleep. So whilst she's asleep, you can play with Wayne and Rory, okay?"

She accepts the compromise without question, but when the boys turn up, I immediately doubt my handling of the situation. Rory's got to be at least 13; a burly boy with what can only be described as a sneer instead of a smile. He seems to bully Wayne at every given opportunity so that his younger sibling just trudges after him doing Rory's bidding without question. Sinead however seems to be flirting with Rory, and that worries me most. So instead of a bit of peace, there's chaos in the garden and the need for me to keep an eagle-eye on them all.

In no time, all three of them – but thankfully minus the puppy – are playing on the trampoline.

"Only one at a time!" I shout, worried about their safety.

They ignore me and I'm sure I hear an Irish swearword from Sinead, which makes them all dissolve into fits of laughter. They continue to jump and bump around on the trampoline and I continue to worry, but after a while, things quieten down, and they're just sitting on the trampoline talking and laughing. I watch from the kitchen window, and can see that Sinead is holding her own with these boys – she's making them laugh and interestingly, she looks Rory in the eye. Something she rarely does with me or Declan.

Eventually, I feel like I can take my eyes off them for a second, leaving me time to bond with my beautiful puppy Carly. I stroke her soft head and offer her rubber bones and she chews on them gratefully. Harry is still a little suspicious of the new member of the family, but he's kind and tolerant and I watch as they wrestle together, the puppy squealing with both delight and fear. Harry has a new companion. I am happy for him.

4.00 pm

It's too quiet – what are those kids up to? I can't see them out of the kitchen window. Jesus – I turn my back on them for two minutes... I chuckle as I catch myself sounding just like a mother.

I find all three of them in the garden shed and they look triumphant. But as I open the door I can smell smoke.

"What on earth's going on, you lot?" I demand.

They look down and shuffle about sniggering.

"Oh my God! Have you been smoking? For God's sake! Make sure they are stubbed out and get out of the shed – NOW! Wayne and Rory – you are going home this instant, and I will have to report this incident to your mother. This shed will be locked from now on." (Note to self: find a safe place for the key and only tell Declan where it is.)

I quickly ring Wayne's mother who has thankfully returned home from wherever it is she's been.

When I tell her the news, I'm surprised by her response. "Wha's the big deal, Bridie? Rory's been smoking for at least a year now – just like that excuse of a father of his! I don't know what the fuck I am supposed to do about it – he won't do a thing I say."

I remain calm and unimpressed. Assertively, I suggest that Sinead is too young at seven years of age to be exposed to this kind of behaviour.

"Don't get all high and mighty with me, Bridie Kelly. You were the one that wanted Wayne and Rory to come round."

I ring-off hastily, feeling foolish and chastised. She's right – I used those boys as impromptu babysitters. I made another mental note never to invite those ruffians around again.

When Declan gets home, he is unforgiving. "Playing with cigarettes at seven years old! Bloody ridiculous." He puts his head in his hands and I detect an, 'I told you so' look on his face. He warns me to keep the shed locked and we agree a hiding place for the key.

Later I tell Sinead how cross I am that she has been experimenting with cigarettes. I explain (feeling somewhat of a hypocrite considering I like the occasional puff) that smoking is for 'eejits'. As a reprimand, she will not be able to play with Carly for one week. Well that's some kind of result, I suppose.

Easter 1999

For the last few days, since the smoking incident, we've been trying to put it all behind us and focus on plans for Easter, and what's more, Bea is coming home for a week or so, which always puts us in a good mood. On Easter Sunday me, Bea and Sinead take Carly and Harry for a long walk on the beach, leaving Declan to cook Easter lunch. We head up to our favourite café for a hot chocolate. We're wrapped up in hats and gloves, and our winter coats and boots as the weather's decided to hit us with one last (hopefully) wintry blast. There are snowflakes peppering down and a dark and lowering sky. And to think, a few days ago, we were sitting in the garden sunbathing! How strange the spring weather can be.

Sinead, however, never seems to notice things like the weather and the cold. As soon as she gets to the beach, she kicks off her boots, pulls off her socks, rolls up her jeans with the little pink glittery hearts on the seams, and runs into the sea for a paddle, eagerly followed by the dogs.

"How're things going, Bridie?" asks Bea. "You and Dad okay now after, y'know... your Dad?"

She looks away from me and kicks at the sand with the toe of her Doctor Marten boots, which I covet madly, but feel I'm too old to wear now.

"I'm fine, but I suppose it did hit me hard"

"Yeah. Dad told me, like, that everything all got too much for you. He thinks..."

"Go on. What does he think?" I am intrigued that my husband and step-daughter have been talking about me in this way.

"I don't know whether I should say really... but, well – it worries me too, so I'm going to say it. We both think that Sinead is too much for you, Bridie."

"Do you?" I'm genuinely surprised. "Why?"

Bea continues kicking at the sand. I grab her hand and pull her round so that she is looking at me in the eye. "Why, Bea?"

"You're not yourself these days, Bridie. You're always feeling sick – that's stress you know, anxiety makes you feel sick – and Sinead bullies you."

I laugh out loud. "No she doesn't!"

"She does. Why won't you face facts? What about last night when we were watching that video and you told her it was time for bed?"

"Oh, that's just because you're here, Bea. She usually goes to bed really well."

"I'm not talking about the fact she didn't want to go to bed, Bridie – I get that she wants to stay up with us – but she pushed you really hard so you fell back onto the sofa when you got up to take her to bed, and then she sat on your lap so you couldn't move. And then, she put her hand over your mouth to stop you speaking. That's not normal behaviour, is it Bridie? Dad doesn't think it is."

"So, when've you two been discussing all this?" I ask, feeling my hackles rise. If Declan has got a problem with Sinead's behaviour, he should be speaking to me about it, not his daughter.

"Oh, it just came up in our conversation this morning, when you were outside, trying to get her off the trampoline. That's another example, isn't it? We saw her kicking at you and refusing to get down. She's quite aggressive with you, isn't she?"

"You've noticed then?" I concede. To be honest, it's good to have someone else to talk to about all this. I don't want to burden Declan with my concerns any more than I have to, but he's noticed and Bea's noticed, and they're right actually. She is quite... physical with me. She hits me and puts herself in my way a lot, so I can't do things like open the door, or get in the bathroom... Oh God, why can't things just be normal sometimes?

"Don't worry, love," I say. "I've spoken to the SS about it. They say she's just pushing at her boundaries – y'know, seeing how far she can push me."

"Well, if she pushes too hard, Bridie, she might just fall flat on her face," says Bea.

For the first time ever, I see Bea as the adult she is, with a growing maturity and wisdom beyond her years. Instinctively, I give her a big hug, wincing a little as my breasts are so tender at the moment – another bloody menopausal symptom.

"Thanks for caring," I say. "I'm okay, truly I am. Sinead – she's very damaged, Bea. She's had a hard life and it's going to take a while for her to really trust us and really feel part of our family. It is difficult and I do worry about her. I do feel stressed, but what can I do? I can't just send her back, can I? But thanks for caring darling, I mean it."

"Course I bloody care, you eejit," she replies, hugging me back.

We walk towards the car, calling Sinead and the dogs as we go. They reluctantly join us, wet, cold and cheerful.

20th April 1999

Sinead has been suspended from school for a day. Apparently she hit a little girl who had called her a Pikey. Frankly, I think they should've expelled the other girl too.

"Bridie, what's a Pikey? Am I a Pikey?" she asked, confused.

I explain that it's not a very nice word; that it's a racist word referring to her background.

"Don't like rapist words," she says.

Christ! "Racist, Sinead. Racist."

But she seems pleased with this new word, like it's some kind of badge of honour. She stomps around the house singing, "I am a Pikey! Pikey, Pikey, Pikey!" at the top of her voice.

I groan, not just at her misunderstanding, but that I've got her with me for the whole day. I'd got so much planned for today – I was going to spring-clean the pantry and chuck out some of the supplements that have gone out of date. I hardly use any of them now, as the thought of taking them makes me feel sick. It's something to do with the way they smell. Yuck! What on earth shall I do with her?

I ring Barry Black and ask for his advice, not about what to do with her, but about the hitting and the bad behaviour, and refusing to come indoors even when it's dark... It's been on my mind ever since my talk with Bea.

Barry is cool with me. "We need to talk, Bridie – are you free this afternoon for a quick visit?"

2.30 pm

Barry arrives and he looks worn out.

"You look worn out, Barry," I say.

"I could say the same about you, Bridie. Are you feeling okay?"

I'm taken aback. "I'm fine thanks. Now, what do you want to see me about?"

Barry shifts uneasily in his chair. I offer him another chocolate-coated cookie to try and put him at his ease. "We've had another meeting with the Fostering Board about Sinead," he says and I can feel my heart plummet into my boots. It's his body language that gives it away: this is not going to be good news. "The Board have had a bit of a change of policy regarding fostering or adopting children from different cultures..." he says, shuffling his papers together unnecessarily, and not looking me in the eye. "It's actually connected to some research that's been done regarding Aboriginal children in Australia who were forcibly removed from their parents and adopted by white families. It had disastrous consequences."

I'm confused. "But I'm Irish – Sinead's Irish... What are you talking about, Barry?"

"She might be Irish, Bridie, but she comes from a totally different culture to you. Her background – what's normal for her is to be part of an extended family of half-siblings, many different mother figures: in essence the traditional Irish traveller communities. The Board has been assessing the Statements from Murphy, Margaret and Patsy, and in light of this new policy that seeks to place children within their community of birth, the Board..."

"They've revoking our fostering placement?"

"Not as such, but they're requesting further assessments and evaluation. You see, this was her culture, Bridie. An outdoor life at Margaret's with lots of other children and role models – play fights, an ability to look after herself, and attachment to the extended family and animals. This type of lifestyle is normal for her, and current thinking is that to take her away from that is to displace her from her culture. I am working to track down her half-sisters at the moment to find out what their situation is and whether there could be an opportunity to reconnect them with Sinead in some way.

I am speechless, yet it explains so much about Sinead's behaviour. She's like a fish out of water. She doesn't feel at home with us, despite everything we can give her that they can't. "But, you seem to be back-tracking on everything you've told me to date?" I say, regaining my composure. "Only last week I spoke to Edna about Peyton and Ginger and she told me that they didn't want anything to do with Sinead..."

"Edna's in a difficult position here, Bridie. She's championed you and Declan as foster parents and potential adoptive parents. Traditional thinking in these cases has been to keep the child separate from the birth family, but policy is constantly changing and evolving – to be honest, it's a nightmare keeping up with it and as I say, there's an emerging new focus on placing a foster-child within their traditional culture, as far as possible."

"We've got no chance of adopting her then?" I ask, deflated and close to tears.

"I'm not saying that, but this is such a complex case. We have to be sure this is the right placement for her. Does she talk about her old family much?"

"No," I lie, "she seems to have forgotten them."

Barry is thoughtful and writes some notes. "Hmmm... that surprises me. She was with them a long time on and off and adopted their lifestyle. Anyway, I will let you all know in due course what the decision is, and we will have a meeting to clarify everything, one way or the other." Barry picks up his briefcase and walks towards the door.

"Barry," I call after him. "She talks about them all the time. Ginger, and Peyton and Cissy... She tries to recreate that culture: she wants to be outside all the time; she nurtures the dogs, she forms gangs with other children, she's confident in that culture. Sorry – I... I just don't want to let her go..." I break down, the tears flowing freely as I accept the likelihood that Sinead will no longer be placed with us.

"Bridie – you have worked wonders with Sinead. Nothing can take that away from you."

No, but you can take her away from me, I think, as Barry hurriedly leaves for his next appointment.

4.00 pm

I feel a curious mixture of relief and sadness. Relief that it's not just me being a crap mother, and that actually Sinead is feeling displaced and insecure; and sadness of course, that this little girl who I love dearly, and who has brought such a whirlwind of energy and fun into our lives, may not be with us for much longer.

When Declan gets home from work, I recount my meeting with Barry. Declan listens pensively, and hugs me when the tears flow again.

"It may not come to that Bridie," he says tenderly. "They might decide that she can stay with us after all..."

"I don't think so somehow D. It was the way Barry wouldn't look me in the eye. It's like it's already been decided. They're going to take her away from us, I know it..." I sniff back the tears as Sinead walks into the room.

"Why crying Mummy Bridie?" she says, walking up to me and pushing my fringe out of my eyes so she can see the tears for herself, in that adult manner she adopts whenever anyone is upset. She plonks herself on my knee and wiggles a bit, then turns and prods my belly. "You're fat!" she laughs.

Christ. That's all I need. Barren and fat!

22nd April 1999

It's Declan's birthday and we celebrate in a local restaurant whilst Anna our Polish cleaner babysits. I've actually asked Anna to move in for a while because, if all goes to plan and Mum's house sells, it won't be long before I'll need her to help with Mum and Sinead and all the housework and cleaning – at least for as long as Sinead is with us, and after that – who knows – we may foster again... She's in the attic conversion which has a nice en-suite and lovely alcove windows looking out across the garden towards the racecourse. I think it's the best room in the house, actually.

However I'm still feeling really odd with these menopausal symptoms. The moment we get to the restaurant I have a hot flush that makes my face feel like it's burning up.

"Is my face red, D?" I ask.

"Yes! You look like a tomato!" is his unsympathetic reply.

"Honestly, Declan, being a GP, I thought you'd take a bit more interest in my symptoms."

"Well, if you're menopausal, darling, there's really not a lot you can do about it apart from live with it."

"Well, that's not what Dr Li says. She's prescribed me Red Clover for the hot flushes and mint and some Chinese herb I can't pronounce for the nausea. They're both disgusting."

"She's not a proper doctor– she can't 'prescribe'."

"Well, she's doing a damn sight more for me than you are at the moment," I retort.

"Great birthday this is turning out to be," my
husband sighs.

We sit there in silence waiting for the first course to turn
up. I've ordered smoked salmon blinis for my starter but when
they arrive, one look at them makes me feel sick. I excuse
myself and rush to the loo.

What's wrong with me? I ask, as I look in the full-length,
fluorescent-lit mirror in the Ladies. Christ on a bike – look at
me! I am fat. My tits hurt. I'm putting on weight. I feel sick
all the time. I'm an emotional wreck... Anyone would think I
was pregnant.

I am quiet in the car on the way home and then feel so sick
I think I'm going to throw-up over the dashboard.

"D – pull over! I am going to puke," I squeak, hand
over mouth whilst frantically trying to wind down the
window to get some fresh air. We pull over into a layby and
illuminated by a beautiful full moon, I am heartily sick. Happy
Birthday, darling!

23th April 1999

Two days later and I still feel like shit. And something has
lodged in my brain. *Anyone would think I was pregnant...*
Anyone would think I was pregnant...

When Declan gets home later that evening, I collar him
when he comes into the bedroom.

"D...?"

"Yes?" He's preoccupied putting his jacket and tie on the
hanger ready for the morning, and changing out of his work
clothes into his jeans and jumper – he's just off out to mow
the lawn before it gets dark.

"Can I ask you something? If you had a 42-year old woman

come into the surgery saying, she feels sick mostly in the mornings, her breasts are enormous and painful, she's having hot flushes, the thought of most food makes her nauseous and she's putting on weight – what would you think?"

He turns round and looks at me, his eyebrows raised in surprise. "Well... when you put it like that, I'd... Well, I'd suggest she has a pregnancy test..."

He looks at me and I look at him.

"Well, we have been shagging quite a lot lately," I say somewhat embarrassed, "and we've never used contraception in all these years because I'm supposedly barren... But – it can't be can it?"

"Have you done a pregnancy test?" he asks.

"No."

"I'll bring one back from work on Monday."

24th April 1999

Happiness Factor: 2/10. It's all going wrong. I feel bereft at the thought that we might lose Sinead, and I just feel dreadful all of the time. There's no way I'm pregnant – I know my body. I'm barren and these are menopausal symptoms. After all these years of trying to get pregnant, I'm not likely to do it in my 40s, when my egg count is lower than ever, and my hormones are diminishing. No. This is the fucking menopause, and I'm going to feel like this for about five years.

Later, I try to talk to Mum about it.

"Mum – how long did your menopause last for?" I ask.

"Oh, I don't want to talk about all that, Bridie, not now."

"But I need to know!" I whine. "I think I'm starting mine already, Mum – I really do."

"Don't be silly – you're too young. What about Lee and

Denise? I don't think they're menopausal yet. Why not talk to them instead?"

"Okay," I agree, and make a mental note to have a chat with Denise next time I see her. I'm not mentioning this to Lee. It would just be another opportunity for her to belittle me.

Later that evening Anna and Sinead are literally having a physical tug-of-war over the remote control.

"In my country, chilren no behave like this," Anna protests. "She is bad chile."

I quickly admonish Anna. "Please don't talk like this in front of Sinead," I whisper.

Sinead however hears me and launches into a sing-song, "Don't speak to me like that!" to Anna who then pointedly gives Sinead the remote control and leaves the room.

"Anna, Anna!" I call after her, running up the stairs, my breasts wobbling like two enormous jellies, and painful too. "I'm sorry – I know Sinead can be stubborn and rude, but she has low self-esteem and control issues. Many adopted children express themselves through control, you know."

"She just rude, Bridie. Naughty girl. In Poland, we not let chilren speak bad like that."

"I know Anna, but we do things a little differently here," I say haughtily, stopping myself from saying, *well, if Poland's so great, what are you doing here then?* "I will speak with Sinead, and talk to her about respecting her elders and sharing things," I add, but Anna just makes a face and stomps up the lovely wooden circular stairway we had especially made to the attic room, with the parting comment, "Pouuf! You too soft."

I administer a warning to Sinead about boundaries and adults and I ask her to have a minute's 'Time-out' to reflect on her behaviour. However she is in one of her defiant moods, folding her arms and adopting an aggressive stance.

"Make me!" she taunts, knowing I'm in no mood for a fight.

I decline. I am too tired to be a good parent.

I am sick all night and even Declan is worried.

25th April 1999

I reckon I am dying. HF: 0/10 I stay in bed all day. As it's
Sunday, I reckon Declan will just have to manage the house
without me, and anyway, he's got Anna to help him now. I
hear all the comings and goings downstairs, and bless Sinead,
she comes up from time to time to give me a cuddle, or bring
me a glass of water. (I can't stomach much else.) But, she
soon gets bored as there's more fun to be had downstairs
taunting Anna.

In the afternoon, Declan comes into the bedroom asking
if I've seen the lighter that he uses for the bonfires – the one
like a flame-thrower that we also use for the gas-burner when
we're having barbeques.

"No... I haven't seen that for ages," I reply.

"Sure you haven't been using it to light your fags?" he
asks grumpily.

I wretch. "Christ Declan, just the thought of smoking at the
moment makes me want to vomit. And anyway, I haven't had
a ciggy for weeks now, so it's not me who's lost it. Are you
sure you put it back in the shed after the bonfire we had when
Timbo was here?"

"Yes, I'm sure. It must've been taken by those bloody boys
– Rory and thingy.... whatshisname – y'know, when you caught
them in the shed smoking your bloody fag-ends."

"Mine and Bea's fag-ends," I retort trying to make him feel
excluded from the occasional girly bonding session I have with
his daughter, smoking like two naughty schoolgirls in our shed.

"So that makes it better, does it?"

"No, Declan! Don't take it out on me just because you've lost your favourite bloody lighter. Use some matches for God's sake."

"I haven't lost it. It's been stolen," he accuses.

"Oh, piss off!" I shout, exasperatedly.

Oh dear...

That evening, I swaddle myself in my dressing gown and make it downstairs to read Sinead's life-story book with her, the one that we've been painstakingly putting together ever since she came to live with us. Tonight she is drawing a picture of a horse.

"Who's horse is that?" I ask.

"Peyton's 'orsey," she replies. "We 'roded on it bareback. When will I see Peyton again?" she asks, as she draws what looks like a five-legged dog, but could just as well be a "orsey'.

"Oh, I don't know, Sinead. Do you really want to see them?"

Her eyes light up. "Yes, yes! Nanna and Magga and Murphy and Ginger, Ginger, Ginger!" she bounces around on the sofa, getting hyperactive and demanding. I wish I'd never mentioned going to see them, but there was just a little tiny place in my heart that thought she might say, "No, stay here with you."

26th April 1999

I wake up feeling most peculiar.

"D – can you get me in to see Dr Clarenson this morning? I just feel so rough. I think there's something seriously wrong with me. I might have cancer or something."

Declan looks at me from the foot of the bed, as he balances on one leg to put his socks on.

"Yes. This has gone far enough. Let's get you in today."

"Thank you, darling."

Dr Clarenson has a cancellation at 11.45am, so I make myself presentable, and drive to the surgery whilst trying not to throw-up on the steering wheel.

"Morning, Bridie. So how are you feeling?"

"Not so good actually," I say and then inexplicably launch into a monologue about my Dad, and my Mum, and maybe losing Sinead... I become tearful.

"Apart from that, what are your physical symptoms?"

"Oh, sorry," I say feeling a bit stupid. I don't know why I had to tell him my entire life story. "If I'm not being sick, I feel sick, and I'm getting hot flushes – but just my face, weirdly – and my breasts are painful... I think I'm menopausal..."

"When did you last have a period?"

"Ummm, not for a while actually, which is another symptom isn't it? Ummm – hang on, I'll have it in my diary." I reach down into my bag for my pocket diary and look for the little sad face symbol that I've used since I was about 25 to indicate that I'm having a period and therefore, not pregnant. I flick through the pages, back and back... I am surprised to see that I haven't had a period since mid-January. "About three months ago, to be precise," I say, a little tiny flutter in my tummy.

"You are how old... 42? It is a bit young for the menopause. How old was your mother when she had her menopause do you know?"

"She was 50," I reply. "Poor Mum – she suffered badly with tears and anxiety. That's why I think it's the menopause with me, because I'm just the same. Always feeling stressed and tearful, even if I'm ten years younger."

Dr Clarenson strokes his chin and asks me to lie on the couch. He wants to feel my stomach. I panic. What if he finds a lump – what if it *is* cancer? Probably ovarian cancer – I knew I shouldn't have taken those fertility drugs." Dr Clarenson probes my fat gut. "That hurt? And that? Any pain? You say your breasts are tender...?"

After a while he finishes his examination and asks me to return to my seat.

"Okay, Bridie – I don't think there's anything for you to worry about. Your symptoms are mostly chronic and could be any number of things – early onset menopause is one, but I want to rule-out some of the major contenders with a blood test, which should tell us a lot more. The results will be back tomorrow morning, so book-in to come and see me again tomorrow and we can take it from there. And I stress again, Bridie, I don't think it's anything major for you to worry about. Oh, and can you leave a urine sample too, before you go?"

Dr Clarenson has been about as non-committal as it is possible to be, and I feel no further forward – apart from the fact that the blood and urine tests will hopefully give me a clue to what's going on. I resign myself to wait another 24 hours. I'm good at waiting.

Chapter 25

It's Never Too Late

27th April 1999

Today is a day I'll remember for the rest of my life. I'm so nervous about the test results that I have a crafty ciggy – the first one for ages, out in the shed after Declan and Sinead have left for work and school. It makes me as sick as a pig. Never again! I wretch and heave and then wretch some more. That's it. I have officially given up smoking. I go into the house and look to see if there's anything in Dr Li's emporium that will help stave off this God-forsaken nausea. I clamp eyes on ginger capsules. That'll do. I down several and drink a glass of water. I throw them up.

My appointment with Dr Clarenson is at 10.00 am and Declan has cleared his appointments so that he can be with me – just in case it is bad news. I'm in the waiting room trying to preoccupy myself with Hello magazine, but nothing can stop my hamster-wheel thoughts. What if it's diabetes? How will I cope with no more trips to Bewley's with Mum? What if it is the menopause? Will it affect my sex-life? Will I get osteoporosis? What if it's cancer and Dr Clarenson was just being nice yesterday to stop me from worrying. What if...

"Mrs Kelly? Dr Clarenson will see you now."

Right – here goes.

I walk into Dr Clarenson's office and I'm surprised to see Declan's already there. I wonder if there's a back passageway that the doctors use privately? Clarenson has a serious expression, but Declan smiles at me as I come in.

Dr Clarenson gestures for me to sit down in the chair and starts shuffling through his notes. Christ. It is cancer, I think, he can't even look at me in the eye. It's probably bladder cancer – I'm peeing every five-minutes at the moment. Who will look after Sinead? Who will look after Mum? I visualise my funeral and decide that I'll prepare for it with special poems and affirmations. I want to cry.

"Okay, Bridie. I'm not really sure whether this is good news or bad news, but the test results show that you are pregnant."

... ??

.... !!!

What?

"What?!" Declan and I exclaim in unison after a pause of total incomprehension.

"Are you sure, James?" asks Declan, moving around to the other side of the desk to read through the test results and various other figures and notes. "Good grief!"

"I'm... pregnant?" I repeat, absolutely unable to take in the enormity of those words. "I think you must've made a mistake Dr Clarenson – I'm not able to have children..."

"Well, Bridie, unless I'm very much mistaken, I think you are."

All these years... all these years I've been waiting and hoping and praying until I'd given up hope. And for the last three months, I just didn't believe that my symptoms could possibly mean I was pregnant. I wouldn't even allow myself to go there – even when Declan said he'd get me a pregnancy test, I thought I wouldn't even bother because it was bound to come back negative like it always did, and then just totally knock me for six. Again. And now here is James bloody Clarenson telling me I'm preg...

"Oh no! Oh no, oh no, no, no...." The men look at me alarmed. I burst into tears. "Declan! I've been drinking and smoking! Oh my God. Oh Jesus Christ! Just my luck to fall pregnant after all these years of trying when I have a lapse back into smoking and bloody drinking! Oh my God – will it have harmed the baby Doctor? Declan?"

"Look, the most important thing is that you're fit and healthy," said Dr Clarenson. "The tests have confirmed that. You don't have any other health issues that we can ascertain, so if you desist from drinking and smoking from now on, the baby should be fine."

At least Declan doesn't say 'I told you so,' which is a huge relief.

I burst into tears again.

"I know this must be a shock to you both," says Dr Clarenson, and then all his words just blur together as the enormity of it hits me. I AM PREGNANT. Oh My God. Pregnant! I want to scream, "I'm pregnant!" I do, I scream, "I'm pregnant! Ahhh!"

Declan is beaming from ear to ear.

"Declan!"

"Bloody HELL!!!" he laughs and we hug and cry and laugh and Dr Clarenson looks embarrassed to see his senior partner acting this way.

After a while, we calm down enough to take some facts on board. "Possibly three months gone; need a scan; possible amniocentesis because of my age; need to book in a meeting with the midwife... The midwife! Oh. My. God."

After a while, I regain my composure. "But how has this

happened, doctor, after all this time? Why now?"

Dr Clarenson smiles. "You're not the first woman to get pregnant in her forties and you won't be the last Bridie. Sometimes – and I know this sounds a bit airy-fairy – but we have noticed that a death in the family is often followed by a birth. It's just nature's way, you know? But it's not all quiet straightforward. If you decide to keep the baby you are at high risk for pre-eclampsia and gestational diabetes. But let's get that scan done and we can take it from there.

"Oh and James," says Declan, "there's no 'if' here. We are keeping this baby."

God, I love him.

Declan deftly rearranges his appointments for the rest of the morning so that he can take me home. We walk out of the surgery like a couple of teenagers, completely high on life.

I stroke my belly as I sit in the car at the traffic lights. "Hello, baby – this is your Mummy talking."

Declan looks over benignly at me. I don't think I've ever seen a look on his face like that before. It's beatific.

I think we are still in shock. We have nothing to say to each other, but just keep holding hands and smiling. After a light lunch, Declan prepares to go back to work.

"Do you think we should keep it quiet for a while, Bridie?" he asks.

"No way, D! I'm not having everyone thinking I'm getting fat! It is going to give me the greatest pleasure to tell people our good news. The only one I'm worried about is Sinead. I wonder how she'll take it?"

"Ummm – good point. Wait until I'm home and we'll tell her together."

Later that afternoon, I walk around to Mum's house. I want her to be the first person I tell – after all, she gave birth to me and she deserves to be the first to know.

I knock at her door and then walk inside to find her snoozing in her armchair, ostensibly listening to the radio.

"Bridie, darling! What a surprise. I was just having a little sleep – I do a bit now, during the day – it helps to pass the time, you know? I do get lonely. I miss the family life, the hustle and bustle... It's too quiet here without your father... nothing going on, just boring old dreary Mrs Leary from next door popping-in for a cuppa every wretched morning."

"Mum," I butt-in, "Mrs Leary is a good friend to you. Don't speak of her like that."

She ignores me. "Hilary and Bunty have been very good to me though. And I like that Anna lady at your house. She is very patient with me. Now what did you want, or have you just come round to keep an eye on me?" she says, as she tries to get up out of her chair. "Let me get you a cup of tea."

"Mum, Mum – it's alright. I don't want a cup of tea, and I think you should stay sitting down."

I steady her onto her specially adapted armchair. Her beloved dog Trixy who is ancient and half-blind immediately jumps on her knee and settles down for a stroke and a cuddle with his mistress.

"Mum, I've got something to tell you."

"Oh no, not more bad news? Don't tell me – Sinead's been excluded again or Bea's got herself into trouble. Nothing would surprise me in your family."

I feel myself bristle at this rebuke. "No, Mum, it's nothing like that. Sinead is up and down as usual, but nothing to worry about and Bea's doing fine. She wants to be a sports psychologist, whatever that is. She's got a new horsey boyfriend – he's rich, I think – and she has been doing some 3-day eventing with him at the weekends. So all's well and good there. Actually, it sounds quite serious with her boyfriend – they're thinking of getting engaged."

Mum claps her hands. "Well that's good." She stares at me. "So, you are not ill, are you, Bridie. You've been off-colour lately."

"No, nothing like that Mum," I say impatiently. "I'm, I'm..." suddenly I can't say the words to my Mum. I become shy and embarrassed. What the... "Mum, I'm not Barren Bridie anymore."

Now it's Mum's turn to look impatient. "What are you talking about? Stop talking in riddles, Bridie. I am getting confused – what did you say?"

I'm leaning over, stroking Trixy, taking some strength from the little dog.

"Mum – I'm three months pregnant."

She looks like she is going to pass out. I hold her shaking hand and look at her tired face but then she suddenly stands up and does a weird little jig. "Bridie! Are you sure? Have you had a test? Oh! I never thought I'd see the day. If only Stanley was here – he'd be so pleased! Are you sure? I can't take this in!"

With that she trots out of the door towards the kitchen, calling back over her shoulder, "I'm just getting those special chocolate biscuits your Dad likes. Come on. Let's celebrate!"

Suddenly, all is well with the world.

Later, back at home, I am like a cat on a hot tin roof. Amazingly, the sickness has abated. Well, perhaps it's because now I know why I'm feeling sick, it doesn't bother me any more.

Next, I phone Bea, who to be fair, has been quite worried about my ill health.

"Bride - are you alright?"

"Are you ready for this, Bea? You really will never

believe what I'm going to tell you!"

"Get it over with Bridie – what's the result? Early menopause? IBS? Colitis?"

"Nope," I reply smirking. "I am only three months pregnant!"

I hear a sharp intake of breath, and then, "Nooo! Kiss. My. Ass!" (which I think is a bit inappropriate, but is probably young-people-speak for 'amazing'.) "How on earth can that happen after all these years? Have you been secretly taking the fertility drugs again? Of course, once you approach the menopause some sort of hormonal surge kicks-in. It's like the body's last chance to procreate!"

"Bea! You make me sound ancient! I'm up the duff!" (I can speak easily like this to Bea, but I see Declan raise an eyebrow at my terminology.)

"Fuck-a-duck!" she says, "I'm going to have a brother or a sister! Wow! I'm so pleased for you and Dad, Bridie, I really, truly am. I know how much you've always wanted this – ever since I saw Dad injecting your ass with those fertility drugs when I was a little kid – remember? I knew then that you had to really want something to put up with that!"

We chat a bit more for a while, and Bea says she's going to try and get home as soon as she can to give us a big hug in person.

We decide not to tell anyone else yet. We'll just get the scan over and done with first to ensure everything's alright, and to be honest, I don't have the energy to go through the whole story again tonight. A couple of times I've thought I'd like a glass of wine to celebrate, but that's a total no-no now.

Once Sinead's asleep, Declan and I curl up on the sofa – it's the first moment we've had together all day to sit and talk and take it all in.

"Hello, baby," I say to my stomach repeatedly. It just amazes me – that there's a baby, a longed-for baby in there.

"What about names, D?" I ask. "NOT Susan or Derek, that's for sure!"

"Or Margaret or Patsy!"

"What about Murphy if it's a boy?"

"Or Peyton if it's a girl?"

"Shhh! Stop it! That's not fair! I like Colm for a boy and Eliza for a girl – what do you think D?"

"Actually Bridie, putting my doctor's hat on, I'd say that we shouldn't get involved in names yet – not until all the tests and the scans have been done. You know there's Downs Syndrome and all sorts of things that can happen as you are an... older mother."

"Declan! I'm going to let that one go! Older mother my ass!" I say, picking up Bea's lingo.

"Actually, darling," Declan continues, "if I'm to use the proper medical terminology, anyone who has a baby over 35 years of age is technically a geriatric mother."

"Declan!" I shout and throw a cushion at him. "Go on, pretty please! Just pick one boy's name that you like," I torment him.

"Well, I quite like Hunter or Charles or Duncan?" he says with a twinkle in his eye.

"Erm, NO! Much too public school-y. Stanley would turn in his grave," I reply smiling. "How about Chuck, or Latham, or Benno? What about Northwest or Heath?"

Now it's Declan's turn to chuck the cushion back at me.

God, I love him.

Last thing at night I find my secret cigarettes stash and matches and I bin them, just like I did with the fertility drugs.

17th May 1999

It's over three weeks since I found out I was pregnant, but
today is the day for the scan. Thank God, as I can't keep this a
secret much longer – I'm getting enormous. I look six months
pregnant already! I'm not taking any supplements because for
once, I'm following Declan's advice. He thinks that as we're
not entirely sure what the supplements do, it's best not to
risk them whilst pregnant. My Happiness Factor is 11/10 and
I think it has rubbed off on Sinead, because she's been a little
angel recently and we're getting on better than ever. However,
I am going to have a baby and it's not all plain sailing. I get
heartburn, incredibly loud flatulence in the most embarrassing
of places, like in the local bakery, overwhelming tiredness,
weight gain by the second and perhaps worst of all, cystitis.
But I don't give a damn. I'm having a baby!

At 10.15 am the phone rings. It's the hospital. Oh, bugger
– it looks like I will have to wait a bit longer now to see my
baby. Apparently the scanner machine is playing-up. I am so
impatient. Three trimesters of pregnancy seems an awfully
long time before I can meet my little one.

21st May 1999

The scan is back on for tomorrow, so only one more day to
go before I see my baby. I'm bursting with joy at the thought.
However, Sinead doesn't have the best of days.

I pick her up from school only to find that she has had a
'toilet accident', poor thing. She hands me the discreet plastic
bag containing her pants and a brown envelope with 'To the
Carer' written on it in firm black ink which gets my back-up for
a start. Why couldn't they have just written to Mrs Kelly – they

know who I am, for God's sake.

At home over tea and biscuits, I am cool about the incident. "Oh dear, Sinead, never mind. Everyone has little accidents now and then. You will get at better timing in the end. You need to practice those muscle exercises I showed you." I demonstrated the squeezing and relaxing of the pelvic floor which is supposed to help with bladder strength. Christ! I think I felt the baby move. Oh my God!

I calm myself without letting on to Sinead. "Now then, let's look at this letter, shall we? I start to read it.

To Sinead Riley's Carer – we note that Sinead is coming to school with nits in her hair. Please kindly deal with this problem immediately, before there is an outbreak in the entire class. My blood boils. How dare they accuse Sinead! They pick on the poor child, I'm sure. I'm usually so careful with her hair – but I have to admit that of late, I've been neglecting the regular, dreaded nit-comb because I've been feeling so ill.

"Wha's it say Mummy Bridie?" Sinead asks.

"Ummm, oh dear, somebody in school has nits. So we will have to give you a nit-comb tonight, okay?"

"No, not nit comb."

"We have to Sinead – it says in this letter."

"No! Go away letter!" she shouts and goes to snatch it out of my hand, but she overbalances and knocks into my stool and I fall to the floor with a bump. My first thoughts are for the baby, but we're okay. Sinead looks horrified.

"Sorry, sorry Mummy!" she pleads, as if I'm going to hit or chastise her, and runs out of the room.

I get up, and regain my composure. No harm done. I devise a plan to secretly nit comb her hair in the sitting room, whilst she watches Teletubbies – still her favourite video after all this time, much to Declan's chagrin. I'll dowse her with T-Tree and conditioner, and then comb out her hair over a bowl of water.

If we've done it once, we can do it again.

But evening comes and I can't find her anywhere. I thought she'd gone to her room after she knocked me off the stool, but she's not there. I search high and low for her, but she's nowhere to be found. I call Anna and ask her to help me look. Anna stomps down from her eyrie, huffing and puffing. "Where bad girl now?" she asks. I wonder whose English is worse: Anna's or Sinead's.

Something tells me to look in the garden shed – call it intuition – and there she is, crouched in a corner, nursing her thoughts. But my only thought is, how the hell did she know where the key was? Declan and I agreed a hiding place and have kept the shed locked ever since. She's a canny one this girl.

I'm too sick and tired – literally – to have another slanging match with Sinead over the key, and I'm certainly not going to give her the nit treatment tonight. She goes off to bed, tight-lipped and tearful and I decide not to tell Declan about the key. It'll only cause a scene.

22nd May 1999

Hurray! It's the day of the scan. I am picking Declan up on the way as they're badly understaffed at the surgery and he couldn't take the whole day off. But that's fine. Today is about me and my baby. Anna can take over the household duties – that's what we pay her for, and it will be good practice because soon, Mum will be moving in and I will be heavily pregnant and I'll need her more than ever. Note to self: Ask Edna if it's okay for Anna to look after Sinead – I don't want to contravene any rules, especially if our chances of keeping Sinead are 50-50. Actually, perish the thought of Anna doing anything with Sinead – those two just don't get on.

I leave a note for Anna detailing her chores for the day and drive off to collect Declan and then on to the hospital, a bag of nerves and excitement.

In the Women's Health Waiting room, I look around me and yes, everybody is much younger than I am, but I don't care about that. My baby is a miracle baby! However, I make a vow to go to Lush and get some more hair-dye. Those stray greys must be consigned to the past. I am Bridie Kelly, 42 years of age and I am about to find out how far gone I am and possibly whether I'm having a boy or a girl.

"Declan – what will it look like, the scan thingy?"

Declan is busy reading the *Irish Times.* "Hmmmm?" he says vacantly. "Oh, well if my experience is anything to go by, it'll look like a little peanut and it'll be so smudgy and unclear that you can't tell if it's got legs, wings or a pointy tail."

I nudge him. "Try and be more enthusiastic, D! I am so excited – and I can't sit down because my back aches from all the meditation you're making me do." If truth be told, I feel sick and hungry at the same time. The worst part is the serious wind I keep getting – I can fart for Ireland. I can hardly tell anybody about that now can I? But I don't care, I really don't. I can't ever remember being this happy in my whole life. HF: One Million!

A smiling receptionist informs me that there is a bit of a backlog because of the problems they've been having with the faulty machine. But I don't care! OMG – I have never been so excited in my life before. My legs are jigging up and down and my eyes are permanently fixated on the receptionist.

"How much longer?" I whisper to Declan after waiting what seems like hours. "Shall I go and check what's happening?"

"No, Bridie! Calm down and read a book – stop thinking about it. Practice some of your meditation techniques."

I obey and give in to the tiredness that is suddenly overtaking me. I close my eyes and dream of babies.

30 minutes later, I am finally lying down and awaiting my scan. The video monitor has arrived, and I tingle with excitement, bracing myself for the cold gel to be spread on my ample belly. I squeeze Declan's hand as Irene the radiographer, applies something that looks like a microphone to my swollen belly.

"How many weeks are you?" she asks, a puzzled look on her face.

"We're not sure. The doctor thinks it could be as much as 12 weeks, but, well like I say, we're not sure."

"Mmmm – it's a big baby for 12 weeks then." I feel a bit hurt about this remark. Is she implying that I am fat?

She scans my big belly. "Now then, ooh ...yes! There we are, look both of you – it's there: a good strong heartbeat. Yep, baby looks very healthy."

I can't see anything really – not even the peanut Declan mentioned. It all seems rather blurry and indistinct to me.

Irene suddenly stops in her tracks and becomes quiet. I try not to panic. She makes a clicking noise with her tongue and stares for what feels like an eternity at the video monitor.

"Is something wrong?" Declan asks anxiously.

She does not answer. I cannot stop the panic rising in me. "There's something wrong isn't there, nurse?"

Irene scans my belly again and smiles. "Nothing wrong, it's just that it looks like double congratulations are in order. Now lets just see if there are two or three babies in there?"

What?

"Bridie, Declan – it looks like you are expecting twins!"

Declan sits bolt upright and peers at the screen. "Are you sure?"

Irene beams and strokes my belly with the scanner. "I am

sure. Look here, can you see?" She points to an indistinct blob and we have to take her word for it. "Do twins run in the family at all?"

We both nod.

Ten minutes later we are at reception booking another scan for two weeks time. Irene does in fact think that I am around 12 weeks pregnant, but because of my age and the fact that I am carrying twins, they want to keep a careful eye on me. I am in shock: numb, scared, ecstatic, tired, delighted and of course, feeling sick.

Bewleys 1.30 pm

Declan is worryingly quiet. He orders two large cappuccinos and two jacket potatoes with salad. I stare at him to try and gauge his thoughts. I ask nervously if everything is okay? He is pensive, biting his nails and staring into space.

"Yes, I suppose so. Sorry darling – I suppose I'm in shock... I just feel a bit too old to be juggling twins. One baby is hard enough, but two... I didn't expect it, not in a thousand years. I thought it was just going to be Sinead and the new baby, y'know? But we will cope. At least we've got Anna to help. Winifred's going to need a lot of care too, but we'll cope, won't we?"

It's rare that I have to console and buck-up Declan, but this time I do. "Of course we'll be alright darling. It's everything I've ever wanted. Two children. It's a miracle! I promise you, we will be fine. I PROMISE you."

We arrive home to find Anna in a bad mood.

"You child very, very difficult. She spit and say she want to go back to her family. I tell her I want to go back to Poland to my family, but I have to stay here."

Oh dear. I am not sure that Anna is suitable as a babysitter after all.

"Where is she now, Anna?" I ask, concerned.

"She in garden shed with her life storybook. She crying – always crying or angry. Never stop talking about her old family."

"What the hell is she doing in the shed?" Declan storms. "She knows it's out of bounds. How on earth did she find the key?"

"Declan, Declan. Leave it for now. Let's speak to her later, eh? Let's let things cool down a bit first shall we?"

I am Supermum.

7.30 pm

We knock on Sinead's bedroom door once she's ready for bed, so that we can try to explain to her what is happening.

I sit beside her in bed and tell her about being pregnant. "Sinead, you know you have been worried about Mummy Bridie being sick? Well I'm not ill but I am going to have twins – that means I am going to have two babies. Isn't that wonderful?" I draw a picture of a Mummy with two babies inside her tummy, making sure that Sinead is depicted beside me smiling.

"That's Sinead," she says, pointing at the picture of herself.

Sinead strokes my tummy and then pouts bowing her head and rocking back and forward. She's confused, obviously. "Will you still be my Mummy Bridie?"

Unexpectedly, I become tearful and upset, because after my last meeting with Barry Black, I know that's something I can't guarantee her.

Thankfully, Declan steps in. "Sinead, we love all our children: you, Bea, the twins – we love you all. Now come and give me a little hug."

Sinead snuggles up to Declan for a while, and I'm thankful to him that he doesn't mention the shed and key incident. But later, once she's asleep, I question him about what he said.

"D – do you really love all the children, including Sinead?"

"Well, we do love them all, don't we? Just in different ways. I love Sinead, but I don't find her easy. Doesn't mean we won't still love her when the twins are born. That's if they let her stay with us."

"What do you mean?"

"Well, don't you remember when we did that course? They said that if biological children were born into an adoptive household it often changes the dynamic and causes problems. That the adopted child felt they were no longer part of the family, and that they had to fight for affection, literally, sometimes. And then what they said to you about us not being a cultural match. Bridie, I think we have to brace ourselves for bad news about Sinead. I just want her to know that whatever happens, we'll always love her."

I am in bits. I know he's right.

9.30 pm

Right – that's it. Everybody knows the news: the cat is most definitely out of the bag. Reactions have varied from:

"Fucking hell!" – Bea

"Oh no!" – Mum

"Fantastic news!' – Flora

"Mum told me actually. How on earth are you going to cope with two?" – Lee

"Right, well Mum told me you were expecting. Just not

twins. I suppose now you've got what you've always wanted – a big family, right?" – Denise

"God bless us and save us!" – Aunty Bernadette

"Oh. I see." Edna

"Oh. We need to talk then." Barry Black

"Yay!" the twins and Mikey

"No, no, not good at your age." Anna

Chapter 26

Worst Nightmare

27th May 1999

6.00 am

The phone rings and jerks me out of a deep sleep where I was dreaming of rows of identical babies in cots, and I was trying to find mine. It was a nightmare actually. I sleepily reach for the receiver, still in a daze from the odd dream, and manage a raspy, "Hello?"

There is no reply except the sound of a little giggle. I curse the caller and fall back into a deep and dreamless sleep.

3.30 pm

I wait tensely at the school gate for Sinead. Other parents avoid me – they assume my child is spoilt, and that her behaviour is due to over-indulgence or lack of boundaries. Little do they know what she's been through in her short life. It's all too easy to make judgments and assumptions without knowing the full facts. Sinead sees me and waves, running gratefully towards me.

"Horrid day. Hate teacher. She put me in another room and I wet myself. Look!" she says, pointing to her soiled pink pants, swinging in a clear plastic bag. I feel for her – they could at least have put the pants in a bag that wasn't see-through. "I got boy's pants on now – look!" she says, boldly lifting up her skirt in full view of the other mothers, and displaying a pair of older boy's white Y-front underpants. Perhaps they're the only spares they had in the school? I make a note to pack a spare pair of knickers in Sinead's schoolbag, as this is becoming a worryingly regular occurrence.

"Sinead!" I hiss. "Little girls don't show their knickers in public."

She frowns. "I do! I like these pants. Can I have boys pants?"

I laugh, despite myself and reply, "We'll see."

I notice that Mrs Hancock, Sinead's new teacher, is making gestures at us. I groan, "What now?"

Sinead picks up on my annoyance. "Hate her too."

Mrs Hancock smiles as she joins us. "If I could have a quick word please?"

My face reddens involuntarily, as if I'm bound to have done something wrong. "Sure – okay, in there?" I say, pointing to the bus shelter, which is now vacated and will give us somewhere private to speak. "Sinead, if you can just go and play on the climbing frame, I will be with you in two ticks," I say, somewhat optimistically. I usher Sinead back into the playground and prepare myself for bad news.

Mrs Hancock smiles. "Lovely little girl," she says patronisingly, as it's obvious she doesn't like Sinead, "but we are having big problems at the moment. She seems to take great pleasure in tormenting everybody, and just makes trouble for herself. I don't like to pry Mrs Kelly, but has anything happened at home that might have upset her?"

For once I am in a good place. "Yes, since you ask," I reply. "We have just told Sinead that I am pregnant – and not only that, with twins," I smile and enjoy the look of total surprise on Mrs Hancock's face.

"Oh, umm, I see. Congratulations, Mrs Kelly. I suppose that is the kind of news that would affect Sinead. So... will she be staying with you?" she asks. I can see her thought process. Maybe they'll get rid of Sinead after all.

I smile and nod. "Yes, Mrs Hancock, yes. She'll be staying with us."

4.00 pm

To make sure Sinead feels loved and secure, I spend more time than usual with her, on her homework. We have to draw a peacock tail, but we decide to do something a bit special. We trace the shape of a peacock onto cardboard and fill in the body and tail feathers with glitter, honesty seed pods, synthetic feathers stolen from an old boa I haven't worn in years, and turquoise-blue paint. The result is fantastic, even though I say it myself! Sinead reaches for her Happy Book Diary and writes, 'i was in truble at scool cuz wain hit me and i hit him bac harder. i got sent out i hate teacher tonite we dun a peecoch i love it.'

Hmm... Art therapy? They do say it works.

At that moment, Bea walks through the back door – true to her word, she has come home to see us and celebrate our news. She looks amazing – a beautiful young woman, but not too old to be excited about the imminent arrival of her new siblings.

"Bridie bloody Kelly," she says hugging me. "I don't even like to think what you and Dad have been getting up to!"

Then Mum arrives with some expensive new baby clothes.

"Bridie," she says, her face flushed with excitement. "I bought these in that new shop in Dublin – Lee helped me choose. I do hope you like them?" I open a carefully wrapped parcel to find six romper-suits, all in a neutral colours. I hug them and hold them up to my face to feel the softness of them.

"Thanks, Mum," I say, overcome with emotion. "I never thought I would see this day. Bridie Kelly, 42 and pregnant with twins!" I realise my H/F is sky high.

Sinead is wary and thoughtful. She leans against me, and hugs Roger Bear, and then unexpectedly, there is a kick from inside my belly, which she feels against her side. Her eyes widen. "Baby kick me!" she says with a smile. "Mummy, can I help look after the babies when they come?" I note that when she wants to get round me, she calls me Mummy.

"That's a long way off Sinead," I say, trying not to make promises I can't keep. "Mummy Bridie has got to get a really big tummy first! Now, how about you go and play with the dogs in the garden, whilst I have a chat with Grandma and Bea?"

"Okay!" she says sweetly, and skips off, her mouth stuffed full of chocolate buttons and toast.

"What was that all about?" Bea whispers.

"It's still not certain we can foster her, let alone adopt her," I say, once Sinead's out of earshot. "The SS think we're not a good cultural match for her, and also, me being preggers may affect their decision."

"Christ. It never rains but it pours in this house!" she laughs, and I'm inclined to agree.

5. 30 pm

The phone rings and a sniggering boy's voice asks for Sinead or Bea. I hear a different, leering voice in the background, grunting, "She's well fit that Bea."

"Who is this?" I demand, wondering how on earth they know that Bea is here. "Did you ring this morning?" I am livid.

"Who the hell are you? Don't you dare ring here again, do you hear me, and you leave Sinead alone..." but the phone has gone dead.

"Something wrong, dear?" asks my mother.

We decide to go outside and relax on the swinging sofa-chair in the garden, basking in the warm sunshine. We watch as Sinead tries to line up the dogs and teach them tricks, but she is soon bored.

"Bridie, can I go to the park on my own?"

I tense up, remembering the stressful time we had with Johnny. "No, Sinead, you're too young to go on your own."

"No I'm not. I go on my own! Wayne and Rory and Tommo do, so why can't I? I am going."

Thinking quickly and predicting either a tantrum or a complete meltdown, I ask Bea to do me a favour and accompany Sinead for half an hour to the park. Bea is reluctant but agrees. "I'm going out with the girls tonight," she says, "so it'll have to be half an hour max." She winks at her Grandma. "Do you want to come out on a girly night with me Grandma?" she asks.

My mother laughs. "I don't want to cramp your style, dear," she says.

Bea and Sinead wander off to the park – peace at last. We study Bea's photos that she brought to show us.

"Oh, is that her steady young man?" Mum asks. "Isn't he handsome!"

"Yes, and rich by all accounts," I add.

My mother smiles approvingly "By the way, Hilary Manson, just up the road, had somebody walk into her garage last night and steal some tools. They forced the door open with a crow bar. It does scare me, Bridie – nowhere's safe these days. Apparently there have been some strange goings on in the neighbourhood. Kids, probably... In fact Hilary and Bunty are in Neighbourhood Watch now."

"Well, you can move in with us sooner rather than later, Mum," I say, trying to comfort her. "Why don't we set a date?"

"Oh, I don't know, love. I've got a lot to do first. I've got to get the attic emptied and sell a load of stuff..."

"But we'll help you do that, Mum. You don't have to do it on your own."

"I know, I know. Don't push me, Bridie."

Mum leaves a little while later as Bunty is visiting her to talk about the Neighbourhood Watch scheme, and as Declan's working late, and Bea and Sinead are in the park, I find myself alone. It's such an unusual occurrence that I feel vaguely uneasy. The house is so quiet you could hear a pin drop. Then, there's a knock at the door. *Probably the girls back from the park, and Bea's forgotten her key,* I think to myself, but when I open the door, nobody's there.

7.00 pm

Thank God for The Railway Children – Sinead's new favourite film, and a vast improvement on Teletubbies. She was exhausted from her foray to the park with Bea, and is now settled in front of the TV with a glass of milk, crisps and a jam tart – all against my better judgment of course, but I feel in a celebratory mood because Bea's here, so I let Sinead have a little feast, all of her own. She's totally mesmerised by the children in the film.

It's not long before Sinead is nodding-off, and I get her up to bed quickly, and before I can even go to kiss her goodnight, she is asleep.

Bea also makes a swift exit for her girly evening out, and at last, I can relax. I talk to my babies and apologise to them for the stresses of the day. I consider whether they are girls or boys or one of each? Note to self: I have missed two scans, so ensure that I talk to the midwife soon to ensure everything is as it should be. Suddenly I panic, a thousand pictures running through my mind: what if there is something else wrong... God after all this wait, that would be just my luck. I would do anything to protect my babies... But then a sereneness descends upon me as I recognise that this is just my hamster-wheel brain kicking in. I observe the thoughts, but let them go. I don't attach to them, and I just breathe deeply through it. I amaze myself, but it works and a calmness floods through me. Tiredness overcomes me and I curl-up on the sofa, in a haze of peacefulness.

And then the bloody phone rings. I answer it, and there's silence on the end, or perhaps I can detect a bit of heavy breathing? I am mature and hang up. I will not stress my babies.

At nine o'clock, just as Declan is coming through the back door, the phone rings again, with the same breathy silence on the other end. I hang up, but Sinead has woken.

"Bridie, can you come up? I had a scary dream."

By ten o'clock, I'm in bed relaxing with, would you believe it, *The Railway Children* book. It's so lovely and wholesome. The children are so... well, so easy.

The phone rings again, and I'm beginning to feel my temper rise. I decide to answer it quickly, before Declan picks-up downstairs, as I haven't mentioned these nuisance calls to him yet. He'll go mental.

"It's me," Bea says. "It's going to be a late one!" I hear the sound of heavy music and people partying in the background.

"I'm having a great time, Mum, so I'm going to stay for a while. You don't mind do you?" There's another one who calls me Mum when she wants to get round me!

"Of course not, Bea! But please don't walk home on your own, okay? Get a taxi," I warn her. "Hilary says that there have been burglaries and funny goings-on round here late at night."

"Oh Hilary! She's such an old fuddy-duddy! Don't worry though – I will get a taxi."

"Okay, love – have a great evening," I say, tiredness overcoming me again. Declan's watching a film downstairs, and I enjoy having the bed to myself for a bit. I make star shapes with my arms and legs and sing a little lullaby to my babies.

I am awoken in the early hours by the front door banging shut. Luckily, Declan could sleep through a Force 9 gale, and doesn't stir. I tiptoe into the hallway to see a rather inebriated Bea negotiating her way up the stairs. She smells of smoke and alcohol.

"I take it you haven't given up then?" I enquire. "The fags!" I add, as she looks confused.

"Oh? Ha ha! All hail, O'Bridie, mother of twins. The miracle of birth, hic..." she sputters and heads for her room, almost hitting the doorframe as she totters in.

Bless her. It's nice to let her hair down with the girls on occasion, I think, but as I close the door to our bedroom, the phone rings again – for the fourth time today. I pounce on it, but this time I just get the dialing tone. Who is ringing my house at this time of night, and trying to talk to my daughters? Could it be anything to do with the break-ins I wonder? I'll tell Declan tomorrow and inform Hilary and Bunty at Neighbourhood Watch.

28th May 1999

It's Saturday morning, so we have a little lie-in. Over coffee, I tell Declan about the four phone calls yesterday. He raises an eyebrow but doesn't seem overly concerned, much to my surprise. "It's just kids, Bridie – probably that Rory and Wayne, getting their own back. Don't rise to the bait," he mutters.

Nonetheless, I ring Hilary and ask her to keep an eye out for anything suspicious. She tells me Bunty is furious about his tools and thinks we should bring back the birch!

If our time with Sinead is going to be limited, then I want her to have as nice a time here as is absolutely possible. So I ask her jauntily what she would like to do today.

"Want Wayne and Rory to come round."

"Ah, no Sinead," I say. "Remember what happened last time?"

"Promise we'll be good."

Declan looks up from his newspaper, and surprises me yet again by saying, "Okay Sinead, they can come round to play later this afternoon for an hour, alright? Now go and get dressed so we can all take the dogs for a walk."

Sinead nods her head and agrees, a broad smile on her face. At the speed of light she dashes upstairs singing, "In and out the dusty blue bells/ Who will be my partner?"

"Declan?" I enquire

"I bet you anything whilst those boys are here we won't get any dodgy phone calls," he says. "Let's call it an experiment."

We have a relaxing morning on the beach, having called around to Wayne and Rory's first to invite them round for tea. I don't really want her to mix with these lads, but Declan thinks it's better to befriend them and talk to them, rather than ban them and alienate them. I think he's getting soft in his old age.

By the time we get home, Sinead is high and can hardly wait for her friends to turn up. When they do though, there are four of them. Wayne, Rory, Tommo and Sean. I look aghast at Declan, who looks aghast at me. So much for his plan to befriend them – this is more like a gang. Tommo looks a bit scared when Sinead puts her arm round him – he's smaller than the other boys and puts me in mind of Johnny a bit. Rory has brought a can of coke and some bubble gum, which makes Sinead's eyes pop out of her head with excitement. He is making it very plain that he's only here because his Mum made him come to look after Wayne, and that he's finding it all very boring indeed.

"So, what do you want to do kids?" I ask, and in unison they chant, "Play on the trampoline!"

Great, I think. An hour outside on the trampoline, a few sandwiches and crisps and they can all bugger-off back home, and Sinead will have had her special day. That's about as much as I can cope with.

They drag the trampoline – which is quite a big one – over to the patio and wedge it by the annexe, so they can launch themselves off it and jump across my flower border, landing on the other side. The winner is the one who can jump the farthest. I'm having kittens as I watch, with visions of broken legs and crushed begonias, but even I have to admit, it's quite a good game, and they're in fits of laughter. Rory wins, but Sinead is second.

By 4.30 the house is in chaos: doors are open, pop music is blaring from Sinead's CD player and the dogs are wary and barking. It is now raining so they're all inside causing mayhem. I suggest a DVD with some popcorn and hot chocolate, which seems to go down well, but when it comes to choosing the film, they sneer at Sinead's selection.

"I'm not watching Watership Down!" says Rory.

"It's better than Teletubbies," says Sean

In the end, they settle for The Railway Children, and I don't hear a peep from them for an hour as they become engrossed in the film. The three younger boys are all on the sofa, with Sinead rather inappropriately wedged in the middle, holding court. Oh, how I wish she had a girl as a friend – would it be too much to ask? Rory is rather surly – perhaps too old for all this – playing on an expensive looking Nintendo Super Mario game. (I know about these because Sinead is forever asking for one.)

I'm sitting in the kitchen with Anna – who is horrified by the mess in the house. She keeps saying, "Not my job to clean after village boys," and I'm too tired to argue. I am nursing a cup of tea when there's a knock at the door. Declan answers, and returns with a face like thunder, saying, "The puppy's on the road, Bridie. Those kids must've left the gate open! John Jarvis has just brought her back. And somebody has been in my study playing with Uncle William's camera. Right, I need a little chat with that lot!" So much for his 'befriend them' technique. He marches into the lounge and switches off the film to moans and groans all round.

"Right! Who left the garden gate open?"

Silence.

"The puppy got out onto the road. She could've been run-over."

Silence.

"Well, please be careful and shut the gate in future," Declan warns. "And who's been in my study playing with the big camera?"

Silence.

"Please don't go into my study in future. That camera belonged to my Uncle William and it's very valuable to me."

"So it's okay to come here 'in future' then, is it Mister?" asks Rory confrontationally.

"Well, I don't know about that, if today's behaviour is anything to go by," huffs Declan. "And it's Mr Kelly, to you."

Tommo and Sean shrug their shoulders and look at the floor. Rory blew a defiant bubble with his gum and Wayne burped. They all collapse, laughing. Declan takes himself off to his study to rescue the camera and get away from all these, "bloody irritating kids."

By 5.30, I am looking at my watch every ten minutes and practicing telling the boys it's home time. The problem is, Sinead does not like it when people leave her, and I don't want a big scene. But when I do suggest it's time to go home, nobody takes a blind bit of notice of me.

Before long, Bea comes downstairs from where she's been trying to work on one of her final assignments from college, and raises an eyebrow at my feeble attempts to restore order.

"Oi! Boys!" she shouts out, and as one they stop their bickering, turn and look at her and go dewy-eyed. "Your parents will be wondering where you are. Off you go now. Home – shoo!"

They all complain, but miraculously do as they're told, and I realise that they're all a little bit in love with her, including Sinead. Oh, the glories of youth!

"Thanks, darling," I whisper as she hands out their coats, and all-but boots them out of the door.

Declan appears from his study and says, "Just like I thought – no phone calls..."

Later that evening, there's a knock at the door, which is unusual for this time of night. Again, there's nobody there.

"Sinead" I shout into the twilight, "is that you messing about?"

"No! I'm upstairs," she shouts back.

By nine o'clock, Anna and I have got the house tidy again, the dogs are fed and have calmed down from the day's activities, and Bea is finishing her assignment in her room, the glow of her laptop screen and the gentle tapping of her fingers the only sign of activity in there. It is just Sinead who is still restless. She peers out of her bedroom window every five minutes and asks if she can go and, "find the boys".

"They'll be in bed by now, Sinead," I say, "like you should be."

"They won't! Rory stays up all night. He plays with the big boys in the park."

My blood runs cold. Christ – he's way too dodgy for her to be hanging about with. I'm going to have to put a stop to all this and try and encourage her to make girl friends.

By ten, I am tucked-up in bed reading a book about baby names – as Declan watches the second half of his film, downstairs. Apparently, he fell asleep half-way through, last night. It's so exciting to be thinking of names. I like Peter, but maybe it's a bit old-fashioned? What about William – that's nice; after Declan's beloved Uncle, the photographer who once had a series of images in National Geographic. William Kelly. Billy Kelly, *Billy Kelly* – bit of a mouthful? Edward? No, too posh. Gareth – hmm, I like that one. Girls names are easier: Jessica, Ellie, Lily... I gaze at the romper-suits and feel their softness, but then notice a splash of paint across several of them. Blue paint, like we were using on the peacock yesterday... Thanks, Sinead.

At 10.30, I get up for my usual dose of Gaviscon – the alternatives do not hit the spot, and indigestion has been plaguing me for weeks. I check on Sinead expecting to see her fast asleep, wrapped around Roger Bear. Wait a minute though – her bed is empty... She must have gone to the toilet? But the bathroom is vacant. I knock on Bea's door.

"Bea? Is Sinead with you?"

Bea is annoyed. "Fuck this assignment! I can't get it right. I shouldn't have drunk so much last night. 10,000 words? Fuck me. And I've got a terrible headache... Sorry? What did you say? No, Sinead's not with me..." She returns to her laptop, tapping furiously.

Getting worried, I shout up to the attic room and ask Anna if Sinead's with her. Anna appears at the door, bleary eyed in her dressing gown, with her hair in rollers. Funny, I just assumed it was naturally curly.

"She not here – naughty girl. Never do as she told."

I suddenly panic, and run around the house calling out her name crossly: "Sinead! Sinead? Where are you? Come on – this is silly, it's late, I need to rest. This is not good for the twins," I add, thinking that might make her feel guilty, but deep inside there's a growing fear that she's gone walk-about to find the 'big boys' in the park.

I walk into the kitchen and find the dogs on edge. They wag their tails and look towards the back door, which is open and creaking in the wind. Christ, no... My mind goes into overdrive. She's so uninhibited around boys... What might she do... oh God. "Sinead!" I scream. Declan's head pops around the edge of the sitting room door – he's obviously not got much further through the film than last night – his eyes are filled with sleep.

"Love?" he asks.

Five minutes later and still no Sinead.

"She in shed!" Anna says, and goes to check but comes

back shaking her head, looking worried herself.

I tell Declan and Bea about her wanting to go and meet the big boys in the park. Declan pales visibly and gets his coat. Before I know it he's out the door, and in the car, reversing dangerously out of the drive, even though the park is only five minutes' walk away.

"Call the Garda, Mum," Bea orders. "Just in case."

I do as I'm told, and they put me on hold, whilst they transfer my call to the local branch. A Constable Cooper takes down details of Sinead's appearance and what she's wearing, and relays it to his colleagues who are out on the beat, or whatever they call it these days.

I look in the shed again, just to make sure she's not crept back in there, but no. It's dark and cold. Sinead was only wearing her nightdress the last time I saw her. I run back up to her room and realise that she must've been planning this as the clothes that she wore today are gone, and so are her trainers.

Where is she?" I sob to Bea as Declan returns saying that there's no sign of her or anyone else for that matter, in the park. "What if she's been abducted? What if they have taken her? It might be Murphy or one of her relatives... Should I ring Edna?"

I am hysterical with worry.

"Bridie!" Declan snaps. "Calm down! The police are looking for her, and me and Bea will get back in the car and carry on searching. Where do you think she might've gone?"

"I don't..." a sob catches in my throat. "Let me think... I don't know, D. "

At that moment, we all see a blue flashing light in the hall as it bounces in through the glazed doorway. Anna goes to open the door and two uniformed Garda arrive, which makes it all too horribly real.

"Mr Kelly. Mrs Kelly," they nod. "Now, let's ascertain a few facts. Have there been any problems at home recently? Any arguments? And she is how old? Seven, nearly eight? Goodness, they are getting younger and younger these days... Now don't worry. She's more than likely looking for these boys you mentioned... So now, where do they live? And if you could just give us a photo of her..."

Tearfully I proffer a photo of Sinead cuddling Hilda.

I pray that Sinead is found quickly. The stress is doing me no good at all. Declan has been taking my blood pressure every day as a precaution and he's already worried that it's a bit on the high side. I pace the house and bite my nails. Declan and Bea return. They've been past the school, past Wayne and Rory's house where the police were already, up to the cemetery and past the shopping precinct. No sign of her. I make tea, but none of us can drink it.

Time ticks by agonisingly slowly. After all the hoax phone calls, I now stare at the phone, willing it to ring. It doesn't. Midnight comes and goes, but still nothing. Declan gets back in the car for want of something to do and starts searching again. Questions pop into my head: was that somebody at the front door, waiting for her? Why didn't I hear her leave? How did she get out of the back door when it was locked and the key was in the larder – does she know we put the key in the larder...?

At 1.30am, when we are low with despair, we get a phone call to say Sinead has been found and that she is cold and tired, but she is okay. She was walking along the racecourse road, but actually the other side of the fence, so nobody driving past saw her.

A little while later, a woman police officer brings her home.

She looks cold and weary.

"Sorry, Mummy," she says, before I can say anything. I am so relieved I just hug and hug her, kissing her head and feeling the coldness of her hair.

"It's okay, it's okay.... You're home now... Sinead! I was so scared. Why did you go? Why?"

"I saw Rory in the park and he told me he played Knock Down Ginger on our door and he smokes. Then Bobby told me to go and find Peyton and Murphy, so I went to find them... and I got lost... and I ... got frighted..." she starts to snivel and then it turns into a full-blown howl.

Anna steps in. "I put her to bed, Bridie. You rest now." Thankfully, without hesitation, Sinead takes Anna's hand and goes upstairs.

It is quite a while before the police are gone and Declan and I are alone in the kitchen.

"It's been a long time since she mentioned her invisible friend Bobby," I tell Declan. "But she's always talking about bloody Peyton... Maybe the SS are right D? Maybe we can't give her what she needs?"

Declan is quiet for a while and then, in his considered way he says, "We'll speak to them first thing on Monday morning. It's only going to get worse, and I can't have you dealing with these stress levels. We have all done our best for young Sinead, but maybe we just have to admit that she doesn't really want to be with us?"

29th May 1999

This morning, I ask Sinead to tell me the story of Knock Down Ginger.

"Rory says you knock on somebody's door and then

you run away," she answers, still pale and subdued from the night before. As I listen I marvel at how well Sinead speaks now after such a short time with us, and how quickly she is growing up. But, I am firm.

"That's not a nice thing to do, Sinead. When Wayne did it to me yesterday, I was worried. It would frighten people like Grandma or Hilary. I don't want you to play that game, okay?"

"Okay."

"And I'm sorry, Sinead, but I don't want you to play with Wayne or Rory any more. They hang out with the big boys, and you are a little girl. I don't want you to come to any harm."

Instead of kicking-off as I expected, she looks worried and bites her lip. "Oookaay..." she says, and slips off the chair and goes to sit with the dogs in the back kitchen. I then ring Hilary to warn her that the boys are in the park late at night and being a nuisance knocking on people's doors and running away. Note to self: keep all door keys on top of cupboard in the back kitchen – there's no way Sinead could reach them there, even with a chair.

I join Sinead and try and engage her again, as I want to talk to her about the dangers of running away – but I find her sobbing, her head buried in the fur round Harry's neck.

"I'm sorry I naughty, Bridie," she sniffs. "I want to be friends but people make me do bad things, like Bobby said run away, and Rory said to smoke in the shed..."

"Okay, Sinead, don't worry now. Just please speak to me first. Tell me what's going on, okay? If you want to see Peyton, tell me and I will see if I can sort it out. You don't have to do it on your own. Okay? Just tell me."

"Okay," she sniffs. All thoughts of grounding her and punishing her go out of the window. She's a vulnerable little girl and I don't think punishment is what she needs.

We return to some semblance of normality and Anna tells me about the course she is attending at the local higher education college to gain some qualifications as a carer. She announces proudly, "I go college and learn to be proper Irish carer and maybe I find boyfriend and live here forever. When Winnie come, I help her in house. Keep her safe from falls, from risks. Old people very vulnerobble," she says seriously, but I know what the subtext is, 'Once I'm qualified, you'll have to pay me more'. She goes on to meticulously list the things that need to be done. "We must have fire extender..."

"Extinguisher," I correct her.

"Bars for the bathroom to stop her fall slip in shower..."

I listen wearily and promise to address these issues.

"Tomorrow, I go on a First Aid course."

I groan silently and make a mental note to buy a new First Aid Kit. I mostly use ours for the dogs.

Since Declan has been promoted, he has to do less 'On Call' duty than previously, but tonight he is 'On Call'. Declan's practice and two other local practices converge for the night duty – they cover a vast area for emergency medical support. It means that usually one night a month, he goes into the surgery to answer the phones and deal with emergencies. As he's a senior partner he usually gets the Sunday shift which is often very quiet, but it does mean he goes into the surgery at 8pm in the evening, and doesn't get back until the following morning. He does get the next day off though. As everything has quietened down, and Sinead is on her best behaviour, and Bea's here to keep me company, he deems it okay to go.

Before he leaves, I ask him to have a look at the window in the en suite because it is jammed open and the sash cord is broken. The window would most likely guillotine my hand off if I attempt to move it. He promises to do it in the morning and kisses us all goodbye. Secretly, I think he likes his On Call nights because he can watch what he likes on the TV, and I know he always gets a Chinese take-away.

Us girls have a relaxing evening watching Coronation Street, doing our nails, dying my hair with henna, which has been only a partial success because there are still lots of determined grey streaks making their presence felt. Sinead seems distracted and takes herself off to bed early, and I too absent myself as I'm still exhausted from last night's shenanigans, so it's bed for me and a good radio play to listen to. Ah, this is the life, peace at last.

I must've fallen asleep because at about ten-thirty, Anna wakes me up. "Sorry Bridie, but dogs not stop barking! I think there is somebody walking around outside. I hear a noise, like bang. I panic, check Sinead's room – she asleep I think".

Anna and I tentatively walk around the garden with a beam torch, but can see nothing. We go right to the back by the veg patch and the fire pit, and into the shed, but can't see anything untoward. Carly and Harry however, are not happy. They growl and their fur stands on end – it shakes me up a little bit.

I allow the dogs to sleep with me in my room tonight. Declan will kill me, but I am nervous, what with the hoax calls and the Knock Down Ginger and then Sinead running away. Note to self: hoover-up dog hairs before Declan gets home.

Just as I settle down, the phone rings twice in quick succession. Only two rings each time, then it stops. Bloody Rory's nuisance calls again. I pray that it hasn't awoken Sinead.

Later, I wake-up for the toilet and as I sit there half asleep-half awake having the longest pee ever, I feel certain that I can hear footsteps on the flat roof below my en suite window – the one that's jammed – and I think I hear someone whisper Sinead's name. It's the roof of the annexe and I think how easy it would be for someone to scale it and climb in through this goddamn jammed window. But the dogs would be barking, wouldn't they? Of course they would. I reassure myself that all's well. Relax, Bridie Kelly – don't let that hamster-wheel brain of yours think of the worst-case scenario.

Both dogs do growl as I get into bed and my heart beats fast, but once again all seems quiet. I am on edge and imagining things. Mindfulness Bridie: remember your meditation. Breathe; relax; breathe; relax... breathe... relax ... br...

"Fire, fire! Fire, fire... Fetch the engines, Fetch the engines..."

This is not a dream. I wake-up totally disorientated. Anna is shaking my shoulders roughly, shouting, 'Bridie, Bridie, wake up!" I hear the smoke alarms ringing, and the dogs are barking. I can smell smoke.

Anna screams, "There is fire downstairs in kitchen. We are locked in – where keys Bridie?"

"Oh fuck..." I say, "they're in the back kitchen. You won't be able to get them. Oh shit! Where's Bea? Where's Sinead?"

"Bea getting Sinead out of bed. What we do Bridie? Can't get out!" she coughs, as Bea and Sinead come into my room

"Stay upstairs everybody – don't go downstairs," I say. Sinead looks worried to death. "Bea, check if the phones are working and ring the Garda." Thank God I brought the dogs up here to sleep tonight, I think.

Bea picks up the phone by my bedside table. "The phone's dead Bridie!" Bea shouts. "The fire must've melted the line and I've left my mobile downstairs..."

"I get my phone!" Anna shouts and goes to leave my bedroom, but comes straight back in, her face ashen. "Fire come up stairs!" she screams. "Oh my God!"

My mind is racing as I take on the enormity of what's happening. My beautiful babies... Oh Christ!

"The window! Out of the window, onto the flat roof. We can wait there until the Garda come. We'll scream until somebody hears us."

We run into the en suite, dragging the dogs by their collars. The smoke in my bedroom is by now choking us and our eyes are stinging. "Shut the door Bea. Now Anna, help me push this window up a bit more so we can get out of it."

Anna and me try with all our might to shove the window up a bit higher, but it is well and truly jammed.

"Help us! HELP!!" Bea screams out of the window.

We try again, but it will not move. There's only about a ten-inch gap between the sill and the frame of the window. Maybe Sinead could wriggle out, but us adults couldn't.

"Help! Help!" Bea screams again.

"Stand back everybody. I have idea!" says Anna and she picks up my bathroom scales, smashes them against the single-glazed pane on the left hand side of the sash. It's about two-foot square and just about big enough to get through. The glass resists.

"For fuck sake!" says Bea, as she scouts around the bathroom for something else to smash the window.

"Declan's dumbbells – in the bedroom..." I shout. I prise the door open and gasp as the smoke hits me in the face. '"Jesus, Mary and Joseph..." I take a lungful of air and hold my breath. Even in the semi-dark, lit only by a streetlamp through the thin material of the curtains, I know my way around this room. I go to Declan's side of the bed, open his wardrobe door and feel around on the floor for his dumbbells which he uses each morning, routinely for about five minutes – his only nod towards exercise all day.

I have to breathe... I have to breathe... I let out the air and take a lungful of smoke. It winds me and catches in my throat. I feel myself start to choke; the acrid taste in my mouth makes me wretch. I grab the dumbbell and make it back to the bathroom. "Shut the... achh.. achh... bloody door," I cough. "Here!"

I hand the dumbbell to Bea and she heaves it at the window. It breaks the glass and falls onto the roof below. Anna clears the jagged shards with the edge of the scales and wipes the splinters away with a towel.

"Sinead – you first," says Bea, all the while eyeing the door as smoke starts seeping under it. "Mind the splinters."

Sinead deftly springs up and through the window with ease, and drops to the annexe roof on the other side, a height of probably four feet, but a big drop for her. I can hear her little voice screaming for help as one or two lights in people's houses go on across the road.

"I'll jump on the trampoline," she shouts. "I'll go and wake next door." Before I can answer, I realise that the children had left the trampoline wedged up against the annexe from their games yesterday, and it easily breaks Sinead's jump. I can hear her running towards the garden gate.

"You next, Bea," I say.

It's not easy for Bea to get out of such a small space, and it dawns on me that there's no way I'll get through the gap. I'm three months pregnant, but as the nurse said the other day, I look like I'm six months gone. Jesus.

"Hurry Sinead," I shout out of the window as Bea drops onto the annexe roof.

"Don't worry, Bridie," Bea shouts up at us. "I'm on it!" She too jumps off the roof onto the trampoline, and Anna and I are left in the bathroom, the smoke wreathing our bodies in a veil of choking, acrid haze.

"You next," I say.

"No! I not leave you Bridie."

"Go on Anna, the fire brigade will be here any minute."

"I wait then," she says. "Here." She hands me a towel soaked in water. "Put over your head. Stop the smoke. Help the babies."

I do as I'm told and she gets under the towel with me. We lean against the window, and feel the heat of the fire under our feet and coming through the door. I feel sick and weak.

"Hurry, please!" Anna shouts out of the window.

I think I can hear sirens in the distance, but I'm not sure. Anna shakes me gently.

Bridie? How you feel?"

"Can't breathe...." I hiss. "The smoke's bad now, Anna – save yourself, please!"

Suddenly I remember the dogs. Oh My God! I come out from under the towel into the smoke-filled bathroom, to see my beloved dogs crouched in the corner by the shower. They are both quiet and I think, overcome by the smoke. Without a second thought, I scoop Harry up and thrust him out of the window. I hear him drop to the floor the other side and start barking madly. Thank God although I worry he may have cut his paws on the glass shards. Then I do the same with Carly, who is much lighter, and much more afraid than Harry. Poor little mite. Then I look at Anna, who is crying. I can see from the streetlight that her face is sooty from the smoke.

"Go Anna." I say, and this time I mean it. She looks at me and hugs me, then turns to the window, but... I can see torchlight flickering in at us, and blue lights flashing too, and I think... I think I must've fainted.

Chapter 27

The Aftermath

7th June 1999

I wake, feeling groggy with a pounding headache, and realise that I am in hospital, and that someone is holding my hand. It is Declan – his eyes the bluest I have ever seen them, and full of love.

"Oh Bridie! Thank God you're okay."

"Am I? What about... the babies, D?"

"They're okay, they're okay. No harm done really. Your blood pressure is high, and they want to keep you in for a few days just to keep an eye on you – complete rest for you now my girl!"

"What happened Declan?" I ask, scenes from the fire flashing-back in my memory.

"Don't worry about all that now, darling. You just rest-up. Everything's okay. The dogs are fine, we're all fine..."

"But our lovely house...?" The tears start to flow. "What about our lovely house?"

I am hospitalised for a week. The doctors tell me my blood pressure is sky high and I risk miscarrying. Fortunately after five days of complete rest, the scans are fine. Slowly, I piece together what happened.

After the fire – which has totally devastated our house – Sinead had to be put into emergency foster care, whilst Declan, Bea and Anna all descended on my mother, who, like in the days of old, has risen to the occasion with a constant flow of tea, cakes, dinners and kind words. The dogs have been lavished with love and seem none the worse for wear – I can't wait to see them.

Declan was very worried about Sinead and arranged to visit her the next day at her emergency placement, and slowly but surely she told him what had happened. Apparently, the night she ran away, she went to see Rory and he told her that he was going to steal Declan's camera and that she should leave the front door open. But of course, I locked it and hid the key. So he jumped onto the annexe roof and called to Sinead to open her bedroom window, which she did. (So, I wasn't going mad when I heard something outside, but if only I'd acted upon it then.) Once in the house, Rory and Sinead went downstairs to Declan's study, which is at the back of the house, off the kitchen, whereupon he nabbed the camera, and as Sinead said to Declan, "Put his doggy end in the bin" – in other words, the stupid sod chucked a lit cigarette into Declan's waste paper basket.

When Declan asked Sinead why she didn't tell Mummy Bridie, she said, "I did, I sung her the 'Fire Fire' song."

Later, we had confirmation from the insurance company that the fire was indeed caused by a discarded, lit cigarette in Declan's study, which quickly spread to the kitchen and then throughout the house. The Garda arrested Rory and found Declan's camera in his possession – which only has sentimental value to Declan, but which is in fact pretty worthless to anyone else.

The rest, as they say, is history.

14th June 1999

I am home – well, if you can call it that. We have moved in with my mother, as our house is condemned. It will have to be knocked down and totally rebuilt. Initially she was delighted and loved our company, and kept making us cups of tea and homemade fruitcake, however I feel the novelty has worn off somewhat! She gets cross with us and tells us we are messy like Stanley was. But she dabs her eyes whenever the fire is mentioned, saying, "I could have lost all of you."

Bea has returned to college, although she's pretty much finished all her exams and has a job in a summer school running an equestrian centre. Anna is still with us, but Declan, bless him, has asked her if she can work for the surgery as the cleaner/caretaker, and she's delighted because there's a small flat that goes with the job. Perfect for one. I will never, ever forget her loyalty to me that night. In fact, I think she saved my life.

My main worry is Sinead, but Edna and Barry have stepped-in to take control of things whilst I'm taking my bed-rest. We have a meeting with them tomorrow, to discuss what the future holds, and I have not seen Sinead since the fire.

15th June 1999

Edna and Barry arrive at my mother's house for our meeting, as I'm still not really feeling well enough to travel. They are obviously concerned for my health, but congratulate us both on our news about the twins. Then they get down to business. I have been bracing myself for this moment, and I think I know what's coming, but nothing can prepare you for the shock of a decision that is taken out of your hands.

"So, Declan, Bridie," Barry says, "we have had several emergency meetings about the situation with Sinead, now that you are in effect homeless, and it has been deemed that the right thing to do is to leave her with her current foster carers until such time as a long-term decision about her future can be made.

I am stunned. I never thought of us as being homeless, but... I suppose we are. This is not our home – we are in temporary care ourselves.

I try to persuade them otherwise. "But Barry, my mother wouldn't mind if Sinead came to live with us here. Just until we found ourselves somewhere to live."

"And then what, Bridie?" Edna says. "More of the same? More of Sinead running away, and bullying you, and struggling at school? Now that you are having twins, the dynamic of your family life will change forever. Sinead as an only foster child may have worked in the long run, with lots of counseling and support from us, but as a foster child in a family with newborn twins? That's a recipe for disaster. And in any case, we feel her best interests are served by placing her in a family that has closer cultural ties to her birth family."

I've been agonising over all these issues for months. They're saying nothing that I haven't considered before, but they're asking us to give-up on Sinead, and I don't want to do that.

"What about love?" I ask desperately. "Does that count for nothing? We've formed a bond with Sinead – won't breaking that bond be detrimental to her?"

Edna and Barry pause and look at each other – a bit like 'good cop, bad cop'. This time Barry takes the initiative.

"Bridie, the fact that you and Declan love Sinead is indisputable. But Sinead transfers her own affections quickly and easily. She's had to do this all her life in order to survive.

She's been with her foster carers just over a week, and she's already saying she wants to stay with them forever. She's more resilient than you think."

That hurts, and I know that I am fighting a losing battle. What is more, I haven't got the strength for it. Declan says nothing, but holds my hand.

"Can I see her, to tell her what's happening please? I need to explain to her that we love her, and that it's not her fault."

"Of course," they say, obviously relieved that I am not making a fuss. "And Bridie," Edna says (good cop), "what you and Declan have achieved with Sinead in such a short space of time is remarkable. She is like a different girl – much more confident with her language and her interpersonal skills... You should be very proud."

I'm not proud. I'm devastated.

21st June 1999

It's midsummer's day, but you wouldn't know it. The weather is grey and cold, to match my mood. I'm feeling fine again physically, but today I feel distraught; it is a day that I have dreaded.

Edna has written down some guidelines about what to say to Sinead, but there seems to be no kind way of telling your foster child that she cannot be with you anymore. Declan and I plan and plan what we are going to say, and we are very sad, but resolute. This is the best thing for everybody. We decide to emphasise that she will be able to see her birth family more often, and that we will hear from the SS regularly about how she is getting on in her new family, just like with Johnny. Most importantly we will tell her that she was a gift to us and that we love her very much.

The dreaded moment has come. We drive to the Family Centre, where the meeting will take place, armed with a box of tissues and some treats. Sinead comes into the room holding the hand of a social worker, chatting amiably. She sees us and stands stock-still, rooted to the spot, her face suddenly a confusion of worry and panic.

"Hello, Sinead!" I say, patting the chair next to me. "Come and sit over here with us."

She looks at her social worker who nods and lets go of her hand, and she walks over to us, her head bowed, looking at the floor."

"Are you okay?" I ask, determined not to say, 'I've missed you' and 'I love you'.

"M'okay," she says, then, "How's Harry and Carly and Bea and Grandma?"

"They're all fine," Declan says.

She looks at the cakes and sweets we've bought with us and then looks up at me suspiciously and says, "Is it someone's birthday, Bridie?"

Despite my best efforts, I dissolve into tears. True to form, she comes to my side and pats my hair saying, "Don't cry, Bridie."

Declan takes over – I just can't look her in the eye. "Sinead," he says, "We both love you very much – I hope you know that? But we can't look after you any more."

"Because of the fire?" she asks, shuffling her feet and fiddling with a pack of sweets.

"Partly because of the fire, yes..."

"I'm sorry! I'm sorry Bridie. I didn't know it would happen..."

"It's okay, Sinead," I say, pulling myself together. "It's not your fault. It was a naughty thing that Rory did, and he shouldn't have made you let him into the house, but the fire is not your fault. I want you to know that we don't blame you at all."

"The thing is, Sinead," Declan says, taking over our version of good cop, bad cop, "we think it would be better for you if you stayed where you are now, because Edna and Barry are going to let you see more of Patsy and Murphy..."

"And Peyton and Ginger?" she butts-in, her face suddenly bright from the mention of their names.

"Yes, and your sisters too, if they can. They are going to try and find you a new home so that you can see all your old family more often."

"And Magga and Nanna?"

"Yes, Sinead."

At that, she starts to hop around the room, singing their names gleefully in one of her funny little songs that we have come to find so charming. My tears do not abate, but somehow, she's making it alright for us.

She stops mid-flow, and comes and stands by my side. I place a little box in her hand that contains a beautiful gold cross on a chain. I thought a present would distract her, but she doesn't even look at it.

"S'okay, Bridie," she says, and then, most unexpectedly, she puts her arms around me, gives me a hug and says, "You go now."

It's like we have been dismissed from her life. I am stunned as she walks over to the social worker, holds her hand and walks out the door. She does not turn to wave goodbye.

Epilogue

October 2010

I was searching for Bea's birth certificate in the bureau today and I found you – my old diary. I tentatively opened you up and read the last entry dated June 1999. Ouch – it makes for painful reading; all about the devastating house fire and the loss of dear old Sinead. I often wonder what happened to her... Around this time of the year, just as we're gearing up for Christmas, I always remember her. We've lost all contact with her now – in fact we never saw her again after the fire, although I did send her a small album of photographs and Christmas cards for the first two or three years, via the social services. I gaze at the last photo we have of her. Thinking about it, she will be about 19 years old now. I just hope she found a family that loved her as much as we did.

Anyway, I have been inspired by finding my old diary to start writing again, joking with Declan that I might turn it into a book. With this in mind, Declan has bought me a sophisticated new computer, teasing me that at this rate, my book might be finished by the beginning of the next century.

I'm going to start with a quick update since we left Dublin. After the fire, it took three months for the insurance money to come through, but well before then we were approached by a local developer, who said he would like to buy the site from us, as he wanted to build a small courtyard of flats there. We weren't sure at first, but realised that if we did sell, it would mean we would have enough money to buy a house somewhere else, and if we were careful, we would have enough savings so that Declan could work part-time and help me with the twins. So that's what we did. We found the house where we live now – a beautifully renovated old farmhouse near a place called Fethard-on-Sea in County Wexford. We chose this house because it has a self-contained little cottage at the end of the garden, which is just right for Mum and Mavis, her live-in carer. More importantly, the house is beside the sea and it has 2 acres of land for the dogs to roam free in, and for Declan to experiment with his new-found passion for organic gardening. Bliss.

I gave birth by caesarean section to twin girls and named them Ita and Belle. It was a rough old pregnancy. I was stressed up to my eyeballs, mourning the loss of Sinead and coping with the after-effects of the house fire and then the move. I developed anaemia and had high blood pressure throughout. Had I not been so determined with all my yoga, meditation, swimming and swallowing every supplement going, I don't think the twins would be here now.

Lee and Denise were an inspiration. They supported me and helped me grieve for Sinead, taking me to the endless scans and hospital appointments, many of which I had missed in the early stages of my pregnancy. This probably accounts for the late diagnosis of Belle's Downs Syndrome. It was a huge shock at the time.

The twins were born at 36 weeks. Belle went into the special baby care unit for 2 weeks and Ita stayed with me. Ita was breast-fed and she latched-on straight away – she just seemed to know what to do automatically. For me, a first time mother, it was an... oh, I can't describe it... It was a sensational experience. I just sat there stroking her and feeling her perfect skin and little soft feet. I had waited so many years for this precious moment. With Belle, sadly things were not so straightforward and she needed lots of extra help to feed. Her tongue was problematic and on top of that, she was a sleepy baby with a very floppy neck. We ended up having to support her neck with a huge pillow and feed her every 2 hours. It was exhausting. In the end, after two months I gave up and opted for bottle-feeding her.

During this time, Mavis – Mum's carer – helped Declan with the running of the house. She would tidy up, walk the dogs and cook big stews and stodgy apple crumbles. I was so grateful for her help. I remember those days well.

Ten years on, and Ita is an academic, quiet little girl – she's what I call, 'low maintenance'. Belle is the opposite! She is larger that life and does not seem to have a stop button! During the week she attends a special residential school, which she loves, learning something new every week. She can now just about read a few words. Her time away gives me special 'mother/daughter' time with Ita, who slightly resents all the attention Belle receives from me.

My step-daughter Bea also has a child, Joshua, now aged 7 years. Bea, though, has recently separated from her partner. I think the stress of the fire changed her in many ways. It was such a shock to her, and she could never find it in her heart to forgive Sinead. For a long time she kept repeating, "We could've died – we could've all died," and she doesn't seem to laugh as much as she did before the fire. I think it took away the feelings of immortality that you have as a young person.

So that's it, and here we are – another Christmas around the corner, and ten year-old twins to enjoy it with. We count ourselves as very blessed.

Epilogue

23rd December 2010

Christmas shopping in Dublin – hooray! What fun! Actually, it's not really, it's a nightmare. Belle gets very high and excited by all the Christmas lights and just wants to stop at every stall to buy food and sparkly things, whereas Ita wants to go to book shops, or to buy some sheet music. It's hard to please both of them. They are so different it can be a challenge, but I love them equally and devotedly. My babies.

Exhausted, we cross over O'Connell Bridge to look for a coffee shop and a sit down. Suddenly, a scruffy, toothless woman interrupts us with, "Buy some heather Mrs? Good luck will come your way." She forces the heather into Ita's hand and asks for a Euro, which I give her just to diffuse the situation.

Shocked, Ita hands me the crumpled and battered bunch of heather. "What's it for, Mum?" she asks.

"It's just a way for people to make some money darling. Sometimes people don't have very much money, so they sell things on this bridge to help them make ends meet."

She nods, knowingly, but I am immediately reminded of Sinead, Margaret and Murphy and a similar situation many years ago.

Lying in bed later, I chat to Declan and tell him about the heather and this leads me on to discussing Sinead as I often do at Christmas.

"I wonder what happened to her?" I muse. "I wonder if she got a job or stayed with that foster family?"

As usual, Declan is not interested. He found it far easier to let Sinead go than I did. "Darling, that's all in the past now. Go to sleep."

But I can't sleep, and for some reason, a memory of

something my Mum said many months ago comes to
my mind.

"Bridie, I think I saw that little girl that we used to know.
I think I saw her in Dublin when we were there last week for
my hospital tests." But I didn't see anybody I recognised, and
because most of the time Mum is in a fantasy world of her
own, due to the dementia, I just nod and agree.

But Mum persists. "No, really, Bridie, I am certain I saw
Sindy, smoking as usual. On the bridge in Dublin, with some
very rough people. Didn't you see her? That little girl, that
rude one?"

"No Mum, I didn't see her."

"You don't believe me, do you? What was she called?
Sindy? Or Susan? Yes, Susan. I was terrified of her." She
frowned at me. "Bridie, I have not lost my marbles quite yet
you know."

31st December 2010

It's seven o'clock in the evening, on New Years Eve – my
favourite night of the year. The twins (well actually only Ita)
have lit lots of scented candles and placed them all over the
house. Declan sternly warns of the dangers of naked flames
and fires. He is always checking the smoke detectors and
says, "Girls, make sure you never put candles near curtains, or
books, or anything that can catch fire, and always make sure
you blow all the candles out before you go to bed." He points
at Ita. "That's your responsibility Ita, okay?"

"Yes, Dad," she huffs, having heard this mantra many times
over the years.

Declan has made a huge roast dinner. As usual there is
a veggie option for me and Ita. There are thirteen of us for

dinner tonight. I can smell Yorkshire pudding and peas. I hear
Declan grumbling as he makes two different gravies. "I don't
know, Bridie – why can't you and Ita be the same as everybody
else and eat meat? I have to do two of everything." He mops
his brow with a dramatic flourish and gives me a wink. Ita and
I smirk, exchanging knowing glances.

Belle is very excited tonight, and she rushes around
grinning and giving everybody hugs, saying in her own way,
"Heppy Yew Year!" She is now instructed to round everybody
up to come to the table. She leaps around prodding
everybody: "Cumon! Now cuuurrm on! M'ungry!"

Aunt Bernadette, Mum, Mavis, Declan, Bea, the twins,
Joshy, Flora, Brendan and Mia – who we haven't seen for a
couple of years as they now live in Germany – and me and
Declan. A full house. A happy family. Declan fusses as much
as Belle, ordering everyone about. He loves cooking our New
Year dinner.

"Winnie, why don't you sit here beside Mavis and Belle?
Bea, Flora? Come and sit next to me, my darlings. Bridie
opposite, so I can keep an eye on you!" he winks at me again.
"Happy New Year, everyone!" he says, raising his glass. "Good
health and happiness to you all!"

The food is very tasty and everybody compliments him on
the meal. To be honest, he is an excellent cook. We all raise
our glasses again – the girls and Josh having sparkling apple
juice – and we toast in the New Year. Aunt Bernadette, who
is now a robust 88, gives us a little blessing: "May you be
blessed with warmth in your home, love in your heart, peace
in your soul, and joy in your life. And let us not forget absent
friends." She looks reproachfully at Bea, upset about her failed
marriage. She crosses her chest dramatically and says once
again, "To absent friends."

It is at just that moment that we all hear the sound of a

van crunching up the gravel drive, coupled with the bass beat of loud music and the slam of a van door. We look at each other enquiringly, but nobody is expecting a visitor tonight. The doorbell trills and the dogs bark madly in the outhouse.

I peer out of the window into the cold, dark night and I can just make out a white, beaten-up old camper van with a bright yellow sun painted on the outside.

As usual Belle runs to answer the door shouting, "Cuuurming! Heppy Yew Yeeaarrr!"

I hear the sound of a heavily accented Irish voice saying, "Sarry to bother youz on this special night but, is Bridie Kelly here please?"

I freeze. OMG. I recognise that accent... It sounds just like... no, surely – it can't be....?

I walk towards the hallway and suddenly, there she is – Sinead! Sinead is in my house, as bold as brass and as large as life. On the lapel of her leather jacket is a little pink spray of heather. I stare at her, completely dumbstruck, as she smiles at me. She has grown much taller of course, and put on a bit of weight, and her thick red hair is matted and tied back with a ribbon, some of it in dreadlocks. I am so surprised to see her.

"Sinead! Oh My God! Come here!" I exclaim, and I hug her. She smells of weed and alcohol, but she's alive and she's here in my home. I am so happy to see her.

"Bridie! It's so good to see youz! I have been trying to find youz since I was 18 and they could tell me where ye went. God it's been difficult. It's okay though is it not – if I say hello to youz all?" She looks nervously around at the family who have gathered in the doorway to see who is visiting us on this auspicious night.

"See!" said my mother, "I told you I saw Sindy in Dublin, but nobody believed me," and she stalks back into the sitting room to settle herself by the fire.

Epilogue

Suddenly, Sinead notices the twins, and kneels down to their level. "Hello! God, I remember before youz was born. One of youz kicked me when you were in Bridie's tummy!"

Belle immediately hugs her and grins a big goofy smile. She offers Sinead her hand and giggles, "Heppy Yew Year!" Ita steps back cautiously, retreating behind Bea who is clearly unimpressed with the visitor.

"Hello Sinead," Bea says formally. "What are you doing here?" Bea is cool, but Sinead is red hot, her green eyes animated.

"I just missed y'all so much, I had to find youz! I've still got Roger Bear y'know! He's in the van with Murphy! Then she fishes out a photo album she carried with her in her handbag. Bridie gave me these as a leaving present an' I've always kept them. It was never the same after I left..." (At least she didn't say, 'After you abandoned me,' I think.)

She gazes around the house misty-eyed, although it's not the place of her childhood. "It's lovely an' peaceful here," she says and wipes her eyes. "Oh, I have missed youz all! I've had so many placements... and none of 'em any good..." she drifts off, then snaps back. "How are the dogs? Still got 'em?" She coughs and looks around for them. Belle runs to the outhouse and lets them out. Harry, who is now 14 and an ancient, fat old thing, waddles towards her. She reaches in her pocket for a dog treat, instantly creating a bond. There's no doubt in my mind that he remembers her. His thin tail wags and his eyes, now full of cataracts, suddenly seem to sparkle – or maybe that's just me. Carly is less confident, probably smelling the weed on her. She eyes Sinead up cautiously and lets out a low-pitched growl.

Next it is Declan's turn to be shocked – he'd gone into the kitchen to fetch the pudding when the doorbell rang, and now he returns to the room, Joshua in tow, with a huge pavlova on a silver tray. I see him freeze.

"Hello, Declan! Remember me? Sinead?" she says, staring at Joshua. "Who is this then?" she asks. Declan stares back. He is speechless and looks awkward. He clears his throat as he plonks down the pavlova.

"Sinead. Happy New Year." His voice is unemotional. "This is a surprise." And I realise at that moment, that like Bea, he blames Sinead for the fire too... despite everything he's said to the contrary. "This is Joshua, our grandson – Bea's son. What are you doing with yourself now?"

Sinead smiles and shrugs her shoulders. "Ah well, God – y'know me! This and that. Met up with the old folks. They said they'd seen youz in Dublin, Bridie. Bought some heather from one of Murphy's old friends, y'did, an' she recognised youz. I see 'em often, God love 'em. Me Dad has a terrible drink problem – always in trouble wi' the law. But I go to mass now every Sunday, God willing. That's when I am not on the Bridge selling this and that... How's Aunty Bernadette?"

"See for yourself," I say. "She's in the sitting room with Winifred and Mavis. They're playing cards." I lead Sinead into the warm, festive lounge. "She is 88 now you know," I laugh. "She'll be happy to see you, I am sure." I am still reeling from the shock that Sinead is here with us.

I hear my mother's triumphant voice. "Everybody, this is Sindy, who I was telling you about. See I told you, I was right! I have not quite lost my memory after all. This is Sindy – she is our granddaughter who lives in New Zealand. She is a doctor."

Sinead giggles and kisses my mother. "You've not changed, Grandma," she says, but she whispers in my ear, "Is she okay?" I wink back and press my finger to my lips.

Next it's Aunty Bernadette's turn to be greeted. They shake hands politely. "I go to mass every week and I always think of you," Sinead tells her. Bernadette nods approvingly. "Sure you'll be wanting to get yourself a home, and settle down. You want to be working hard and staying out of trouble. I will pray for you."

Suddenly, Sinead seems shy and nervous, and she strokes a gold cross and chain around her neck. I wonder if it's the one I gave her all those years ago. She announces that she has to leave. I think she senses that there's a bit of an atmosphere in the lounge, mostly emanating from Bea and Declan.

"Got to go – my lot are outside in the van. Sean, Murphy, Ginger... and Sean's probably doing me a rollie right now. I just wanted to find youz all and wish youz a Happy New Year!" And with that, she get's up to leave, saying, "Bridie, can I have a private word?"

We go into the hall and I shut the door behind us. I kiss her once more and look at her straight in the eye. "What is it, Sinead? Are you happy? Are you safe?"

"Well, Bridie, I am wit Sean now and he is much older than me, so he looks after me. He's..." she hesitates and whispers, "He's 30 would ya believe! And has a son, same age as young Josh in there. But, Bridie, I wanted to tell youz in person – I am 3 months pregnant! Sure, did I not get the shock of me life when I found out. Me! Blessed with a baby. Mind, I've been praying for one of me own. A family all of me own. I just wanted you to know Bridie, because, well – I know how much you wanted a baby all them years ago."

I didn't think she knew... How did she know that? "Thank you, Sinead. Thank you for telling me. So where are you living now?" I ask her.

She points outside to the battered old camper van where I think I can see a dirty Roger Bear squashed into the front window! "We're living in the van for now," she says proudly, "like proper travellers! But Sean's going to get a job and a house for us before the baby comes."

The occupants of the van must've seen the front door being opened because the passenger window was wound down and a scruffy head appeared in the dim light of the porch lantern.

"Is that you Bridie Kelly?" a voice shouts out. "S'me, Murphy – Murphy Riley! Happy New Year to youz one and all, and thanks for all ye done for my Sinead years ago. She's a beautiful girl now, isn't she?"

"She is that, Murphy," I shout back. "Happy New Year to you too."

I look at Sinead, all grown up. I want to say, 'Don't be a stranger' but I know that Declan won't thank me for that. Instead I say, "I love you, Sinead – I always have done. You were the one who helped me to become a mother – and now you're becoming a mother too. Take care of yourself, and take care of your little one. That's all that matters now."

"I will," she says, as she heads out the front door. She gives me one final hug and runs over to the dilapidated vehicle, jumping in the van and taking a deep drag on the cigarette that a stocky young man passes her.

"Bye Bridie!" she shouts out of the window, as she drives off back to Dublin or wherever it is they're all living.

"Send me a postcard!" I shout after her. "Don't be a stranger..."

91672418R00212

Made in the USA
Columbia, SC
21 March 2018